"So good to finally meet some of Dhamon's old friends!" Rikali cut in, cracking a forced smile and stretching out her hand. She glided toward the Solamnic Knight. "You must be Fee-ohn-a," she said, her tone almost polite. "Dhamon has told me so very much about you. And you're. . . ."

"Very angry," Rig stated. He ground the tip of the glaive into the dry earth. His eyes, like daggers, were aimed straight at Dhamon.

By Jean Rabe

DRAGONS OF A NEW AGE
The Dawning of a New Age
The Day of the Tempest
The Eve of the Maelstrom

BRIDGES OF TIME
The Silver Stair

DOWNFALL

The Dhamon Saga · Volume One

Jean Rabe

DOWNFALL
DRAGONLANCE

©2000 Wizards of the Coast, Inc.

Distributed in the United States by St. Martin's Press. Distributed in Canada by Fenn Ltd.

Distributed to the hobby, toy, and comic trade in the United States and Canada by regional distributors.

Distributed worldwide by Wizards of the Coast, Inc. and regional distributors.

Cover art by Jerry Vander Stelt
First Printing: May 2000
First Paperback Printing: March 2001
Library of Congress Catalog Card Number: 00-190763

9 8 7 6 5 4 3 2 1

UK ISBN: 0-7869-2032-7
US ISBN: 0-7869-1814-4
620-T21814

U.S., CANADA,	EUROPEAN HEADQUARTERS
ASIA, PACIFIC, & LATIN AMERICA	Wizards of the Coast, Belgium
Wizards of the Coast, Inc.	P.B. 2031
P.O. Box 707	2600 Berchem
Renton, WA 98057-0707	Belgium
+1-800-324-6496	+32-70-23-32-77

Visit our web site at **www.wizards.com/dragonlance**

DEDICATION

For the Saturday evening dungeon-delvers:

Annette, who leads her friends
into the clutches of vampires,

Dean, who portrays wizards able
to defeat those toothy foes,

Tracy, who swings a mean sword,

Bill, who will fall for any trap . . .
no matter what world he visits,

And Bruce, who collects flying carpets
and paladins and who once fancied himself a king.

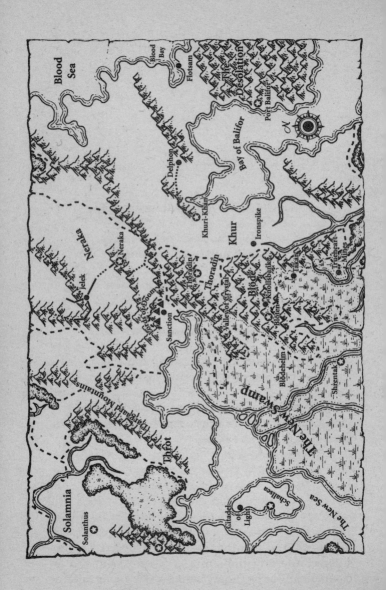

Chapter One
Healthy Earnings

"A dragon chew on you for a while and spit you out?" Rig Mer-Krel asked as he leaned against the doorframe, eyeing a patient who was almost completely sheathed in bandages.

The mariner scowled—not from the lack of an answer or at the patient's sorry appearance, though the latter was more than a little disconcerting—but from the smell that permeated the small room and clung to his nostrils. Rig swallowed and nearly gagged, a nasty taste settling in his mouth that he attributed to the odd odor.

The heat made things worse, he decided. He was certainly miserable from it, his clothes drenched with sweat. This was the middle of an exceptionally hot summer, a month called the Dry-Heat by the area's residents, and the air in this place felt brutally heavy and close. The narrow gap beneath the drawn shutters allowed only the suggestion of a breeze. Rig considered opening the shutters wide to get the air circulating. But he didn't intend to stay long, and he had no desire to make the patient more comfortable.

"This being such a big hospital, it's a wonder they couldn't have found you a longer bed. And somehow a room that didn't . . ." Rig sniffed hesitantly, trying futilely to identify the scent,". . . stink quite so much. But maybe the folks who run this place don't especially like you, either."

Only the man's head and feet weren't bandaged, and the latter hung well over the end of the bed frame. A pair of scuffed boots rested beneath his heels on a violet rug. The mariner edged farther into the room and studied the man's sweat-slicked face. His cheekbones were high and hollow, his skin tanned, and his overall appearance was slightly gaunt, as if the patient hadn't been eating properly for some time. A thin, crescent-shaped scar Rig didn't remember ran from just below the man's right eye and disappeared into the start of an ill-trimmed beard as night-black as the tangled mass of hair splaying out like spilled ink over the small pillow. The man twitched fitfully in his sleep, eyes moving beneath closed lids, jaw working, and long fingers alternately clutching.

Rig found himself nearly overwhelmed by the smell. He retreated a few steps and coughed, a useless attempt to clear his lungs. "You hardly fit on that," the mariner told him, though he understood now the man wasn't listening—hadn't been listening to a single word.

The mariner shrugged his broad shoulders and continued to speak for his own benefit. "Well, what do you expect? Ironspike's a dwarven town, so I guess all the furniture's dwarf-size." He tilted his head toward a stunted chair, where an attempt had been made to neatly fold the shredded remains of the patient's clothes. "Man in the hall said something clawed you up pretty bad."

"A big mountain cat, most likely." This from behind the mariner.

Rig whirled to see a thickset dwarf dressed in gray, framed by the doorway. Her hair was pulled tightly back from her ruddy face, and the wrinkles of several decades fanned out from her narrowed eyes to add to her unpleasant countenance. She tapped her foot and glared at the dark-skinned man. "You shouldn't be here," she lectured, adding a finger wag to emphasize her point.

"How is he?" Rig asked, offering his best congenial smile.

Her expression didn't soften. "Your friend's wounds aren't at all deep, but they are numerous. He was delirious when they found him at the edge of town early this morning, and he hasn't regained consciousness since his cuts were dressed."

The mariner let out a low whistle and crossed his arms. "When will he . . ."

"Regain consciousness?" It was her turn to shrug. "A day, two. It's hard to say." Her voice reminded Rig of gravel bumping around in the bottom of a bucket—coarse and unappealing. "If he does wake up, we'll probably keep him for a day or two longer—to make sure he hasn't caught something foul from whatever clawed him. It was quite lucky for him we had this vacant room."

"He doesn't look so lucky," Rig muttered under his breath. Louder, he said, "Must be a dozen rooms in this . . ."

"Hospital." The eyes eased wider a bit. "On this floor. Two dozen rooms all together, and all of them filled. We're the largest hospital east of the Kalkhists."

"You get lots of folks clawed up these days?"

She shook her head and huffed, the air escaping

from her lungs like a kettle left too long on the fire. "I wish animal attacks were all we had to treat. A couple'a days ago some Legion of Steel Knights fought an army of goblins a few miles outside of town. The wounded are being tended to here. A couple'a the wards upstairs have as many as a dozen patients each in them."

Rig turned his back on the woman and regarded the patient again.

"And our beds aren't *dwarf-sized*," she continued. "This room was intended for children, and its former occupant was released yesterday afternoon. A youngster fully recovered from the pox." Her eyes twinkled with an inner light, and she almost smiled. "A good lad. We burned the sheets, cleaned, and . . ."

"Ha!" Rig let out a clipped laugh when he finally noticed the pastel blue paint on the walls and the crude chalk drawings—a string of frogs and bunnies circling the room at waist-level.

The sun was setting outside. The pale orange light slipped beneath the gap in the shutters and stretched toward an upended crate on which sat a one-eyed rag doll with scraggly yarn hair. Nearby were cornhusk soldiers and colorful wooden blocks. There was another bed in the room, empty and even smaller, covered with a quilt dotted with pink and yellow kittens. He laughed again. "Wait'll Fiona sees this. She'll be greatly amused. 'Course she'll probably have to visit the Knights, too, while she's here."

"The Knights won—in case you're interested," the dwarf added. Her foot tapped a little louder and she made a harumphing sound. "What few goblins weren't killed were driven . . ."

"Must be keeping your healers busy. All these patients. Probably exhausted with all the conjuring and magical muttering."

He didn't see the dwarf ball her hands and set them on her wide hips. However, he couldn't miss the sound of the kettle steaming again. "We don't have *healers*, sir, not the kind who use magic. None of those *gifted* folks are within a couple hundred miles of here. Not that we need them. We know how to take good care of people. *Very good care.* A lot of the nearby villages bring their sick here. We've men who make strong poultices from herbs and . . ."

"Ah, so that's what's responsible for that remarkable fragrance."

". . . that work just as well as any magic. Probably better."

Rig made a sound in his throat that could have passed for agreement.

"Your friend is receiving excellent care. Just wish we knew what to do about that *thing* on his leg. Might try to cut it out tomorrow."

"It's a dragon scale," Rig volunteered, as he held his breath and bent over the bed again. "And you may as well leave it alone." The patient moaned and twitched as if in the throes of a fever, his fingers clawing at the sheets now. The mariner retreated to join the dwarf. "I didn't expect to find him. Fiona heard he was in the area, but you never know. We were close by and she wanted to track him down, so I came along. She's stabling the horses now, and then she'll be . . ."

". . . *not* coming in here," the dwarf finished evenly. "Visiting hours have been over for more than an hour, and our doors are closed—to the healthy. Spotted you slipping in a side entrance, and I came by to chase you out. Visiting hours start again tomorrow at midmorning. Sign says that quite clearly. If you'd bothered to read it. You and . . ."

"Fiona."

". . . can come back tomorrow." She backed into the hall and pointed to a far door. "Your friend might be better then."

"Ma'am, I've never considered Dhamon Grimwulf my friend." Rig politely nodded and walked past her, his boot heels clicking rhythmically against the tile floor.

When the footsteps faded to nothing, a shadow slid out from under the smaller bed and glided toward Dhamon. "Thought that man would never leave," the stranger whispered in a breathy voice that sounded like a hot breeze over sand. "Standin' in that doorway and just lookin' at you, not sayin' nothin' worthwhile, and then that stumpy woman came by. Pigs! Where were his manners? Didn't even bring you any flowers or sweets."

The figure was slight, draped in a hooded gray cloak so dark it looked like a piece of the night sky come to ground. From inside the hood came a sharp intake of breath. "Och, but that stench is strong."

Dhamon stopped his twitching act, opened his eyes, and gave his visitor a slight smile. "One gets used to it."

A thin-fingered hand reached up and disappeared inside the hood, muffling a gagging sound. "I could never get used to *that*," came the muted reply. "Good thing it's you layin' there, Dhamon Grimwulf, and not me. Phew!"

"Mal?" Dhamon ventured, changing the subject.

"He and the little man are in town. They'll be makin' their rounds tonight. Like me. Just as we planned." Then the figure dropped a small leather pouch into one of Dhamon's boots and glided silently out into the hall.

◇ ◇ ◇ ◇ ◇ ◇ ◇

Shortly before midnight, Dhamon rose and stretched and rubbed the backs of his calves, which were achingly sore from resting against the too-small bed's footboard. He crept to the doorway, listening for noises.

Nothing worth worrying over, he determined. Just the faint hiss of his own breath and an occasional moan from patients in other rooms. No one was about. It seemed even the caregivers had finally gone to bed.

The Legion of Steel sentries had just made another pass down the hall, which meant they'd be patrolling the grounds within a moment or two. Three predictably monotonous and slow circles the Knights always made, vigilantly guarding their injured brethren. Dhamon had been "listening" to the hospital since he arrived shortly after dawn and had the Knights' dull routine memorized. He knew he would have a little more than a half-hour to work undiscovered.

More than enough time.

Dhamon padded to the window and opened wide one of the shutters, breathing deep the warm fresh air that offered him some respite from the pungent salve they'd smeared all over his body. He wondered how even an unhealthy man could bear the stuff, the cure seeming worse than the malady. Craning his neck this way and that, he spotted no one out on the street. Only indistinct sounds reached him, muted music and off-key singing coming from a tavern down the block. He began to unwrap the bandages, the moonlight revealing his lean, athletic body glistening with a sheen of sweat. His chest was well defined, his stomach taut, his legs muscular. On the center of his right thigh sat a dragon scale, glossy black and shot through with a line of shimmering silver. Around the scale and all over the rest of his tall form were dozens of crisscrossing claw marks. Only his face had been spared the assault, and it was angular and handsome—despite the unkempt hair crowning it.

Dhamon blotted some of the foul mixture off his chest and arms with the ends of the bandages and took one more glance up and down the street. The grounds weren't empty any longer. His dark eyes flashed as he studied a stubby form walking awkwardly on the dried grass that made up the narrow lawn of the hospital. He continued to watch until he was certain it was a drunk dwarf trying to find his way home. When the dwarf finally stumbled onto the street and out of sight, and after he watched the Legion of Steel sentries begin to make their first pass, Dhamon reached for his clothes. They were in bad shape. Even his leather vest bore the crisscrossing cuts. Beyond that, they were worn, the color faded so badly and the fabrics so thin they should have been discarded long ago.

He retrieved the leather pouch from his boots and left them sitting on the carpet at the end of the bed. No use putting them on and clomping through the halls, he thought. His bare feet would be more silent. He carefully closed the shutters and returned to the doorway, again listening for sounds beyond. Still nothing. *Good*, he mouthed, as he slipped into the hall and padded by a string of lanterns, hung evenly along the wall. Only one was lit, however. As the night got older, all the others had been extinguished and the only one that remained burning had its wick turned down to a soft glow.

Dhamon glanced in two open doorways as he went, picking through the shadows to spy Knights in thick bandages, some softly moaning even in their sleep. A few were missing legs and arms. Then he passed by a door marked "Caregivers Office," where soft light seeped out along the floor. With a little effort, he could make out the muffled conversation of two dwarves. They were discussing the status of a patient. Not his concern. Dhamon moved on.

Heartbeats later he reached the end of the hall, where a wide curving stairway stretched into blackness. Like a cat, Dhamon silently glided up the steps and soon found himself on the top floor, where another lone lantern provided ghostly light. He started toward the opposite end of the hall—he knew from eavesdropping on the caregivers that this was where he needed to go. Then suddenly he stopped and pressed himself against a wall as a young dwarf carrying a bucket filled with soiled bandages emerged rather noisily from a room and nearly brushed against him. The dwarf didn't see Dhamon; his wide, glum face was fixed on the bucket, and he was grumbling to himself in his native tongue. The dwarf didn't smell Dhamon either—an even worse odor was coming from the room he'd just vacated.

When the dwarf disappeared down the stairs, Dhamon poked his head inside the room to make sure nothing there would upset his plans. There were a dozen men stretched out on beds, in various states of injury and all being treated with one reeking balm or another—the redolent mix competed with the repugnant smells of gangrenous flesh and blood, fresh and dried. The form on the nearest bed was not breathing and gave off the almost-sweet odor of death. Dhamon had been on enough battlefields to recognize this scent. Deciding this fatality was perhaps what the dwarf was so glum about, and none of his concern, he edged toward his goal.

The hallway was eerie, still and hot. Wheezing,

moans, coughs, and snores echoed hauntingly, raising the hairs on the back of Dhamon's neck. Each
step he took was a cautious one, for in places the tiles
were slick, with perhaps blood or sweat, or from
something the dwarves had used earlier for cleaning.

At last he reached the end of the hall and stood in
front of a closed door. This was it, he was certain, the
only door on this level that boasted a padlock. The
heavy iron lock straddled two thick metal strips connecting the frame to a very sturdy-looking door.

Dhamon opened the leather pouch. Too far from
the lantern, he relied on his well-practiced fingers to
locate what he needed. Kneeling in front of the door
and slowing his breathing, he selected two thin metal
picks and went to work. His large, sweaty hands and
long fingers made the task difficult, but he persisted
and the mechanism finally rewarded him with a faint
click. He cupped his hand behind the padlock so that
when it swung open it wouldn't strike the wood,
then he carefully removed the lock and laid it on the
floor, hesitating only when a loud, throaty moan cut
through the air. It was followed by a string of deep
coughs, then the patient quieted. Dhamon waited a
moment more, then opened the metal strips and tried
the door handle.

He scowled and cursed under his breath. *Padlock
wasn't good enough by itself*, he mouthed, as he brought
the picks up to the keyhole and worried them inside.
One snapped off, a quick, sharp sound, and he sucked
in a breath and waited again. Nothing. Just snores
and soft whimpers of pain, a bed creaking as someone rolled over. Another moment and he selected a
longer pick, nearly dropping this one in his clumsy
fingers. Silently reproving himself, he wiped his
hands on his pants and resumed the job.

It seemed like hours rather than mere moments

before he finally defeated the second mechanism. He replaced the tools, dried his hands again, and tried the handle. This time the door opened—into pitch blackness. *Damn my human eyes*, he thought. But he wasn't to be undone. Not after going to all that trouble of getting inside the hospital. Rising, he slid down the hall, ever alert for waking patients and more dwarf caregivers, glancing in the rooms he passed to make sure no one was stirring.

He plucked a lantern from the wall and lit it, quickly and quietly returning to the dark room. Then Dhamon slipped inside and closed the door behind him. He breathed deeper now, uncomfortably so. There was no window in here and the room was as small as a pantry, the air inside dead and stifling. He worked the wick, coaxing more light and revealing shelves upon shelves from floor to ceiling, all containing wooden bins, satchels, coin purses, and more. There was little space to move. Each item was painstakingly labeled with the owner's name—safe from thieves who might slip into patients' rooms and steal their valuables while they were too sick to resist, safe until their owners were well enough to leave, or in the most unfortunate circumstance, until survivors arrived to claim them.

A smile spread wide across Dhamon's face as he noted that the shelves had built-in ladders to accommodate the short dwarves. He wouldn't need the ladders. He guessed ten minutes had passed since he left his room. Twenty minutes or more left. Still more than enough time.

Setting the lantern on the floor he began opening one pouch after the next, swiftly collecting pieces of jewelry—rings mostly, but also a few thick gold and silver neckchains that belonged to the wealthier Knights. There were a few feminine pieces, one an old dainty ring set with tiny pearls, another a delicate cloak pin. They either belonged to lady Knights or were keepsakes from wives and lovers.

Dhamon discovered a small velvet purse filled with loose black pearls—a good find, as most of the pouches contained only coins. Behind the purses he found a sizeable leather bag and two well-worn backpacks, one with a crude broken arrow lodged in it. He set the bag and the largest backpack carefully on the floor, trying not to make a sound, opening them and nudging the lantern close. A neatly folded spare tabard was inside one, bearing the Legion of Steel emblem. He discarded it and emptied the other backpack, too. All they carried were garments.

Then he returned to the shelves and moved faster. Within moments rings and bracers found their way into one backpack, along with coin purses filled with steel pieces, daggers with ornate handles, and a variety of other small, valuable objects. He used the tabard for padding so the baubles wouldn't "chink" together. Coins and jewels were stuffed into the sack.

Dhamon ignored swords and axes labeled with patients' names. Too cumbersome, he decided, and many a man would let his coin purse disappear but would hunt forever for a favorite weapon. Ah, but not this sword. Dhamon decided he would not be leaving this behind. He paused for a moment in front of a broadsword sheathed in a scabbard covered with the fine-tooled images of flying hippogriffs and pegasi. He drew it, noting it was sturdy and elegant and well balanced, undoubtedly belonging to a Knight of some importance. The pommel was inlaid with brass and ivory and bore a hallmark.

"Now it belongs to me," he whispered, "until I gain something better." He strapped it around his waist and left his own sword hanging on a hook, the tag dangling from it reading "unknown human patient, Room Four." Then he made his way to other bins. There were more coins inside, a ruby brooch that he snatched up and thrust in a pocket, and a heavily jeweled Legion of Steel ring that he decided must belong to a commander laid up here—perhaps the same owner of the broadsword. Dhamon pushed the ring on his index finger and continued.

When he could fit no more in the leather bag and when the backpack was straining its seams, he filled his pockets with small pouches, tying a few to his sword belt. A final pouch, small, but made of expensive material, he clenched between his teeth.

Able to carry no more, he blew out the lantern, opened the door, and peeked into the hallway. Still empty. He wriggled into the heavy backpack and hoisted the sack over his shoulder. He stood like a statue for a few moments, listening intently, picking through the soft moans and snores for noises of alarm and getting used to the weight of his new possessions. Satisfied all were soundly asleep, he closed the door behind him, glided down the hallway, and reached the stairwell. His goal was to return to his room as quickly as possible, retrieve his boots, and slip out the window.

But the Legion of Steel sentries coming up the stairs altered his plans.

Dhamon's throat went dry. He couldn't have guessed wrong on timing the sentries. What had happened? Hugging the shadows, he skittered down the hall, sweaty feet softly squeaking against the tiles as he strained to hear the Knights' hushed conversation.

The body he spotted a few minutes ago! They were coming upstairs for their dead comrade. And eventually, their dead comrade's personal effects.

Dhamon scowled and slipped into the next doorway, one of the large wards filled with a dozen patients and the smells of balms, blood, and soiled sheets. He held his breath and headed toward the back of the room where the shadows were thickest, and where he knew a window would be—a stirring of air told him so.

Have to hurry, he urged himself. *Come on!*

"Who're you?" This from a patient only a few feet away. The Knight was propped up on several pillows.

Come on! Dhamon had the shutters open. Another moment and he was standing on a narrow stone ledge.

"Who?" the patient persisted. "What're you doing?"

It was hard to navigate the ledge with the bulging pack on his back. The fingers of one hand dug into the cracks between stones, the other hand gripped the heavy sack on his shoulder. Shuffling along on the balls of his feet as his heels hung over the edge, he worked to keep his balance. The ground was roughly ten feet below.

"A wild man," he heard a patient say, likely the Knight who spoke to him. "A wild mountain man with hair like a bear went out there . . . out the window."

Dhamon balanced the sack on his shoulder and reached for his knife. Not there. He had forgotten. Damn. Lucky for the man, Dhamon thought to himself, for his instinct was to climb back in to slit his throat.

Dhamon hoped the patient was talking to himself or to another bedridden fool, not one of the passing Knights or caregivers. Time was wasting. He scurried along the ledge toward a drainpipe. Testing the pipe with his weight, he slid down, his knees thunking and the small pouch falling from his teeth.

"Damn!" he spat at the falling pouch and the noise he'd made.

Crouching behind a low, wide bush and releasing the large sack, his hands flew across the ground around him searching for the lost item, his fingers pushing aside twigs and rocks. "There!" he whispered to himself. The dirt stuck to his feet and fingers. Dhamon idly rubbed his hands on his trousers and caught his breath.

I've not been discovered, he told himself. *Maybe I can sneak back to my window, get my boots . . . then be on my way.*

He could still hear music drifting faintly from the tavern. It sounded better this time, with no one singing along. He peered out from behind the bush. There were three dwarves on the street, just wandering into his line of sight beyond the hospital's brittle lawn. Two of them were supporting the third. Leaving his plunder hidden behind the bush, Dhamon crept like a crab along the wall, back to the center of the hospital where he judged his room to be. He paused beneath the window for only a moment—but it was long enough. Dhamon heard voices inside— two dwarves talking worriedly about a missing, delirious patient who'd unbandaged himself. A search was to be immediately mounted with the aid of the Legion of Steel Knights.

"Splendid," he hissed. He would miss those boots. Whirling, he hurried back to the bush and snatched up the sack and backpack, holding the small pouch in his free hand. The dwarves were still on the street. One of them was sitting stiffly, the other two were trying to tug their woozy friend to his feet.

Certain they were too full of spirits to notice him, Dhamon strolled nonchalantly toward the trio, the dry grass softly crackling beneath his feet. A moment later, he was beyond them, heading for the far end of town where he knew the stables sprawled. *Walk normally*, he told himself. *Be calm. Arouse no suspicion.*

He had nearly reached Ironspike's main thoroughfare when he heard a loud, shrill whistle from behind him. It was followed by the pounding of several pairs of feet.

CHAPTER TWO
A CHANGE IN
THE SCENERY

Hmm?"

"Rig, I think I heard something."

"Just got to sleep," he protested. "Didn't hear anything. I . . . wait . . ." The mariner stifled a yawn, reluctantly slipped away from Fiona, and shook off a wonderful dream. He'd been captaining an impressive galley on the Blood Sea, and all his old friends were in the crew—Palin and his son Ulin, Groller and Jasper. Two women were draped on his arms—Shaon, an ebony-skinned beauty who dressed in tight, colorful garb, the other a fair-complected, red-haired Solamnic Knight in gleaming plate mail.

He stretched his legs and wrapped a long red curl around his thumb, inhaled its flowery scent and released it, then climbed out of the cramped bed.

There was a whistle, soft at first, repeating a pattern. It grew shriller and came from somewhere outside. Footsteps—someone running. Rig groggily gathered the sheet about his waist and shuffled to the window, brushing aside the canvas curtain and looking down onto the street below. The collection of century-old wood and stone buildings that stretched away beneath him was illuminated by the full, bright summer moon. Only a few lanterns burned outside a handful of taverns.

He worked a kink out of his neck and yawned wide as the whistle blew again. "Couple'a dwarves," he observed. "They're running down a side street. One of them's blowing a whistle. Nothing to . . . wait a minute. One of them's putting on a jacket. I think it's a town guard. And I see two more following them. Ah! There's a Legion of Steel Knight. And another one!"

Behind him, Fiona started to don her armor.

◇ ◇ ◇ ◇ ◇ ◇ ◇

Dhamon was running now, ignoring the gravel that bit into the bottoms of his bare feet. A slight, gray-cloaked figure cut toward him from an alley, a large satchel slung over its shoulder.

"Pigs," came a breathy curse, as the figure closed the distance between them. A gust of warm summer wind caught the hood and threw it back, and a mass of long, curly white hair spilled out, sparkling like spun silver in the moonlight. "Pigs!" she repeated. "Damn you, Dhamon Grimwulf, for your clumsiness. Yours was supposed to be a quiet job, though the riskiest. Slip into the hospital as a patient. Then slip out with . . ."

Dhamon thrust the small pouch at her, freeing his hand so he could draw his new sword. "How many are following?"

"Five. Three dwarves. Two Knights. Knights! Truly wonderful, Dhamon," she said as she shook the pouch at him and continued to run at his side. "I visited the silversmith all nice and quiet." She jiggled the satchel over her shoulder so he could hear metal clinking inside. "I should've handled the hospital instead. I could've done it nice and quiet. I should've been the one to . . ."

"Rikali, you couldn't have carried all of this," came the reply.

I could've, she mouthed, as they ran. "But I wouldn't've liked the stink," she added aloud.

The whistle blew behind them again, and it was punctuated by shutters being flung open, questions flung into the darkness. The number of pounding feet grew, all the sounds eerily muted by the dwarven buildings.

Several blocks away, beyond Dhamon's vision, a small crowd was assembling on the street—a few members dressed in guard jackets and tabards. The majority of them were curious late-night revelers who'd come straggling out of the taverns to see what the to-do was about. These latter were marked by their staggering gaits and loud voices. "Did someone say Sanford's was robbed?" One of them hollered. "And the bakery?"

Among them were two distinct figures, strangers to Ironspike—one with a considerable collection of pouches and water skins hanging from his waist. He was dressed in deerhide breeches and a shirt, and he seemed overly large and imposing compared to the cloaked one at his side, who was barely taller than his knee.

"The bakery?" a few of the revelers repeated.

Meanwhile, Dhamon and Rikali raced along and turned onto the main street, outdistancing the dwarves and the armor-encumbered Knights chasing them.

"There they are—Mal and Fetch! I hope they did as well. Worthless, Fetch is," Rikali stated, spitting on the ground, her eyes on the small man. "Fetch is nothing but worthless."

"Maldred!" Dhamon shouted.

His back to Dhamon, the larger figure raised a hand, then reached behind him and pulled a two-handed sword from a latticed sheath that hung between his broad shoulders. He turned.

"Thief!" A cry cut through the air from behind Dhamon and Rikali. One of the Legion of Steel Knights had caught up and was rounding the corner. "They've robbed the hospital!"

"Pigs! They're comin' at us from both sides of town!" Rikali noticed the growing tavern crowd near Maldred and Fetch. "We should've ducked in an alley."

"Full moon," Dhamon shot back. "They'd have seen us."

"Should've been more careful." She sucked in a breath, increasing her pace.

"I really didn't think they'd discover my handi-work so soon," Dhamon offered.

"C'mon," Rikali urged him. "Move your big feet faster. We've got to get out of here before the whole stinkin' town wakes up." She closed on Maldred and Fetch, Dhamon following her with hobbled feet.

❖ ❖ ❖ ❖ ❖ ❖ ❖

Rig was struggling into his pants and boots while gazing out the window. The mariner saw that other windows were opening, lanterns were being lit. Dwarves were sticking their heads out and trying, like himself, to figure out what was going on. Rig heard shouted questions and the faint cry of "Thieves!"

He hurriedly finished dressing as he glanced up and down the streets from his third-floor vantage point. There! His mouth dropped open. Rig spotted none other than Dhamon Grimwulf, running off to his right toward the main street. There were three others with him. "Dhamon! He's . . . he's out of the hospital!"

"You're sure it's him?" Fiona was strapping on her leg plates.

"Of course it's him! And it looks like he's being chased," the mariner said. He fumbled about behind him for his belt. "They're . . . no!"

Beneath his window a dwarf was readying a heavy crossbow, steadying it on a horsepost and aiming it in Dhamon's direction. Though it would be a long shot, Rig didn't want to take any chance that the dwarf might be successful. He muttered a string of curses, acting without thinking.

Rig dashed to the bed, reaching under it and grabbing the brass chamber pot. He slid to the window, quickly took aim, and hurled it down, soundly striking the dwarf and cracking the stock on the weapon. The mariner ducked his head back inside and reached for his sword. He glanced at his plethora of daggers all laid out neatly on his chair and bit his lip. He looked wishfully at his precious glaive propped up against the wall. "No time," he muttered, heading toward the door.

Fiona snatched her shield and was quick on his heels.

❖ ❖ ❖ ❖ ❖ ❖ ❖

Four jacketed dwarves had reached the large man called Maldred. All three were brandishing short swords. The fourth was blowing away on a whistle, red cheeks puffing out almost farcically.

"Outofourway!" the lead one huffed so fast the

words buzzed together like an angry hornet. "Move-movemove!"

"Move!" another shouted more distinctly, waving at Fetch. "Move! Damnable kender, move! What's all this about? Who sounded an alarm?"

"I ain't no kender," the small man spat.

"Movemovemove!"

The large man smiled wide and brushed a lock of short ginger hair out of his eyes. "Public street," he said, as he maneuvered himself in front of them just as they tried to cut around toward Dhamon and Rikali. Dhamon was back to back with Maldred in a fighting stance. Dhamon eased the sack of purloined treasure off his shoulder, setting it on the ground and taking a practice swing with his stolen blade. Satisfied, he readied himself for the men approaching from the other end of the street.

Fetch made a growling noise and took a few steps away from Maldred, grasping a hoopak, an odd-looking oak weapon of kender design that consisted of a staff with a "V" at one end, to which a red leather sling was attached.

"Mal, we don't have time to play games with dwarves," Rikali warned. "Just kill 'em quick."

The lead dwarf heard that and cursed. He spun to the big man's right, but Maldred was faster, cutting him off. He brought his leg up, striking the dwarf in the chest and punching the wind from his lungs. As the dwarf gasped, Maldred kicked him in the chest a second time, stunning him. A second dwarf paused, which was his undoing. Maldred tripped him, stepping on his sword as it struck the ground and snapping the blade. The third opponent pivoted to the big man's left and found himself face to face with Fetch.

Fetch sneered, stopping the dwarf in his tracks.

"Th-th-that ain't no kender. It's a weird little monster," the dwarf stammered.

"How rude," the small man returned, snarling and kicking out ferociously. Fetch missed, however, and landed on his rump, his hoopak tangled in his cloak.

At the same time, the fourth dwarf took a few steps back, continued to blow on his whistle, and frantically pumped his arms up and down at the crowd down the street, as if he were some kind of bird trying to take flight.

"Mal . . ." Rikali said again.

"Put your blade away," Maldred advised the dwarf who was still standing in front of Fetch. He leveled his great sword, facing the dwarf. "Take a deep breath, go back to bed, and live to see tomorrow."

"Mal, we don't have time . . ."

"Thieves!" hollered a Legion of Steel Knight, the lead of the growing pack approaching from Dhamon's direction.

"We're gonna get trapped in the middle!" Rikali spat.

"Your sword. . . ." Maldred warned the dwarf again.

"Put your *own* sword away," the guard retorted. "Thieves!" The dwarf feinted to his left, but Fetch was quicker, jumping to block the guard's path. The small man twirled the hoopak ahead of him to keep the dwarf at bay.

"I'd prefer not to kill any of you," Maldred said ominously. His voice was deep, rich, melodic, almost hypnotic. "Your deaths would not profit me." He lashed out with his foot, tripping one of the dwarves who was trying to get up.

The approaching crowd was only a few hundred feet away now.

"Pffah!" taunted the guard in front of Fetch. He thrust the sword at the small man and grumbled when it was parried with the hoopak. "Maybe I'd prefer not to kill you—or your tiny monster!" He spun to his right, avoiding a jab from Fetch and ending up in front of Maldred.

"I'm warning you," Maldred cautioned.

The dwarf ducked beneath Maldred's sword and made another attempt to get around the big man.

"Mal!" Rikali was bouncing back and forth nervously on the balls of her feet, looking up and down the street and appraising the charging mobs.

"I'm sorry," Maldred said to the dwarf, a tinge of regret in his sonorous voice. "Truly." He drove the pommel of the sword down hard on top of the guard's head. There was a disturbing crack, and the dwarf fell and lay still. Maldred turned his attention to the other weaponless guard who had finally struggled to his feet. The big man intended to repeat his peaceful offer, but Rikali darted in front of him and thrust out with her knife. The guard sidestepped her, though the blade cut through his jacket and fear made the color drain from his ruddy face.

Maldred nodded significantly to the one who continued to blow the whistle. *Stop that ruckus*, he mouthed. At the same time, he kept an eye on the crowd that would be upon them in a moment. "I said I'd prefer not to kill you."

"Thieves!" A Legion of Steel Knight was shouting orders. "Catch them!"

The dwarf facing Maldred growled. He spit out the whistle and risked a glance at his dead companions— Rikali had just finished off the unarmed one. He fumbled for the sword at his waist, tugged it free and drew back. "There's too many of us. We'll stop you!" Then he ducked beneath the swing of the big man's blade. Too late, the dwarf realized his opponent was a master. Maldred's sword swept wide and down in the opposite direction, and the guard's head fell with a dull thud.

"Hurry!" someone hollered. The crowd was only a few yards away.

"Yes, hurry," Rikali said.

"Where're the horses?" Dhamon gasped as he grabbed the leather sack and slung it over his shoulder. He parried the swings of the first Legion of Steel Knights who'd reached him.

"Mal didn't bring any horses," she answered, as she, too, engaged one of the Knights. "Rode our last ones out til they were all but dead and thought we'd get some new ones here. You know I like a little shopping now and then."

"Wonderful," Dhamon said. He was besieged by Knights and looking for openings. He found one and swept his sword past one man's guard, cutting deep into his leg. The Knight dropped to his knees, hands pressed against his thigh.

The others were equally beset.

"Surrender!" someone hollered. "Surrender and you'll live!"

"That man! He has the commander's sword." This from a Legion of Steel Knight.

"Kill him!" A gravelly dwarven voice. "Kill the thief!"

"Guess surrender's not an option now," Rikali said.

Dhamon was exchanging blows with two dwarves.

"I'd prefer not to kill you," Maldred announced to the dwarves who had reached him.

"Don't be so polite," Rikali shouted to the big man. "I repeat, let's kill 'em quick and be on our

way—before even more come." She gathered the
hem of her cloak in her free hand. In one fluid
motion, she danced forward and whipped the cloak
about the sword of a charging dwarf. At the same
time, she thrust up with the knife into a Knight's
vulnerable neck, whirled, and slashed at another
dwarf, cutting through his tabard and deep beneath.
"Look at the lights bein' lit about town, Mal. Can't
you hear all the voices? Everyone's wakin' up! These
odds are ugly enough, but in another few minutes
they're gonna be too ugly to handle. There's lots of
Knights around. Do somethin'!"

Dhamon drove the pommel of his sword down on
the helmeted head of a dwarf, denting the metal and
stunning the man.

"Yeah, do something, Mal," Fetch parroted.

The big man growled deep in his throat and
instantly dispatched two in front of him, spraying
the crowd with blood. Those next in line backed up
and held their swords in front of them in an effort to
keep him at bay and take better stock of the situation.

Fetch thwacked his hoopak soundly against the
hands of his foe, the blow causing the dwarf to drop
his sword. "I'd prefer not to kill you," Fetch sneered,
imitating Maldred. The dwarf held his arms out to
his side in surrender and backed up, and Fetch let
out a victory whoop.

A few of the other dwarves were retreating, trying
to push the crowd back so the Legion of Steel
Knights who had come from the hospital could circle
the thieves and deal with them. But there were a
dozen town guards in the mix, and they continued to
press forward. It was on these that Maldred and
Fetch concentrated.

Rikali sliced at the dwarves on her side, who
slightly outnumbered the Legion of Steel Knights.

She guessed there were more than a dozen in the group facing her and Dhamon, and she wasn't going to look over her shoulder to see how many more there were. One of her attackers was an especially good swordsman, and she couldn't quite manage to upset the rhythm of his swings nor wrest the blade from his grasp. "Mal, more're comin' fast. I hear them! Knights all a' clangin'! I don't want to die in this town! Do somethin', Mal!"

The big man finally mumbled an acknowledgment, then let out a keening cry that sounded like a chorus of angry gulls. He swung his great sword in an arc over his head, the metal fairly singing and catching the moonlight. The light skittered along the blade and a shower of sparks—like swarming fireflies— leapt into the crowd, catching hold of the dwarves' garments. Maldred ran forward into the mass of startled dwarves. Unnerved by Maldred, or more likely frightened by the rash of fires, they parted like a wave. Fetch was quick to follow the big man, swinging his hoopak against the backs of those who were too slow to get out of his way and accidentally striking Rikali in the process.

On Dhamon's side, the dwarves also retreated. But the Knights, though momentarily stunned by Maldred's magical display, stood their ground.

Rikali spotted more dwarves emerging from their homes, most toting weapons of some kind—even makeshift ones, torches, a few crossbows—and these latter especially worried her. There would be too many now for Maldred to chase or to scare. Or to fight.

Dhamon saw Rig and Fiona running down the street. The mariner was shouting something and waving. Fiona was moving quickly despite her Solamnic armor, the torches illuminating her disbelieving, wide-eyed face.

Rikali and Dhamon ignored all of them, capitalizing on the momentarily stunned Legion of Steel Knights and whirling to follow Maldred, who had chased a group of dwarves beyond the stable.

As Maldred stopped and threw open the stable door, Fetch darted inside. The big man gestured at Rikali and Dhamon. *Hurry*, he mouthed. Behind the pair, a half-dozen Knights were running toward them. More dwarves were charging, cursing as they came, hollering "Thieves!" at the top of their lungs. Only the dwarves' stubby legs kept them from overtaking the Knights. A quarrel struck the stable, inches from Maldred's hand.

In the middle of the dwarves could be seen Rig and Fiona. The Solamnic Knight's eyes were fiery, and she was resolutely threading her way through to the front of the angry crowd.

"Inside!" Maldred urged, ducking as a quarrel whizzed over his head.

A heartbeat later he followed Rikali and Dhamon into the stable and slammed the door shut, throwing the bar across it. Maldred motioned for Dhamon to do the same with a side door that was barely discernible in the dark, cavernous interior.

"Oh, this is great!" Rikali jeered. "You've trapped us, Mal! Like rats, we are. And it stinks in here. Pigs, I see there's a Solamnic Knight in town on top of the dozen or so Legion of Steel Knights who aren't laid up in the hospital! That's all we need. A shining-in-armor Solamnic Knight!"

"She's an old friend of mine," Dhamon said as he brushed by.

"Friend?" Rikali put her hands on her narrow hips. "You have bad taste, lover. Least you used to. No one needs a Knight for a friend. They're trouble—at least for the likes of us."

"Quit complaining," Fetch said. He was huffing and wheezing, rolling a barrel to prop against the door. "Give me a hand."

"Oh, that'll work, wee man," Rikali said wryly.

"No. Fetch has the right idea," Dhamon said. He gestured to the center of the stable, where they could see the outline of a big wagon.

Maldred patted Rikali's shoulder as he rushed by and grabbed the front beam of the wagon. The muscles in his arms bunched, the veins on his neck stood out like ropes as he began to pull. The horses started whinnying nervously as Dhamon, dropping the backpack and leather sack, got behind the wagon and pushed.

Fetch scampered up into the wagon bed, tugging free a half-dozen canvas sacks. "Coins from the bakery, which was my idea to rob," he said as much to himself as to Dhamon. "Coins from the weaponsmith's. Spoons and candlesticks from an old manor. Stuck it all in here, Mal and me. Thought we were gonna use the wagon to ride out of town on."

Outside, the dwarves pounded on the doors, frightening the horses further. That was nothing compared to the tremor that suddenly shook the building. Someone outside shouted "Earthquake!" Another cried "Sorcery!" Finally the ground stopped trembling.

Fiona's voice cut above the din, shouting to be heard. "Dhamon Grimwulf! Come out at once!"

Rikali braced her back against the doors and gritted her teeth as blows continued to rain against the entrance. "Hurry, fellows," she urged. "This stable is sturdy 'ole dwarven construction. But it ain't gonna hold forever. Not with them poundin' on it, and not with the ground grumblin' so." Fetch joined her and copied her stance, small legs spread wide. "Oh, you're a great help," Rikali said sarcastically, looking down at the small-sized one.

Then the ground trembled again.

"Is there another way in?" came the cry from outside.

"The hayloft!" came an answer. "An' the side door!"

"I've got an axe! Let me up front! I'll chop the door down."

"That's my stable! Don't ruin it! Talk 'em into coming out!"

"Boost me up. Human! Boost me up!"

"Find a ladder!"

"Thieves! They stole from the wounded Knights! Kill them!"

"Hurry, Mal!"

"Yeah, hurry!" Fetch added.

Dhamon and Maldred braced the wagon against the door and locked the brake in place just as an axe-head started breaking through the wood. They heard scrabbling against the wall outside, as if someone were trying to climb the wall. They heard the strangled cry of a dwarf. Then a thump.

"Try again. Boost me this time!" It was a human's voice, though not Rig's or Fiona's. Probably one of the Legion of Steel Knights.

"Where's the ladder?"

"Forget the ladder." It was Rig's voice, laced with anger. "Move aside. I'll open your damn door."

"My stable!"

"Not going to hold them for long," Dhamon observed.

"Really?" Rikali said in feigned surprise. "Have you a next move, Dhamon? Mal? I'd rather not die in this dungheap."

"Dhamon Grimwulf! Come out! This is Fiona!"

"The planks! Pry the planks free!"

"Damnable thieves!"

Dhamon dashed to the side door and began sliding crates and barrels in front of the door, anchoring the mass with pitchforks he thrust into the ground. There was pounding on this door, too.

Maldred retreated to the back of the stable, ignoring the jittery horses, Rikali's complaints, and Fetch's apologies. He splayed his fingers wide over the wood and felt the coarse grain.

"It's hard to see in here," Fetch grumbled. "For Mal and Dhamon especially." He jumped when an axe blade smashed through a plank. "I'll get us some light."

Dhamon joined Maldred, dragging the sacks that had been in the wagon. "I'll saddle some horses." He had noted a dozen full-sized steeds, two exceptionally large. If the Legion of Steel Knights had other horses, as Dhamon suspected they did, they were likely kept at a camp outside of town. The rest of the stalls contained ponies, stocky ones ideal for dwarves. He hurried at his work, selecting the two largest and leading them to the back of the stable.

Maldred closed his eyes and started humming, a low sound that came from somewhere deep in his throat and that fluctuated in pitch and tempo like a complex piece of music. His fingers fluttered up and down the planks. His fingertips lingered on the nails that held the wood together, and as he continued humming, the nails grew warm and faintly glowed.

"There, that'll help!" Fetch announced. The small man had started a fire with a pile of hay in the center of the stable. "Now we can see better."

"You scaly little idiot!" Rikali screamed when she realized what he had done. The light revealed the anger on her face. Her skin looked like smooth alabaster in the fire's glow, her wide eyes a pale watery blue outlined heavily with kohl, her lips thin and painted crimson. She snarled to reveal a row of tiny, pointed teeth, so small and uniform they looked filed. "You're worthless!"

Before she could reach the fire and attempt to put it out, it had begun to spread, racing along the floor on the scattered straw, then jumping from bale to bale. The horses' nostrils flared in fright. They were neighing anxiously in their stalls, pulling on the ropes that held them. The fire was spreading toward the animals, was spreading toward everything, and Rikali's efforts to stamp it out were ineffectual.

"Mal!" Rikali called. "We have another problem! Fetch decided to burn down the buildin'."

Maldred continued humming.

Cries of "Fire!" resounded outside. A dwarf hollered to start a bucket brigade. Another was yelling to leave the blaze be, to let it kill the thieves who would steal from the wounded Knights who risked their lives to save the town from the goblin army.

Dhamon had the two largest horses saddled and was returning to select another one or two. He sucked in his breath when he heard one of the center beams groan and saw the flames rising. "Riki!" Dhamon hollered. "Saddle one more for you and Fetch. Be quick."

She grumbled but complied, futilely kicking dirt on the flames as she turned and made a grab for a saddle. An axe splintered the door. She decided bareback was a better idea. Coughing and blinded, she cried out. Fetch tugged on her cloak.

"Sorry," he said. "Didn't think about the fire spreading. Wanted to try out that fire spell Mal taught me."

"You're always wantin' to try that spell."

"Just wanted everyone to see better."

She reached down and grabbed him about the waist, hoisted him up onto the horse, then got on behind him. "Shut up," she said. "Just shut up and hold on." She snatched the rope of another horse and jabbed her mount in the ribs with her boot heels, urging it forward and tugging the other one to follow. The other ponies were fighting their ropes, rearing frantically in the face of the fire and billowing smoke. The sound of the panicked animals and the crackling flames, the hacking of the axes against the front door, the shouts of the dwarves and of Rig and Fiona all made it difficult for her to think. "Dhamon!" Rikali screamed. "I can't see you. Dhamon!"

Dhamon followed her voice and managed to grab her horse and lead it to the back, where he began loading up the other horse with the sacks that had been in the wagon. Rikali was coughing deeply, Fetch, too, and Dhamon's eyes stung from all the smoke.

Then Dhamon spun and ran to retrieve his own precious plunder, relying on his memory as the smoke and flames obscured everything.

"I've got the door down!" Rig's voice called. "Help me move this wagon!"

"Thieves! Let them burn!"

There was a dwarf's voice—staccato and commanding—shouting orders. Voices swelled with the billowing smoke, angry and curious and filled with fear and outrage. A Legion of Steel Knight issued orders to his men.

Maldred was humming louder, his fingers moving faster, dancing in the air now. His fingers beckoned to the nails as they worked themselves out of the wood, the planks groaning in the process. The air all around was hot, the flames were growing wilder behind him. The wagon shifted, dwarves and Knights spilled inside, and some were immediately trampled by horses trying to escape.

Dhamon hoisted the leather sack onto the largest horse and thrust the reins into Maldred's hand. He struggled to slip on the backpack and heaved himself into the saddle of the other horse.

Maldred formed a fist with his free hand and struck the back wall of the barn. The wood groaned a final time, then the entire back wall of the stable began to topple.

In an instant the world was consumed by fire and chaos, and by heat as intense as red dragon's breath. The great gout of fresh air fed the flames, sending them dancing into the upper reaches, into the hayloft, onto the thatch roof. A hellish orange blaze devoured the wood and sent a billowing mass of thick gray smoke high into the night sky. The fireball chased Rig, the Knights, and the dwarves back outside, where they gasped and choked.

"Dhamon!" Rig's voice. Then Fiona's. But the words were drowned out by the thundering hooves of their stolen mounts as Dhamon, Rikali, Maldred, and Fetch escaped Ironspike, driving a handful of freed horses and ponies before them.

"So hot," Rikali moaned. She shuddered as she looked over her shoulder at the fire that had spread from the town's stable to a half-dozen other buildings. "I stink with smoke. I've blisters on my arms. My face! Fetch, is it. . . ."

"Your face is lovely as ever, Riki, though that garish stuff you paint on your eyes is running down your cheeks like black rain. Hey, my robe!" Fetch started squirming. The hem had caught on fire. He slapped at it with his diminutive hands.

Rikali hissed and helped him put it out. "Worthless," she pronounced. "Absolutely worthless, Fetch."

"Sorry," he answered. "But at least nobody'll be following us. Ponies and horses are either dead or long gone. The humans have nothing to ride. Dwarves are gonna be trying to put out the fire rather than worrying about us. Gonna have to work hard to keep the whole town from burning. Summer's made everything so dry. Water's not so plentiful."

"The Knights, though. . . ." Rikali suggested.

"Yeah, the Legion of Steel Knights aren't gonna forget that their wounded brothers were robbed. Them, we can worry about."

The four didn't slow their horses until the fire and smoke were far behind, the scent of the blaze a memory, and a rose-petal dawn was creeping over the sky.

The land that stretched directly before them was barren and scrubby and flat. There were clumps of prairie grass, scattered like tufts of hair on a balding man. They were dry and rustling in the scant breeze, and balls of dried weeds spun recklessly across the quartet's path. Summer, never kind to Khur, had been especially brutal this year—the rains more infrequent than usual, the temperature higher, the wind too slight to grant any measure of relief.

A little distance to the west the scenery changed dramatically. Foothills rose toward the towering Kalkhist Mountains, jagged and imposing upthrusts of granite shielded by steel-gray clouds There were a scattering of stunted oaks and bushes. All of the plants looked like they were dying, except for the aromatic gray-green sage that thrived in such heat.

Maldred shrugged out of his shirt, tying it about his waist. His muscles gleamed with sweat. He tugged one of the waterskins free from his belt, drained it, and snatched free another, which he passed to Dhamon.

Dhamon looked thin riding next to Maldred, and his ropy muscles were dwarfed by the big man's thick arms, barrel chest, and square shoulders. Some of his cuts had been healed completely by the hospital's medicine, but the deeper ones had opened during the fight in town and glistened with oozing blood.

"Rikali," Maldred called, "you didn't need to scratch him quite so much."

"You said Dhamon had to look in a bad way," she cut back. "You said he needed to be convincing."

"Not *that* convincing," Maldred softly returned.

She shrugged, tossing her thick mass of hair. "Dhamon didn't complain."

"I was more than convincing," Dhamon admitted to the big man. "I *should've* pulled it off without a hitch. I'm not sure just what went wrong. I hadn't taken into account that patient dying, I guess."

Maldred grinned and lowered his voice. "Yours was the riskier venture in town. The rest of us robbed closed businesses. Besides, it added a little excitement in our lives. No harm done to us. And we've fine horses to show for it." He took a long look at Dhamon and sniffed. "You need some new clothes, my friend. Rikali pretty well shredded those, and they . . . stink. All of us could do with some new outfits. I doubt the smoke will leave these."

The miles fell away as the sun clawed its way into a slate blue sky, pushing the temperature higher. To the north Rikali spotted a small copse of trees and tall green grass, a virtual oasis for Khur. At first she truly thought it a mirage, blinking furiously, believing it would disappear, but then she spied a raven suspended above a tall tree. It climbed upward into the sun, where she lost track of it for a moment, then it dropped, banked, and dove into the canopy and vanished. She urged her exhausted horse in that direction, releasing the reins of the other, which continued to follow her. As the first shadows touched her, she slipped from her horse's back, complaining about her sore back and stiff legs and her smoky clothes and Dhamon's medicinal stench. She led the animal through the dozen trees that grew here and along the small stream that lazily wended its way along the base of the Kalkhist foothills. "Blessed shade," she said as she stretched, lifted Fetch to set him on the ground, and watched the horses drink.

"I could use a little rest," Dhamon confessed to Maldred.

"No argument." The large man looked over his shoulder. "At least not for the moment." He slid from the saddle and led his horse to the bank. "Probably feeds a tributary of the Thon-Thalas River," he said, gesturing with his head at the water. The famed river wound its way through part of Khur and into the Silvanesti Forest, where it eventually joined up with the Thon-Rishas, which meandered deep into the swamp on the other side of the Kalkhists.

"The stream's half of what it would normally be," Dhamon noted, pointing at the dry bank where part of the ground was cracked and patterned like shingles. "But at least the summer hasn't dried it up completely."

Maldred shook his head, the sweat flying from his face and hair. He took off his boots and lowered his thick toes in the water. Then he bent and filled two skins and clipped them on his belt. He passed a third skin to Dhamon. "For when you really need it," he said. "It's all I have, so take care."

"Thanks."

"*Was* your friend," Rikali said, interrupting their conversation. She had her hands on her hips and her head was cocked to one side, as if she was lecturing a naughty child. "*Was. Was. Was your friend.*"

Dhamon pursed his lips and tethered his mount to a low branch that overhung the bank. He wondered what she was talking about, but knew he didn't have to ask—she'd explain sooner or later.

"The Solamnic. I was thinking about her as we were ridin', hair as red as them flames. I'd say she *was* your friend. Them rigid types don't forgive thefts and murder. She'll be your enemy now."

"I didn't kill anyone in that town." Dhamon patted the horse, running his fingers through its tangled mane. "I might have, but I didn't," he added.

She shrugged and made sure he was watching her, choreographed a graceful display of slipping off her cloak and then squirming out of her tunic, dropping them and her small satchel on the bank to reveal her petite, pale form. She slowly waded into the stream and began bathing, making it a point to tend to her face first and remove the kohl that had run from her eyes. "Dwarves died in that town, Dhamon Grimwulf," she said, cupping her hands to catch the water and throwing it over her hair. "And maybe some Knights who aren't Solamnics. Doesn't really matter how many or by whose hand. Dead is dead. And you were there in the middle of it." She tucked her hair behind gently pointed ears that attested to her half-elf heritage, then she splashed water at him and wriggled her nose. "I tell you, you stink!"

"Aye," Dhamon said softly, as he arranged his boots and new sword on the bank, peeled off what was left of his trousers and joined her in the river. "I certainly do." The water swirled around his calves and then thighs. He waded in as deep as the stream bed allowed, until the water came up to his waist. There were scars on his body amid the scratches that Rikali had administered. They were older and thick, and most had faded so they were difficult to discern.

The half-elf traced some of the scratches. Her nails were long, clawlike, and they were covered with a thick black lacquer that stood out starkly against her parchment-hued skin.

"These will heal, lover," she said huskily, fingers fluttering over her handiwork. "And they were your idea." She kissed one of the longer scratches on his chest, her pale face and white hair contrasting markedly with his sun-bronzed skin.

"Everything heals, Riki," he said softly.

Maldred was inspecting the four horses, announcing that two of them were especially fine and would bring a good price if they decided to sell them. Fetch followed him, pretending to study the big man's ways with animals and apologizing profusely for accidentally setting the fire in the stable.

"You stink, too," Maldred said, looking down and wrinkling his hawkish nose.

Fetch furiously shook his hooded head, backing away from the stream. But Maldred scooped him up with one hand and plucked away his smoky robe with the other. The hoopak and a small belt pouch fell free. Beneath the scorched fabric was a creature.

It was less than three feet tall and had the form of a man, but more resembled a cross between a rat and a lizard, with a rusty brown hide that was a mix of scales and skin. His stunted, dog-shaped snout had a smattering of reddish whiskers growing haphazardly from the bottom jaw that nearly matched the color of his long, pointed, batlike ears that hinted at his goblin ancestry. A kobold, Fetch was a poor cousin to the ancient and more powerful goblin race that often employed his kind as footsoldiers and lackeys throughout Khur and other desolate parts of Krynn. He had beady eyes set beneath a pair of short, curved white horns, and they glowed red like hot embers. "Please, Maldred," Fetch implored in his thin, scratchy voice. His ratlike tail whipped about nervously. "You know I don't like water. I can't swim and I. . . ."

Maldred laughed loud and deep and pitched the kobold into the stream. "See that he washes behind his ears, will you Rikali?" With that, the big man settled himself beneath a tree, his hands resting on the sack and backpack Dhamon had stuffed. Within moments he was asleep.

"That Knight," Rikali persisted after she had finished washing Dhamon's back. Her voice was soft so she wouldn't wake Maldred and Fetch who, like a dog, now was curled in a ball between the big man's feet. "Do you think she'll follow us? She looked so . . . angry."

"Jealous?"

The half-elf shook her head, water flying in an arc from her waist-length hair. "Me, jealous? Hardly, lover."

"You're always jealous, Riki. Besides, Fiona is with Rig—has been for about as long as I've known her. Last I heard, they were to be married this fall, on her birthday."

"You know her first name. . . ."

"I said we *were* friends. Rig was the dark man with her." Dhamon had turned his back to the elf, was studying something in the water. He spread his legs and bent over slightly, letting his hands sink quietly beneath the surface.

"Is he a Solamnic Knight, too?"

"Hardly! Shhh."

"Hardly," she tittered. She watched him carefully with an appraising eye, then she grinned as he tried futilely to catch a fish that dove between his legs. Droplets arced away from him as he smacked the water and quietly cursed.

Quick as lightning, she drove her slender arm into the stream, then pulled it up to reveal a trout speared on her fingernails. She flicked the fish high onto the bank. "You used to be a Knight, Dhamon Grimwulf. Or so you claim."

"Not a Solamnic," he said, as he watched the fish flop about.

"And I'm *not* jealous," Rikali cooed as she moved closer to him, spinning him around to face her. The half-elf's finger snaked out to rub a spot of dirt off his nose. "Have I a reason to be?"

Dhamon said nothing, but he pulled her close.

◊ ◊ ◊ ◊ ◊ ◊ ◊

It was early afternoon when Dhamon woke. He gently lifted Rikali's arm off his chest. He rolled away and reached for his trousers. Before he could finish dressing, a wave of pain struck him and he grabbed for the scale on his leg, digging his heels into the earth. It felt like nails were being driven into his flesh. He bit his lip to keep from crying out and weathered the pain for several minutes. His skin grew feverishly hot and his muscles cramped tight.

He convinced himself it wasn't so bad. Roughly two years ago a dying Knight of Takhisis had removed the scale from his own chest and bestowed it on Dhamon.

Dhamon fought to stay conscious as his mind propelled him back to the forested glade in Solamnia. He was kneeling over the mortally wounded Dark

Knight, holding the man's hand and trying to offer what comfort he could in the last moments of life. The man beckoned him closer, loosed the armor from his chest and showed Dhamon a large scale embedded in the flesh beneath. With fumbling fingers, the Knight managed to pry the scale free, and before Dhamon realized what was happening, the Knight had placed it against Dhamon's thigh.

The scale adhered, molding itself around his thigh and feeling like a brand thrust against his unprotected skin. It was the most painful sensation Dhamon had experienced in his life. The scale was the color of freshly drawn blood then, and Malys, the red dragon overlord from whom it came, used it to possess and control people. Months later a mysterious shadow dragon, along with a silver dragon who called herself Silvara, worked ancient magic to break the overlord's control. The scale turned black in the process. And shortly thereafter it had begun to ache periodically. At first, the pain was infrequent and fleeting.

Dhamon figured pain was preferable to being controlled by a dragon. But lately the spasms had been getting worse and lasting longer. He noticed Maldred watching him, the big man's expression asking if Dhamon was all right.

Dhamon returned the stare, but his unblinking eyes were indifferent and implacable, hiding his attitudes, feelings, keeping everything a mystery. Then he blinked, the pain finally passing. He reached for the skin Maldred had given him, took a deep pull, his throat working hard, and replaced the cork.

"Bad?" the big man asked.

"Sometimes. Lately," Dhamon answered, gingerly rising to his feet. The scratches on his chest and arms were healing. He was clean-shaven, his hair had been combed and tied at the nape of his neck with a black leather thong—compliments of the half-elf. His face looked youthful with all his hair pulled away from it.

Maldred, however, refused to abandon his troubled expression. "Maybe we can find a healer who. . . ."

"A healer can't do anything. You know that." Dhamon changed the subject, pointing to the back-pack and leather sack and the small pile of coin purses he'd brought out of his trousers, and the sacks filled with coins from his companions' heists. "An excellent haul," he pronounced. "A small fortune."

Maldred nodded.

"Gold jewelry studded with gems, plenty of coins, pearls. Enough, hopefully, to purchase that. . . ."

"Not enough," Maldred interrupted flatly. "Not close, Dhamon. I know him."

"Then the hospital . . . the risk . . . was wasted time."

The big man shook his head. "We didn't know how little or how much would be locked away. You did very well."

"Not enough," Dhamon parroted.

"Ah, but it might be *just enough* to purchase an audience with him."

Dhamon frowned.

Maldred gestured at the haul, then opened his backpack and stuffed the smaller pouches into it, keeping one of the larger coin purses out and tossing it to Dhamon. After a moment, he reached back inside and selected a second pouch. "Better give these to Rikali and Fetch for their trouble." He nodded toward the pair, both sleeping soundly a few yards away, close to each other. "Otherwise we'll never hear the end of it."

Dhamon gazed at Rikali for a moment, saw her eyelids fluttering in a dream, then he stretched and turned back to Maldred. "How long should we let them sleep? I know Riki's not worried about any dwarves coming after us, but I'm not so unconcerned. Especially regarding those Legion of Steel Knights. They won't let this go unavenged."

Maldred glanced back the way they had come. Away from the stream the land looked as dry and inhospitable as any desert. "Ah, my friend, this is a most pleasing spot. I could stay beneath that great tree for a few days. It is cooler here, a more restful a place than I've known for a while." His face looked serene, almost gentle, as he glanced at the stream and followed the progress of a floating leaf. It quickly clouded over as he said with a frown, "But don't worry, my friend, such idling is not to be. We can't afford to stay in any one spot too long. Not people like us. Not here. Because of those Knights and others we've crossed. And—most importantly— because we've quite a bit of work ahead of us."

Dhamon cocked his head. "You've a plan?"

The big man nodded. "Oh, yes."

Dhamon's dark eyes glimmered. "Whatever it is, we'll need to move quickly."

"Aye."

The half-elf made a sound, rolling onto her back as her thin arms moved like the wings of a butterfly.

"So this plan. . . ." Dhamon prompted, when he was certain Rikali was still asleep.

"Will bring us great wealth. Gems, my friend. Some as big as my fist." Maldred grinned, showing a wide mouth filled with pearly, even teeth. "We're not terribly far from a valley in Thoradin, to the north and west, cradled by the high spires."

"A mine?"

"So to speak. It will take us a week to reach it. Less, perhaps, as these horses are fine ones. We'll take that trail." His finger indicated a line that ribboned through the hills. He arranged the skins on his belt and adjusted the two-handed sword on his back. "We'll get enough to purchase what you want, and we'll likely have a good bit left over."

"That's a merchant road up there," Dhamon observed.

"Where hopefully we'll find a merchant wagon," the big man added, a gleam in his hazel eyes. "We're going to need something to haul all of our riches in."

CHAPTER THREE
WINDFALLS

I'd prefer not to kill you." Maldred stood in the center of a well-beaten trail that cut through the heart of the Kalkhist Mountains. He was bare-chested, with his deerskin shirt tied about his waist. The midday sun was baking his already-tanned skin and had brought out beads of sweat that slowly ran down his chest and gathered at the waistband of his trousers. The steady breeze that teased his short ginger hair spun the dirt around his boots into dust devils. He gripped his two-handed sword in damp hands, wielding it as if it were no heavier than a twig and pointing it in the direction of a stoop-shouldered grizzled man who sat on the driver's platform of a bulging covered wagon. "Your death would not profit me, old one."

The man sputtered but said nothing, gripped the reins even tighter and stared in disbelief at Maldred. He blinked rapidly, as if doing so might make the big man go away.

"Now," Maldred warned.

"By all the vanished gods, no," the man said—not in response to Maldred's command, but to the unthinkable and very real situation he found himself in. "This cannot be real."

"It's as real as this damnable, rainless summer. Get down off the wagon. Now. Before I lose my patience."

"Gran'papa, don't listen to him!" A gangly youth poked his head through a slit in the canvas and climbed up front. "He's only one man."

"He *should* listen to him, son." Dhamon stepped from behind a boulder, broadsword in hand, blade catching the sun and reflecting it so brightly that the old man squinted. The skin was red and peeling on his shoulders, cheeks, and nose, the rest of his sweaty skin so darkened from the sun that it looked like he was carved from oiled cedar. He looked unkempt and primitive, with his feet bare, remnants of thin scab lines across his naked chest, dressed only in the shredded remains of his trousers—which did little to hide the strange-looking scale on his leg. He'd not shaved since Rikali tended to him, so his jaw looked shadowed, clouded by his new beard. When he curled his lip upward in a snarl and narrowed his black eyes, the youth quivered.

Rikali slid from behind an outcropping on the other side of the pass, long knife outstretched and pointed at the dark-skinned man sitting atop the second wagon. Fetch was at her side, growling and clawing at the air in a reasonable effort to appear menacing.

"Get down, old man, and raise your hands," Maldred's voice was steady and commanding. "And tell the others to do the same. Your lives are worth more than whatever it is you're hauling. We need your cooperation. I don't want to have to say it again."

There were three wagons stopped in the pass, each heavy and each pulled by several large draft horses. A "sumptuous find," Rikali eagerly pronounced it when she spotted the small procession on her scouting trip.

The old man swallowed hard, dropping the reins. He whispered something to the boy and shakily climbed down from the wagon, trembling from fear and casting his eyes back and forth between Maldred and the weird kobold creature. The youth followed him down, glaring at Maldred and casting worried looks Dhamon's way.

"Brigands," the old man wheezed when he'd found his voice again. "Never been robbed in all my life. Never." Louder, he said. "Better do what they say, son. Everybody out!" To Maldred he added, "Don't you hurt none of my people. Not a one! You hear me?"

"Hands away from your sides," Maldred continued, nodding to Dhamon. In response, Dhamon crept forward, taking a thin knife from the old man's belt, tossing it to the far side of the trail, cautiously eyeing the youth for weapons.

"Now stand over there. And be quiet," Dhamon ordered. He gestured with his sword to the opposite side of the trail, where a gray rocky wall stretched toward the cloudless, bright blue sky. "All I want to hear is the sun baking your sorry faces."

Fetch scampered around to the back of the small caravan, hoopak in hand, using it to prod the rest of the merchants forward. The man who climbed off the last wagon moved too slowly for the kobold's liking, so he thwacked him across the back of the knees. The man fell, and Fetch whacked him with the hoopak a few times. He was quick to rise.

Without his hooded cloak, which Rikali said had

to be thrown away because it was so smelly, the kobold presented a frightening figure to the humans, despite his small size. He spat at a portly middle-aged woman who clutched a canvas sack in front of her, and he pointed with his hoopak, indicating she should drop it on the ground. She shook her head furiously, held it tighter, and shouted "Demon!"

"Leave her be," Rikali said as she joined the kobold. "There's plenty of other things for us. Let the ol' bag keep her precious ol' bag." She chuckled at her own keen sense of humor.

Rikali and Fetch shoved the merchants forward. There were nine all together, eight adults and two of those, by their dusky skin, Ergothians like Rig—a long way from home. All were alternating expressions of fear with whispering curses. The grizzled man was the loudest.

"You can't earn an honest way in the world! Shame!" he muttered.

"This is honest enough to suit us," Rikali shot back. She lined the merchants up and looked each one over carefully, her hand darting out to snatch the arm of one of the Ergothians. "The silver bracelet. Take it off. That's it. Now hand it over to me. No tricks. Slow. Ah, it's a beauty." She tried to slide it on her wrist, but found it much too large. She hollered for Fetch, and the kobold scrambled over and hooked the bracelet around her knee, just above her boot cuff.

"Yer welcome, Riki dear," the kobold told her, grinning when a few of the merchants gasped to hear that the demon-creature could speak.

"Fetch!" This time Dhamon was calling for him. "Check the wagons. Make sure there're no surprises inside." Dhamon and Maldred turned their full attention to the line of merchants, hot and defeated and looking for some measure of mercy.

Dhamon sneered at the Ergothians and drummed the fingers of his free hand against his belt. His eyes narrowed, as if telling them "give me an excuse for a fight."

"No need for anyone to get hurt," Maldred said, offering the merchants a bit of reassurance.

A few of them relaxed at his words. But the Ergothians watched Dhamon warily. The old man showed a little courage and ground his heel into the edge of the trail. "Hurt? Stealing from us isn't hurting us? You're taking everything we. . . ."

"Shush, Abril," the portly woman whispered. "Don't provoke them. They've a little demon that serves them."

Without warning the mountain rumbled. But rather than quickly dissipating, the quake grew in intensity, pitching the old man to the ground and causing Dhamon and everyone else to scramble to keep their balance. Fetch had been climbing into the lead wagon when the trembler struck, and he cursed shrilly in his odd language as his head thumped against a crate inside. He cursed again and poked his head out from under the canvas flap, hollering in an odd, snarling language.

"It's nothing," the big man consoled Fetch. "A slight tremor. Happens all the time in the Kalkhists— ever since the Chaos War."

"It's not a tremor. It's the very earth angry at you!" the portly woman said. "Stealing from good people! The spirits of the gods are furious with you!" She instantly stepped back and rounded her shoulders, terrified of the bandits and that her words might provoke them.

The others seemed cowed too, except for the old man who continued to glare as Maldred explained that there was a stream about two days away by foot, perhaps a little more, where they could get something to drink and rest for the night before moving on. He tossed them his largest waterskin to share sparingly until they got there. And beyond that, Maldred said, there was a trail to the south that would eventually take them to either of two dwarven towns—though the farthest might have fewer accommodations available.

"But likely you know about those towns," he finished. "You were probably heading to one of them, or to a larger human settlement even farther south."

"No. They were heading to the coast," Dhamon guessed, smiling thinly when a surly look from the youth acknowledged the correctness of his suspicion. He padded by the Ergothians, noting they too had relaxed a bit. *All bluster*, he thought. "Maybe to Kalin Ak-phan. It's got some size to it. They're toting enough goods to sell to a ship captain there. Especially with all these horses."

"Well then," Maldred said. "We've saved them quite a trip, haven't we? The coast is a considerable distance, too far to travel in this heat."

"So feel free to thank us," Rikali taunted. She dug the tip of her boot into the gravelly ground and stirred it up. "Indeed, we . . ." She stopped as she spotted a flash of gold peeking out beneath the sleeve of one Ergothian, and she slipped closer to examine it. In a heartbeat, the once-seemingly acquiescent man darted forward and managed to grab her, spinning her toward him and snatching the knife from her grip. He was surprisingly strong. He shoved the blade under her throat. "Stay still!" he barked to Maldred.

"Let her go!" the big man snapped. "Now!"

"Not all merchants are easy marks!" The Ergothian returned. "We don't all give up our goods to brigands!" His companion reached under his shirt and pulled two wavy-edged daggers from hidden sheaths. "We heard about robberies along the trails, and we came well prepared. Now *you* back away! And *you* drop *your* weapons."

Maldred and Dhamon didn't budge. Neither made a move to surrender their weapons.

"If you kill her," Dhamon said flatly, "that'll just mean fewer ways to divide the spoils." He noted Rikali's outraged expression but kept his blank face. "Besides, she complains a lot. And we could do with a bit of blessed silence."

After what seemed like several long minutes, where the only sound was the wind rustling through the pass, Dhamon rolled his shoulders, a signal to Maldred that he had sized up the Ergothians and was ready.

Maldred took a step closer to the two Ergothians, watching the other merchants out of the corner of his eye. "You'll be dead before you can cut her throat," he stated. "I'm faster than you. And I'd really prefer not to kill you. Certainly you have relatives somewhere who would prefer you stay alive. So why not drop the blades? You'll live to see tomorrow."

The Ergothians held their position for a heartbeat, then Dhamon flinched, forcing their hand. The one with the twin daggers lunged. Maldred effortlessly swept his sword up, slicing through the man's right arm. The limb fell to the ground, and the Ergothian dropped to his knees, screaming and holding the stump while blood sprayed the horrified merchants.

At the same time, his companion pressed the knife into Rikali's throat, but the half-elf was quicker. Before the Ergothian could cut her, Riki's hands shot up to grip his arm. Throwing all of her strength and weight against it, she pried his arm back. The half-elf scrambled away just as Dhamon stepped forward and swung his sword, cutting deep beneath the man's ribs and killing him instantly.

The portly woman shrieked in terror. The boy sprang into action, his feet churning over the gravel until he was close to Maldred. He launched himself at the big man's back and grabbed hold of him by wrapping his arms around Maldred's thick neck. His grandfather moaned with fear. Rikali spun back to the corpse, plucked the gold bracer off its wrist and fitted it high on her arm. Then she retrieved her knife.

Dhamon held his bloodied sword out, directing the rest of the merchants to stay in line or they'd be next to die. "I'm not as charitable as my large friend," he hissed. "I've no qualms about killing any of you."

Everyone nervously complied, their eyes locked on the scene playing out before them, the old man begging for his grandson's life. The youth's arms were wrapped around Maldred's neck, his knees pummeling the big man's back. But Maldred seemed unaffected.

Rikali slipped behind the pair and pried the youth off, tossing him to the ground and grinding her boot heel into his stomach. "I'd hate to see Maldred kill you, boy," she hissed, waving her knife for emphasis. "He'd keep us up for days fretting about it, moaning about how sacred life is and all that rot. 'Course, Dhamon could do it and save Maldred the grief. Dhamon wouldn't moan over the likes of you." The boy struggled for a moment more, until he was silenced by her icy stare. He lay still.

"Fetch!" Dhamon wiped the blood off his sword onto the dead Ergothian's shirt. "What did you find?"

The kobold's head poked out of the second

wagon, a dark red cap resting awkwardly on his small head. "First one's filled with clothes and such!" he called out, hooting when Rikali let out a whoop. "This one's got some food and spirits and boo-ti-ful smoking pipes." He held out an exquisitely carved sample of a bearded old man, the stem rising from his head. "Pipes for me, tobacco. Lots of tobacco. There's some crates I can't get into. Lots of nails in them." He scampered out of the wagon and ran to the third. "Maybe our luck'll be better here."

"Clothes. Good. You need some clothes," Rikali told Dhamon. "And you could do with some, too," she added to Maldred. "Of course, I can always . . ." She grimaced. The Ergothian missing an arm moaned louder. "Shut up!" She pounced on him, cracking him in the side of the head with the haft of her knife and knocking him out. He lay in a pool of spreading blood which seeped under the toes of Rikali's boots. Turning to the portly woman, who had broken out sobbing, she added, "If you don't want him to die, you better lose some of your skirt and tie off that stump. Put some pressure on it. Don't need to be wearin' so much in this heat anyway." She pivoted and returned to Dhamon, rubbing her soles on the ground in an effort to get the blood off. "Now, about some new clothes . . ."

A cacophony of high-pitched screams from the third wagon cut her off. "Watch them," she said to Dhamon and Maldred, pleased with herself that she gave an order for a change. "He's worthless, Fetch is." Then she was dashing toward the sound.

"Monster!" Rikali shrieked a moment later. "There's a horrible monster in here!"

Dhamon, holding his position, glanced among the merchants and the small caravan. He gestured with his head to the last wagon, and Maldred jogged toward it. The big man thrust his head in the flap and immediately pulled it back out. Rikali scrambled out behind him, holding only the haft of her knife. The blade was missing. Fetch was close behind her, thin cuts crisscrossing his small torso.

"Pigs!" Rikali fumed. "Pigs, but there's some odd-looking beastie tied up in that wagon." She glared at the merchants, waving her knife handle.

"It's not a monster," one of the men quickly offered. "It's just an animal. Leave it be. Please."

Dhamon singled out the wailing merchant and directed him to the wagon. Maldred pushed the man inside, while Dhamon tried on the boots of the dead Ergothian and pronounced them a reasonable fit.

A few moments later the merchant came out leading an unusual creature by a thick rope he had looped about its neck. The thing was as large as a fat calf, but looked like an insect for the most part, with six chitinous legs and feelers that twitched slowly in the air. It had saucerlike black eyes that swiveled back and forth to take everything in, and a small nose that quivered and was aimed toward Maldred. It began to sniff, its purple tongue darting out to lick bulbous lips.

"Bring it over here!" Dhamon called. "Mal, stay back from it. I heard about them when I was stationed in Neraka. The thing eats metal."

"So I discovered," Rikali complained. "That was my favorite knife. Filched it from a handsome noble in Sanction last year. Had lots of sentimental value."

The merchant led the creature like a dog, keeping it in line with the rest of the merchants and clucking softly to it and calling it Ruffels.

"You want *it* to live . . . *you* want to live . . . you start heading down the mountain," Dhamon demanded. "Now. All of you—and that beast. Keep

going and don't look back. As I said, I'm not so generous as my large friend. I've truly no qualms about
killing each and every one of you."

The youth grabbed his grandfather and started
down the trail, the portly woman following, still sobbing hysterically, and two men bringing up the rear,
carrying the injured Ergothian. The man with the
insect-pet was last.

"Wait!" Rikali called, bounding after them. "Is
that beastie valuable?"

The man kept walking and shook his head. "No."

Her eyes narrowed and she scratched her chin,
deciding she was being slighted, that he hadn't at
least properly answered her. She waited a moment,
then ran to catch up. "Then if it's not worth anythin',
you won't mind leavin' it behind."

He tugged the beast closer and clucked to it.
"Please," he said. "You've taken everything of value.
Don't take Ruffels. He's a pet."

She leaned forward and jerked the rope away,
pushing the merchant with her free hand. "I'll have
this, too. He's worth somethin', this beastie is. I'll just
bet. Sell him somewhere for a good turn of coin." She
shook her fist at the odd-looking creature. "And he
owes me for my sentimental knife." Then she waved
the merchant down the hill. "You'd best catch up
with the rest before we decide to sell you, too. You're
not so old and ugly. I could get me a few steel for you
in an ogre town!"

It took some maneuvering to turn the wagons
around in the pass and point them west. While Maldred, Dhamon, and Fetch handled that job, Rikali
inspected the metal-eating creature. "Gonna sell you, I
am," she told it. "Buy me some fine rings with the
coin. Someone'll want a peculiar beastie like you. Rich
people're always wantin' peculiar things. Ruffels.

Gonna change your name first. Call you Fee-ohn-a, I think. Yeah, I like that. Fee-ohn-a the peculiar beastie."

"This won't be enough either, eh?" Dhamon had been in the wagons, eyeing the contents, picking up objects and running his fingers over them. He noted makers' marks on some, which in some circles added to their value. But he could find nothing especially worth all the trouble.

"Valuable, to be certain, but not wildly so. And not what we need to deal with a certain man. We'll still need to visit the valley. But . . . I know a bandit camp where we can sell all of this. Should give Rikali and Fetch enough to stop complaining for a while," Maldred told Dhamon as they made sure the merchants' horses were tied tightly. "We might make more in a town."

"No." Dhamon drew his lips into a thin line, his dark eyes flashing. "We don't want to risk running into people who saw these merchants earlier—or saw others we've run across."

Maldred nodded his agreement. "Very well, then. We'll keep one of these wagons, or get a new one—which is my preference. In the bandit camp. We'll need at least one good wagon for the valley."

"The gems you mentioned, and the mine . . ." Dhamon's face became serious, his eyes intense. He brought a hand up to scratch at the stubble on his chin, then he met Maldred's gaze.

"If fortune favors us, we'll be done with robbing merchants for a while. This is the first time one of these caravans has put up a fight. Next time we might come across mercenaries."

"I'm spoiling for a good fight!" Fetch was dancing around the big man and twirling his hoopak. "We can take on anything. Can't we Dhamon? You've never lost a fight!"

Dhamon ignored the kobold, jumping into the second wagon. There was a large water barrel inside, and he nudged the lid open, drank deep, and splashed water on his face and chest. Then he began prying at the crates that Fetch couldn't open, while Maldred retrieved their horses and tied them to the last wagon.

A scream interrupted them.

Rikali stood in the middle of the trail, yelling at the metal-eating creature and waving her fists. The buckles on her boots were gone, so was the bracelet about her knee and the gold armband. Her right hand was devoid of rings. "I'll kill it!" she hissed. "My jewelry. Quick as a rabbit that cursed beastie grabbed and ate it!"

The creature's nose twitched, and its tongue snaked out to lick its lips. It trundled toward her, eyes locked onto the rings that still sparkled from her left hand.

"Dhamon!" She swung at it wildly, clawlike fingernails raking the beast's tender skin. The creature made a sniffling sound and skittered back a few feet, but its nose continued to twitch. "Dhamon, get over here!"

He peered out of the wagon, grinning at her predicament. "Fetch!" The kobold hurried over. "You've got nothing metal on. Take that thing and tie it back in the wagon where you found it."

Fetch grumpily did so, getting some help from Maldred to boost the creature up and under the canvas, keeping away from its front legs and its metal-devouring mouth. This wagon was held together with wooden nails and there wasn't a trace of metal anywhere on it. "We don't keep this wagon," the big man said. "Or this creature for long. Let's get moving."

❖ ❖ ❖ ❖ ❖ ❖ ❖

Dhamon picked his way along the mountain trail, scouting ahead as the sun melted into the horizon, painting the Kalkhists with a soft orange glow. He relished his time alone, no one to badger him with small talk and questions he didn't want to answer. No one to make any demands of him.

When he was in the company of Maldred and Rikali he often ranged ahead, as he was doing now, seeing if there were any obstacles along the course they would take in the morning. Or if there were any strangers in the area who might bother them during the night. It was his excuse for some silence and peace.

Despite the approaching evening, the heat didn't seem to be letting up. The air was thin this high in the mountains, and coupled with the temperature, Dhamon found it a little discomfiting. He paused to rest on a flat rock, fishing about in his pocket for a piece of candy. Fetch had found a small bag filled with sweets in one of the merchant wagons, and Dhamon made sure it was divided—before the kobold could manage to devour it all.

He stared at the vanishing sun for several moments, breathing as deep as was comfortable and savoring the sugar on his tongue. Then he glanced down the trail. It was just wide enough for the wagon. They would be taking the fork to the north, according to Maldred's directions. The man he needed to see was to the south, but there was the matter of gaining more treasure before they could take that trail.

The north fork appeared less-used, with scrub growing in patches here and there, and wheel ruts so shallow he could barely make them out. Dhamon scooted off the rock and headed north. Just for a few minutes, he told himself, just for a little more time alone.

It wasn't that Dhamon didn't like his current company, he simply believed he needed some solitude once in a while. Maldred had become his closest comrade and partner, and Fetch had a few endearing and useful qualities. Rikali . . . well, she wasn't at all like Feril, the elf he used to keep company with and whom he often thought of. But when he looked past the cosmetic paint and her constant prattle, Rikali was all right. She was here, and Feril was. . . .

"Gone," he stated softly. He was staring at the ground, at a feather from a jay that had fluttered to the side of the path. Feril had a tattoo of a bluejay feather on her face. Dhamon closed his eyes and pictured the Kagonesti, the memory bittersweet. A part of him wished she was with him. But she wouldn't approve of his current lifestyle. She might like Maldred, however, he mused.

Dhamon scowled as he continued to follow the trail around a bend and discovered it was blocked by fallen rocks. The tremors likely had caused it, he decided, as he clambered up the pile and peered over the top, trying to see just how much of the trail was obstructed. A rock wall rose on the east side of the path, and much of its face had crumbled loose to block the way. Dhamon could tell it should pose little problem beyond this point—after this pile was cleared.

Maldred was strong. Between him and Dhamon, and with some help from Rikali and Fetch they should be able to manage it without too much trouble. And provided there weren't any more tremors in this section of the mountains. The tremors had bothered him more than a little, as a force of nature was something he couldn't stand up to. But apparently the tremors were something he had to put up with here, including the results—such as this blocked path.

Dhamon bent to the task of clearing the way himself, the activity feeling good and keeping his mind off Feril and all manner of other things that festered at him when he grew introspective. He worked until dark, the heat letting up only a little. He hadn't cleared all of it, but the worst was out of the way. He could tackle it again in the morning to finish the job. Exhausted, sweat-soaked, and very hungry, he retraced his steps along the trail and back to where he'd left the others to make camp.

❖ ❖ ❖ ❖ ❖ ❖ ❖

Night didn't soften Dhamon's features. The angles of his face still looked hard, his eyes were dark, his demeanor as usual unreadable. His stubble had thickened, and he rubbed his fingertips across it, making an almost imperceptible sound. His jaw worked and the muscles in his sword arm tensed and relaxed as he considered the plunder from the wagon and the sale of the goods. He was silently cursing the merchants for not having more wagons or anything of extraordinary value inside.

He and Maldred sat just close enough to a small fire that they could see the coins they were counting. Fetch materialized every once in a while to turn the meat roasting on the spit and to make sure he wasn't being cheated of food or money. Rikali was nearby, trying on garment after garment she'd claimed as part of her spoils from the wagons and trying unsuccessfully to catch Dhamon's attention.

"Acceptable," Maldred announced when he'd

made four piles of coins and placed them in four leather pouches. Two were larger, and he tossed one to Dhamon and tied the other large one on his own belt. "Coin and food."

"Drink," Dhamon added, his darker thoughts abandoned. He gestured to a jug of strong, distilled spirits that sat within his reach. He reached toward the jug, his hand folding about the handle. "Good drink."

"And new clothes, my good friend." Maldred had abandoned his deerskin breeches and shirt in favor of lightweight trousers and a thin, billowy tunic the shade of pale lilies. He'd found only a few things to fit him in the merchant stores, enough for two changes of garb with one shirt to spare and a cloak that hung just past his knees. Though he was only a few inches taller than Dhamon, his shoulders were much broader, his chest, arms, and legs thick and heavily girded.

Dhamon had more to choose from, and he had selected expensive, dark-colored garments that draped his lanky frame. He'd also helped himself to a ropelike gold chain, at Rikali's insistence. Hanging from his neck, it gleamed in the firelight.

Fetch had managed to find some children's clothes to fit into, though the colors and design made him hiss—sky blue with embroidered birds and mushrooms along the sleeves. Fortunately, he also managed to find a kender-sized wool cloak the shade of charcoal with a hood. He vowed to wear this when they came close to civilization—no matter how hot it was. Though others of his kind rarely bothered with clothes, Fetch had come to appreciate well-made garments—if for no other reason than because they helped to disguise his race. He muttered that he needed to find more appropriate attire down the

road. He certainly didn't want to stride into any sizeable city looking like this.

At the moment, he was getting ready to smoke his
prized acquisition, the old-man pipe, as he called it.
Humming and gesturing with his fingers, he began
to execute a simple spell. He fingered the intricately
carved beard and tamped the tobacco down tight.
The spell magically helped the tobacco catch fire. He
puffed to get it going, and let his teeth click comfortably against the stem.

Rikali fared the best, in her opinion, discovering
all manner of tunics and skirts and scarves and
baubles. She'd been occupied for more than an hour
since they'd stopped, trying things on again and
again and twirling to unheard music.

Those things that didn't suit her sense of fashion,
along with practically everything else in the wagons,
had been sold at the bandit camp. Dhamon conducted the bargaining, gaining more than Maldred
had guessed likely for the lot. They'd purchased a
different wagon there, one that had high sidewalls
and a big canvas tarp. Maldred contended it was
even sturdier and more appropriate for the trip to the
valley than the ones they sold. And they'd kept two
draft horses to pull it.

"The trail you want to take is narrow," Dhamon
told him.

"I know, I've used it before. It's my favorite route
to the valley. Not so easy to navigate, and therefore
not often used."

"So, are you going to tell me precisely what's in
this valley?" Dhamon prompted. "Diamonds, you
say?"

"Yes."

"Why so secretive?"

"I thought you liked surprises."

"Never said that. You must be thinking of Riki."

Maldred grinned and shook his head, reaching forward and tugging free a hunk of meat. "There will be windfall profits, partner," he said, "if we can pull it off. I wouldn't even consider attempting it without you."

Dhamon's dark eyes gleamed, reflecting the light and his curiosity.

"It will be easy, I think. All we have to do is. . . ." Maldred caught Rikali listening and shook his head. "Best I keep the details to myself until we get there." He lowered his voice until Dhamon had to strain to hear him. "Fetch'll do whatever we want, go wherever we tell him. But we don't need Rikali getting all excited and upset. Trust me?"

"With my life," Dhamon said. "Keep your surprise for a while longer."

The big man rose and stretched and cocked his head back to take in the night sky. A riot of stars winked down, and he raised a finger to trace a design in them. "I, too, trust you with my life, my friend. I've not said that to another man before. But in the four months since you've drifted into my company I've come to think of you as a brother."

Dhamon reached for the jug and unstoppered it, drank greedily for several moments. "I've had . . . few friends I could trust like that, either."

Maldred chuckled. "I can read your mind, my friend. What are you thinking about? Palin Majere and the mystic Goldmoon?" Maldred stopped tracing stars. "I'd say your travels at their behest added to your character, Dhamon Grimwulf. And taught you the true meaning of friendship."

"Aye, perhaps," Dhamon agreed, raising the jug in toast. "Friendship is important." He drank deep again, then met the big man's gaze. Dhamon's eyes were unblinking. "I've told you considerable about my past," he said evenly. "But I know little about you."

"Nothing much to tell. I'm a thief. Who dabbles in magic." He padded from the fire and stretched out on a blanket, hands cupped behind his head as a pillow. Fetch scampered over, took a last puff on his pipe, shook out the tobacco, and carefully put the pipe away. Then he curled up between Maldred's feet and in an instant was softly snoring.

Dhamon tugged free a hunk of charred meat and chewed on it almost thoughtfully. The odd beast called Ruffels was tasty and tender. He had slaughtered it himself on his return from the scouting trip. No one in the bandit camp would buy the accursed creature, and it had gobbled down a few more pieces of Rikali's jewelry.

"Do you like this?" Rikali had slid behind him, draping a gossamer-fine scarf in front of his eyes.

"Very pretty," he replied, craning his neck and glancing up at her.

The half-elf's face was heavily made-up, her eyelids and lips painted the color of a ripe plum, her silver-white curls piled high atop her head and held in place by a jade comb she'd found in one of the wagons. She was wearing a dark green tunic made of a satiny fabric. It was a little too tight, which seemed to suit her. "And don't you think I'm very pretty, too?"

Dhamon nodded and made a move to rise. But she dropped the scarf over his face and eased down next to him. He gazed appreciatively at her somewhat hazy and celestial form. "Riki, you're very pretty." He gave her a hint of a smile. "And you know it. You don't need me to tell you that."

She waggled her fingers at him, showing off the new rings she'd claimed from the merchant stores.

She had tried unsuccessfully to talk him out of the old pearl ring he'd stolen from the hospital—and out of any of the best pieces from that haul. But the hospital booty had not been fairly divided. Still, there were several new bracelets on each of her wrists and around one of her ankles. She'd discarded her boots in favor of soft leather sandals that she also appropriated, and she had managed to find a thick gold ring to fit around one toe.

"You don't need all that . . . decoration," he said.

"Ah, lover, but I do." She kissed the jeweled Legion of Steel ring on his hand. "It's easier to carry my baubles than a heavy sack of coins. And they're much lovelier to look at than minted pieces of steel. But some day I'll trade all of this in for a fine house far from the dragons and Knights and this insufferably hot weather. On an island, I think. One that catches the cool breezes when the summer tries to get too unbearable. One where it never snows. A perfect, beautiful island. It'll be just me and *you* there—and company when we invite them. And we'll have a big strawberry garden ringed with a field of daisies." She leaned close and kissed him, lingering so he could smell the sweet musky perfume she'd liberally applied. "And maybe we'll have a babe or two to cuddle and watch grow up." She shuddered and giggled. "But not for quite a while, Dhamon Grimwulf. I'm much too young for all of that, and I've too much o' the world to see first." She tugged free the scarf and kissed him again.

When she pulled back, her face was serious. "Tell me you love me, Dhamon Grimwulf."

"I love you, Riki." He said the words, but there was no ardor in them, and his eyes did not meet hers.

She smiled wistfully and teased the hair that hung over his high forehead. "Someday you'll mean it."

They settled down, nestled together, but Dhamon's mind was elsewhere. Once again he had felt the scale begin to burn. It was a slight sensation at first, a not unpleasant warmth. It always started this way, the gentle warmth, almost comforting in a way, teasing him. And after several minutes, sometimes as much as an hour, the warmth began to build.

Now he gritted his teeth, trying to focus on Rikali's sensual ramblings, but all he felt was the growing heat. Hot as a flame now, it felt like it was melting his flesh. All he heard was the pounding of his heart, so loud in his ears it was deafening. The jabs of cold started next, alternating with the burning until fire and ice pulsed outward from the scale with each breath he took. The pain was consuming him. Despite his best efforts, he started to shake. He slammed his mouth shut and felt his teeth involuntarily grind together, felt his fingers twitch and the muscles in his legs move uncontrollably.

In the back of his mind he saw the red dragon and the Dark Knight who, long ago, had cursed him with the scale. "Remove it and you'll die," the Knight had said, repeating the words in a whisper that sounded like a chorus of maddened ghosts. He saw, too, a glaive, the glaive that was now carried by Rig, though it had once been borne by Dhamon. Saw the glaive in his hands, saw it bearing down on Jasper Fireforge, cleaving into the dwarf's chest and sorely wounding him. Saw his arms raise the glaive again and strike down Goldmoon, slaying her—or so he thought. He felt something then, in a small faraway place in his mind, grief and horror and a desire to be dead in Goldmoon's stead.

As the pain mounted, he watched and watched. He saw it all happen again, watched the months melt away until a shadow dragon and he were in a cave.

A silver dragon used her magic to alter the scale. Then memory vanished as the pain intensified, making it impossible for him to think of anything more.

Rikali snuggled even closer and kissed his damp forehead. Tears welled up in her eyes, her fingers closed about his arm. "It'll pass, lover," she said. "Just like always."

Chapter Four
The Vale of Chaos

No wonder you had us travel at night, Mal, so none but your ill-tempered self would know where we were goin'." Rikali was whispering, her voice biting, buzzing around Maldred's head like a cloud of annoying gnats. "Why, if I'd a clue we were comin' here, I'd have . . . well, I wouldn't't've come along. And neither would've Dhamon. I'd have told him all about this place, and for a change he would've listened to me. We'd be cuddlin' up somewhere nice, where it ain't so damnably hot and dry, and . . . well, I'm tempted to turn right around now and. . . ."

"Where are we exactly?" Dhamon prompted, understanding why Maldred had kept their destination secret, but now wondering if he should have pressed his partner for some information about this mysterious mission.

They were picking their way down the side of a mountain, Dhamon and Rikali following Maldred and Fetch and trying, save for Riki's mumbled complaints, to be reasonably silent. The footing was quite precarious, with jagged rocks stretching up like crooked fingers everywhere and abundant patches of loose gravel that threatened to send them sliding to the bottom. It was dark, well past midnight. A touch of gray in the east alluded to dawn being only an hour or so away.

"By my breath," Rikali persisted in her hushed voice, "this is idiocy, Mal, worse scheme you've ever come up with. First Dhamon steals all of the treasure kept at a hospital and then makes it clear it's not to be properly split—a "door opener," he calls it. Must be some helluva door. Where's the door, I keep askin'."

"Where are we exactly?" Dhamon repeated, raising his voice.

"Shh!" Maldred and Fetch warned practically in unison.

Dhamon paused, watching the three thread their way down the mountain. It looked like they were heading into a great, black pit of the Abyss at the bottom of the vale. Through the soles of his procured boots, he could feel the summer's heat baking the land. Still, he felt better than he had in quite some time. He'd had no episodes with the scale for the past several days, and his spirits were high—too high to continue to put up with Rikali's grumbling and this mystery. "Tell me exactly where we are, Mal, or I'm not taking another step."

Maldred continued down the mountainside, oblivious to Dhamon's threat. Fetch shrugged and followed the big man. But the half-elf stopped, huffed, and put her slender hands on her hips. She cast her head over her shoulder again, her mass of silvery-white hair fluttering, and she glared up at Dhamon. "We're just south of Thoradin, in the heart of dwarf lands. Satisfied?" Then she started down again, motioning for him to follow.

"I know that much . . . dear."

"The Vale of Chaos," she added, still talking so softly he had to strain to hear her. "Smack in the middle of the Vale of Chaos."

When Dhamon finally caught up to them, Maldred signaled they'd made it halfway down the mountainside, and he directed them behind a massive boulder.

"Never heard of it," Dhamon muttered. "This Vale of . . . Chaos?"

"That's 'cause you never lived around here," Rikali said. "That's 'cause before your head was always filled with notions of Knights and dragons and honor and such. And with . . . what was that lady's name . . . Fiona." She spat at the ground and cut Maldred an evil look. "Gonna all die, we are. Gonna die right here in this damnable Vale of Chaos."

Fetch looked nervous, but kept silent, his small hand clutching a pouch of tobacco.

"Ruled by dwarves, this place is," she continued, her voice even lower. "It don't make sense to seek out dwarves after Ironspike."

Jasper Fireforge, Dhamon thought, meeting her gaze. That was a dwarf Dhamon had considered a friend.

"Pigs, but this place is supposedly patrolled by an army of them stubby, hairy men."

"There *are* patrols," Maldred finally spoke, his voice low. "But it's not an army. And they can't be everywhere. The valley's too big for that. And the dwarves don't *own* the land, they just *claim* it."

Dhamon gave him a look that said, what's the difference?

The big man sighed and glanced around, ran his fingers through his hair and considered his words.

"Dhamon, Thoradin is always skirmishing with Blöde . . ."

"The ogres," Rikali cut in.

". . . over ownership of this vale. It is a struggle with a long history, made more bloody in recent decades."

"All 'cause of the Chaos War," the half-elf added.

"The ogres have a legitimate claim, since they roam freely over the rest of these mountains. The vale truly should be theirs."

"Tell that to the dwarves, Mal," Rikali whispered.

"But the ogres don't care to press the issue at the moment. They can't. They must direct their efforts against spawn and draconian and other minions of the black dragon who constantly encroach upon their time-honored territories."

"Why is this valley so damned desirable?" Dhamon asked.

"Wait until the sun comes up, lover," Rikali said. "You'll see, or so the tales say. All of us will see. And then all of us will die."

When they lay down, Rikali snuggled against Dhamon and rested her head against his chest. She told him to wake her at dawn if the dwarves hadn't found them before then. Maldred closed his eyes, too, but Dhamon could tell the big man wasn't sleeping. The knob in his throat was going up and down, his teeth softly clicking together, his fingers tracing intricate patterns in the dirt. Fetch glanced back and forth among the three of them, and occasionally, very nervously, poked his head out from behind the boulder. Dhamon dozed fitfully and briefly, keeping an eye on Mal and Fetch. When, hours later, the sun struck the top of the canyon walls, the kobold was the first to see and gasp in amazement.

Dhamon too found himself at an uncustomary

loss for words. The stoical mask fell away and his face glowed with childlike wonder. He nudged the half-elf awake.

"Forget what I said earlier, Mal," Rikali said in a hushed voice. She shielded her eyes with her hand. "This was a glorious idea. Glad I followed you here."

Crystals of every imaginable color dotted the steep canyon walls, catching the light of the rising sun and reflecting it in near-blinding patterns. The valley was an immense dazzling kaleidoscope of shifting colors—shades of amethyst; a riot of peridots and olivines; mesmerizing quartz spires that sparkled rosy pink one moment, sky blue the next; diamonds that twinkled like ice; gems nobody could ever put a name to. The rocky mountains down which they had picked their way last night were laced with rubies and opals and tourmaline, and topaz shards and garnet and . . . all kinds of gems that wouldn't normally be found together but somehow were together. All in this Vale of Chaos.

The wind picked up as the sun inched higher. The breeze sounded like windchimes as it wound around the rocks, slipped down one side of the vale, and then up the other to warm the ground. It was a warmth that, as the day went on, would become miserable heat.

Dhamon found himself caught up in the pure beauty of the place. He shaded his eyes, then blinking and turning, he looked all around at the mesmerizing display of colors. Rare, priceless, bountiful, unending colors.

"By my breath. Paradise," said Rikali. She reached out toward a large green crystal and managed to close her fingers around it, just as Maldred grabbed her by the ankle and pulled her back.

"An emerald," Rikali said, turning it over in front

of her wide eyes, oblivious to her scraped and bleeding knees. The rough gem was a few shades darker than the paint she had applied to her eyelids yesterday. "By my breath, I'm gonna have a jeweler cut it for me." She thrust it in her pocket and whirled on Maldred. The big man stopped her with a finger pressed to her lips.

"I've been here before, Riki," he began, "a few times—alone. Always before it was only my own neck I risked. There *are* patrols. I've seen them. They mainly cover the top of the vale, catching people who come down while the sun is out and they're readily visible. That's why we hid the wagon and horses."

"So that's why we came in at night," Fetch mused. His tiny eyes were flitting about, lighting on one patch of gems, then moving on to the next. His gaze was like a bee, never resting one place for any length and his breath was coming ragged from excitement.

"We can avoid the patrols," Maldred continued, "And the miners. But we have to be careful—very careful, and alert. Rikali's right. They will kill trespassers."

Rikali's fingers were in her pocket, the clawlike nails clicking against the edges of the emerald. "I can be careful," she whispered. "And I can be rich. Very."

Maldred nodded. "I don't care if some of these gems find their way into your pockets. Take whatever you can stuff in your pouches and clothes. But we're here *first* for Dhamon."

She shot Dhamon a curious look, turned back and raised her eyebrows questioningly.

"We'll explain later," Maldred said.

"You'll explain now," she returned, her voice a little louder than she had intended.

"We need to harvest as much as we can from the vale," Maldred continued.

"And I will use our treasure trove to buy us something very old and even more valuable. Something that will tremendously profit all of us," Dhamon added.

"I can't imagine more profit than this."

Maldred softly chuckled. "Then Riki, you don't have much of an imagination."

She scowled and looked again at Dhamon, who was preoccupied by the shimmering beauty of this place. Her expression softened as she smiled wistfully. "For Dhamon, then. Anything for Dhamon."

"And ultimately for us," Maldred added. "We load up our sacks with the finest gemstones, hide behind boulders until it's dark, then carry everything back to the wagon. Two days of this, we don't want to press our luck for longer, and the wagon will be reasonably full and we'll be on our way to Blöten."

"Blöde's lovely capital, in the heart of ogre land," Rikali hissed, her sarcastic voice less caustic than usual. She edged closer to Dhamon. "What could the ogres possibly have that you want, lover? And why haven't you told me about it?"

"Because you can't keep secrets, dear Riki."

"Now let's get to work," Maldred advised. "And remember, be careful." He crept out from behind the boulder and headed farther down into the valley, trying to hide behind outcroppings and large spires as he went.

He stopped to squat between a pair of natural granite columns which were flecked with chunks of aquamarine. Glancing about, he dug the tips of his fingers into a patch of loose soil between them. A hum came from deep in his throat, high in pitch, the sound resonating musically off the columns and accompanying the wind. His fingers stirred the dirt, then suddenly his right hand started clawing, digging a hole and uncovering a chunk of rare pink topaz as big as his fist. Nudging it aside, he continued to hum and dig, finding more and more, keeping up his enchantment until he was fatigued. Leaning against a column to regain his energy, he took a deep pull from his waterskin, practically draining it. Then he opened a canvas sack and carefully filled it with the precious crystals he had unearthed.

Fetch went in another direction, making sure he could keep the big man in sight for a sense of security. The kobold was small enough to easily hide behind jutting rocks, and he picked up pieces of crystal as he went, turning them over to check for imperfections. He quickly discarded the ones that didn't meet his considerably high standards. The pockets of his sky blue pants were bulging before long, and well before he started filling up his canvas sacks.

Rikali motioned Dhamon to follow her. "I know what's valuable, lover. 'Course so do Mal and Fetch. By my breath, but this is all so wonderful." She took his hand, her clawlike nails softly raking his palm, and tugged him southward. "All of this has worth. But some crystals are superior." She pointed at a crevice, and they quickly made their way there. Partially hidden by the shadows, she inhaled deep, thinking the air much sweeter in this place, and leaned her back against Dhamon's chest, her head turning from right to left to watch the colors dance. "Good thing Mal hadn't told me we were comin' here," she confessed. "I truly wouldn't have gone along with it. I wasn't foolin' him. I wouldn't have followed even you here, Dhamon Grimwulf." She grinned at Dhamon. "But I am glad we're here. Amazin'. I don't believe the dwarves should have this all for themselves, don't believe the ogres need it either. Can't none of them ugly lookin' folks truly appreciate this beauty. They're warlike and mean-tempered people, they are, and they don't deserve anything this exquisite."

Dhamon hadn't spoken since the sun came up. He was still mesmerized by what his eyes beheld.

Rikali nudged him hard with her elbow to break the spell. "And what's this about usin' all of this wealth, well, most of it anyway, to buy somethin' special for you? What could you possibly want more than this?" She gestured with her hand. "Tell me, lover. You shouldn't be keepin' no secrets from me."

"A sword."

She paused, clearly surprised at the answer. "A sword's gonna make us all rich?" She spat at the ground and shook her head. "You've got a sword. A pretty one that you picked up in that hospital. And worth a very pretty steel piece, it is."

"A better sword."

"Ain't no sword worth giving up these gems for."

Dhamon cut her a sharp look.

"Well, where is this sword? I could help you steal it. We'd slip into whatever ogre camp it's in, slip away with not a one of them the wiser. And then you'd have your old sword *and* we'd keep all these gemstones for ourselves."

"Stealing it would be too risky."

Riskier than this? her face asked. She poked out her bottom lip. "Must be a very big ogre camp. And you couldn't've told me about all of this? I truly don't like you keepin' secrets from me. I don't keep a thing from you, Dhamon Grimwulf. I never have." She turned to stare fully up into his face. "But then, you're nothin' but secrets, are you, lover?"

His eyes were unblinking. So dark, she could hardly discern the pupils in his eyes. Mysterious and brimming with secrets upon secrets, she decided, and certainly worth losing herself in. His eyes could catch hers as fast as any manacle, holding them until he wanted to break the moment. She wished he would look at her now.

Rikali also wished he was as taken with her as he was by all these crystals. Finally his eyes met hers, and he began to ask her a dozen questions—not about her, but about this place. He was trying to keep his mind off his leg, Rikali thought with a sigh.

"A product of the Chaos War," she told him, "or so the tavern tales say." The half-elf nodded to indicate some gems that protruded from the ground, which she stopped to pick up and examine and thrust in her pocket. She discarded only a few. "During the war they claim this vale burst with priceless crystals. Oh, dwarves and ogres had been minin' it before then, findin' some opals and silver now and again and fightin' over them more because they were fightin' to expand their home territories. But there was no real reason for all o' these gemstones comin' to the surface when they did. I guess the gods must have did it before they left, wanted to really give the dwarves and ogres somethin' to tussle about." She waved her hand and sighed. "So beautiful."

"And . . ." Dhamon's voice cracked as his throat was going dry. Rikali was right. The scale on his leg had started to tingle, and he fought against the sensation, concentrated on the shimmering crystals to keep his mind occupied, tried to focus on her voice.

"The dwarves claimed the vale, of course, and the ogres claimed it, too—just like Maldred said. But this rocky hole is in Thoradin, dwarf country. Now, Blöde wraps around Thoradin like a glove. And the ogres run all of Blöde. So who knows—or cares—who it really belongs to." She cupped her hand around a chunk of topaz. "But, like Mal will tell you, there're plenty more dwarves than ogres, and the ogres have the black dragon and her spreadin' swamp to worry about, too. So the runty dwarves're winnin' this particular turf war. And accordin' to every tale I ever heard, the dwarves do indeed have an army guardin' this place. Greedy little hairy men." She spat at the ground. "I've had my fill of dwarves, I have."

"What do they do with all these gems?" Dhamon forced the words out, then he gritted his teeth and clenched his fists.

"The dwarves export gems and minerals to Sanction and Neraka and are gettin' steadily richer. Miserly little toughs, they are. But they're careful not to take out too much at a time, keepin' the price for gems and such still horribly high. They put too many on the market, and the gems're just not worth as much—supply and demand and all, you understand."

Dhamon nodded. He was sincerely interested in Rikali's story, but it was getting more difficult to hear her. His leg was burning. The pounding of his heart was filling his ears.

"Regular folks stay far away from here—and for good reason. I had friends tell me about corpses of trespassers staked out around the vale entrance. Some twisted and mutilated, barely recognizable to their kin. Heads on poles." She shuddered and made a face. "I don't want to die, lover, but if I'd have known the tales didn't do this hole in the ground justice, I would have risked my life a dozen times over before now. This is worth the risk."

She stooped again, her clawlike fingers digging into the scree at her feet. Giggling, she tugged free a rose quartz crystal the size of an apricot. Rikali held it up so the sun would catch its natural facets, held her breath and stared at it a moment, then exhaled with a soft whistle and quickly put it in her pocket.

"Not especially valuable, that one, a little too milky. But it's a very pretty shade, and I fancy it cut just right and polished and hangin' on a gold chain around my neck. Follow me, lover, and I'll show you how to spot the good pieces, the ones that'll cut the best. I'll teach you how to picture 'em all finished and more beautiful than they are now. Teach you how to look for flaws."

Dhamon didn't move. He had wedged himself into the crevice and slammed his eyes shut. "I'll catch up with you, Riki," he managed to gasp. "You go on ahead and find the best crystals."

The half-elf stopped chattering, her shoulders sagged, and she moved closer, wrapping her arms around his waist. "You made it nearly five days, lover, without one of these spells. Some day you'll beat it." She held him tight and felt his body tremble, a sympathetic tear sliding down her face. "You *will* beat it," she told him. "I just know it. Everything will be all right. Here, concentrate on this."

She held the rosy gem in front of his face, turning it this way and that as if to hypnotize him. He tried to fixate on it, staring unblinking, telling himself how beautiful it and Rikali were, how beautiful this vale was. But the heat on his leg, increasing now, was concentrated on the scale, and it was somehow worse, different from the times before.

He tried to swallow, but found his throat had gone utterly dry. He tried to move and found himself paralyzed, the strength vanishing from his legs.

"Lover?" the half-elf asked.

Dhamon reached for his thigh, where the scale was covered by the expensive black trousers gained from the merchant robbery. "Ow!" He pulled his fingers back. It was hot, practically scalding! He doubled over from the pain. "Riki. . . ." was all he managed.

"I'm here." She forgot the gems and threw her arms around his shoulders, brushed his cheek with her lips. "Ride it out. Just ride it out."

Dhamon sucked in his lower lip, cursing himself for acting like a wounded child. There was an acrid taste in his mouth he couldn't get rid of, and his lungs burned. He looked up so he could see over the half-elf's shoulder, trying to find something to concentrate on—anything to occupy his mind and diminish the pain.

Then, suddenly, his mind was flooded with an image, and as if in a dream he saw in front of him a wall of gleaming copper plates that reflected his face back at him. Hundreds upon hundreds of Dhamon Grimwulfs. And all of those faces contorted in pain.

"Riki . . ." he repeated, reaching up with his hand and turning her face and pointing. "Do you see it? The scales? The dragon?"

The half-elf looked up with a shudder, her eyes spotting something not in the air in front of her, where Dhamon's eyes remained fixed, but in the sky far overhead. "Pigs, lover! There is a dragon! So high up in the sky. Hard to see it. Wouldn't've noticed it if you didn't. . . ."

She pointed and Dhamon saw it, the image in his mind melting away. Dhamon squinted up into the bright summer sky and saw the form arcing over the valley, dipping lower, then climbing higher and higher and higher, finally disappearing altogether from view.

A heartbeat later, the agony in his leg dissipated.

"It was a copper dragon, Riki."

She cocked her head. "It was too high to see what kind, the sun too bright."

"*It was a copper dragon*," he repeated.

"How do you . . ."

"I just know, that's all."

A moment later they emerged from the crevice, Dhamon a little shaky but intent on doing his share of harvesting the crystals.

Determined to keep his mind off the strange episode, Rikali pulled a wavy dagger from her belt, one taken from the slain Ergothian, and used it to pry free chunks of green peridot. She held one of the precious gems up to the light and began explaining to Dhamon, with a gemologist's expertise, about imperfections and coloration in rough material.

❖ ❖ ❖ ❖ ❖ ❖ ❖

Late the second morning Fetch sat in front of a piece of pale yellow quartz shaped like a rounded tombstone. Its large, flat facet reflected his doglike visage as if the kobold were staring into a tinted mirror.

He craned his neck this way and that, admiring his diminutive, craggy features, then he scowled when he saw the embroidered birds and mushrooms on his clothes reflected back at him. "Baby clothes," he hissed. "I'm wearing human baby clothes." After a moment, his scowl turned into a wide smile, revealing his uneven yellowed, pointy teeth. "A baby," he whispered. "Goochie goochie goo."

Fetch started humming, a scratchy, off-key tune mingled with occasional gargling sounds. His scale-covered fingers started dancing in the air, as if he were conducting an invisible orchestra. The air shimmered around him, the heat rising from the ground. The shimmering closed around him like a cocoon, until flashing and sparkling motes frolicked over his cheeks, growing and winking ever brighter. He swallowed a snicker, the sensation of the enchantment tickled him, and then he increased the tempo of his strange melody. Finally the music stopped and the motes disappeared, and the only sound was the wind playing against the crystals like distant chimes. Staring back from the mirrorlike quartz was the cherubic face of a young human boy with wispy blond hair and rosy cheeks. He opened his mouth to reveal two upper teeth cutting their way through petal-pink gums. "Goochie goochie goo!" Fetch stuck his thumb in his mouth, winked, and wriggled happily.

"Getting good at this," Fetch congratulated himself. "Wish Maldred could see me." The kobold twisted his neck around to make sure the big man was still in sight. "Good indeed!" Soon he was humming again, his crystal-gathering chores forgotten for a moment in favor of the magic. A few minutes later, a vacant-looking gully dwarf was reflected in the crystal. "Dwell, dwat do you dknow," he said, imitating the nasally sound of gully talk. Next, an ancient kender with deep wrinkles and an impressive gray topknot appeared. "Most unfortunate I left my hoopak in the wagon. It would complete the image." Try as he might, the kobold could not change the appearance of the clothes. He worked to see how long he could hold a face, guessing that almost ten minutes had passed before his own craggy countenance reappeared. "I am indeed getting much, much better," he pronounced. "What next? Hmm. I know."

He concentrated again, humming something now that sounded like a funeral dirge as his fingers twitched in the air along his jaw line. The motes sparkled with a darker light this time, concentrating around his brow, which was broadening, and his jaw, which appeared to melt in upon itself and widen. The scraggly clumps of reddish hair that dangled from his chin multiplied and thickened, growing longer and forming a dense, auburn beard. Heavy brows developed over eyes that were becoming larger and as blue as the sapphires he had stuffed in his canvas sack an hour ago. Fetch's nose was swelling, taking on the bulbous shape of a large onion, and his scaly skin was turning a ruddy flesh color that made his blunt white teeth stand out. When the metamorphosis was complete, a stunted dwarf was reflected in the crystal.

"Too bad Rikali can't see me," he mused. "Says she's had enough of dwarves. This'd give her a good chuckle." The image's eyes widened in surprise, and Fetch gulped. Above his mirrored face was the image of a real dwarf, one with narrowed steely gray eyes, and one with thick fingers wrapped around the haft of a battle-axe that was plunging down toward him.

"Mal!" the kobold sputtered as he whirled away.

The dwarf had swung his axe hard and missed Fetch only by inches, striking instead the crystal and shattering it. Shards pelted Fetch as his image was melting off him like butter. The kobold rolled again, squealing when the axe sliced through his butterfly sleeve.

"Mal! Company, Mal!" The kobold sprang to his feet and started scrabbling down the mountainside, feet slipping on gravel as he went. A quarrel whizzed over his head as he ducked behind a hornblend spire. He risked a peek out the other side. "Th-th-there's four of 'em," he sputtered. "Four very angry dwarves. And me without my hoopak."

❖ ❖ ❖ ❖ ❖ ❖ ❖

"This one must weigh close to three pounds, huh?" Rikali tossed over a pear-shaped crystal that was uniformly pale yellow in color.

"What is it?" Dhamon caught it and hefted it in his palm, then carefully placed it in his canvas sack. He was using the scraps of a shredded cloak to pad the crystals so they wouldn't jostle against each other and chip. Three already-full canvas sacks sat at his feet. There were nearly three dozen more large sacks already loaded on the wagon.

"Citrine," she said. "A type of quartz. Not as valuable as some of the other stuff we've been takin', but that one'll cut really fine. More valuable because of its size, though."

"How'd you learn so much about gems?"

She puffed herself up, smiling. "Dhamon Grimwulf, I decided at a very young age that I wasn't gonna be poor like my parents. So I fell in with a small guild of thieves. My dad . . . my parents're both half-elves . . . anyway, my dad disowned me, he did, not that I minded. Said he didn't approve of how I made my livin'. My folks were horribly poor, barely makin' their way as fishermen in a village on the shore of Blood Bay." She shook her head as if casting off the inconvenient memory. There was no trace of regret in her eyes. "The guild schooled me—in all the things important to becomin' wealthy. Such as how to recognize good stones, how to tell which houses are likely filled with the most valuables, where to fence things, how to pick pockets and cut coin purses from a man's belt. I'd still be with them if I hadn't tried to pick Mal's pocket when he was strollin' big-as-you-please along the Sanction docks. Caught me, he did—and took me in and taught me other things, like how to rob merchant wagons and scam folks and to always be movin'. No roots sproutin' from the bottoms of my feet anymore. No percentage to give the guild." She studied his face a moment. "Why hadn't you asked me before now?"

Dhamon shrugged. "I guess I wasn't curious."

She discarded a cracked chunk of opal, picked up another large piece of citrine and passed it to him. "Wonder how Mal is doin'?" she mused, looking around a gypsum outcropping and searching for the big man. "There he is. Way down there." She watched Maldred a moment, enjoying the view his sweat-slick, muscular body presented, then she waved. But Maldred wasn't looking in her direction. He was staring up and to his right, and his hand was reaching for the great sword strapped to his back. "Trouble," she hissed, turning her head to see what had caught his attention. "Fetch got himself into more trouble. He's worthless."

Dhamon sped by her, navigating around the gypsum spires, dropping his sack of gems as he tugged the broadsword from his belt.

❖ ❖ ❖ ❖ ❖ ❖ ❖

Maldred reached Fetch just as another two dwarves appeared. "A half-dozen," the big man growled. "And there'll be more coming if we don't take them out quick. Might be more coming anyway." He immediately sized up his opponents. "Stay down," he told the kobold. Then he was dodging quarrels from their crossbow bolts, bringing his sword around to parry some that "thwanged" off the blade as he scrabbled over the loose gravel and gems. As he neared, he shouldered his sword, bent down, and scooped up a handful of rocks, bringing his arm over his back and hurling them at the closest dwarf. Several found their marks, and one of the dwarves dropped his crossbow and rubbed furiously at his eyes.

The others were loosening battle-axes from their

waists and readying to meet Maldred's charge. He shouted as he closed the distance. "You haven't a chance against me! Lose your weapons and I'll spare your lives!"

The thickest of the quartet laughed loud and deep. He stopped only when Maldred was upon them, swinging his massive blade. The sword practically cut the lead dwarf in two, and then Maldred drew back the weapon and brought it down to cleave off the arm of another dwarf. One of the others started scrambling up the hill, calling for support, this being the one who had laughed so heartily. The rest gritted their teeth and one hollered, "Die, trespasser!"

"Life is precious," Maldred said as he drew back his blade again, muscles tensing and veins bulging. "You are very foolish to throw it away."

The dwarves were dead by the time Dhamon reached Maldred. Dhamon sheathed his sword, knelt, and tugged a thong free from one of the dwarves' necks. Dangling from it was a large, beautifully cut diamond, the largest he'd seen. Dhamon hung it around his own neck and started searching the other bodies, retrieving finished stones set in gold and silver and stuffing them into his pockets.

The big man was shielding his eyes from the light of the crystals in the rocks and craning his neck up the mountainside, looking for the dwarf who got away. "Can't see in this glare. But I know we'll have company soon," he told Dhamon.

"Aye. Let's take what we've gathered and get out of here. And let's be quick. We certainly have more than enough to buy the sword. We could buy all of Blöten, I suspect, with what we've gained."

Fetch grabbed his sacks, struggling under the weight and making his way slowly up the mountainside. Maldred glanced back at his collecting spot, where four bulging bags waited. "Very quick," he added to himself.

Dhamon whirled and headed toward his own sacks, noting Rikali was continuing to stuff gems into one, her arms practically a blur, her tunic plastered against her back with sweat. He scrabbled over the rocks and spires and was almost at her side when two steel-tipped quarrels shot through the air, one whizzing by his shoulder, slicing through his sleeve, the other lodging itself in his right thigh, finding its way to the scale affixed there.

He shouted from surprise, falling back and clutching at his leg.

"Remove the scale, and you'll die," he heard the long-dead Dark Knight say. Then the Knight was gone and Dhamon was writhing on the mountainside in the Valley of Crystal. A wail escaped him, long and unnerving, one that brought a choked sob from the half-elf.

She threw herself on him, wrapping her slender fingers around the quarrel and tugging gently. "Maldred!" she called, "By my breath, Mal, help me!" She continued to tug, mindless of the dozen dwarves who had loosed the last of their quarrels and were now charging down the mountain toward her and Dhamon. "Maldred!"

Dhamon gasped for air. All he could feel was intense heat and excruciating pain covering every inch of his body, turning him into a human furnace. "Damn this scale!"

Within moments the dwarves were on the pair, gleaming axes raised, intent on slaying the two trespassers. Rikali tried to shield Dhamon. "I said we were gonna die, lover," she muttered, as the first axe came down . . .

And clanged loudly against Dhamon's upraised

sword. Despite the pain, he'd managed to scramble away from her and rise to his feet. "I'm not going to die today," he told the half-elf as he pushed her away. He whipped the blade about and shoved the tip through a dwarf's wrist. Maldred raced to his side, and the big man gave no warning to the dwarves this time. He waded into their midst and began swinging. "Join us, Riki!" he shouted. "Any time, please!"

The half-elf picked herself up and drew her wavy-edged dagger, hurling it deep into the throat of a dwarf coming her way, one who wrongly had decided that fighting her was an easier proposition than taking on Maldred or Dhamon.

All of the dwarves were heavily armored despite the summer heat. The half-elf tugged free her blade and moved on to another one. She had to look for openings in their defenses, jabbing her blade at the joints in the thick plates.

Three lay dead at Maldred's and Dhamon's feet before one managed to land a blow against the big man. The tallest of the dwarves cut deep into Maldred's arm, bringing a groan from the big man. The great sword clanged to the ground, as Maldred could no longer hold it with both hands. His wounded arm hung limp at his side.

Two dwarves darted in and raised their axes, thinking the large human an easy mark now. However, Maldred's good arm shot forward, his massive fingers closing on the haft of a battleaxe and ripping it free from the dwarf's grip. Without pausing, he pulled the axe back and brought the weapon down on the other dwarf, cutting through his helmet and lodging in his skull. He tugged the axe free as the dwarf fell and swung it against its previous owner, dropping him.

Dhamon dispatched one dwarf by shoving his

blade through a gap in the armor beneath the
dwarf's arm. Releasing his sword, which he couldn't
easily tug free, he scooped up the dead dwarf's axe
and swung it around hard, chopping into the neck of
another dwarf and sending an arc of blood flying.
His immediate opponents dead, he worked quickly
to retrieve the broadsword and buried the axe in the
chest of a corpse as more dwarves moved in.

Although the odds were turning against them, the
dwarves who remained showed no signs of retreating,
save the one who found his beard on fire—courtesy of
Fetch, who had just arrived on the scene. The kobold
grinned maliciously and shouted to Rikali that his fire
spell was indeed a great boon. The half-elf ignored
him and threw her efforts into parrying the attack of a
particularly thickset dwarf who had a scattering of
medals affixed to his armor.

Maldred felled one dwarf and was preparing to
strike another as the ground started shaking beneath
their feet. It was a gentle tremor at first, but it quickly
gained energy, and within a heartbeat even the
nimble Rikali was struggling to stay on her feet.

Dhamon slammed his blade into the thigh of one
of his opponents, then felt the haft of the weapon
start to slip from his sweaty fingers. He put all his
effort into keeping the blade, tugging it free and
sheathing it just as he felt his feet lose purchase
against the jarring ground. An instant later his legs
were pitched out from under him, and he was rolling
down the mountainside, unable to cushion himself
from the spires he was thrown against along the way.
Fetch dropped to the ground and wrapped one of his
spindly arms around a rock that didn't seem to be
going anywhere, the other arm snaked out to latch
onto one of his bags of crystals. The dwarves and
Maldred fared worst, not able to keep their balance

and joining Dhamon on a pell-mell descent toward the bottom of the valley.

"Dhamon!" Rikali screamed. She half-slid after him, doing her best to avoid the rocks careening down the mountainside, and crying out when sharp ones seemingly jumped up from nowhere to slam against her arms and legs.

The mountainside thundered. Cracks appeared along the rocky slopes—small at first, like spider veins beneath pale skin, then widening until they resembled the jagged maws of monsters. Two of the dwarves screamed as they were swallowed by one of the growing fractures.

Rikali felt the ground give way beneath her feet as she slipped into one of the widening chasms. Her slender hands thrashed about until her fingers found a spiny tooth of rock. She held on tight as her body was hurled against the rockface, the breath rushing from her lungs. She coughed and blinked furiously as a cloud of dust settled in the chasm, threatening to smother her, then she gasped in terror as the ground began to seal itself. She instinctively propelled herself up the trembling rockface, finding nooks to slip into that an ordinary man would overlook. She hauled herself over the lip and rolled away just as the fissure rumbled one last time and closed.

"Dhamon!" she hollered, though she couldn't hear her own voice. All she heard was the echo of the quake, so loud it was painful to her keen ears. Again she scrambled down the mountainside, kicking up gravel and chunks of crystal. Her heart leapt when she spotted Dhamon's body wedged between a pair of granite columns. Maldred was hanging onto one of the columns with his good arm, his eyes shut in the face of flying rocks.

The other dwarves who had tumbled down the

mountainside were nowhere to be seen. Only one helmet was comically perched atop a gypsum spire. Fetch was high above Rikali, still clinging to his half-buried rock with one hand, the other somehow still holding fast to a sack of gemstones. Rikali had dashed to the columns and was holding on tight, suffering the fist-sized stones that battered her and riding out the quake until it mercifully stopped.

She sagged next to Dhamon, gasping for clean air. "Lover?" She barely heard the word, perhaps only imagined it. Tears rolled down her face as she felt for him and her hands came away smeared with blood. "Lover? Please, oh please." Sobbing, she put her head to his chest and cupped a hand across his mouth, hoping to find some trace of breath. "He's alive!" she called a heartbeat later to Maldred, who slowly pushed himself off the pillar and dropped to his knees. The big man was mangled, his one arm hung limp, his sleeve covered with blood. But just *how* badly he was injured didn't sink in, as her concern for Dhamon took precedence. "Help me, Mal! Dhamon's hurt bad."

Rikali was struggling with the quarrel again, which had broken off and was protruding only a few inches above the scale in Dhamon's thigh. Her claw-like nails were broken, and her fingers were bleeding. "I can't pull it out, Mal!"

He pushed her hands away, and with his good hand ripped Dhamon's pants to fully expose the scale. Then he grunted, and with considerable effort he pulled the broken quarrel free.

"What do we do, Mal? I'm afraid he's dyin'." Her hands fluttered over his face and chest. "Help him. I love him, Mal. I really love this one. Don't let him die."

"He's not dying, Riki." Maldred shook his head,

fighting a wave of dizziness that threatened to overwhelm him and send him rolling to the valley floor.
The side of his shirt was growing darkly crimson.
He'd lost quite a bit of blood, and his wounded arm
was so numb he couldn't move it. "Indeed, he
doesn't look like he's hurt bad at all. Just unconscious." He pointed to a gash on Dhamon's forehead.
"Hit a rock, knocked himself out. He'll be fine. Me,
on the other hand . . ."

"You've got magic. I've seen you mend things.
You can heal yourself, I know you can. Make sure
Dhamon's all right. Please."

"Oh, I can mend things, Riki. But nothing living."
His hand touched the scale, his thumb centering on
the small wound. "I'd wager the bolt was enchanted,"
he said, "else it wouldn't have pierced this. Good
thing more of us didn't get skewered."

"I don't care what the damn thing was," Rikali
cursed. "Enchanted. Lucky shot. Let's get out of here.
Please. Let's leave and everythin' will be all right.
Won't it?"

"I care about him, too, Riki," Maldred said, his
voice too soft for her to hear. He cast a glance up the
mountainside to make sure Fetch was still there and
that no more dwarves had arrived. Then he looked
down at Dhamon, noticed blood gushing out of the
hole in the scale. "All right. Maybe I can mend this.
But maybe I should just rip the damn scale off."

"No! You do that and he will surely die. I'll help
you carry him."

"Wait." The big man concentrated on the hole in
the scale, started humming and directing his magical
energy. Several minutes later Maldred sagged
against the rocky column, and where the hole once
was could be seen a flat black circle near the center of
the otherwise glossy scale. The ground had flowered

red around Maldred's limp arm. "I sealed it, and he's not bleeding anymore."

"Damn the dwarves," she said, bending over Dhamon and running her fingers across his damp forehead. "And damn the dragons. A dragon did this to him, you know." She touched his scale.

"I guess so." Maldred's voice had lost its sonorous power. He felt dizzy and terribly weak. "I don't know how or why, but the red overlord did it."

Rikali cast a glance at Maldred. "By my breath, you're more than just hurt. I'm sorry. I'm so selfish. All the blood you've lost, Mal . . ."

Ignoring her, he pushed himself to his feet, then bent to shoulder Dhamon with his good arm. Another wave of dizziness struck, threatening to pitch him to the ground.

"You need to rest, Mal," she protested. "You shouldn't be movin'. I can carry Dhamon. I can! All of us need . . ."

"We need to get out of here," he gasped. "Just like you said. There'll be more dwarves soon, wondering what the quake did to their blessed valley. Time to heal later, Riki—provided we can get out of here alive."

The ground trembled again. Maldred had braced himself, but the half-elf wasn't as quick to react. She tumbled to the ground and managed to catch herself on a spire. The ground shook a moment more, then quieted.

You coming? Maldred mouthed, as the half-elf picked herself up. He turned and started up the mountainside again.

They recovered two bulging bags of gemstones on their way up, Rikali carrying them when Maldred insisted he could handle Dhamon by himself. Even so, he stumbled a half a dozen times as they continued on. The mountain rumbled twice more as they climbed—aftershocks of the first quake or precursors to another. Fear made them drive themselves faster.

"It's still here," Rikali said when she spotted the wagon. "Pigs, but I figured the horses would be long gone—takin' all of our gems with them." A moment later she saw why the horses hadn't bolted. A boulder had tumbled down, blocking the horses' path. There had been nowhere for them to flee.

Maldred nested Dhamon on top of the bags in the wagon bed, using their stolen clothes to pad him. Fortunately, the wagon had received little damage. Maldred sagged to his knees and closed his eyes. He sat back, opened his mouth to say something, then passed out and fell onto his back.

"Mal!" Rikali struggled to pull him up, but he was dead weight and too much for her. Fetch deposited the bag of gems he had somehow managed to hold onto, then scurried to Maldred's side and began tugging on his shirt trying to help. "Worthless," the half-elf spat at the kobold. "You had a hard enough time with the sacks of gemstones. Ain't possible for you to lift Mal." Undaunted, the kobold put his effort into pinching the tight flesh of Dhamon's face and chittering at him in his odd native tongue, which he knew the human found irritating.

Dhamon's eyes fluttered open as he softly moaned. "What . . ." Fetch nodded toward the back of the wagon.

"Help me," Rikali urged him. "C'mon, you can do it."

Dhamon shook off the dizziness and reached over the back of the wagon, wrapping his arms around Maldred's chest. Muscles bunched and his jaw tightened as he tugged the big man into the back of the wagon. "Heavier than he looks," Dhamon huffed, his arms momentarily numb from the effort. "Much heavier." He slumped next to Maldred and his fingers felt about his own forehead, finding the gash and pressing tentatively on it.

"Get us out of here, Fetch," Dhamon snapped. "Before we have more company."

The kobold scampered to the front of the wagon and put his shoulder against the boulder blocking it. He grunted and cursed, his muscles straining. Rikali joined him and pushed hard. The earth helped the pair's efforts, rumbling slightly with another aftershock and providing just enough impetus to budge the rock. It rolled slowly down the mountainside, careening into natural pillars, sending shards of crystal into the air and breaking apart as it went.

Panting, the kobold climbed up onto the wagon, his feet dangling. Rikali passed him the reins, then scrambled up and ripped open Mal's shirt, tearing the sleeve and fashioning it into a tourniquet for his injured arm.

"I can't feel my arm, Dhamon," Mal said, his voice so hoarse and soft he had to lean his face over to hear. "I can't move it."

Rikali offered him soothing words as Dhamon searched about beneath the canvas sacks and found a jug of hard cider. He poured some on the wound, and Maldred shuddered at the stinging sensation.

"There, you *can* feel something," she said. "That's a good sign." Softer, she said, "Isn't that a good sign, Dhamon?"

Dhamon didn't reply. Holding his forehead, he was scrutinizing his big friend, his eyes unusually wide and sympathetic, but he was frowning. "I hope so," he finally whispered.

Rikali regarded Dhamon for a moment. "Perhaps this should be me layin' here instead of Mal," she said too softly for him to hear.

Then she returned her full attention to the big man and tried to blot some of the blood away with a section of her own tunic. "Where should we go? Someplace to get him help. Someplace. Dhamon, I don't know what to . . ." she started.

"We have got to get away from here," Dhamon said, wincing slightly as he poured more cider onto Maldred's arm. "Toward Blöten. Fetch knows the way."

◇ ◇ ◇ ◇ ◇ ◇ ◇

Four nights later they sat around a fire roasting a large rabbit. Despite the late hour, the air was still hot. The ground was so starved for water that it had become powdery like ash. Fetch risked a few sips from his last waterskin and grumbled that they'd be even richer if they could find a way to make it rain in these mountains.

Many of the clothes they had claimed from the merchant wagon had been fashioned into bandages for Maldred, replaced as they were needed.

Dhamon refused Rikali's attempts to bandage him, saying he wanted all the available cloth saved for Mal. He convinced the half-elf that he looked far worse than he felt—though he was certain he'd either bruised or broken a few ribs. He moved carefully, and breathed shallowly. His oily hair was matted with blood, and it was badly tangled and streaked gray and brown with dust and dirt. The stubble on his face was becoming an uneven and unsightly beard, and his clothes were soiled and tattered. He'd managed to save one shirt from the merchant haul, tucking it away beneath a sack of gems so the others wouldn't find it and rip it into bandages. But there was no reason to wear it now—it was for

later, he decided, when he reached Blöten and
needed to look better.

All their clothes were dark with sweat stains and
dried blood. Fetch had fared the best, escaping with
only a few scrapes, though his clothes were riddled
with holes. He was playing nursemaid to the rest of
them, inspecting the cuts and bruises they'd picked
up from their ride down the mountain, and serving
as their sentry.

Now, with his good hand, Maldred was tracing
patterns in the dirt. His wounded arm was wrapped
close to his chest to keep it immobile. The kobold
intently watched the big man, thinking the symbols
mystical and part of some spell. He tried to copy the
patterns, then grew bored when he couldn't fathom
them and instead busied himself by passing out
wooden plates.

After Fetch finished waiting on them, and after he
wolfed down his own meager share of the cooked
rabbit, he recovered the last jug of distilled spirits
from the wagon and placed it next to Dhamon. In a
great show he withdrew the old man pipe from its
pouch, tamped tobacco into the bowl, and lit it with
his finger in an effort to demonstrate to all that he'd
truly perfected the fire enchantment.

After that, the kobold paced in front of them, clicking his pointed teeth on the stem and gently thwack-
ing his hoopak on the ground while he waited for a
magical request. When none came, he took a deep
puff on the pipe, blew a smoke ring into the air, and
broke the silence. "At least I didn't lose my weapon in
that quake, like Maldred and Riki did. Didn't have to
take one of them dwarven axes like Mal," he stated.
"At least Dhamon's pretty sword stayed in his belt. So
we had some good fortune after all. My 'old man'
didn't get a scratch on him. And we got all these

rough gems . . ." He frowned when he saw Maldred glaring at him. "Oops. Well, I'm sure you'll find another sword just as big and heavy and sharp," he said quickly. "And we'll get some more daggers for Riki. In Blöten." When he figured out that nobody was appeased, the kobold finished with his pipe, carefully replacing it in the pouch, and then he excused himself to patrol the grounds around their camp—just to make sure no dwarves were tracking them.

"I'm still a little sore," Maldred quietly admitted to Dhamon after a long silence. "And a little weak. But I guess I should just be happy I'm alive."

"Ah, Mal," Riki said. She slid closer, cringing when Dhamon wrinkled his nose at her. "Mal, don't you worry. You're too mean to die."

Maldred rubbed the muscles of his injured arm and was barely able to make a fist. He frowned. "Had never been hurt like that going into the valley before. But then I'd never stayed as long, or had an earthquake to contend with on top of the dwarves. Never came away with as much, either."

"Are we going back?" There was hope in the half-elf's voice. "I mean, if we need all these gems to buy Dhamon his sword—which we shouldn't 'cause nothin' in the world should be that expensive, maybe we could take a big old wagon back just for us and. . . ."

He shook his head. "Not for a while, Riki. The dwarves will double their patrols. Maybe in a few months, perhaps right before winter sets in. Or maybe we'll wait until just after the first snow. They wouldn't expect anything then."

Her eyes gleamed merrily.

"At least I'm on the mend," he continued. "And thankful to feel at least something in my fingers. I know a good healer in Blöten who will finish the job. Have him take a look at the two of you also."

"Doubt you'll need him, Mal. Riki's right, you're too mean to be down so long," Dhamon joked. His words were slurred, heavy with the alcohol he'd been drinking. An empty jug lay on its side at his feet. He awkwardly moved the new jug to between his thighs, his finger playing around the lip. "Besides, being hurt like this is a good excuse to take it easy for a while."

Rikali slid over to sit between them, tugged Dhamon's jug away and took a long pull from it, then coughed and sputtered. She handed it back and studied her fingernails. Sighing, she reached up and draped an arm across each of the men's shoulders. "I figure we're two days from Blöten, maybe less. I wonder if there're grand shops to visit. Maybe Dhamon can't buy his sword with all of that on the wagon. And if he can't, we can keep all of that for ourselves, right?"

Maldred disregarded her. He glanced at a battle-axe that lay within reach, the firelight dancing off its blade, which held his attention. Finally, he looked away into the darkness and said, "Riki, we'll have a grand time in Blöten celebrating our good fortune. And we'll get you some new knives. And we'll get Dhamon his sword, too."

"I want to buy some more clothes. And perfume. And . . . Mal, did I ever tell you about this grand house I want built? On an island far . . . did you hear something?" Quick as a cat, she glided away from the men and peered off into the darkness on the far side of the camp. The fire cast tendrils of light toward the rocks and scrub grass, and the grass moved lazily to an almost imperceptible breeze.

Dhamon struggled to his feet, fighting to keep his

balance. His hand fumbled for the sword at his waist, his fingers were thick from the alcohol. He favored his right side, and reached for a cane Fetch had fashioned from a tree branch. Maldred was a little slower to rise, hefting the battle-axe in his good hand.

"Did you hear it? Dhamon? Mal? It's Fetch. He's . . ."

There was a crashing in the dry brush, the sound of cursing, and the shrill voice of the kobold. A moment later a disheveled-looking black man tramped into the clearing, the kobold clinging to his leg. The man was soaked with sweat. In addition to a knapsack that hung from his back and several skins of water that dangled from it, he had a large sword strapped to his waist, and more than a dozen daggers in sheaths crisscrossing his chest. He was swinging a great two-handed polearm at Fetch while at the same time trying to shake the snarling creature off. But the polearm was much too long and unwieldy, and the kobold would not be dislodged. More crashing followed, the clang of metal and the hiss of a sword being drawn.

"Rig!" Dhamon shouted, his tongue feeling swollen from the distilled spirits. "Leave him be!"

The black man growled and kicked out with his leg, trying again to remove the kobold who bit down through the fabric and found his calf. Rig howled as Fiona charged into the clearing. She was quick to lower her weapon the moment she spotted Dhamon, though she didn't sheathe her blade, and she kept her shoulders squared, ready for trouble.

"Call the little mutt off," Fiona told Dhamon, glowering at him as her fingers tightened on the pommel of her sword. "Call him off now, or I'll cut him off and toss him on your fire." She raised the tip of the sword for emphasis, and her eyes narrowed and locked onto Dhamon's like a vise.

"Fetch," Dhamon said almost gently, "Let the man go."

"Trespasser. Spy," the kobold grumbled as he released Rig, swatted him for spite, and scurried to Dhamon's side. The kobold puffed out his chest and bared his yellowed teeth, hissing. "Good thing I was patrolling, Dhamon. Otherwise them two *defenders of justice* would've snuck up on us and stole all of our . . ."

"So good to finally meet some of Dhamon's old friends!" Rikali cut in, cracking a forced smile and stretching out her hand. She glided toward the Solamnic Knight. "You must be Fee-ohn-a," she said, her tone almost polite. "Dhamon has told me so very much about you. And you're . . ."

"Very angry," Rig stated. He ground the tip of the glaive into the dry earth. His eyes, like daggers, were aimed straight at Dhamon.

CHAPTER FIVE
TALK OF REDEMPTION

Give me one good reason why I shouldn't haul your loathsome carcass back to Ironspike and let them hang you. One reason! Hell, I ought to supply the rope and pick out the tree. Robbing a hospital—from injured Knights no less. Knights, Dhamon! Big-as-you-please Legion of Steel ones." Rig sat heavily on the ground. Dhamon glanced over his shoulder at the jug of spirits, contemplated hollering for Fetch to bring it to him.

The mariner rested the glaive on his knees and glared at the Legion of Steel ring on Dhamon's hand. "One damn reason! And don't you even think about saying 'for old time's sake'."

Dhamon looked away toward the dying campfire, where Maldred, Rikali, and Fetch were attempting to entertain a furiously pacing Fiona.

"Maldred wouldn't let you s'haul me anywhere," Dhamon finally said. His words were slurred a little. He nodded toward the big man. "Tha's Maldred."

Rig snorted. "Right. Maldred. You've told me his

name three times now—whoever in the deep levels of the Abyss Maldred is. He's worse off than you are, arm all bandaged like that. You're limping—and dead drunk. A fine pair of cripples you are. An' that elf . . . "

"Rikali's a half-elf."

"She's hurt, too. An' the clothes she's wearing, the paint on her face, all that jewelry."

"Leave her outta it."

"The whole lot of you stink worse than three-day-old fish."

Dhamon shrugged, his face unreadable.

"Where's Feril?"

No answer.

"And that . . . creature?"

"Fetch," Dhamon said, blinking and trying to bring Rig completely into focus.

"He's a . . . *kobold.*" The word sounded like the mariner was spitting out a bad piece of meat. "A two-legged rat. A damnable, stinking little monster the likes of which me and Shaon fought more than once in the Blood Sea Isles and . . ."

"Aye, that he is. A s'kobold. But he works for Maldred, and he's harmless enough."

"Harmless. Ha! You're all a wretched bunch of thieves as far as me and Fiona're concerned." Rig shook his head in disgust, the sweat flying off his face. "Stealing from the hospital. Burning down a stable and taking half the town with it. Did you know that? Half the town burnt to cinders. Do you care? And stealing horses. Where are *our* horses? The ones we rode into Ironspike. You were riding mine out of town last I saw. Your elf . . . half-elf . . . had Fiona's. *Our horses!* All I can see are what you're using to pull that old wagon."

"Sold those horses some days ago to a camp s'of bandits."

"You stranded us in that dwarven town!" The mariner tightly gripped the haft of the glaive and narrowed his eyes. "Wouldn't have even been there if Fiona hadn't heard you were in the area, heard what you'd been up to. Probably had it in her pretty head that she could redeem you. Ha!" The veins in his neck bulged like thick cords, and he let out a deep breath between his clenched teeth. "Those were damn good horses, Dhamon. Expensive. What we're riding now're. . . ."

"If I recall, we got quite a s'few steel pieces for your horses."

"Why, I ought to . . ."

"Kill me?" Dhamon's expression lightened and he laughed, rocking back on his haunches and almost losing his balance.

"That'd be too good for you," came Rig's clipped reply. Another breath of steam. "Too easy. I ought to drag your sorry self off to prison and let you rot there for the rest of your miserable life. No Palin Majere or Goldmoon nearby to save you. And neither you nor that man you call Maldred would have a hope of stopping me."

"Me? Stop you? Not at the moment s'anyway."

Rig growled from deep in his throat and ground his heels into the dirt. "I don't understand, Dhamon. What's happened to you?"

Dhamon's fingers unconsciously worried at a thread hanging from his shirt. His fingers felt thick and clumsy from the alcohol. "The Dhamon Grimwulf you knew is dead. I'm a different person, Rig. You have to accept that."

Rig was silent for several moments, probing Dhamon's face and waiting for him to continue. He'd seen Dhamon Grimwulf ragged before, wearing the dirt of a hard-traveled trail. But this was different—

far worse, his hair tangled, face covered with stubble, fingernails cracked and caked. Rig shuddered.

When it was clear Dhamon wasn't going to volunteer any explanation, the mariner pressed him on a different matter. "So you're with that woman over there. I can tell by the way she watches you. Interesting looking company. But where's Feril? She know what's going on with you?"

At this repeated mention of the Kagonesti Dhamon once claimed to love, his dark eyes flashed with anger, then he dropped his gaze to study the tip of his worn boot.

The mariner made a clicking sound, shook his head, and finally relaxed his grip on the glaive. "You know that Fiona'll demand you go back to that town and stand trial for what you did. It'd be only right. Me, I think they'd hang you. And I think maybe I'd help."

"No, you wouldn't." Dhamon lifted his head to stare at Rig. "Besides, I'm not going back s'there."

Rig closed his eyes and tried to calm his temper, counted three breaths, then opened them again and nodded. "Yeah, you're right. But only because I've got too many other things to worry about right now than carting a dirty drunk back down through the mountains. You're just not worth it. But it'd be the right thing to do. The honorable thing. Remember that word, Dhamon? Honor? You used to say it often enough. 'Live by honor.' And you got me to believe in it."

"Honor's a hollow s'word, Rig."

The mariner's next words were slow and deliberate and drawn out. *"You owe me an explanation."*

Dhamon tipped his head back and stared at the night sky. A growing number of clouds hid most of the stars, but a few twinkled through. He thought he saw a tongue of lightning and the flash, real or imagined, made him recall Gale, the blue dragon he once rode when he served with the Knights of Takhisis. "I owe no one. And you trailed me s'here for nothing. Your horses are gone. And you'll get nothing out of me for them." He felt some of the alcohol's effects fading away, his head starting to throb, and he wished the jug were within arm's reach so he could make himself thoroughly numb again. He glanced over at Maldred—the jug was at his feet. Not that terribly far away.

Rig slapped his thigh, pulling Dhamon's attention back. "Wish we hadn't found this camp. Wish Fiona and me. . . ."

"I wish you weren't here either."

"Damn fate."

"What, Rig? You blame it on fate that you happen to be in the same stretch of mountain? Coincidence?" There was another flash in the sky, this one real. Dhamon's eyes sparkled at the possibility of rain. He shook his head. "I don't believe such a faerie story. I believe you were looking for us."

Rig snorted, rubbing the bridge of his nose. "You think you're so important," he mumbled. The mariner closed his eyes. A moment later he opened them. "We took the first decent trail we could find through the Kalkhists and we met up with some merchants—offered them protection in exchange for a ride. They were quick to take our offer, seems the folks who still have to travel these passes are skittish with all the recent robberies and are taking on sellswords. Seems there's a thieving band that's been raiding wagons up and down this range—a giant of a man, a black-maned brigand, a painted woman, and a . . . creature."

"Guilty," Dhamon cut in, squaring his shoulders as if in pride.

"The merchants took us to the next town and we bought a couple of old draft horses there," he said, pointing toward the south, where Dhamon squinted to make out two big mares. Even in the darkness it was obvious they weren't as well bred as the pair Rig and Fiona had in Ironspike. "And then we continued on this trail. Saw your fire when we intended to stop for the night and thought we'd take a look. Thought you might be the merchants we befriended. But it was purely a coincidence we crossed paths."

"Pity we weren't the merchants."

Rig stared at him for several minutes, his brow furrowing with a dozen thoughts. Then his eyes trailed away to watch Fiona.

The Solamnic was sitting on a log near Maldred, occasionally glancing Rig's way and steepling her fingers—a gesture she practiced when she was uncomfortable. The half-elf was standing at Fiona's shoulder, alternating between inspecting the Knight and casting flirtatious looks at Dhamon. She strolled the length of the wagon, hips undulating and shoulders swaying. The kobold was sitting cross-legged at the big man's side, his glowing red eyes focused solely on the mariner.

"You're welcome to share our camp tonight, Rig." Dhamon finally broke the silence. His mouth felt dry. Another glance at the jug. "This is ogre country, and you're safer with us than on your own, especially this late at night. In the morning, we'll go our separate ways. You should head back into Khur—if you're smart."

Rig's eyes cut into Dhamon. "You owe me an explanation," he repeated with more force. "Why are you acting like this? What happened to you?"

Dhamon sighed. "And then I suppose you'll let me get some sleep?"

The mariner said nothing, continuing to stare.

"All right," Dhamon relented. "For old time's sake." He settled himself into a more comfortable position, but grimaced when he heard the scrabble of small feet.

"Dhamon's gonna tell a story," Fetch said with glee, revealing that he'd been using his acute hearing to eavesdrop on their conversation. The kobold picked a spot near Dhamon, just outside the reach of Rig's glaive, then he waggled his bony fingers to get Rikali's attention. He pulled out the 'old man,' already filled with tobacco, hummed at his finger and thrust it into the bowl, lighting it. Then the kobold puffed away, blowing smoke rings in the mariner's direction.

The half-elf glided over, kneeling behind Dhamon, and languidly wrapped her arms around his shoulders. She nuzzled his neck and winked slyly at Rig.

The mariner looked across the camp to Fiona, who nodded as if to say, "I will stay here and keep an eye on Maldred." She turned her attention back to the big man, intending to learn something about this band of thieves.

❖ ❖ ❖ ❖ ❖ ❖ ❖

"You've questions, Lady Knight," Maldred began, his expression gentle and his good hand relaxed on his knee. He let the silence settle between them before continuing. "I can tell it from your face. It's a beautiful face, one that is most easy on my weary eyes. But you've some unbecoming worry wrinkles here. All those questions surfacing." He reached up and tenderly touched her forehead, where her brow was creased in thought. "Your mind is working far too hard. Relax and enjoy the evening, it's finally cooling a bit."

Her stiff posture proved she wasn't yet willing to do that. She steepled her fingers again and sucked her lower lip under her teeth.

"We'll not hurt you."

"I'm not afraid of you," she said almost angrily. They were the first words she had spoken to the stranger.

He raised an eyebrow. "I can see that," he continued, his deep voice soothing and melodic, almost hypnotic. Fiona found herself enjoying listening to it, and that disturbed her more than a little. "Though perhaps, Lady Knight, you *should* be afraid of us. Some call our small band cutthroats, and many decent folks around here fear us. Still, I'll not raise a weapon against you, at least not unless your rash friend over there . . ."

"Rig," she said.

"Rig. That's right. An Ergothian, correct? Dhamon mentioned him several times before. He's a long way from home. Unless Rig starts something." He traced her steepled fingers, his eyes still capturing hers.

"You've already hurt enough people," she said. She shook her head when he offered her a drink from the jug of spirits, and she brushed a stubborn, sweat-soaked curl from her forehead. "In Ironspike, you killed several dwarves. Knights. And many buildings were burned." She closed her eyes and let out a deep breath, clasped and unclasped her hands, as if her fingers needed to be doing something.

"Lady Knight," again the sonorous, musical voice. She relaxed just a little, opened her eyes, and found herself looking straight at him. His face seemed kind, yet rugged, and his nose was long and narrow like the beak of a hawk. "Lady Knight, I never killed anyone who didn't deserve it—or who didn't ask for it by raising a weapon against me and our friends. All life is precious. And though I readily admit I am a thief, life is the one thing I am loath to steal." He edged closer and smiled when her expression calmed. He stretched his good hand up and brushed away another damp curl. "Lady Knight, I won't lie to you and say I'm an upright man. But I'm a loyal one." He gestured to Dhamon and Rikali. "I stand by my friends and by my principles. To the death, if need be."

"Ironspike. Justice would demand . . ." She was having trouble getting all the necessary words out and was getting lost in his eyes. She blinked and focused instead on his strong chin.

Maldred nodded. "Ah, yes, justice." He laughed softly, melodically.

Her eyes narrowed, and the big man frowned and shook his head. "You've spirit. Your hair like flames, your eyes filled with fire. Spirit *and* beauty—and I'll wager skill with a sword, else you wouldn't have *that* armor. But don't mar your face so with troubled thoughts." Then his eyes caught hers again and held them unwavering. "Life is far too short for that, Lady Knight. Fill your mind with pleasant ideas instead."

She felt her cheeks flush and mentally chastised herself for keeping civil company with the handsome rogue. "Dhamon stole from wounded Knights," she said, her tone instantly hard.

"And you think he should be tried for that? I couldn't let that happen," Maldred interjected. "He'd be found guilty. And then I would lose my friend."

She shook her head, her eyes still locked to his. "You don't understand. That's not why I'm here."

"Ah, I see! You're here to redeem your old companion. He's not the same man you knew. But he's the Dhamon I've become close to." Maldred offered her the jug again, and this time she took it, surprising herself and drinking deep, then passing it back and glancing across the camp at Rig, who seemed caught up in whatever Dhamon was saying. She blinked, not used to drinking the alcohol, then it went to her head, making her hotter than the summer.

She made a move to join the others, feeling oddly vulnerable in the company of Maldred, but he put a hand on her knee. The warm, light touch was somehow enough to hold her in place.

"You can't redeem Dhamon," he said.

She drew her lips into a thin line. "I'm not here to redeem him." Her hand drifted down to the pommel of her sword.

❖ ❖ ❖ ❖ ❖ ❖ ❖

Rikali snuggled as close to Dhamon as she could, making a display of her affections for Rig's benefit. She traced Dhamon's jawline with her fingertips, then her thumb stretched down to rub the thong around his neck. It held the dwarf's diamond that she coveted. The gem was hidden beneath his tattered shirt, and her teasing threatened to reveal it. Dhamon brushed all hands away. She scowled, then winked at him, amusing herself by toying with his boot laces. "Is this a tale I've heard, lover? Not that I mind hearin' the same ones again. But if it's a new one, I'll pay more attention."

Dhamon shook his head and looked at Rig. "There's not any one thing that changes a man," he began. "No *one thing* made you righteous and turned you away from being a pirate."

Rig met his gaze. "And with you?"

"With me it was a lot of things. More than I care to

remember or perhaps more than I care to count. We fought the dragons at the Window to the Stars. We lived, but we didn't win. Nothing can beat the dragons. I guess that was the start of it—the realization we can never win."

"The start?"

"Something else happened a long ways from here. Not too long after all of us parted company."

The mariner raised an eyebrow.

"Seems like it was the other side of the world," Dhamon mused. "In dragon lands. A forest held by Beryl, the great green overlord some call The Terror. There was terror, all right," Dhamon said. "And death. And the tale is quite a long one."

"I'm not going anywhere."

Chapter Six
Death and
Elven Wine

Dhamon closed his eyes, the blackness swallowing Rig and Rikali and the kobold. He focused on the incident, shivering slightly from the memory, and shutting out the sounds of the crackling campfire and the hushed conversation of Fiona and Maldred. At length, he opened his eyes and reluctantly began his story.

◊ ◊ ◊ ◊ ◊ ◊ ◊

Dhamon Grimwulf looked different, his face fuller and form a little thicker. His ebony hair hung only to the bottom of his jaw. It was trimmed evenly and well combed. His face was smooth and clean-shaven, his skin only lightly tanned, his clothes were in excellent repair. Beneath his wooly coat, he wore leather breeches and a chain mail shirt. And strapped around his waist was a recently forged long sword, a gift from the Qualinesti for taking on this difficult task.

The mountains were different, too, not as steep, though still craggy and made perilous because of winter. Ice coated the narrow trail that Dhamon was leading a group of men and women down. Bundled in furs and weighted down with supplies and weapons, they picked their way tediously along the western ledge until they reached the bottom of the foothills where the snow and ice gave way to forest that was somehow more hospitable.

"Your orders, Sir!" the lead mercenary snapped. He was young and eager to please, and stood rigidly at attention.

Dhamon eyed his line of charges, nearly four dozen mercenaries gathered at the request of Palin Majere in the city of Barter, deep off Ice Mountain Bay. Most of them were battle-tested Qualinesti elves. The Qualinesti had sought Palin's help against a young green dragon.

One of the mercenaries was an Ergothian, who by the number of daggers he carried and his confident swagger reminded Dhamon of Rig. And there were a few other humans in the mix.

Three elves were women, so small and slight they looked like children. By their cold eyes and the numerous scars on their arms, Dhamon was certain they were the most seasoned warriors in the group. He intended to rely heavily on them.

It had been several years since Dhamon commanded men, and that was for the Knights of Takhisis. But issuing orders and not second-guessing his own decisions still came easy, and he spit out commands as if this collection of mercenaries—volunteer and paid—were Dark Knights. His experience leading men had prompted Palin to approach him about this mission. That, and his experience with dragons.

"It'll be dark soon. Set up camp and we'll rest for

a few hours," Dhamon told them. "We'll break before dawn. Gauderic, assign a watch." *No watch for me this night,* he decided. He was so very tired. Just a few hours of sleep would put him back in top form. A few hours' respite from the walking and the wind and the memories that gnawed at his mind. There'd been no time for rest since he and his companions—Rig, Fiona, Feril, Jasper—fought the dragons at the Window to the Stars portal in Neraka nearly four months past.

At the Window, an ancient stone ruin that had once held enough magic to act as a passageway to other realms, Malystryx had summoned all of the other dragon overlords. Gellidus the White, Beryllinthranox the Green Peril, Onysablet from the swamp, and Khellendros the Storm Over Krynn—agreed to help Malys ascend to godhood. All of them had been collecting powerful magical artifacts, intending to use the energy released in destroying them to turn Malys into the next Takhisis, god-queen of the dragons.

Dhamon, Rig, and their small band of heroes had likewise been collecting artifacts, to keep them from the Red. And they traveled to the Window to the Stars in an effort to stop Malys's transformation.

It was a foolish undertaking Dhamon realized even then, a handful of mortals going against dragons—the most powerful dragons on Krynn. Still, his heart burned with a righteous fury the night that they made their way up a winding path to the plateau that held the Window. Then his heart nearly stopped at the terrifying sight of the massive dragons gathered there.

One of the overlords spotted them as they were hunkered down behind some rocks. Fortunately, Malys was in the midst of some intricate enchantment and was pulling energy from the gathered artifacts. She refused to be distracted, which bought Dhamon and his comrades precious seconds.

Dhamon rushed forward, intending to fight Malys. He vowed to exact revenge for the scale that was on his leg and to end her tyranny. He also expected to die. Help came from an unexpected source—The Storm Over Krynn. The great blue dragon tossed a lance Dhamon's way, one of the original dragonlances and one of the most arcane weapons ever forged on Krynn.

Amid all the fire and the chaos of that terrible night, the great red overlord was seriously wounded by the lance Dhamon wielded. And she was tossed into the Blood Sea by her blue dragon rival. The massive blue gained the power Malys sought that night.

Dhamon was certain Khellendros could slay them all with a single swipe of his claw, and that the dragon with but a thought could become as powerful as Takhisis. However, rather than using the mystical energy to ascend to godhood, the blue used it to activate the ancient portal, the Window. The dragon, called Skie by men, gave Dhamon and his companions leave—his boon to recognize their contribution in foiling the red dragon's plans. Then the massive blue flew through the Window and disappeared.

After Dhamon and the others left the Window to the Stars, some of them vowed to continue their struggle against the overlords—in their own fashions. His beloved Feril returned to her Kagonesti homeland of Southern Ergoth, saying she needed some time alone to think matters over, and some time to study the White called Frost. For a time, he told himself that she would return and they would be together again. That thought helped to bolster Dhamon's spirits and keep his fire kindled against the dragons and their minions. But the weeks passed without any word from her, and then a few months strolled by carrying whispers that she'd found another.

Rig and Fiona, who'd sworn their love for each other and vowed to marry, traveled to the coast of the Blood Bay on the Blood Sea of Istar. Dhamon had made no attempt to stay in contact with them.

The sorcerer Palin and his wife Usha went to the Tower of Wayreth to pursue their studies of the dragon overlords. It was Palin who remained closest to Dhamon through magical and mundane messages and who asked the former Knight to assist with various tasks.

The kender Blister went to the Citadel of Light to study the healing arts under Goldmoon's expert tutelage. Dhamon had heard she was doing exceedingly well, but he had not visited her since they parted company after the Window.

Groller went to who knew where. The deaf halfogre had his own personal demons to deal with. Dhamon suspected Palin knew where Groller was, but he never bothered to ask the sorcerer. It wasn't his concern.

And Dhamon . . . who went away on this mission prompted by Palin—a mission to slay a young green dragon who was tyrannizing the Qualinesti in this part of the forest—was so very tired. Just a few hours sleep was all he needed. A little time.

But there was no time to himself. No time to think. No time to forget about the dragons. Dhamon and his men were at the edge of the forest now.

"Sir?"

The lithe elf named Gauderic roused Dhamon from his musings. Gauderic was his second-in-command, and in the short time they'd been together the elf had earned Dhamon's respect and friendship.

"Windkeep is along that river." Gauderic pointed to the southwest, where a thin ribbon of dark blue cut through the trees. The setting sun sent just enough light through the canopy to fling sparkling motes of orange across the swiftly moving water. "Sir, we'll be able to get . . ."

"More mercenaries there, Gauderic, " Dhamon finished. "I know. Forty or fifty, Palin told me. We'll be there before noon tomorrow. Get some rest."

The air was chill as they struck out before dawn, cold enough to make their cheeks rosy and to keep their bare hands buried deep in their pockets. Still, it was not near so cold as what they breathed on their arduous trek through the Kharolis Mountains to get here. The air smelled rich and so full of life.

The men would follow Dhamon without question, most admiring him to the point of hero-worship—he'd shaken off the mantle of a Dark Knight, dared to stand up to the Dragon Overlords, and was the chosen hero of Goldmoon and Palin Majere, two of the most powerful and influential people on the face of Krynn. Dhamon Grimwulf was a living legend, his deeds whispered regularly, and in his company they envisioned being part of some grand and glorious feat that would be the stuff of tavern tales. Their spirits were impossibly high.

However, it did not take long for those spirits to plummet.

Dhamon led his men into Windkeep and discovered that the elves who were to join them were dead—as were all the rest of the villagers. Nothing stood in Windkeep. The birch log homes, so lovingly constructed by their owners, appeared as so much wreckage. Bolts of fine cloth flapped like pennants amidst splintered furniture and broken dishes. Toys were pressed into the earth, as if the people had carelessly stepped on them in their panic—not realizing there really was nowhere to run. The dead were everywhere—old and young, innocent infants, dogs that had stayed with their masters to the very end.

At first glance, it looked as if the bodies that littered the area around what was once the great house had been dead for a few weeks. Dhamon and his second knelt by the corpse of an elven woman. Both fought to keep from retching. What was left of her tunic had practically melted into her colorless flesh. Her hair was oddly brittle, crumbling like spun glass when they touched it. Her exposed skin was bubbled and grotesquely scarred. Bone showed through in places where the flesh had been eaten away—not by animals or insects. No living creatures of any size could be found in the village remains.

"A dragon," Dhamon whispered.

"Sir?" His second stepped away from the corpse only to find himself staring at another body equally as ghastly, made worse on closer inspection because it cradled a dead babe to its rotting chest. Gauderic whirled and doubled over, vomited until he was weak. Several minutes later when he regained his composure, he found Dhamon kneeling by an uprooted tree, studying something on the ground.

Dhamon pushed himself to his feet, his hand pressing into the scale on his leg. The scale was tingling faintly. It was a warm sensation he dismissed as nerves. "The wind from the dragon's wings destroyed the homes and uprooted a few saplings. Its breath slew these people. I'd say it was recent, within two or three days."

"No large tracks," a young elf argued. "A dragon would leave tracks. Any creature that size would. I've seen dragon tracks! I don't think there's any . . ."

Dhamon padded away from the center of the village, careful not to step on any of the bodies. At the edge of the pines that ringed what was once Windkeep, he looked outward and motioned for the young elf.

"Out here." Dhamon pointed several yards away to a clearing. He headed toward it, the young elf silently on his heels.

"For the love of all the firstborn," the elf breathed. He was staring at a depression, a footprint nearly as long as he was tall. The clearing he gaped at, one filled with small trees and bushes, had been flattened by a great weight.

"The dragon stood here," Dhamon said, then he turned and pointed toward Windkeep. "And he managed to kill all those people."

"How?"

Dhamon gestured for his men to join him at the edge of the village. The troop of humans and elves stood at attention, their eyes—wide in disbelief— continued to scan the ruins and bodies. "This dragon is fairly small."

"Small?" he saw Gauderic mouth. The once-brave man had grown pale.

"I would guess from the footprint that he's less than sixty feet long. Palin was certain we could best him with all of you and the men who were to join us. I agree. He's far from an overlord, and he's not a brave dragon, taking on this village from such a distance. Perhaps he fears men. The hunting parties he has been attacking have been small."

"Sir!" It was one of the human mercenaries. Dhamon recalled the man had an elven wife, and though she was safe in their home in New Ports far to the north and on the other side of the mountains, she had close ties to this land. "If we turn back, the dragon will keep on killing. It's bad enough that the Green Peril holds this realm. But she . . ."

"Doesn't so wantonly slay her subjects. At least not anymore," Dhamon finished. "Aye. But perhaps this young one is simply beneath the notice of the Green."

"Or perhaps not," Gauderic muttered. "Perhaps the Green Peril does not care about her 'subjects' and . . ."

Dhamon cleared his throat. "I say we press on and find this dragon and deal with him."

A chorus of murmurs from most of the men indicated they weren't eager to face a dragon without adding to their number. But Dhamon began issuing orders, and they nervously fell in line, some continuing to stare mutely at the bodies. Gauderic was quick to assign his two brothers and his friends the task of digging graves, using the few tools they could salvage. And the following morning, after a simple ceremony to honor the dead had been conducted, the mercenary band continued on.

The Qualinesti Forest, called Beryl's Forest by those who lived outside it, as well as by some of those who lived within and claimed fealty to the overlord, was truly impressive. Even before the dragon staked a claim to the land in the midst of the terrible Dragon Purge, it was a vast, ancient woods with more than a thousand varieties of trees.

But after the dragon arrived and began altering the land, the forest turned strange and primeval. Now, trees stretched more than a hundred feet toward the sky, their trunks thicker around than a bull elephant. Vines choked with flowers that could handle the coolness of winter wound their way up maple and oak giants and scented the air with an almost oppressively sweet fragrance. There were a few patches where something wasn't growing. Moss was thick everywhere, however, and spread in all directions in dazzling shades of emerald and blue-green. Ferns as tall as a man overhung streams and shaded dense patches of fist-sized mushrooms. Leaves were green and vibrant. Life was teeming.

The birds were plump and healthy from the abundance of fruit and insects. Gauderic pointed out several types of parrots that would normally be found in tropical lands. Small game thrived and skittered out of the path of the men. Rabbits and other animals had multiplied in staggering numbers. There were a few trails, made by the Qualinesti who traveled from village to village or who hunted along the Windsrun River. But the magic of the forest kept the trails from becoming well worn. Moss and vines grew across them almost as quickly as they were tramped down by booted feet. Each trail Dhamon found looked like it had been newly forged.

Dhamon recalled that Feril had talked about this forest, which she had ventured into with Palin and the dwarf Jasper Fireforge. The Kagonesti considered it intoxicating. He could almost picture her face in the whorls of a great oak. His eyes took on a softness when he thought of her, and his fingers reached up to touch the patch of bark he envisioned as her cheek.

"Sir! I've found tracks! Over here!" The excitement was high in the human scout's voice. He was one of four who had fanned out from the main trail. "Look, they're difficult to make out, sir, and I almost missed them. But here's an impression. And here's part of another one."

Dhamon shook off his musings, knelt, and traced the impression of a print. He was a skilled tracker, schooled by the Knights of Takhisis when he joined their ranks as a youth, taught more nuances by an aging Solamnic Knight who befriended him and lured him away from the dark order. His time with the Kagonesti Feril had further improved his mastery. *Feril*, he thought again.

The young man waited for Dhamon to say something.

"Aye, they are dragon tracks," Dhamon confirmed, his voice even but hesitant. "Hard to tell how old they are."

"And our course follows these tracks!" The young man beamed. He was saying something else, but Dhamon wasn't listening. He was studying the flowering ground cover that had been pressed into the earth. The tracks belonged to a larger dragon than the one that apparently destroyed Windkeep, and already the forest was recovering from the weight of the dragon's tread. Moss had sprung up, small broken branches were mending.

Dhamon felt the scale on his leg tingle uncomfortably. "Nerves," he whispered. He rose and scanned the brush for more prints, noting that the young tracker was doing the same. The man gestured to the west, toward what looked like a tamped-down patch of fern grass, and the pair started for it. But they stopped in a heartbeat when a strangled cry cut through the air behind them.

Birds shot from the trees in a great cloud of squawking color, and small animals that had been hidden by the undergrowth burst away in a wave. There was a thrashing to the south, larger animals also running, and there was the pounding of boots across the ground—the mercenaries were also fleeing.

Dhamon whirled and sped back toward the trail, mindless of the branches that whipped at his face and tugged at his cloak. The young tracker did his best to follow.

"Run!" Gauderic was hollering to the men. "Spread out and run!"

"Fool elf!" Dhamon cried as he rushed toward the river bank. He hurried past a thick clump of willow birches, leaping over a large rock and sidestepping a stagnant puddle. The green of the forest was a blur as he raced toward his men.

"Charge the dragon!" he bellowed. "That's an order, Gauderic! Charge and fan out! Come at the beast from several directions! Don't you dare turn tail!" It took him only a few moments to corral the men and force them forward.

And it took another few minutes for half of his men to die.

Those charging well ahead of Dhamon were caught in a cloud of foul chlorine. They fell screaming, twitching, clawing at their faces and clothes, sobbing uncontrollably. A few thought quickly to roll into the river, where the chill water helped to wash away the horrible film of the green dragon's breath. But most just gave up in the face of all the pain and succumbed.

Dhamon raced toward the front of the line, nimbly avoiding the fallen mercenaries. Bubbles spread across their chins and foreheads like those he'd seen on the elven villagers. Those at the very front had fared even worse, as they had shouldered the brunt of the dragon's breath. The chlorine gas was deep in their lungs, the chemical so caustic it was eating away at them inside and out.

"Murderer!" Dhamon cried to the dragon.

The great beast cast a long shadow across the trail. It was half-in, half-out of the river, had probably lain in wait for them, rising to surprise them with its cloud of deadly gas. It was indeed much larger than the rogue dragon they were hunting—roughly a hundred feet from nose to tail tip.

The supple plates on the dragon's belly glimmered like wet emeralds, catching the morning light that seeped through the branches. The scales on the rest of its body were shaped like elm leaves and ranged from a drab olive shade to a dark, bright blue-green that nearly matched the needles of the tall spruces nearby. The dragon's eyes gleamed dully yellow, and were cut through by black catlike slits. A large crested ridge the color of new ferns ran from the top of her head down her neck, disappearing in the shadow of leathery wings. She had one horn, on the right side of her head, black and twisting away from her, misshapen like an accident of birth. There was no nub where the second horn should have grown.

The few mercenaries left were backing away, mesmerized by the sight of her, afraid to turn their backs to her.

"Fight her!" Dhamon heard himself scream. "Don't back down! Don't run!"

The mercenaries paused for just an instant, looking to Gauderic, who was still standing. "No," he mouthed to Dhamon in disbelief. But Dhamon furiously shook his head at his second-in-comand and gestured for them to move forward.

"Fight her!" Then Dhamon charged, his feet churning over the ground, then flying out from under him as he slipped in a muddy puddle.

In the same instant, the dragon darted forward, brushing against the forest giants and somehow not harming them. Her tail cracked out like a whip, striking the trio of elven women who were advancing on her, swords shining and wet from the chlorine that still hung in the air.

Dhamon's lungs burned. The chlorine threatened to suffocate him. He made a move to rise, but stopped, watching from his prone position the horrifying tableau that was playing out before his eyes. The sounds were overwhelming—the moans of the men, the shrill cries of the birds, the pounding of his heart. Louder still was the sharp intake of the dragon's breath. The tingling warmth of the scale on his leg was becoming increasingly uncomfortable. Not nerves, he realized. Something else.

He saw one of the elven women leap at the dragon, swinging her sword wildly. The dragon exhaled, a second whirling gout of the chlorine gas. Dhamon managed to avoid the brunt of it, rolling behind a dead mercenary and feeling the caustic mist settle on his clothes and chain mail. His skin stung harshly.

But the elven women were not so lucky. The sickly yellow-green cloud billowed and enveloped them. As one they screamed, a horrid chorus that made Dhamon gag. The thumps of their bodies hitting the ground was soft. The cloud continued to drift outward.

"Damnable beast!" Dhamon heard Gauderic cry. His second-in-command drew in close to the dragon's belly and struck out with his blade. The weapon bounced off the plating and Gauderic nearly lost his grip on it. He redoubled his efforts and struck harder, putting all of his strength into it and this time meeting with more success. The dragon issued a tremendous roar that momentarily deafened everyone.

Only a dozen of the mercenaries had survived the dragon's last onslaught and had angled in close enough to strike. As far as Dhamon could tell, those brave ones were trying to follow his orders.

"Stay away from its mouth!" Gauderic was shouting. "Stay close to its body. Hit it low and keep moving! Circle and strike!"

The dragon was sweeping her tail through the foliage, brushing the corpses into the river. Out of the corner of his eye, Dhamon saw blood trickling down the dragon's green scales. Gauderic had opened a wound inside the beast's rear leg, and its blood ran freely, pooling on the ground. One of the elven mercenaries had managed to plunge his sword between the large scales on its front leg. Not able to pull the blade free, he reached for twin daggers at his side and continued the attack.

Suddenly the dragon reared up and roared. Hope swelled in Dhamon's chest. There was a chance! However, the scale was becoming increasingly painful. He gulped in the caustic air and tried to move forward, but a knifing pain shot up his leg and rooted him to the spot.

The dragon's roar changed pitch and faltered. Gauderic cried jubilantly. Through a haze of pain, Dhamon realized his second-in-comand was practically covered with the dragon's blood, and brave Gauderic was continuing to worry at the dragon's wound.

The dragon thrashed about, head twisting this way and that. Then eyes locked onto Dhamon, and her great, mottled lips pulled back in a sneer. For an instant Dhamon's heart froze. He managed to scuttle to the side, leaning behind a tree and trying to blot out the burning sensation on his leg.

"Can't fight like this," Dhamon spat. "Worthless. I'd be throwing my life away. No help to them." Then, though a part of him knew better, he turned away from the battle and from Gauderic and hobbled off through the ferns. "No hope for them."

The sounds of battle grew dimmer. Not only because Dhamon was putting distance between himself and the dragon but because the last of his men were dying. He heard a loud sizzling sound. Then he heard Gauderic's voice, little more than a whisper now, cry, "She commands magic! The dragon has magic!"

Then Dhamon heard nothing else but the snapping of twigs beneath his feet and the pounding of his heart. The pain in his leg seemed to decrease with every yard he put between himself and the dragon. He wandered in the woods for several days, fully expecting the dragon to track him and kill him, too. But when that didn't happen, he found his way back to Barter.

It was late at night. Only one tavern was open.

None inside seemed to recognize him, or notice his tattered clothes and matted hair. He'd abandoned the chain mail shirt at the edge of town. Settling himself at an empty table, Dhamon Grimwulf began drinking. Drinking a lot and considering what he would tell Palin Majere.

"Ale!" Dhamon slammed his empty mug against the table, shattering it.

His outburst quieted the crowded tavern for but a heartbeat, then dice games and muted conversations resumed. An elf serving girl, so slight she looked frail, hurried toward him, fresh mug in one hand, pitcher in the other. Expertly dancing her way through the maze of tightly packed tables, she sat the mug in front of Dhamon and quickly filled it.

"S'better," he offered, his voice thick from alcohol. "I'm thirsty tonight. Don't let me go dry again." He took a long pull from the mug, draining it as she watched, then thumped it on the table, though not so hard this time. She poured him another and wrinkled her nose when he loudly belched, his breath competing with his sweat-stained clothes to assault her acute senses.

"Tha's a good girl," he said, reaching into his pouch and retrieving several steel pieces. He dropped them in her apron pocket and noted smugly that her eyes went wide at his substantial generosity. "Leave the pitcher."

She put it within his reach and busied herself brushing at the ceramic shards of his first mug, sweeping them into the folds of her skirt.

"You're quiet," he continued. His dark eyes sparkled in the glow of the lanterns that hung from the rafters and softly illuminated all but the farthest corners of the dingy, low-ceilinged establishment. "I like quiet women." He stretched out a hand, his armpit dark with sweat, and wrapped his fingers around her wrist, tugging her onto his lap and sending the gathered shards to the floor. "An' I like elves. You remind be jus' a bit of Feril, an elf I was in s'love with." He waved his free arm in a grand gesture, knocking over the pitcher and bringing a curse from an old half-elf whom he splashed at an adjacent table. Save for himself and the glowering old half-elf, and two men chatting in front of a merrily burning fireplace, the tavern was filled with full-blooded Qualinesti.

"Barter is primarily an elven village, Sir. Most everyone who lives here is Qualinesti." She smiled weakly at the irritated half-elf, who was wringing the ale from his long tunic. He softly cursed in the Qualinesti dialect and fixed a sneer at Dhamon with his watery blue eyes.

"Aye, tha's true, elf-girl. There aren't many humans aroun' these lands," Dhamon said. "They'd make the chair legs an' the ceilings a might s'taller if there were. Not many humans at all." His expression softened for a moment, his eyes instantly saddened and locked onto something the serving girl couldn't see. His grip relaxed, though he didn't release her, and with his free hand he reached up to gently trace a pointed ear. "Or s'maybe there's one too many humans. Me."

She took a good look at him. Had it not been for the tangle of long jet black hair that hadn't seen a comb in days, and a thick, uneven stubble on his face, she would have considered him quite handsome. He was young for a human, she guessed, not yet thirty. He had a generous mouth that was wet with ale, and his cheekbones were high and strong and deeply tanned from hours in the sun. His shirt and leather vest were open, revealing a lean, muscular chest that shone from sweat as if he'd oiled it. But his eyes were what captured her attention. They were compelling and mysterious, and they held her gaze like a vise.

"Let me go, Sir," she said, though she did not struggle, and though her words held no conviction. "There's no need to cause any trouble here."

"I like *quiet* women," Dhamon repeated. For an instant there was a brightening in the eyes, as if a secret thought were working behind them. "Quiet."

"But she don't like you." It was the ale-spattered half-elf. "Let her go."

Dhamon's free hand dropped to the pommel of the sword at his waist.

"No trouble," the girl urged, still staring into his eyes. "Please."

"All right," Dhamon finally agreed. He released the girl and the sword, wrapping both of his hands around the mug. He narrowed his eyes at the half-elf, then shrugged. "No trouble." To the girl, he added almost pleasantly, "Bring me another pitcher. And not this rot you've been serving me. How about some of that fine elven wine I'm catching a whiff of. The stronger the s'better. The kind you've been bringing the rest."

"Maybe you'd better leave," the old half-elf suggested as soon as the girl was gone. His voice was uncharacteristically deep and scratchy. "You've had more than enough to drink already."

Dhamon shook his head. The muscles in his back tensed. "I haven't had near enough to drink—still awake, ain't I? But don't you worry about me. I'll be on s'my way soon enough. With first s'light I suspect. Then you and none of the s'other Qualinesti will have to stomach me anymore."

The half-elf took a step closer, and Dhamon saw himself reflected in a large polished medallion that dangled from a fine chain about his neck.

He scowled at the disheveled image.

The half-elf lowered his voice to a harsh whisper. "Go drown your sorrows somewhere else."

A hint of a smile tugged at Dhamon's face, then he opened his mouth to argue, but a gust of chill evening wind interrupted him. The tavern door flew open wide, banging loudly as two more elves entered. They were dusty and haggard-looking, the one carrying a gnarled staff a stranger to his eyes, the other very familiar and decorated with dried blood stains.

"Gauderic," Dhamon whispered. His face grew ashen as if he'd seen a ghost.

Gauderic likewise noticed him, nudged his companion, and pointed. "That's him! That's Palin Majere's worthless champion!"

At the same time, a colorful skirt swished loudly. "Here's your elven wine, Sir!" the serving girl musically announced. She gasped as the two elves charged toward them, pounding across the hard-packed dirt floor as they made their way around the tables.

Dhamon stood up, cracking his head on a beam of the low ceiling and bumping into the girl. She fell back against the ale-spattered half-elf, soaking him again as the pitcher slipped from her fingers and shattered against the floor.

The half-elf cursed and tried to help the girl to her feet, but they both slipped on the spilled wine, fell in a heap, and became tangled in her skirt. Dhamon ignored them and grabbed the edge of his table, upending it and positioning it as a shield against the two newcomers. The stranger collided with the tabletop and made a sickening thud, as Gauderic nimbly sidestepped the obstacle and raised his sword high.

"Dhamon Grimwulf!" he shouted. "You ordered us to charge the dragon! Charge and die!" He swung the sword in a wild arc above his head, sending the nearby patrons scrambling for cover, wine mugs in tow. "We shouldn't have listened to you!"

Dhamon kicked Gauderic in the stomach and sent him careening into an abandoned table.

"Noooo!" the serving girl hollered, as she finally managed to pick herself up. She awkwardly scampered through the maze of tables to the back room. "Silverwind! We've got trouble! Silverwind! Call the Watch!"

"I didn't want trouble," Dhamon grumbled. "I just wanted something to drink."

Both of the elves had recovered and were coming at him now, though the stranger was a bit groggy and blood ran from his nose. Furniture was being moved toward the walls to better accommodate the fight, and whispers and murmurs of speculation filled the room. Out of the corner of his eye, Dhamon saw the two human men wagering coins. A few of the elf patrons had their hands on their weapons, and

Dhamon had no doubt whose side they would take if they decided to join in.

"My wife and sister!" the stranger spat. "Dead! Dead because of you!"

"My brothers and friends!" Gauderic added.

"I didn't force anyone to come with me!" Dhamon returned. He stooped to keep from bumping his head against the six-foot ceiling. He swung his own blade down, using the flat edge of the weapon and striking the stranger on the shoulder. "Dragons are dangerous! They kill people, dammit! That's just the way of it and you know it, Gauderic!"

"The green didn't kill you!" Gauderic returned. "You were lying on your belly, avoiding the fight! You were busy watching your men die!" He wiped the blood that ran from his lip with one hand and drove his other fist hard into Dhamon's stomach. Dhamon doubled over, and the stranger followed through by swinging his staff solidly into his side.

"You're coming with us, Dhamon Grimwulf," the stranger added. "We're turning you over to the authorities. You're going to stand trial in Barter! And there won't be anyone to speak in your defense. I want your death for the death of my wife and sister."

"Death for death," came a cry from a corner of the room.

"Try him here!"

"We don't need a trial!" another patron shouted.

The stranger swung the staff at Dhamon again.

Dhamon felt his ribs crack, the pain instantly sobering him. "I didn't kill those men. The dragon did. I've no quarrel with you," he hissed between clenched teeth. "I don't even know you." This he directed to the stranger. "Leave me be!" Favoring his side, he crouched and spun, somehow avoiding blows from both elves. "Leave me be!"

"You ordered them to fight the dragon!" Gauderic repeated. "Ordered them! You should have at least fought and died with them! Coward!"

"You didn't die either," Dhamon argued flatly. He brought his sword up to parry another swing of the stranger's staff. Dhamon's leg shot up, cracking his boot hard against the chin of the stranger and stunning him. The elf fell to the floor and Dhamon kicked him hard for good measure. He wouldn't be getting up for quite a while. "I didn't force anyone to go against the dragon, Gauderic. I didn't force you."

"Didn't you?" Gauderic sneered. He took a step back and caught his breath. Both men eyed each other, chests heaving and knuckles white on their sword pommels. "Palin's champion! A real hero. You ordered. . . ."

"So I was wrong!" Dhamon spat. "Maybe. But you lived. You lived!"

"Only me!" Gauderic retorted. "And only because the dragon let me!" The elf's breath was ragged now, green eyes narrowed to slits. "She'd killed them all. All! And I was next. She dropped her head down so close I could see my face reflected in her eyes and feel her breath so hot against my legs. Stared at me and left! At first I thought I was just too inconsequential to be bothered with. Then I realized she was leaving me alive so word of her deeds this day could be spread to other men. I spent hours searching the river, hoping to find at least one more survivor, hoping to find you. All I found were corpses. I eventually found every mercenary—save their glorious leader. And I buried every one of them. It took me days. In that time the dragon came back twice to watch me."

Dhamon lowered his sword and shook his head.

"I wanted to bury you, too."

"Kill him!" came a wine-thick voice from a corner. "He let our brothers die! He should die, too!"

Gauderic snarled. "Told me you were a Dark Knight. That you gave it up. Maybe that was all a lie. Maybe you're still one of them."

"Dark Knight?" echoed throughout the room.

"Dark Knight of Neraka?" cried the old half-elf.

"That's what they're called now," Dhamon said flatly.

There was a second wave of murmurs, the sound of a few swords being drawn, the creak of wood as patrons leaned against the tables to better take everything in. There was the clink of more coins being wagered, shouted words in the elf tongue, a faint cry from the back room. This last voice was the serving girl's, summoning the guard.

"Get the Dark Knight!"

"Kill the traitor!"

Suddenly plates were crashing to the floor. Chairs and benches were tipped over. Someone behind Dhamon hurled a mug, the heavy tankard striking his back. A boisterous curse of "death to the Dark Knight of Neraka" sounded. And from somewhere outside he heard a shrill whistle.

A silvery-haired elf was coming at him, using a chair for a weapon. Another had tugged free a table leg and was trying desperately to wield it like a club. Dhamon easily sidestepped this slightly inebriated pair and moved straight into the path of the old ale-drenched half-elf. The man lowered his head and lunged, ramming into Dhamon's stomach and momentarily dazing him.

Despite the pain, Dhamon forced himself to react. He brought his sword pommel down with a thud against the old half-elf's head, sending him to the floor. Dhamon swept the sword in an arc in front of him, keeping several other patrons at bay. He kicked out to his side, connecting with the jaw of a young elf who was merely trying to escape the press of bodies. Blood and teeth flew, and the unfortunate patron changed his mind and decided to join the fray, drawing a dagger and cursing loudly in several languages. The young elf angrily flung the blade at Dhamon, scowling when it bounced off the human's right thigh and nearly struck another patron.

The edge of a short sword bit deep into his left leg. Dhamon tottered, then dropped to his knees, and a pitcher crashed against his head. Sweet-smelling elven wine soaked his hair and clothes, and rivulets of blood ran down his face from where the ceramic shards had cut his scalp in several places. He shook himself and sent a few shards thunking to the floor as he fought to remain conscious and pushed himself to his feet. He swung out wildly at an elf who was trying to skewer him with an iron poker, knocking the poker aside and bashing the man in the side of the head.

"Stop this at once!" the serving girl cried. She was somewhere behind the mass of elves and shouting as loud as she could manage.

"Stop this!" Another voice joined hers, likely the tavern owner's. He was banging on a pot and adding to the cacophony, "Don't break that! Put that down! Please stop!"

"I didn't start it!" Dhamon cursed as he clumsily leapt over a charging elf wielding a long kitchen knife. He lost his footing and accidentally bowled over three others who were scrambling toward the door. He brushed against a table, and his right pant leg caught on a protruding nail. The fabric ripped, revealing the large midnight black scale on his leg. It was shot through with a vein of silver that caught the lantern light and shimmered.

There was a collective gasp when the elves spotted it, and from deep in the press of bodies someone cried, "Sorcery!"

"It's from a dragon overlord!" Gauderic bellowed. He was standing on a chair at the edge of the fray, waving his sword. "A black dragon put it on him!"

"No, a black dragon didn't," Dhamon futilely corrected. *It was the Red.*

"He's an agent of a dragon!" someone else hollered. "Kill him!"

"I'm no one's agent!" Dhamon screamed as he drove the pommel of his sword down on someone's head. Then as a dagger tip sliced into the back of his leg, he reflexively struck out with all of his strength at anyone who came close while trying to reach the door.

A half-dozen elves lay sprawled around him, with more dead or unconscious toward the center of the tavern where the fight began. The dirt floor was spattered with wine and blood. Nearly two dozen elves remained standing.

Mugs were hurled against Dhamon's chest, some rebounding to strike the elves around him. Dhamon kicked out against those nearest to him, noting they seemed wary of the leg with the scale. And he continued to rain blow after blow with the blade and the pommel of his sword, shattering teeth and bones and spattering himself with elf blood.

Suddenly a log was heaved through the air, coming from one of the humans who had up to this point stayed out of the fray. As Dhamon ducked and watched it sail over his head, he was rammed in the back. The impact drove him forward into several elves, who started clutching at him. It was all he could do to hold onto his sword.

"Don't kill him!" a cry rose above the din. It was

Gauderic, who was forcing his way closer. "I want him to stand trial for his atrocities!"

Dhamon vaguely heard another shrill whistle, then another, heard the girl desperately pleading, heard an elf moaning. He felt fist after fist slam into his face, his chest, booted feet kick at him. He thrust forward with his sword just as Gauderic reached him. The blade—given to him by the Qualinesti of Barter—sank deep, crimson flowering on his tunic as the astonished elf dropped to his knees, then pitched forward eyes wide in disbelief. Dhamon's sword was lodged in him.

As the elves turned their attention to the fallen Gauderic, Dhamon snatched the opportunity to shove past the last few patrons blocking the door. A heartbeat later he was out in the chill night.

◇ ◇ ◇ ◇ ◇ ◇ ◇

The mariner swallowed. "Palin . . . what did he have to say about the green dragon and all the lost men?"

Dhamon shrugged. "I didn't look for him."

"But . . ."

"I'm done with Palin. I'm done with facing dragons and trying to make things right in this world. Nothing will ever be right again. I told you—we cannot win against the dragons."

Rig shook his head. "You can't mean that, Dhamon. After all we've been through and all we've seen! After all we've fought for!"

"I've seen enough. There's no hope, Rig. I'm surprised you haven't realized that by now. There're no gods. They've abandoned Krynn's children. There're only dragons. Jasper was killed by a dragon. Shaon was killed by one I used to ride. All those men—and all the men and women I never knew. *We've no chance against the dragons.* Are you so blind that you don't see that? Everyone will eventually fall to them. Everyone! So I'm making full use of whatever life I have left. *I* come first now. *I* do what *I* want. Take what *I* want. Work for whoever *I* please."

"That's wrong," the mariner started.

"Wrong?" Dhamon laughed.

"Aren't you ashamed of what you've done? The thefts and . . ."

"No."

"Ordering your men to fight the dragon?"

"Fight or flee, the outcome would have been the same. The dragon would have hunted them down and slain them anyway."

"Surely you regret killing Gauderic. . . ."

"I have no regrets," Dhamon snorted. His eyes were so dark, no pupils were discernible. "Regrets are for fools and for heroes. And I'm neither."

"Feril would be shocked," Rig muttered, trying to find some way to reach him.

Dhamon's face was cold and dispassionate. "Feril is lost to me."

"No." The mariner shook his head, dismissing the notion. "I don't believe that. I saw the way she was always looking at you. Why, you and her were . . ."

"Last I heard, she was keeping company with another Kagonesti elf on the isle of Cristyne. They're probably married by now."

❖ ❖ ❖ ❖ ❖ ❖ ❖

"And so that's how I met Dhamon," Maldred was telling Fiona. "In a rundown tavern in Sanction. He was drunk and gambling, arguing with a half-ogre over a few pieces of steel. As bad of shape as

Dhamon was in, he took out the half-ogre. Didn't even have to draw a weapon."

"And that impressed you?"

Maldred shook his head and let out a clipped laugh. "Not especially."

"Then what?" Fiona seemed genuinely curious.

"It was his eyes. Like yours, they were filled with fire, and there was a mystery burning behind them, just waiting to be unraveled. Decided I wanted to get to know him, so I waited around until he sobered up. He and I have drifted in and out of each other's company ever since. Dhamon saved my life twice—once about a month ago when we were far south in these mountains and accidentally came upon a pair of red spawn."

"Dhamon's fought them before."

"That was evident." Maldred turned his arm so Fiona could see the back of it, where just above his elbow a thick pink scar stretched toward his shoulder. "My souvenir of the day. Dhamon didn't even get a scratch. Of course, if I hadn't've set my sword down before they pounced on us—I was gathering some herbs for dinner—it would have been another matter. No one can beat me when I've a weapon. Anyway, I owe him. And I don't mind the owing. I think we're kindred spirits."

Fiona heard a clap of thunder, tipped her face to the sky, and felt the first few drops of rain splash against her.

Fetch began to hoot.

"Blessed rain," Maldred pronounced. "Been far too long since it rained in these mountains." He looked skyward, stood, and stretched his good arm out to the side to catch more of the rain, opened his mouth wide to drink it in.

Fiona started toward Rig, but a second clap of

thunder stopped her. It was followed by another, this once coming from beneath her feet. It was the mountain rumbling again, and she nearly lost her balance. The horses neighed nervously and the wagon creaked as the tremor intensified. Overhead, the lightning danced between the clouds, and the rain fell harder.

"It's the lightning one has to fear, not the thunder," Maldred said, lowering his head and catching Fiona's gaze again. He bent his knees to help keep his balance as the mountain continued to shake. Concern was etched on the big man's brow. "The earthquakes are different, Lady Knight. Another matter entirely. There've always been quakes in these mountains. Was a big one a few days ago. There's been quite a bit more rumbling lately than I'm used to. Bothers even me."

The ground stilled for just a moment, then it rumbled again, faintly at first, then growing stronger. Fiona lost her balance and fell against Maldred, who was quick to wrap his arm around her. The tremor lasted a few more minutes, then dissipated. She continued to stare into Maldred's enigmatic eyes, then berated herself for being so slow to extricate herself from his arms.

Across the camp, Rig gaped at her. Dhamon brushed by the mariner, Rikali and Fetch on his heels. Dhamon opened an empty waterskin and held it out to catch the rain as he headed toward the wagon, intending to camp underneath it. "Fiona, I told Rig you're welcome to share our camp tonight."

She stepped in front of him, eyes bright, blocking his path.

"You're not taking me back to Ironspike." His head was still a little muddied by the alcohol, but his words were coming clearer and quicker.

"Not my plan."

"You're not taking me anywhere else to 'atone' for my crimes. I won't let you."

"I wouldn't think of it."

Dhamon tipped back his head and chuckled. "And you're not going to change my ways, dearest Fiona. I've been through this with Rig. No redemption. I rather enjoy the way I've turned out."

She took a step closer until the stink of his sweat and the alcohol on his breath stung her eyes. "I don't want to redeem you, Dhamon Grimwulf. I want to join you."

Chapter Seven
Grim Kedar's

You're crazy! Join him?" The mariner's eyes were wide, mouth working soundlessly as he tried to figure out what else to say to Fiona.

"Join me?" Dhamon, too, was momentarily stunned. Then his face quickly slipped into its stoic mask and his eyes grew hard. His teeth clicked lightly together and he alternately clenched and relaxed his fingers as he waited for Fiona to explain herself.

"Join a band of brigands? I'd say that's hardly the Solamnic thing to do. Might tarnish your shinin' plate mail." Rikali sidled up close to the Knight. "Besides, Fee-ohn-a, we don't want you to join us. The four of us do just fine by ourselves. The two of you wouldn't fit in. And wouldn't be welcome."

Fiona none-too-gently nudged the half-elf away, causing Rikali to puff out her chest, thrust her chin up, and make a defiant fist. Maldred put a hand on the half-elf's shoulder, keeping her from taking a swing at the Knight.

"I need coins, Dhamon. Gems, jewels, lots of

them. I need them quickly. Immediately. And you
seem to know how to get them."

Rig slapped the heel of his hand against his forehead. Softly, he said, "It won't work, Fiona. You can't
make a deal with evil. I can't believe you're considering this. By all the vanished gods, I had no idea this
was going through your head." The mariner
watched the Knight, a myriad of emotions playing
on his face—above all, annoyance.

The Solamnic had everyone's attention. "My
brother is one of several Solamnic Knights held captive in Shrentak," Fiona began. "He's been there for
nearly two months. And I mean to see him free."

"Shrentak, the heart of the swamp," Rikali whispered. "Now that's a right foul place to find yourself
in." The half-elf wrinkled her nose and leaned against
Dhamon, who in turn leaned more heavily on his
cane.

"Sable, the black dragon overlord, holds them—
and others—in her lair. And I intend to free my
brother and as many other Knights as I can. I'll have
to use plenty of coin to ransom them."

Dhamon stood silent for several moments, the
rain and her words sobering him. His dark hair was
plastered against the sides of his head, the grime on
his face and hands slowly vanishing under the constant torrent. The fire behind him was out, plunging
the camp into darkness. Still, there was just enough
light from the lightning that danced overhead to register his grim expression. A touch of anger burned in
his eyes, the skin on his face was taut like a drum.

"You should listen to Rig," Dhamon told her.
"Ransoming them, making a deal with a dragon,
that's foolishness indeed. You should know better."

"I've no choice."

"Contact your mighty Solamnic Council. Doubtless

they ordered the Knights into the swamp in the first place. They can send more Knights to rescue them."

She shook her head. "Yes, the council sent my brother and the other men. For what purpose is a mystery. And yes, the council has tried to rescue them. Twice garrisons have gone in. And twice, no one has returned."

"Send another." His words sounded hard and brittle. "It would be an *honorable* cause."

Rikali thrust out her bottom lip and nodded agreement.

"The council refuses," Fiona practically hissed. "In all its infinite wisdom it has decreed that no more lives will be . . . 'thrown away,' were the words."

"Then hire mercenaries." This from Maldred.

"We've tried," Rig added. "But no amount of coin, it seems, will lure people into Sable's swamp."

"Smart people," the half-elf cut in.

"But coin will get my brother out," Fiona continued. "One of the dragon's minions recently contacted the council and said Sable would ransom the men for enough coin and gems. Dragons horde treasure."

"But you can't trust a dragon." Dhamon's words were ice.

So I've told her, Rig mouthed.

"I don't have any choice," she repeated firmly. "He's my brother."

Dhamon shook his head. "And he's probably dead. Or for his sake you should hope he is."

"I don't believe that. I'd know if he were dead. *Somehow I'd know*."

Dhamon let out a breath between his clenched teeth and cocked his head to catch a glimpse of a long fork of lightning. He squinted through the rain. "And the council, Fiona, what did they contribute for this ransom?"

Thunder rocked the camp and the lightning over-head intensified, jagged fingers bouncing from cloud to cloud. The rain was drumming down even faster now.

"Nothing," she finally said. "Not a single piece of steel. They said they would have no part of this, didn't believe the minion's offer to ransom the men. They've written off the Knights, the council has, con-sidering all of them lost. Dead."

"Then why—" Dhamon began.

"I'm doing this on my own. And I'm risking my standing as a Solamnic Knight." She crossed her arms, looking more defiant than Dhamon ever recalled seeing her. "I don't care how I get this treasure, Dhamon Grimwulf. I'll rob hospitals with you. Mer-chant wagons. I'll do whatever it takes short of killing. I'll . . ."

" . . . be joining our fine, but humble company of thieves, it seems, Lady Knight," Maldred finished. Rikali spat at the ground, and Fetch's eyes glowed red. Dhamon's expression was unreadable, though his unwavering eyes were on Maldred now, not Fiona. "Pity, however, that we have no wealth at present to contribute to your worthy endeavor, Lady Knight," the big man continued. "Nothing. We squandered nearly everything Dhamon recovered from the hospital. But we are traveling to Blöten, to drop off some supplies. And there, I am certain we can arrange for a way to gain considerable wealth. Enough for your ransom."

Fiona's stiff posture relaxed just a little. "I am to meet Sable's minion in Takar. He lives there, some-where. It shouldn't be hard to find him and . . ."

"And this man is. . . ." Dhamon prompted.

"Not a man, Dhamon. A draconian. The dragon has assigned him there."

"Lovely," Rikali interjected. "And you'll recognize him, I suppose."

Fiona nodded. "He has a gold collar welded about his neck. And a deep scar on his chest. I'd recognize him."

"A charmin' fellow, I'm sure," Rikali added.

Fiona ignored the half-elf, who was now grumbling about the swamp and the Knight, and about four thieves being more than enough for their small company. The Solamnic continued to watch Dhamon and Maldred. "Blöten is not very far out of the way," she said finally. "I'll go with you."

Behind her, Rig cupped his face with his hands.

❖ ❖ ❖ ❖ ❖ ❖ ❖

The rain turned soft, but maintained a steady downpour until dawn, a sheet of driving gray that kept them thoroughly soaked, and turned the trail that wound between the rocky ridges into mud.

"You should return to Khur," Dhamon told Rig as the mariner was saddling his big mare. The horse was not as good as the one Dhamon had stolen from him. Its back swayed and there was a large lump on one rear leg. "The country's more hospitable, safer for you and Fiona. Talk her out of this nonsense. Dragons . . . and draconians . . . are not to be trusted. She's wasting her time."

The mariner cinched the saddle and made a clucking sound in his throat. "Glad to see you're so concerned about our safety."

"I'm not." Dhamon's face was impassive, his voice steady. "I'd just rather not have your company."

"All the more reason, then, for Fiona and me to come with you. I know once she gets her mind set on something I can't change it. But I'm not going to help any of you swipe a single steel piece."

"A waste of time," Dhamon repeated.

"It's our time to waste."

The trail they followed had become a meandering brown snake that rippled with thick rivulets of water. At times it gently wound its way through the mountains, with steep rocks rising on both sides. But often it coiled around the edge of the western slope, as it was doing now, climbing a near-vertical cliff face, the top of which disappeared into dark gray clouds on one side, on the other a two-hundred-foot drop-off that yielded to Sable's immense swamp. A thin strip of cloud hovered above a section of the swamp, a few of the giant cypresses stretched through it, their tops decorated with large parrots.

Rikali sloshed ahead, probing with Dhamon's cane to make sure the way was safe for the horses and wagon. Though complaining about the task, she had suggested that it be done and that she be the one to handle it.

"My eyes're better'n yours," she had said to the men. Softer, so Rig and Fiona could not hear, "and I don't want anythin' happenin' to our gems. No tumble down the mountainside to lose them after all we went through to get 'em." She knew Dhamon was still favoring his ribs and that Maldred couldn't use his right arm. And although her own scrapes and bruises hadn't yet healed, she recognized she was the best choice for guide. The only thing wrong with Fetch seemed to be the repulsive odor he was exuding from being so thoroughly wet, but Rikali didn't trust the kobold to lead the wagon.

Maldred sat on the wagon bench, eyes trained on the half-elf, his wounded arm still tucked close to his chest. Dhamon, who sat next to him, could tell he was feverish. Dhamon had the reins and was watching Rikali carefully, too, though it was clear from his blank expression his mind was elsewhere.

Fetch was behind them, sitting cross-legged on the tarp that covered the bulging bags of gemstones. He'd fastened the tarp down tightly at Maldred's orders. Rig had been eyeing the tarp, and the kobold felt certain he was trying to guess what was underneath. Supplies, hah! Fetch had decided from the very beginning that he didn't like the dark man—didn't like the way he swaggered, the way his eyes flared from time to time with belligerence, the way he dressed, and the kobold certainly did not like all the weapons he carried.

The kobold didn't care for the Knight, either, but he knew Maldred was at least mildly interested in her, so voicing too much resentment there would be wasting words.

Fiona and Rig rode side by side behind the wagon, the entire procession moving slowly, the mariner frequently glancing at the tarp.

"They're talking," the kobold informed Maldred, his beady red eyes fixed on the mariner, hoping to unnerve him. "All this rain, the patter, making it too hard fer me to hear what they're saying. Something 'bout Knights an' prisoners an' Shren-something, can't make out the rest. Wagon's creaking, too. Hope it doesn't fall apart. Loaded down with gems and water. Water. Water. Water."

"I thought you wanted it to rain."

The kobold made a noise that sounded like a pig snorting. "Not this much, Mal. Can't even light up my old man. Tobacco's all damp. In all my days I've never seen it rain so much at one time in these mountains. It ain't right. Ain't natural. It could stop anytime now an'. . . ." As a booming clap of thunder cut the kobold off, he dug his small claws into the tarp. "An' what's this business about you helping that Solamnic Knight get coins an' gems an' such? Since when do we share our booty with the likes of her?"

Maldred chuckled. "I truly have no intention of helping her. And I certainly won't share any of what we have in the wagon."

"Yeah, yeah, it's for Dhamon's sword," the kobold grumbled. "Damn expensive sword."

"But she believes I will help her," Maldred continued. "And that thought warms my heart."

"And keeps her hanging around." Fetch made a face. "But she's a . . . well, she's a Solamnic Knight. Trouble. Very big trouble. Besides, she's going to marry that man."

"But she isn't married yet. And I fancy her."

"Fancy." The kobold snarled again. "The last woman you fancied was the wife of a rich Sanction merchant an' . . ."

"She didn't have so much spirit as this one," Maldred returned. "And wasn't quite so pretty. Besides, Lady Knight and the dark man are heading toward Takar, and eventually, deeper into the swamp. I suspect we could turn a good profit by going along—at least part of the way."

At mention of the swamp, Dhamon snapped to attention. He shot the big man a protesting glance. "You can't. . . ."

"What's this about profit?" Fetch cut in. "How much profit?"

"There are people in Blöten who are concerned about Sable and her swamp. They'll pay well for any information garnered from a scouting party."

"I'm not going on your little scouting party," Dhamon said. "Bad enough you invited Rig and Fiona along."

Maldred shrugged. "If I hadn't, they'd have followed us anyway. Lady Knight is headstrong. Better we keep track of them."

Dhamon found himself agreeing. "But I don't

have to like it," he said. Then he reached behind the seat and for the jug. Shaking it, he scowled. There was little left. He unstoppered it, drained the last of the spirits, then tossed the jug over the side of the mountain and watched it disappear into the mist.

Just then, Rikali slipped, the cane flying from her fingers and clattering over the edge. Dhamon pulled back on the reins, stopping the horses before they could trample her. Spitting and cursing, she picked herself up and brushed at the mud on her back. The half-elf looked up at Maldred and vehemently shook her head. Her long white hair was plastered against the sides of her body, streaked with mud. "It's like a damn stream ahead!" she hollered. "Pigs, but water is gushing down it. It's too slippery. We'll have to stop."

"Fetch!" Dhamon gestured to the kobold.

Muttering all the way, the small creature clambered down from the wagon and skidded toward the half-elf, falling twice before he reached her. He glanced down the merchant trail that continued to wind its way along the edge of the Kalkhists, his red eyes looking like tiny beacons through the gray sheet of rain. He skidded past Rikali and glanced around the next curve, scowled, and looked up, squinting as the rain pounded against his face.

"She's right. It's pretty bad," he called to Dhamon. "But waiting ain't gonna help." He pointed. "No sign of this letting up anytime soon. Only gonna get worse."

The big man gestured down the trail, and Rikali and Fetch moved slowly ahead, stopping at the bend to wait for the wagon to catch up, and guiding the horses around the next outcropping. It was difficult going, as a significant portion of the trail was washing away, and what was left was barely wide enough for the wagon. When the wagon rounded another curve, Fetch let out a whoop. His feet flew out from underneath him. Hands flailing in the air, the kobold slipped toward the edge.

Rikali grabbed his bony wrist just as his body shot over the side. She let him dangle in the air for a moment, treasuring the terror-filled look on his face before hauling him to safety and hoisting him up on the back of one of the horses. "Worthless," she muttered, turning and resuming her task as solo guide. "You are completely worthless, Fetch."

What would have taken them only a few hours, took them nearly the entire day and almost resulted in a catastrophe when a wheel slipped off the trail. It required Rig, Fiona, and Dhamon to set it back on.

They camped that night on a small plateau that was free of mud—the rain had washed all the earth away, revealing a layer of slate that gleamed slickly black when the moon made a brief visit. The rain was also threatening to dislodge the few saplings that sprouted from the cracks in the cliff face. The small trees were whipping about unmercifully in the wind that had picked up and that was driving the rain nearly horizontally.

The deluge continued throughout the night, lessening with the morning and then increasing again at sunset. The sky was masked with clouds, billowy and dark and rumbling with constant thunder. Occasionally the ground shook beneath them, and though it was not as threatening as the earlier tremors, it unnerved Fetch, Rikali, and Maldred. Dhamon remained impassive to the weather and small quakes.

Rig and Fiona kept to themselves for the most part, and Dhamon managed to avoid their company by losing himself in Rikali's arms. The half-elf was suspicious enough to wonder why Dhamon had become so devoted all of a sudden. She couldn't help but notice the mariner's eyes narrow every time she kissed Dhamon.

"I know you love your brother," Rig said in a low voice to Fiona. "But I don't think he'd approve of this. Hell, I don't approve." They sat side by side on a flat rock, inured to the rain. "Keeping company with these people, heading to Blöten. That's the heart of ogre country. It doesn't feel right. And it's damn dangerous."

"I need to raise a ransom, Rig. How else can I get it? These . . . people . . . are my best chance. I have nothing—through the years I've tithed it all to the order. You haven't enough. And you haven't a better idea."

The mariner snorted and draped an arm around her shoulders, frowning when she didn't sag against him as she usually did. Her posture was as stiff as her armor. Water trickled out from between gaps in the plates and spilled over the lips of her boots. "I don't trust Dhamon. And what about this man Maldred? We know nothing about him other than that he's a thief."

"I recall you telling me you were a thief once."

The mariner shook his head, grinding his heel against the slate. "That was a lifetime ago, Fiona. Feels like it anyway. And I wasn't a thief. I was a *pirate*. There's a big difference. At least to me there is."

"Those whom you stole from might disagree." She sighed and softened her tone. "Look, Rig, I really need to raise this ransom. And soon. This is my best idea. Maybe if there was more time . . . but there isn't. His life is at stake."

"Do you really think this draconian will be waiting around for us?"

"He told the Solamnic Council he was stationed in Takar."

"And you trust him?"

She shrugged. "What choice do I have? Besides, there's no reason he'd lie to the council about his whereabouts if he really wanted to collect some treasure for Sable. And there's no reason he would've approached the council about a ransom in the first place if the dragon wasn't interested in adding to her horde."

"And if you can manage to raise the ransom, and get to Takar, you've still got to find this draconian. I'd wager there are quite a few draconians and spawn there."

She let out a deep breath. "That, I'm certain, will be the easy part. I will recognize him, Rig. I know it. His name is Olarg, and the scar was singular."

"Fine. So you're sure you can find him. And are you as certain this draconian will simply hand over your brother for a big sack of—"

"I've no alternative but to believe it. And Dhamon and Maldred are our best chance of raising the coin. Maybe our only chance. My brother must be set free. Then we can put all of this behind us and be married."

Rig raised his eyebrows and leaned forward to look into her face. She was watching the bare-chested Maldred, who was resting against the wagon, his face tipped up into the rain.

"And what about Dhamon? After this is all over— one way or the other?"

"Dhamon needs us to believe in him, and you know it. He needs another chance. He's a good man, Rig. Deep down. Too good to cart off to prison, no matter what he's done recently."

Her words genuinely surprised him. "Doesn't sound like you, Fiona. I thought you told me justice demands people pay for their wrongs."

"Justice," she repeated. "Where's the justice in this

world? My brother is in Shrentak. And Dhamon is going to help me get him released. That's the justice I want—my brother free. Besides, Dhamon is really a good man. Deep down good."

I'm a good man, too, the mariner thought ruefully, as he picked a spot on the ground and settled down for another drenched and sleepless night.

Two days later, the rain still falling, though more gently now, they stood at the gates of Blöten, a once-great city nestled high in the Kalkhists, the mountains ringing it like a spiky crown.

A crumbling wall nearly forty feet high wrapped around the ancient capital. In sections it had collapsed, the gaps alternately filled with boulders piled high and mortared in place, and with timbers driven deep into the rocky ground and held together with bands of rusted iron. Across the top where the walls seemed in the worst repair, spears were jabbed in, angled outward and inward.

"Broken glass and caltrops are spread across the top everywhere," Fetch informed the mariner. "For the purpose of keeping the uninvited out."

"Or to keep everyone in," the dark man returned. "It looks like an enormous prison to me."

Atop a barbican that seemed so weathered it might crumble at any time, stood two grizzled ogres. Stoop-shouldered and wart-riddled, their gray-green hides slick with rain, they glowered down at the small entourage. The larger had a snaggly tooth that protruded up at an odd angle from his bottom jaw. A dark purple tongue snaked out to wrap around it. He growled something and thumped his spiked club against his shield, then growled again, issuing a string of guttural words lost on all save Maldred and Dhamon.

Maldred eased himself from the wagon, swaying

a little from the effects of his fever, and padded to the massive wooden gates. He looked up at the pair and raised his good arm, balled his fist and circled it once in the air, then brought it down against his waist. Then he spoke, nearly shouting, his words sounding like a series of snarls and grunts.

Next, Maldred motioned to Dhamon, making a gesture Rig recognized as "wealth," or "coin," a signing word his deaf friend Groller taught him. Rig instantly thought of his companion, wondering if he'd found work on a ship somewhere or had elected some cause to champion. Perhaps he was assisting Palin Majere. The mariner regretted not staying in touch with Groller and found himself wishing the half-ogre were here. He would be handy in this city, though he would not be able to hear what was being said, and he was someone Rig could trust. *If I get out of this*, he mused, *and after the matter of Fiona's brother is settled, I'm going to find my old friend.*

Dhamon tugged the Legion of Steel ring off his hand and tossed it to Maldred. Again Maldred issued a string of growls and grunts, punctuating it by hurling the ring up at the ogres. The larger's arm shot out, warty fingers closing over the bauble. He brought it up to his eyes, then smiled, revealing yellowed, broken teeth. He snarled back happily.

"Not good," Rig whispered to Fiona. "That man Maldred knows the ogre tongue. Worse, it seems Dhamon does, too. And don't tell me ogres are deep down good. I know better. I don't like it."

"Good that *someone* can understand the brutes," she softly returned. "Otherwise, I doubt we'd get past the gates."

"Oh, we'll get in all right," the mariner smugly replied. "But we might not get back out again." He watched the doors swing wide, as the pair of ugly sentries gestured for them to enter. "I really don't think this is a good idea."

Fiona ignored him, kneeing her horse to follow the wagon. Rig cursed, but tagged along, keeping his eyes alert. The doors creaked closed behind them, and a great plank lowered to lock them in place. They saw large crossbows mounted at the crest of the walls, and ladders leading up to them. "Wonderful," the mariner muttered. "This is such an enchanting place we've come to. We should vacation here."

The city spread out before them, too large for them to take it all in at one glance. Massive buildings, the facades of which were deteriorating from age and lack of repair, stretched toward the clouds overhead. Signs hung from some of the buildings, drawings indicating taverns, weaponsmiths, and inns, though whether the buildings were actually open and operating businesses was doubtful—some looked as though they might topple at any moment and few lights shone from within. The words on the signs were in some foreign language, looking like faded and chipped bugs dancing in an uneven line. Ogre tongue, Rig guessed, though he had never seen it written down before.

Growing puddles dotted wide streets lined with wagons and massive draft horses with sagging backs. A large ox was being groomed by a one-eyed ogre woman outside what appeared to be a bakery. The woman glared at the Solamnic and brushed the ox harder as the group streamed past her.

Nearly all of the other citizens they spotted were ogres, manlike creatures nine or more feet tall. They were all broad-faced with large, thick noses, some of which were decorated with silver and gold hoops and bones. Their brows were thick, shadowing large, wide-set dark eyes that glanced at the newcomers, then looked away. Their ears were overlarge and misshapen, most pointed like an elf's, but not gracefully so. And their skin ranged from a pale brown to a rich mahogany. A few were green-gray, and one who strolled slowly across the street in front of them was the color of cold ashes. They milled about sluggishly, as if the unusual wet weather had managed to dampen their spirits.

Many were in hide armor and toting large spiked clubs. The shields that hung from many of their backs were pitted and worn, some with symbols painted on them, others with hash marks that attested to victories, or crudely painted pictures of fearsome animals they'd likely slain. Some ogres wore tattered clothes and ragged animal skins, and were sandaled or had bare feet, all looking filthy. Only a few were dressed in garments that appeared well made and reasonably clean.

There were some half-ogres in the crowd, and these were also dressed raggedly, their features closer to human-looking. One was a peddler hawking smoked strips of gray meat from beneath an awning that swelled away from a boarded-up building. A trio of ogre children hung around him, alternately begging for food and taunting him.

"Our good friend Groller's a half-ogre," Rig said, his voice low and his words intended only for Fiona. "But he's far removed from these creatures."

She nodded. "*These people*, Rig. Ogres were once the most beautiful race on Krynn. It is said no other race equalled their form."

"Beautiful. Pfah!"

"They were beautiful. But they fell from the grace of the gods during the Age of Dreams. Now they're ugly and brutal, shadows of what their ancestors were."

"Well, I don't care for these *shadows*," Rig said.

"And I wouldn't be here if it wasn't for you." His hands tightly gripped his mare's reins, the wet leather cutting into his finger joints, and his eyes drifting from one side of the street to the other, looking for a face with the tiniest spark of friendliness. "We're definitely out of place here, Fiona. I'm so uncomfortable my skin feels like ants're crawling all over it."

"Wait, there're some humans here." Fiona leaned forward in her saddle and pointed west, down a side street they were passing.

Indeed there were about a dozen men, dressed even worse than the ogres. They were toting sacks from a building and tossing them into a wagon that sagged and looked stuck in the mud. There were words cut into a sign that hung from the building, but Rig and Fiona had no clue what they meant. Two mountain dwarves were working with the humans—and unlike the ogres and half-ogres, none of them seemed to be carrying visible weapons.

"I truly don't like this," the mariner continued. "In fact . . ." He cast his head over his shoulder, looking at the gate receding behind them. "Fiona, I think we should—"

"Maldred! You handsome swine!" A booming voice cut through the air, followed by loud, sloshing footsteps. "It has been too long indeed!" The speaker was an ogre, one of the better dressed of the lot, who was splashing his way through the puddles toward them. He had massive shoulders, from which draped a black bear skin, the head of the animal resting to the side of his thick neck, the rear claws dangling down to rake the mud. He continued talking loudly, though in the ogre tongue now, the bear head bobbing along with his broad gestures.

Maldred walked into the ogre's embrace. But the

ogre quickly backed away when he noted Maldred's
condition. Gesturing at Maldred's bad arm, the creature eyed the rest of the entourage, quickly determin-
ing that the half-elf and the other human were also
injured. He chuckled deeply when he spotted Fetch.
The kobold scampered down from the wagon and
practically swam through a puddle to reach the pair.

"Durfang!" Fetch squealed. "It's Durfang Farn-
werth!"

"Fetch! You stinking rat! I haven't seen you in
years!" the ogre boomed in the common tongue—
apparently for Fetch's benefit. He bent over and
scratched the kobold's head. "Seems you have not been
taking good care of my friend—or his companions."

The kobold shrugged and cackled shrilly.

"You folks need a healer," the ogre continued,
standing and meeting Maldred's gaze. "A good one."

Maldred nodded, pointing to Dhamon and Rikali.
"My friends, first."

The creature scowled and wriggled his lips. "As
you desire, Maldred," Durfang finally said. Then his
eyes drifted to Fiona, narrowing with curiosity. He
returned to the ogre tongue, speaking to Maldred
quick and low, his face animated and concerned—
relaxing only after Maldred said something evidently reassuring. "Okay, all of you, follow me."

"To Grim Kedar's?" Maldred asked.

"He is the best."

"Then I will meet you there shortly, Durfang. I
have a cargo to arrange safe-keeping for. And that
takes precedence over my well-being."

The large ogre scowled, but didn't argue.

Dhamon leapt from the wagon, cringing at the
strain. He sloshed toward Maldred, using gestures
rather than talking, the quickness of hands hinting at
an argument.

"The cargo will be safe with me," Maldred whispered.

Dhamon's eyes became slits, flickering between Maldred and Durfang.

"On my life, Dhamon," Maldred added. "You know we have to keep the wagon somewhere tonight, or maybe for the next few days depending on when Donnag will see us to negotiate over the sword you want. He might not be available immediately. And we just can't leave the wagon out on the street. Not in this city. And if we guard it, the scurrilous element will only become curious. We can't take that risk."

"How about a stable?"

Maldred shook his head. "Not safe enough. Too public. Too many people going in and out."

"Where then?" Dhamon asked, his voice difficult for Maldred to hear above the rain.

"I have friends in this city whom I can rely on and who owe me a few favors. I'll see who among them seems the most trustworthy today."

Dhamon nodded. "On your life, then. But just in case, I'm keeping some trinkets with me." He returned to the wagon, tugging a backpack from beneath the seat and throwing it over his shoulder. "And be quick about it, Mal. You need tending far more than Riki and I."

Rikali and Fetch each claimed a small, gem-stuffed satchel before Maldred drove the wagon away, cleverly ignoring the mariner's persistent questions about what kind of supplies they had brought to Blöten to sell. Dhamon knew Rig didn't believe for a moment there were genuine supplies under the tarp.

Rig and Fiona walked their horses behind the trio, the mariner cursing softly and repeating what a bad idea this was at every opportunity. Their ogre guide, who had not uttered a word since Maldred left, took them down one side street after another. Some buildings had been boarded up, others were in ruins because of fire. A few ogres sat on a bench in front of one gutted building, talking and grunting loudly and eyeing the small group. One rose and thumped a club against his leg—but sat back down quickly after Durfang snarled in their direction.

"You hungry?" Fetch asked, glancing up at the Solamnic. "I'm starving. We haven't eaten for at least a day."

Fiona, who hadn't realized the kobold was talking to her, kept walking.

"I've lost my appetite," Rig answered for them both.

Grim Kedar's was a squat building—compared to those that rose around it. Its front was as gray as the skies overhead, and a wood plank sidewalk that had once been painted red sagged in front of it beneath a canvas awning that looked as hole-riddled as Karthay cheese. A weather-beaten sign out front depicted a mortar and a pestle with tendrils of steam rising from the bowl to form a ghostly ogre skull.

"Very bad idea," Rig growled as he tied the horses to a post and followed Fiona inside.

They were ushered by Fetch to a table with over-large chairs that tottered on uneven legs. Two ogres commanded the only other table in the room, clutching steaming mugs that released a bitter smell into the air. They flaunted a collection of small pouches and daggers. Fetch, who climbed up the table leg to sit next to Fiona, explained the ogres were busy bartering for something—he couldn't tell what because he didn't know hardly any of their language—and that the daggers were being displayed in the event of a double-cross. The kobold's eyes gleamed eagerly, hoping to witness a fight.

Rikali and Dhamon stood at a small counter, behind which rose, at merely eight feet, a pasty ogre with a smattering of dark green hair on his mottled head. His pointed ears were pierced with dozens of small hoops, and a metal stud pierced the bridge of his nose. He grinned at his customers, revealing yellowed teeth so blunt and even it appeared as though they'd been filed.

"That's Grim," Fetch whispered to Fiona. The kobold didn't bother addressing the mariner, though he shot the occasional dark glance at him. "He's a healer. The best in Blöten, probably the best anywhere on Krynn. Sells tea said to ward off diseases and he's known for having herbs that'll counteract most poisons." The kobold gestured to the mugs the ogres were drinking from. "Maybe we should get some, too. All this rain can't be good for you humans. Might be something goin' around."

Rig growled.

"He'll fix Dhamon and Riki up good as new. Maybe even do something about the scale. . . ." The kobold stopped.

"We know all about the scale on Dhamon's leg," Fiona said.

"But you don't know that it. . . ." The kobold let the words hang, his gaze following Rikali and Dhamon, who walked behind the counter and through a beaded curtain that clacked noisily as they passed through it. "That's where Grim does all of his serious healing. I went back there once with Maldred after he got cut up bad in a tavern brawl. Course, the other ogres in the fight were beyond repair."

Rig made a move to rise and follow Dhamon, but the kobold scowled and shook his head.

"Let's stay here," Fiona suggested. She dropped her hand below the table and rested it on Rig's leg. "And let's stay alert."

"I don't like this place," the mariner said. "I'm only here because of you." His eyes wandered from the front door to the ogres and back to the beaded curtain, his jaw working tensely. "I don't like this at all."

Behind the curtain were a few large tables stained with blood and other unidentifiable substances. Dhamon climbed up on one of the cleanest ones and tugged free his shirt, revealing that the right side of his chest was a massive purple-black bruise.

Grim stood silent, his eyes fixed on the injury. Dhamon in turn inspected the ogre more closely. He was ancient, his pale skin covered with small wrinkles. The flesh sagged on his arms and around his jaws, giving him the visage of a bulldog. Veins were visible on his forehead, which was knitted in concentration. Only his hands looked smooth, seeming incongruous to the rest of his body. The nails were well manicured and not a speck of dirt was visible. A simple steel ring circled his right thumb. There was writing on it, but Dhamon couldn't make it out. There was an odor about the ogre that Dhamon found vaguely reminiscent of the hospital in Ironspike, but it was not near so pungent.

The half-elf was chattering softly to Dhamon and the ogre, though both were ignoring her. She climbed atop another table and sat watching the ogre shove Dhamon onto his back and inspect his ribs.

Grim prodded Dhamon's ribs and muttered in the ogre tongue—to himself, not his patient. Then he turned his attention to the scale, which he could see through Dhamon's tattered pants. The ogre curiously touched it and traced its edges, ran a thick fingernail down the silver line. Dhamon sat up and shook his head.

"There's nothing you can do for it," he explained. He tried the words again, in a broken ogre dialect.

But the ogre healer pressed him down on the table again, waggled a finger and pointed to Dhamon's lips indicating he should be quiet. Grim pulled a thin-bladed knife from a sheath on his back. When Dhamon realized the ogre intended to cut the pants off, he rolled away, wincing. He quickly undressed, placed his tattered clothes, satchel, and sword aside, again trying to explain about the scale while being pressed back on the table, harsher this time.

The ogre knew how to handle difficult patients, and he made Dhamon feel vulnerable and uncomfortable as he continued his brusque examination, which must have taken at least half an hour and included ogling the diamond that dangled from the thong on Dhamon's neck. Then he made a clacking sound. Reaching into one of the many pockets in his patched robe, he tugged free a root and snapped it, letting the juice dribble onto Dhamon's chest where he smeared it into a pattern.

The clacking continued and became primitively musical as his long, knobby fingers worked over the obvious wounds and bruises, always returning to the scale. The ministrations reminded Dhamon of Jasper Fireforge, who had healed him more times than he cared to count. Jasper's work had seemed much more caring, however, the actions of the ogre healer were uniform and practiced, yet detached and sometimes almost harsh.

Dhamon fervently wished either Maldred was here or that he, himself, was elsewhere. Then he felt a warmth begin to flow through him. It wasn't the painful sensation associated with the dragon's

scale, however, but one similar to the relaxing calm
he had felt when Jasper tended him. The ogre
stopped his clacking and welcomed Maldred, who
had arrived, and who had quite a mastery of the
strange language. Dhamon started to drift off
toward sleep when the pain intensified all of a
sudden. The ogre healer was tugging at Dhamon's
scale.

"No!" Dhamon shouted, sitting bolt upright and
throwing his hands over the scale. "Leave it!"

Grim tried to press him down again, but Dhamon
successfully fought against it, arguing with words he
was certain the healer couldn't understand but
couldn't mistake their meaning. The pasty ogre
shook his head and snarled, pointed to the scale and
made a surgical gesture that was clear.

"Remove the scale and you'll die." The words
repeated inside Dhamon's head. Then the scale was
heating up like a branding iron again, sending ago-
nizing waves through every part of his body. There
was no gentle, teasing warmth to warn him this time.
The pain struck like a hammer, over and over, seeming to drive him into the table. His muscles con-
stricted and he shook uncontrollably, his teeth
grinding together and his hands clenching so tightly
that his fingernails cut into his palms. He raised his
head and sucked in great gulps of air. He tried not to
cry out. But a strangled moan escaped his lips and
his head fell back hard against the table.

Rikali was at his side, fingers moving over his
face, alternating stern and worried looks between
Grim and Maldred.

Maldred's hand was on the scale now, and he was
arguing with the healer. Dhamon wished he could
understand more of what was being said. Finally
Grim backed away, shaking his head and making an

almost-human tsk-tsking sound.

"What's going on in here?" Rig's head poked through the beaded curtain, and immediately all eyes were on the mariner.

"Nothing," Maldred said. "Wait outside."

"What are you doing to Dhamon?" The mariner could see Dhamon shaking, the sweat covering Dhamon's limbs and the odd-colored liquid on his chest that had come from the discarded root.

The ogre healer took a step toward Rig, eyes narrowed and a hiss of growled words issued rapidly from his mouth.

"It's all right," Dhamon breathlessly cut in, the episode finally abating. A part of him was bothered that the mariner seemed concerned for his well being. He wanted to sever all his ties with the man.

Rig grumbled, but slipped outside to rejoin Fiona. His eyes grew wide when he realized the beaded curtain he had moved aside wasn't truly beads. It was a collection of painted finger bones.

"Rig's a little jumpy," Dhamon explained to Maldred. "Always has been a jumpy guy. I told you we should have stole their horses again and not let them follow us."

The big man passed Dhamon his clothes. "Feeling any better?"

"Remarkably better." The ogre passed him a cloth. Dhamon wiped the concoction off his chest, eyes widening when he discovered the bruise was gone, and no mark was left behind. Even a few of his old scars had disappeared. "Remarkable," his whispered. "What do I owe this man?"

The ogre healer turned and pointed to the diamond that dangled about Dhamon's neck.

"So you can understand the human tongue after all," Dhamon said, tugging the gem free and passing it over—despite Rikali's protestations. "Will that pay for Mal and Riki too?"

Grim nodded and set to work on the half-elf, while Maldred undressed and, with Dhamon's help, climbed on another table. Rikali's wounds were easy to cure and required little time. When Grim finished with her, she glided toward Dhamon and prodded him here and there, pronouncing the healer's work more than satisfactory.

"Mal, what about the wagon?" She was whispering, fearing those in the outer room might hear her. "All those . . . uhm . . . our cargo. What did you do with the wagon and . . ."

Grim waved a hand at the half-elf, trying to silence her as he worked. But Rikali would not be dissuaded. She hovered around Maldred's table, just out of the healer's reach, dodging when he made a move to push her.

The healer snarled when he removed the bandage on the big man's arm and saw traces of gangrene. Dhamon recognized the seriousness of the injury, too, as he had tended many fallen Knights of Takhisis on battlefields and had been forced to amputate limbs. He drew Riki away and held her close as Maldred moaned. The healer busied himself applying another root to the wound.

Grim glanced over his shoulder, meeting Dhamon's gaze. "Tomorrow," he said, the first word he'd spoken in the common tongue. "Come again then. For Maldred. After mid sun." He suggested several reasonably safe areas they might go to pass the time, and then he dismissed them with a wave of his hand.

But Maldred beckoned Dhamon closer, then gave him quick and quiet directions to the wagon. "In the event Grim isn't able to put me wholly right, you'll be on your own with it."

The big man intended to say more, but the ogre healer growled and spun Dhamon away from the table, then forcibly guided him and Rikali through the bead curtain after they'd retrieved their satchels. Fetch was waiting for them atop the counter. Rig stood and put his hands on his hips, as if to say, "well?"

"Maldred needs to rest here a while," Dhamon began, not intending to tell them the big man was most certainly going to have to have his arm amputated. "Rikali and I are going for a long bath, at something that serves as a bathhouse down the street. Then we've some shopping to do—that is provided we can find the right stores and some clothes in Blöten that might fit us."

"Dinner," the half-elf chimed in. "Rare meat and somethin' sweet." She wrapped her arms about Dhamon's waist and stretched up to nuzzle his shoulder. "And wine, the expensive kind."

"I'm coming!" Fetch decided. Softer, he said. "But ya ain't gonna find anything better here than bitter ale."

"I doubt Rig and Fiona will want to follow us around for the rest of the day," Dhamon said. "So. . . ."

Fiona cleared her throat. "On the contrary, Dhamon. Rig and I wouldn't think of abandoning you and the fair Rikali in this ogre den."

"Thank you for speaking for me," Rig said under his breath. Louder, he said, "A warm bath sounds like a wonderful idea."

The following day found Dhamon in different clothes. They were not new and not the best fit, the pants being too baggy for his lithe frame. Still, they were clean, a dark yellow, the shade of dying birch leaves. He also wore an oddly striped, faded blue-and-red tunic that was overlarge and draped to his

knees. With the application of a few steel pieces he'd
managed to talk an ogress, who was an adequate
seamstress, into fashioning ties about his ankles so
the pantlegs ballooned out and fell in folds. A fine
leather belt wrapped about his waist only twice.
Somehow the seamstress was also able to provide a
deerskin vest that fit him nearly perfectly. It showed
little wear, and was decorated by polished brass
studs that formed a half-moon in the center of the
back. Human-sized boots, which he'd spied in her
shop, completed his new outfit. He suspected the
boots had been taken in a raid or removed from an
unfortunate soul who found his way into slavery
here. But they were superbly fashioned and would
have cost four times as much in a human city.

"So handsome, you are, Dhamon Grimwulf.
Haven't seen you lookin' so fancy since that day I met
you," Rikali told him. "We look quite fine together,
you and I." The half-elf's hair was piled in locks atop
her head. She'd decorated it with jade clasps in the
shapes of butterflies and hummingbirds, bits of jewelry she'd taken from one of the merchant wagons.
Her face was again painted, eyelids a bright blue,
lashes made long, and lips a rich crimson.

She tucked her arm beneath his, expecting to
accompany him to get the wagon, but he instead
directed her and Fetch to meet him outside Grim
Kedar's later.

Alone, Dhamon strolled down a street that led to
the east, where the tops of the towering Kalkhists
disappeared into low-hanging clouds. Indeed,
Dhamon mused to himself that he hadn't seen clear
sky since the night Rig and Fiona stumbled upon
their camp.

He stopped at a squat building, one in far better
condition than its neighbors. It appeared the ogre

who maintained the place took a little bit of pride in it. Stepping inside, he was met with a growl and narrowed eyes. The ogre behind a great table that served as a counter pointed a stubby finger and gestured for Dhamon to leave.

But Dhamon shook his head and jiggled a small pouch on his belt.

The finger dropped and the growling stopped, but the eyes narrowed even further. The ogre cocked his head and glanced at the rear wall, from which hung all manner of long-hafted weapons—all too unwieldy for Dhamon.

"I want a bow," Dhamon began, jingling the pouch again.

The ogre shook his head and shrugged a misshapen shoulder.

Dhamon let out a deep breath. "So I'd better learn a bit more ogre-speak if I traipse around these mountains any longer or ever come back to this cesspool," he muttered. He drew his lips into a thin line, met the ogre's stare, and pretended to draw a bow and nock an arrow as he said a few words in broken ogre.

Minutes later, Dhamon was continuing down the winding, narrow street, a long bow and a quiver filled with arrows strapped across his back. Following the incident with the dwarves in the valley, he'd resolved to acquire a distance weapon.

Another stop, and he purchased three skins of the strongest liquor available in the city. Two dangled from his belt. And the third was in his hand. He took a long pull from it before he clipped it onto the belt.

The several ogres he passed gave him a wide berth. It was clear they had no respect for humans, as they spat at the ground when he neared, snarling, and wrinkling their warty, hooked noses. But there was something about Dhamon's bearing and expression that kept them from accosting him. He dropped his hand to the pommel of his sword, and they moved to the other side of the street, not daring to look over their shoulders until they were several yards behind him.

His next stop was where the street dead-ended at a large building. There was no roof, only walls of stone and wood, and a double-wide rotting door that rested slightly open.

Dhamon poked his head inside, then instantly pulled it back out. There was a whoosh and a thud as a great two-handed battleaxe descended in the space where his neck had been a moment before. Mud and water flew when the blade struck the ground, spattering Dhamon's tunic and causing him to curse loudly.

He kicked the door open and drew his sword in the same motion, darted inside and braced himself to meet an impressively large ogre. The creature was easily ten feet tall with broad shoulders and a considerable paunch that swelled over a thick leather belt. The ogre hefted his axe again, a yellowed, crooked smile spreading across his pudgy face, his drab green eyes gleaming.

Dhamon stepped back, into a deep puddle. With no roof, it was raining as steadily inside the building as it was outside. "Maldred!" Dhamon shouted, oblivious to the muck. "I am with Maldred!"

The ogre paused a moment, smile disappearing. His shaggy brow furrowed. His hands still clenched the axe, but the menace had lessened in his eyes.

"Maldred," Dhamon repeated, when the large brute took a step forward with a threatening snarl. In broken ogre-speak, he added, "Our wagon. Maldred asked you watch. You have. I have come to claim our wagon."

The ogre looked to the back of the building—the glance was enough to let Dhamon know he understood clearly. The wagon was cloaked by the shadows. Dhamon walked toward it, careful to keep an eye on the ogre and to keep his sword at the ready. Only one horse was tethered nearby. Dhamon worked quickly to harness it to the wagon while he scanned the area for the other horse.

"Damn," he swore softly when he spotted blood against the back wall. There was a hank of mane, and from beneath a pile of wet, moldy straw, a hoofed leg protruded. "Got hungry, didn't you?" He didn't expect the ogre to understand or answer. "Picked out the biggest one to eat."

The creature padded closer, sloshing through the mud. He still held the axe in front of him, his eyes darting back and forth.

Dhamon busied himself checking beneath the sodden tarp, keeping an eye on the brute. "Got greedy too, didn't you? Or at the very least, curious." He noticed the sacks had been rearranged in the wagon bed, and though he couldn't be sure if there was anything missing, he decided to play a hunch. He pointed the sword at the ogre. "Give back. Sacks you took. Give back."

"Thwuk! Thwuk!" The ogre snarled as he closed in, bringing the axe up over his head in a great threatening show. "Thwuk not take from Maldred!" But Dhamon wasn't in the mood to be intimidated. He darted in and swept his sword across the creature's belly, then leapt back as a film of dark blood sprayed out. The ogre howled, and the axe slipped from his fingers, which were now furiously clutching his stomach. Blood spilled out over the brute's hands as he dropped to his knees, a mix of anger and surprise on his ugly face.

He growled deeply at Dhamon, red spittle trailing over his bulbous lip. Then he cried out once more as Dhamon stepped in again and slashed the blade across his throat. The ogre pitched forward dead.

"Hope you weren't too good of a friend to Maldred," Dhamon mused, as he wiped his sword on the brute's clothes and sheathed it. He quickly tossed the straw over the dead ogre, avoiding the insects that swarmed over the horse haunch.

Then he used the rain to wash his hands and take a good look around. There were tall plants growing along the northern half of the building. They appeared well tended, and their tops nearly reached to where the roof had been. There was a huge hammock strung between what had served as the roof's support beams, and beneath it was quite a collection of small barrels and satchels, likely the ogre's possessions.

Dhamon tugged off his newly purchased tunic, sprayed with blood and mud, and tossed it behind a row of plants. Searching around in the wagon beneath a sack of gemstones, he recovered the fine shirt he had saved from the merchant haul and was quick to don it. Black, it complemented his baggy trousers and deerskin vest. He admired his dark reflection in a puddle near the ogre's hammock.

Dhamon searched through the ogre's possessions, finding only a small sack of gemstones—which the ogre might have stolen or more likely had been given in payment for watching the wagon. Dhamon tossed it in the wagon and continued to pick through the dead creature's worldly goods, finding a pouch heavy with steel pieces, an ivory pommeled dagger, and bits of dried foodstuffs, which Dhamon sniffed unenthusiastically. There were a few other odds and ends, a small broken jade mermaid, and a bronze bracelet, thick with mud, which he sloshed about in the water that had filled the hammock.

Deciding there was little of value, Dhamon led the horse and wagon from the barn and propped the door shut.

"One final stop," he told himself. "The most important one."

An hour later, he found his way back to Grim Kedar's.

Rig was across the street, leaning against an abandoned stone building and watching the entrance to Grim Kedar's. His eyes appeared sunken, the circles beneath them dark, proving he'd slept little the previous night. A disheveled-looking human was cowering next to him, nodding and shaking his head as Rig grilled him with questions. The mariner had not spied a single human who was not shabbily dressed or who appeared remotely happy.

Fiona motioned for Rig to join them, but the mariner shook his head and continued talking to the stranger. She shrugged and turned her attention to the kobold.

"An unusual name," she said, bending over until her face met his.

"Not my real name," Fetch returned. "I'd guess you'd call it a . . ." He scrunched his features and tapped on his nose ring.

"Nickname?" Fiona risked.

He nodded. "My real name's Ilbreth. I'm just called Fetch 'cause—"

"Fetch!" Rikali was standing on the sagging walk and crooking her manicured fingers at the kobold. "Bring my satchel and get inside. Hurry up!"

" . . . I fetch things," he finished, scampering to do her bidding.

Dhamon urged the horse toward the sagging

wooden sidewalk, tethered it to a post and brushed by Rikali, whom he told to guard the wagon—with her life. Entering the establishment, he noted that even though it was just past lunchtime, there were no tea-drinkers or apparent patients. He rapped on the counter. The others came in behind him. A few moments later, Maldred emerged from behind the beads.

A wide grinn was splayed across the big man's face, and his arms were spread to his sides. He turned once for inspection. There was no indication of injury, and Dhamon stared wide-eyed at his large friend.

"I thought he'd have to cut off your arm," Dhamon said evenly.

"So did Grim," Maldred replied. "Indeed, he tried! But I wouldn't let him. Told him he had to work his magic and make me whole or I'd tell everyone he was nothing but a simple charlatan. And he could not afford such a reputation—at least not here. Of course, this cost me a bit more than what you gave him yesterday."

Dhamon winced.

"Worth it, my friend. Grim is the best. Unfortunate, however, he is not so powerful as to stop all of this rain. I doubt these mountains have seen this much in the past few years. At least it's giving all of Blöten a much-needed bath," Maldred chuckled, then instantly grew serious. "The wagon?"

Dhamon nodded toward the street.

"Did Thwuk demand anything else for watching it?"

Dhamon shook his head. "Nothing else. I'm a shrewd negotiator."

"That's why I like you." Maldred strolled toward Fiona, his eyes sparkling merrily and catching hers. "Now on to that matter of gaining you some ransom, Lady Knight."

Dhamon cleared his throat. "We've an appointment this evening."

Maldred raised his eyebrows as if to say, "you negotiated that as well?"

"We're to have dinner with Donnag this evening to discuss various matters."

"Then I'd best find something presentable to wear," Maldred returned. "Join me, Lady Knight?"

"My ransom?" Fiona's face was still wrinkled with worry. "Is the ransom part of the *various matters*?"

"Yes. We should gain you some wealth tonight, I think." Maldred did not see Dhamon's hard expression and narrowed eyes, as he was devoting all of his charm and attention to the Solamnic. The big man extended his arm, and she took it, strolling out of the shop with him and meeting the glare of the half-elf. Fiona looked across the street, but the mariner was nowhere in sight.

Rig had wandered down a cobblestone side street, one of the very few of its kind in Blöten. Nearly all of the streets seemed to be wide streams of mud. He skirted the largest puddles, avoiding them entirely was impossible. As the cobblestones ended and another swath of mud began, the businesses and dwellings that lined it became more rundown. He could tell a few of them were owned, or at the very least operated, by humans and dwarves, and they seemed to cater to the nonogre population. None of these shops had awnings or planks out front, just strips of deep, muddy clay. He glanced at his reflection in an overflowing horse trough. His stomach rumbled. He'd barely touched his dinner last night, while his companions ate heartily. He'd had nothing to eat today, not wanting any part of this place. But he was feeling a little weak, his head aching and hands shaking, and he knew he was going to have to eat something. He glanced up, looking for an establishment that might sell identifiable foodstuffs.

"Gardi? Izzat you Gardi?"

Rig realized that a gangly young man who had leaned out on a crooked stoop was speaking to him.

"Oh, sorry. Thought you wuz Gardi." He turned and disappeared in the doorway, as the mariner sprinted forward and his arm shot out to catch the man's wrist. The young man spat a foreign-sounding word, then gulped and his eyes grew wide when he took in all of the mariner's weapons.

"S'okay," Rig said. "I'm not going to hurt you. Just want to talk. I'm new to town, and I was wondering . . ."

"Too bad," the man said, relaxing a bit when Rig released him.

Rig cocked his head.

"Too bad you came here," he said, a genuine look of sadness on his face. "Blöten's not a good place to be—if you have the choice to be somewheres else. And I haven't time to dawdle with you. Got money to earn. Taxes to pay. Taxes and taxes and taxes and taxes."

Rig pulled a steel piece from his pocket and pressed it into the man's hand. "Tell me about this place."

"Taxes," the young man repeated.

"Yea, I know," said Rig. "So tell me where I can get something good to eat."

CHAPTER EIGHT
DONNAG

E vening found Rig and the others across the city, at the home of Chieftain Donnag, the ruler of all of Blöde.

The manse, a palace Fetch called it, was a little incongruous compared to the buildings that sprawled around it—and to all of the buildings they'd seen so far in Blöten. It was three stories tall, ogre measurement, making it appear nearly five stories to the humans. And it extended across an entire city block. The exterior was in good repair, the stonework patched and painted a bright white that looked pale gray in the continuing drizzle. Orange-painted wooden trim rimmed the corners, carved in the images of dragons with their wings spread and heads to the sky. Ornamental bushes thick with weeds and in desperate need of pruning spread out beneath windows that were fancifully curtained, and thorny vines were trimmed away from a meandering cobblestone walk that led to massive front doors nestled beneath an arched overhang.

Two ogres stood on either side of the doors, attired in pitted armor and carrying halberds longer than Rig's glaive. Protected from the rain, they were dry and sweating from the summer heat, and they smelled strongly of musk. One stepped forward and pointed to a crate.

"He wants your weapons left outside," Maldred explained.

"I will not!" Rig stepped back and shook his head. "I'll not leave myself defenseless in . . ."

Fiona slid by him, unfastening her swordbelt and placing it in the crate. She pulled a dagger from her boot and added that weapon. After a moment's thought, she set her helmet next to the crate, combing her hair with her fingers. Dhamon tugged at his sword belt, dangling it and the attached ale skins over the crate as he glanced at the ogre sentries. Then he carefully set it inside. Rikali followed with the ivory-pommeled dagger Dhamon had given her, and Fetch grudgingly deposited his hoopak. The four of them waited for Rig.

"I won't."

"Then suit yourself and wait for us out here," Maldred said. The big man gallantly extended his arm again to Fiona, his eyes sparkling and warm and bringing a slight smile to her heart-shaped face. The Solamnic paused for just a moment before she took his elbow and entered the manse, not giving Rig a second glance.

Rikali waited for Dhamon to copy Maldred's gracious gesture, pouting when he didn't and slipping inside just behind him. "Lover," she whispered as she nudged him. "You should learn better manners. Watch Mal. He knows how to treat a lady." Fetch had squeezed in just ahead of the pair.

"Awh. . . ." Rig rested his glaive against the front

of the manse. "This better be here when I come out,"
he warned. Then he proceeded to drop his more
readily visible weapons into the crate and join the
others inside.

The interior was impressive. A long cherrywood
table dominated the dining room into which they
were escorted, ringed by ogre-sized chairs with
deeply stuffed cushions and intricately carved backs.
None of the furniture was polished or in the best of
condition, but it was better than the furniture at Grim
Kedar's and the other places they'd visited. Paintings hung on the walls, rendered by human artists of
widespread reknown. Rig's eyes narrowed and fastened on one. It was painted by Usha Majere, Palin's
wife—he'd seen enough of her work when he'd visited the Tower of Wayreth to recognize it, and he
knew she wouldn't have painted this for an ogre
chief. *Stolen*, he mouthed. Probably like everything
else in this room.

A lanky human woman, scantily dressed in pale
green scarves, bid them to select a spot at the table,
and whispered that they should wait to sit. Then she
clapped her hands and an ogress entered with a tray
of drinks served in tall wooden cups. Behind the
ogress came Donnag.

The chieftain was the largest ogre they'd observed
since entering the city. Nearly eleven feet tall, he had
wide shoulders on which sat shining bronze disks
festooned with military medals—some recognizable
from the Dark Knights and Legion of Steel Knights, a
few with Nerakan markings. He wore a heavy mail
shirt, which glimmered in the light of the thick
candles that were spaced evenly throughout the hall,
and beneath that an expensive purple tunic. Though
dressed as regally as any monarch, he was nonetheless obviously an ogre, with warts and scabs dotting

his wide, tanned face. Twin fangs jutted upward from his bottom jaw, and several gold hoops were pierced through his broad nose and his bulbous lower lip. His ears were hidden by a crownlike gold helmet embellished with exquisitely cut gems and grotesquely angled animal talons.

He moved gracefully and silently, however, gliding to the thronelike chair at the end of the table and folding himself into it. The human woman stood to his right, awaiting his orders. A nod from Donnag, and Maldred pulled out the chair for Fiona, then sat himself. The others followed, with Rig the last to comply. The mariner continued to look suspiciously about the room, noting the paintings and candelabras and knickknacks that were certainly not fashioned for an ogre. A former pirate, Rig was quick to recognize plunder when he saw it.

The mariner's gaze occasionally rested on Fiona, who did not seem as concerned about her surroundings. But then the mariner reminded himself, she was being ruled by her belief that being here would somehow get her the coins and gems with which she could ransom her brother.

"We have not entertained a Solamnic Knight before," Donnag began. His voice was deep and scratchy, hinting at advanced years, but his command of the human tongue was precise. "We are honored to have you in our most esteemed presence, Lady Fiona."

Fiona didn't reply, although she was surprised he knew her name. And Donnag, perhaps sensing her uncertainty, was quick to continue. "It is good to have you in our humble home again, Maldred, and servant Ilbreth." The kobold nodded, smiling. "And friend of Maldred . . . Dhamon Grimwulf. Your glorious exploits are known to us, and we are impressed. And you are. . . ?"

The mariner had been glancing at another painting, one depicting the eastern coast of Mithas, the Black Coast. The artist had rendered an early evening sky, and three moons hung suspended above the water—from a time before the Chaos War when Krynn had three moons. Lost in the painting, which stirred thoughts of the Blood Sea Isles, Rig was unaware the chieftain was talking to him.

"He is called Rig Mer-Krel," Fiona offered.

"An Ergothian?"

Rig nodded, his attention finally on Donnag. The mariner stifled a chuckle, finding Donnag's visage, royal speech, and attire greatly at odds.

"You are a long way from home, Ergothian."

Rig opened his mouth to say something, and then thought better of it. He nodded again and prayed to the absent gods that dinner would go quickly.

"Lady Fiona, our advisors tell us you've need of a considerable amount of coins and gems to serve as a ransom for your brother. That the chieftains of the Solamnic Knights will not aid you in this."

She nodded, another hint of surprise in her eyes that he knew so much about why she was in his city.

"Your brother is being held with other Knights in Shrentak?"

Again a nod.

"And you intend to go to Shrentak? It is a very deadly place."

She shook her head. "No, Chieftain Donnag. I'll not need to travel that far into the swamp. One of the Black's minions, a draconian, will meet me at the ruins of Takar. It is there I must deliver the ransom. My brother will be brought there and handed over to me. Perhaps other Knights will be handed over with him if I can raise enough."

Donnag cleared his throat. "It is a most admirable

task you've assigned yourself, as family is most important." He paused to take a sip of wine and to clear his throat again. "We are not opposed to slavery and the keeping of prisoners. Always the weaker and the unfortunate must serve the stronger. Still, we have no love of the Black and her spreading swamp. Indeed, our army journeyed into the swamp but a month ago and destroyed a growing legion of spawn—my general believed he found a nest where they were being created. The cost was heavy for us, but not one spawn remained. Fortunately for us, the Black was not there at the time."

Donnag slowly turned his head to make certain everyone was paying attention to him. "And so, because of our love of family and because of our hate of the Black, we will provide you with coins and gems, more than enough to gain the release of your brother."

"Why?" This came from the mariner.

Donnag looked irritated, as the human woman at his side filled his wine glass to the brim. "Too, we will give her men to accompany her to the ruins of Takar. The swamp is dangerous, and we will help insure she reaches her destination. In aiding her, perhaps we will be striking a blow against the one we call Sable. We can spare forty men."

"And what's this gonna cost us?" Rig wished he could swallow those words when he caught the fierce look of the chieftain. Still, he continued, "Everything costs in your country, doesn't it, your majesty? Licenses, taxes, fees. I understand you even charge humans and dwarves for the water they pull from the wells. Oh, I forgot, you tax half-ogres, too, just not as much."

"As you said, Ergothian, everything has a price. Including our help," Donnag said coldly, as he turned his gaze to the Solamnic Knight. "In the hills to the east are goatherding villages that provide us with milk and meat. We do love milk. One village in particular has been raided heavily, goats carried off in the night. Wolves, we suspect, or a great mountain cat. Nothing to a warrior such as yourself. These villagers are my very loyal subjects, and it troubles us greatly that they are so plagued. If you will visit this village, Knollsbank, and put an end to the raids, a fortune in coins and gems—your ransom—will be yours. Knollsbank is not far, a long day's travel."

"You've an army of ogres," Rig cut in. "Why not have them help your *very loyal subjects*?"

Donnag narrowed his rheumy eyes. The fingers of his left hand clutched the table edge while his right reached for the wine. He downed the glass in one swallow. The woman quickly refilled it. He repeated, eyes fixed on Rig, "As you said, Ergothian, everything has a price. Consider this as a favor to me—a payment in kind."

The kobold dropped his napkin. He'd only been half-way listening to the exchange. *Goats?* he mouthed to Maldred. "When did *we* agree to rescue goats?"

"Yes," Fiona said. "I will agree to help in exchange for the ransom and the assistance of your forty men."

"It should take but a few days of your time," Donnag added. "And the men will be outfitted and ready upon your return."

"Waitaminit!" Rig rose from the table, tipping over his wine glass. "You can't be serious, Fiona. Helping a . . . a. . . . You can't mean it."

Fiona glared at him. "I intend to free my brother. And this is my means to do so." Her tone was quiet but tense, as if she were scolding a little boy. "We need the coins and gems, Rig. *You know it.*"

"Would that I could go with you into the mountains, Lady Knight," Maldred offered. "I have other things to tend to in town. But I will look forward to your return."

Rig sat heavily in the chair as the ogress servant busied herself cleaning up his spilled wine and casting disapproving glances his way. His glass was righted, but not refilled.

Donnag harumphed. "Very well, Lady Fiona. You and the Ergothian will set out in the morning for Knollsbank." The chieftain pushed himself away from the table. "We've eaten already. But our cook has a fine meal ready for you, Maldred, when we are finished. And now perhaps you and Dhamon Grimwulf will join us in our library, so we can discuss other matters."

Rig continued to stare, refusing to eat any of the sumptuous fare that Donnag provided. "I don't like this at all," he muttered. "You've no clue who you're dealing with, Fiona. Donnag's cruel. He taxes the humans and dwarves who live here to the point of breaking them. What he does is. . . ."

"His concern," Fiona said. "This is his country. What would you have us do, overthrow him?"

Not such a bad idea, the mariner thought.

The library was at the same time grand and appalling. Three walls were covered with shelves that stretched to the top of a fourteen-foot-high ceiling. Each shelf was crammed with books, the spines of which were labelled in the common tongue, as well as elf, dwarf, kender, and a few languages Dhamon did not recognize. Some were histories, others fanciful tales of fiction. A thick tome embossed with gold was about the art of warfare. On a quick inspection, it appeared none were marked with the buglike characters that could be found on Blöten's business signs. Perhaps ogres did not write books, Dhamon mused.

The books smelled musty and were covered with dust and cobwebs, hinting that none were ever read, only looked at and possessed. Had they been well cared for, they would have been worth a veritable fortune in any reasonably sized city of Ansalon.

The fourth wall was decorated with helmets of silver and black plate—souvenirs from Solamnic Knights and Dark Knights. A full suit of Dark Knight armor stood vigilant behind an overstuffed armchair that Donnag settled himself into.

Near the chair hung a great two-handed sword, which Maldred lifted down from a rack. Its pommel was shaped like a knobby tree trunk, and chunks of polished onyx were set into the whorls. He checked it for balance and swung it in a level arc, nearly tipping over a pink marble column holding a bust of Huma.

"Take it. The sword is yours, Maldred," Donnag said. "We give it to you to replace that which Dhamon Grimwulf said you lost in the valley of gemstones."

Maldred ran his thumb along the blade, cutting the skin and drawing blood.

"And the sword I am seeking, the one I sought this audience for?" Dhamon stood in front of the chieftain, facing him with his hands on his hips.

Donnag cocked his head.

"The sword that belonged to Tanis Half-Elven."

"Ah, *that* sword. The one that can find treasure. We have heard of the weapon."

"In your stables is a wagon loaded with—"

"Uncut gems from our valley," Donnag finished. "We know. Our guards informed us before dinner. A most admirable haul. We are quite pleased. And impressed."

"And it's more than enough to purchase the sword that tales say is in your possession."

Donnag drummed his long fingers against the arms of the chair. Dhamon noted the fabric was frayed in places and bits of stuffing threatened to spill out. "Indeed, the tales are true. We have the sword of Tanis Half-Elven."

Dhamon waited patiently.

"But why should we give up a sword that can find treasure? We love gold."

"I've brought—"

Donnag waved a ring-encrusted hand to silence him. "Yes, yes, you've brought us more than enough for its purchase. Indeed, we will be glad to be rid of the thing. We fear if you learned of it, others will, too. We do not wish the notoriety nor the steady stream of humans, elves, and whoever else might deign to come here in search of it—and who might demand it by force rather than offer to pay. We are too busy to cope with such nonsense." Almost as an after-thought, Donnag said, "Besides, our hands are too large to wield it. We prefer weapons of greater sub-stance." The chieftain glanced at the sword Maldred was still admiring. "And we haven't the time to plod through ruins trying to use it to gain more wealth."

After a moment more, Maldred eased the two-handed sword into the latticed sheath on his back. "How did you come by it? This sword Dhamon wants?"

A deep chuckle escaped from Donnag's doughy lips. "We come by many treasures. This one from a little thief with no spine. He stole from the dead rather than from the living. And then he sought to sell his prize to me." Softer, he added, as a smile spread across his stern face, "The little thief is with the dead now."

Donnag rose to tower over Dhamon. Dhamon didn't flinch, tilting his head up to meet the steely gaze of the chieftain. "We will consider this fabled sword yours, Dhamon Grimwulf—more because you are a friend of Maldred, whom we accept as one of our own, than because of your wagonful of gems. Still, before we hand it over, we must require an errand of you."

"And what is this errand?"

"We want you to accompany your two human friends into the mountains. To the goatherders' village, Knollsbank. We want you to make sure they live up to their word of stopping the raids. Help your friends deal with the wolves."

"Rig and Fiona are not my friends."

"But they are your *kind*," Donnag swiftly returned.

"I've no desire to remain in their company. All I want is the sword. You've said I more than met your price."

"But we do not trust the Knight and the dark-skinned man. If they indeed make good on their word of helping the village, we will give the Knight her ransom—only because her notion of buying her brother's freedom amuses us. Then, too, we will give you the sword."

Dhamon frowned.

"And more," Donnag continued. "We will give you a few other trinkets from my treasury to sweeten the deal. For your trouble of helping my loyal subjects in Knollsbank."

Dhamon's jaw clenched. His eyes darkened and narrowed and his voice grew threatening. "I'll take the sword now and accompany Fiona and Rig. But I want the sword up front."

Donnag shook his head. "We make the rules in

this city, Dhamon Grimwulf. You can demand nothing of us."

"You do not trust them," Dhamon said evenly.
"How can I trust you?"

"Oh, you can trust him." This came from Maldred,
who stepped from behind the ogre to join them. "On
my word, Dhamon Grimwulf, you can trust Chieftain Donnag."

"Done, then," Dhamon said, extending his hand.
"We will tend to your village of goatherders, and
then we'll conclude our deal." He pivoted on the
balls of his feet and strode quickly from the room.

When he was out of sight, Maldred turned to
Donnag. "I don't understand. Why the interest in
helping a village of goatherders? I've never known
you to be so concerned about the peasants in the
mountains. Or to be concerned about anyone, for
that matter."

"We are not concerned," Donnag returned, gesturing with his fingers as if he were shooing away an
insect.

"Then why . . ."

"You are not to go with Dhamon Grimwulf and
the others. Do you understand? Neither is Ilbreth.
Stay here, Maldred, in our palace."

Lines of curiosity spread across Maldred's forehead.

"Those three will not be returning from Knollsbank," Donnag continued. "We've sent them to their
deaths. We will keep the precious gemstones and the
sword of Tanis Half-Elven, and we will rid ourselves
of all of those bothersome people in the process."

Chapter Nine
Life From Death

he rain made the rockface cruelly slick, and Maldred had to use all of his strength to struggle up it, digging fingers into cracks, his feet scrabbling, arm muscles bunching, and finally pulling himself up onto a wide ledge. Catching his breath, he tossed his rope over the side, braced himself, and pulled Fiona up to join him. He held her in his arms for a moment, the others waiting below.

"It is fortunate you decided to join us," Fiona told him.

"Yes, I decided the matters I needed to address in town could wait." Maldred's face was cloudy, recalling Donnag's orders to stay behind. The chieftain would find out soon enough that Maldred and Fetch joined the mission to Knollsbank. Maldred wondered what could be so dangerous in these hills, and he hoped his presence and sword skill would be enough to keep this from becoming a death's errand.

"Something troubles you?"

"Wolves, Lady Knight. The wolves that raid the

goats." Maldred doubted wolves truly were the cause of the goatherders' problems.

"We will send the wolves hunting for food elsewhere," she said.

His face lightened as he banished his thoughts of death and Donnag. "You are indeed fair," he said, his eyes capturing hers and twinkling with an inner light. "I swear by all I hold dear you surely take my breath away." His words sounded achingly sincere.

"I think it is this height that is making it difficult for you to breathe, Maldred."

"No," he chuckled. "It is you, Lady Knight." He dipped his head and met her lips, the kiss long and forceful.

When he pulled back she blushed and eased herself away, tucking a strand of hair behind her ear and glancing down the steep ridge. They were too high to see the crumbling buildings, the misshapen ogres, and the poor humans and dwarves struggling to barely eke out an existence in Blöten. The rain, coupled with the heat of summer, had engendered a mist around the ogre city, a pale pink and gray halo that made the place look serene and beautiful and very remote from this high vantage point—a magical city from children's bedtime stories where everyone lived well and happily. Not used to the altitude, a feeling of dizziness overtook her and she stepped back to lean against Maldred.

"Are you all right, Lady? Not that I mind."

"I don't look like much of a lady in these clothes," she said. He'd managed to convince the Solamnic to leave her plate mail at Donnag's, since it was not proper attire for climbing mountains. She had staunchly disagreed, and Rig voted with her just to side against Maldred, but then she got a good look at just how sheer and dangerous the mountain was.

And so she was wearing a pair of tan breeches and a long-sleeved black tunic, man's garb, tucked in at the waist. Rikali had grudgingly offered to share her more fine and more colorful clothes, and was secretly pleased to discover them too small for the muscular Knight. "In fact, Maldred, I look like an old field hand."

"You do not take compliments well, Lady Knight," he said, dropping the rope over the side. "Perhaps that is because the company you've been keeping does not think to offer them. And perhaps they do not have the good sense to realize what they have in their presence. I mean the big stupid mariner—Rig. You cannot marry him, Fiona."

"People really live up there?" she asked, changing the subject. Her eyes remained locked on Maldred.

"Goatherders in the village of Knollsbank—and from other smaller villages. They know better ways around these mountains than I, and likely would have chosen a much simpler path. Chieftain Donnag says they climb these rocks easier than most people walk. And, of course, goats live up here too."

"And wolves, apparently," Rig added. The mariner was the next to arrive, using the rope primarily as security, climbing as Maldred had done, as if he was born to the activity. Like scaling the masts of a ship, he fondly mused as he finished with this portion of the ascent. He was weighted down with his weapons, the glaive strapped to his back. Dhamon followed him, Fetch on his shoulders.

Maldred started up the next section of rock, Fetch accompanying him this time, while Dhamon stayed behind to wait for Rikali. The half-elf skittered up the mountain like a spider, not needing the rope, as her fingers and sandaled feet found cracks and crevices the others had somehow missed. It was a skill she

learned from the thieves' guild in Sanction, fitting
her fingers and toes into the narrow crevices between
the bricks that made up the exteriors of the nobles'
walled houses. Dhamon helped her up on the ledge,
just as Fiona turned to go.

Just then, the mountain rumbled slightly, as it had
a few times since they began their climb. Rikali clung
to Dhamon, feigning fright and then becoming genuinely afraid when the tremor continued unabated.
Her hands nervously massaged the muscles in
Dhamon's arms. When the tremor finally passed, she
let out a deep breath and grinned slyly.

The rain had continued steadily for the past several days, at times pounding down, and at other
times, like now, a fine drizzle, the sole purpose of
which seemed to keep them from bearing the brunt
of the otherwise hot day. Rikali now turned her face
up to catch some of the rainwater in her mouth, then
dropped her chin to his chest again. "Dhamon
Grimwulf, I love you."

"Rikali, I—"

"You lovebirds joining us?" Rig had made it up to
the next ledge and was peering down at the two.
Fetch was at his shoulder, red eyes twinkling mis-
chievously.

Dhamon reached for the rope, not noticing the
clouded expression on the half-elf's face. He had
nearly made it to the next ledge when he felt his leg
tingle with warmth from the scale. It gave him little
warning this time, turning instantly to a fiery heat.
He gripped the rope, his eyes squeezing shut, teeth
digging into his bottom lip. He tasted blood in his
mouth, then put all of his effort into simply hanging
on as he was wracked by wave after wave of intense
heat and bone-numbing cold.

Each time the pain was profound. And each time

it was different, hotter, then so cold, shifting violently back and forth. Now from behind his eyelids he saw nothing but red, the flames of a fire, the breath of the dragon overlord who had cursed him with the scale on his leg. He fought to focus on something besides the flames, real or imaginary, it didn't matter. Anything that might lessen the pain. For an instant he saw the face of a Kagonesti, soft and beautiful. But then the red overwhelmed it and he saw a pair of blinking red eyes.

"Dreaming," he croaked. He bit down hard, almost relishing that pain.

"Dhamon?" Rig was looking over the side, waiting to hoist him up.

Rikali was nervously prancing about on the ledge below, realizing what was happening.

"Dhamon!" Rig shouted.

"You leave him be!" she hissed to Rig. She started up the rockface. "Hold on," she urged him. "Lover, you just hold on." The half-elf caught up with him, reached out and grabbed the belt that held his sword and ale skins. His trembling threatened to pull her off the cliff face.

In the span of a few heartbeats Dhamon started shaking even more. Rig pulled on the rope, Rikali climbing up with it, one hand in a vertical crevice, the other still clutching Dhamon's belt. Between the two of them, they were able to drag him up to the ledge, where they tugged free his bow and quiver and laid him down away from the lip. Rikali hovered over him and pushed Rig away, clucking like a mother hen. "You keep going," she told the mariner, waving her arm. "Dhamon and I will be just fine here. We'll catch up in a few minutes." Then she quickly thought better of the situation. "Mal!" she screamed. "He needs help!"

It looked as if Dhamon was having a seizure. The half-elf tugged a skin free from Dhamon's belt, raised his head, and poured the liquor into his mouth, a good portion of it dribbling down his chin and onto his shirt. She massaged the muscles of his throat, helping it go down.

"That won't help him, Riki." Maldred had climbed down from the higher ledge, nudged Rig aside and squatted next to Dhamon. "It just makes him a little numb, is all." He took Dhamon's arm and gripped it as Dhamon gripped him back with all his strength, fingernails digging into the big man's muscles. "That's it," Maldred coaxed, concern etched deeply in the lines around his eyes and mouth. "Ride it out, my friend."

Rikali replaced the skin, pointedly ignoring the mariner and Fiona, who was calling down from above. "It's none of your business about Dhamon," she finally told them.

A few minutes later, Dhamon stopped shaking. He gulped in the damp air and opened his eyes. "I'm all right now," he said, not arguing when Maldred helped him to his feet and helped him strap the quiver and bow on his back. He met Rig's stare. "*I am all right*," he repeated more strongly.

"The hell you are," the mariner argued. "It's that damned scale, isn't it?"

Maldred brushed by the pair and started climbing again, dropping the rope when he got to the top and bracing himself to lift Dhamon.

"Aye, it's the scale." Dhamon grabbed the rope, relying almost entirely on Maldred's strength to pull him up. The episode had exhausted him.

Rikali motioned for the mariner to go next. "Dhamon has these shakes once in a while. That's all," she said. "He gets over them and is good as new.

Mal helps him through it. Mal's his best friend. Dhamon doesn't need your sympathy."

The rest of the climb was in silence, and by late afternoon they reached a narrow plateau, where the goatherders lived. It was a small community, the homes a collection of tiny caves and lean-tos constructed of pine logs and skins set against the side of the mountain, which rose up for at least another four hundred feet. The residents were humans and mountain dwarves, the former short and thin, almost spindly, but obviously agile as monkeys. The latter were ruddy and stocky, somehow equally at home in this high outlook. All the men wore short, pointed beards, as though they had taken on the appearances of their four-legged charges. The air carried a pungent scent of wet goats, wet people, and something unidentifiable—and most unpalatable—that was cooking in a covered fire pit.

Rikali dug about in her satchel for a vial of perfumed oil and liberally applied it, adding a drop beneath her nose. "Better," she pronounced.

"I'm Kulp," an older human said, extending his hand to Dhamon. The two were near the fire pit, where several goatherders had gathered. "I lead this village, called Knollsbank, and I'm the one who sent word to his exalted Lordship Donnag that our herd is dwindling. Our gratitude to the lord for any help you can provide. Truth, though, I am most surprised he sent us aid. His lordship is not known for caring about these villages' well-being."

His lordship? Rig mouthed.

Maldred walked around the village, Fiona at his side, looking for some sign of the dread wolves. They made pleasant small talk with the people as they went, answering questions about the town far below, the styles of dress for the women, the music that was popular, the threat from the Black called Sable, what was going on in the world to the east of the Kalkhists. When Maldred revealed that Fiona was a Solamnic Knight who had stood up to the Dragon Overlords, all attention turned to her and the questions focused on the great dragons. The villagers had all heard of the overlords and knew what they'd done to Krynn. Yet none of them had seen a dragon, save a rare silhouette high overhead, and all of them were in disbelief that Lord Donnag would send someone as important as Fiona to help them.

On the opposite side of the village, Rikali locked her arm with Dhamon's as he introduced himself and the half-elf. "These wolves that are slaughtering your goats, Kulp. . . ."

"Wolves?" The goatherder scrunched his face in a question. "Wolves don't live in these mountains. It's giants. Giants are stealing our goats." There was instantly a great sadness on Kulp's face, as if he had lost a child. "Our herd is half of what it was in the spring. If it continues, by winter we'll be finished. They took four kids last night who were being mothered on that ridge."

Dhamon's mind was working, his fingers drumming against his belt in irritation. "Giants?"

Kulp nodded. "So our messengers told Donnag."

Dhamon drummed faster. *Trust Donnag?* he said to himself. *Maldred said to trust him.* Anger flared in his eyes, and Kulp stepped back, startled.

"So they haven't actually hurt you, these giants?" Dhamon finally asked.

Kulp looked shocked. "Hurt? They hurt us most horribly! Taking our goats is hurting us, our livelihood. The goats are all we have. We won't have the goods to pay Donnag's taxes if this continues. We will have nothing to barter with and we will lose our home."

"Pay Donnag?" Rig interrupted. The mariner had been edging over during the conversation.

"We pay the chieftain in milk and meat for the right to live on his mountain. Certainly that is why he sent you—to stop the giants so we can continue to meet his fees and taxes."

"Giants?" The mariner growled and looked about for Fiona. Where was she—she ought to hear this evidence of the ogre chieftain's fiendishness. He spotted her and Maldred leaning over a small pen where a mother goat and three newborns rested.

Dhamon cleared his throat. "And where are these so-called giants. . . ."

"We believe the giants live in those caves, Mister Grimwulf." Kulp was pointing toward a peak that rose up high away from the village. "Some of our young herders fought one and thought they'd killed it. Said it was a massive creature with long arms and wicked claws. It must have only been stunned and then came to, escaping as they tried to drag it here. A few of them tracked it, heading toward that peak." He dropped his gaze and shook his head. "But those young men did not return."

"Tracking the giants now—tracking anything—is not possible," Dhamon said, looking at the ground. What earth there was consisted of broad patches of mud from which sprouted tall grass. There were small gardens, reasonably protected from all the rain by a network of skins and lean-tos. But mostly there was shale and granite and goat droppings.

Dhamon looked toward the lofty peak, squinting through the rain to spot caves where the goat-raiding giants might live. "Kulp, that's another several hours climb, at the very least. We'd like to stay here the rest of the day, get an early start."

The village leader clapped his hands loudly. "We

will make accommodations for Donnag's men,"
Kulp said. "And we will feed them well." Then he
was off to evict a family to make room for the companions for the evening.

The rain had stopped for a few hours during the
night, and beneath the scant stars that poked through
the wispy clouds they were fed a meal of boiled
roots, spicy broth, and hard bread. The broth was
what had been simmering throughout the day and
tasted surprisingly good despite its strong smell. The
bread was among the foodstuffs the herders received
regularly in barter from Blöten. There was a strong
liquor, which the herders made themselves and
Dhamon pronounced acceptable.

Maldred instructed the half-elf not to let the kobold
out of her sight while they were in the village, not
wanting him to stir up any trouble. He spoke in whispers to Dhamon, vowing that when they returned to
Blöten he would make sure Donnag kept his part of
the bargain. The sword would be his—along with
plenty of baubles for dealing with giants rather than
wolves. When the big man left their company, Fiona
followed him until they were alone beside a spindly
rock. That is when Maldred drew her into his arms.

Dhamon spied them, casting a glance at Rig who
was engrossed in a conversation with one of the villagers. He looked back at Maldred and Fiona, who
were kissing. Maldred's fingers were wound tightly
in the Knight's hair.

Dhamon shrugged and sat facing Rig, engaging
him in conversation to keep him distracted.

Dhamon asked the mariner about his wedding
plans and about whether Fiona had managed to convince him to join the Knighthood.

Rig was quick to talk about the former and preferred to avoid the latter. "We are to be married on

her birthday, a tradition among the women in Fiona's family," he happily explained. Yet there was an edge in his voice. "It's not so long from now. Two and a half months. In fact, we. . . ." His words trailed off as he spotted the Knight walking toward them.

"Where've you been?" Rig was quick on his feet and took her hand. "You've been . . ."

". . . visiting with some of the villagers," Fiona returned.

Dhamon was startled at the lie and strolled away, finding Rikali perched on a ledge overlooking Blöten. He looked over his shoulder to see Fiona and Rig engaged in conversation.

"Fiona, that Donnag is far from a good man," the mariner said, keeping his voice low. He told her about the milk and meat tax here, the heavy taxes the humans bore in Blöten, the fear all the people had for the ogre chieftain, how oppressed everyone was in his realm. How wolves had become giants.

"I know," she said finally, her face soft and a little sad. "And it is good that it bothers you. It bothers me, too. But we can't right all the wrongs in this world, Rig. We have to choose our battles. And bad as Donnag is, the Black in the swamp is far worse. The ogre protects these people from her, and his forces work to keep the swamp from swallowing up these mountains. So by helping Donnag, in one respect we are fighting her. And if you get rid of Donnag, being overtaxed would be the least of these people's worries."

The mariner sat silently, digesting her words. "I still don't have to like it, and I don't have to agree with it," he said, sighing as raindrops trickled down the end of his nose. "I don't have to like the fact we're going to accept coins and gems for the ransom of your brother from that evil . . . creature. Provided he comes through, which I still doubt. And I don't have to like all this rain. This isn't right. These mountains should be dry as a desert."

"A while ago you were complaining it hadn't rained in weeks."

"Didn't mean I wanted it to rain *for* weeks."

He tried to slip his arm around her, but she was on her feet and heading toward their borrowed lean-to, from where they watched the rain pound the rocky plateau for the rest of the evening.

Morning was no different, the rain continuing, slapping against the rocks and drenching everything and everyone. Only the goats seemed not to mind. Lightning arced through the sky, and the thunder that chased it sounded loud and eerie in the mountains.

"Up there," Maldred said, pointing toward a series of black holes. "Maybe the giants are in all of them if they're spread out, maybe all bunched together in one—but I hope not. I'd rather deal with them one at a time. In any event, we'll have to search a little until we find them. The dwarves I spoke with last night are certain there are only three because of the tracks they spotted."

"Only three," Rikali murmured. "They're *giants*. I would think three are plenty more than enough."

"Well, at least we know what we're up against," Dhamon said.

"Have you ever fought giants?" Rikali asked mockingly as he started up the ridge.

"Once. When I was with the Knights of Takhisis. There were two of them, and each had two heads. Ettins, my commander called them."

"Well, you obviously came out on top. You're here. Were they very tough? How big do giants run?"

He shook his head, not caring to answer her

stream of questions until they reached level ground again. After a few dozen feet of climbing he motioned to her, pointing to evidence of the giants—the gutted carcass of a goat wedged tightly between two rocks, the bones of another goat some fifty feet above.

Rikali covered her mouth and gagged.

"Messy eaters," Fetch observed as he yanked a twisting horn off the carcass and held it up to his ear as if he might hear the ocean. Picking off a few pieces of rotten flesh, he stuck the horn in his belt. "Parents never taught them to clean up when they were done eating. Bad giants."

◇ ◇ ◇ ◇ ◇ ◇ ◇

"Three caves, and nothing. Nothing but rain and goat bones. They've been here, but they're not here now. Doesn't look like they've been here for a couple of weeks." Rig leaned against the cliff and looked up at Dhamon who was climbing higher, his clothes looking dark as charcoal against the glowering sky. The mariner patted his stomach as it grumbled. "Sky and my gut tell me it's about sunset. An' there isn't much left of the mountain." He tugged a piece of boiled root from his pocket, snapped it in two, and popped a piece in his mouth.

Fetch scampered up after Dhamon, Rikali following him and scolding the kobold about something.

"Perhaps they've moved on," Maldred suggested.

Fiona's shoulders sagged. "I need the reward Donnag promised. I need those forty men."

"Ogres," Rig cut in. "He promised you ogres, Fiona." Softer, he muttered that the chieftain's promise was worth about as much as the goat carcasses they found.

"Ogres *are* men, Rig," she returned. "And I would welcome their help."

Maldred stepped between the two of them, eyes twinkling at the Solamnic. "You'll get the men, Lady Knight. We will search in one or two more caves and then leave. I will explain to the chieftain that we did our best, and that maybe they've moved on and will pose no more threat to Knollsbank. As long as the menace is gone, Donnag will keep his word about the men."

Will he? the mariner's arched eyebrows asked.

"Up here!" Dhamon called. He was standing on a ledge before a high, narrow slash in the rocks. The cave mouth looked jagged and irregular, as if the talon of some great creature had torn the mountain open.

"Find a trace of them?" Maldred called from below.

Dhamon shook his head. "No trace. But I did find something else very interesting." And then he vanished inside the cave, with Fetch and Rikali behind him.

"Lady Knights first." Maldred bowed to Fiona, who started up the ridge. He made a move to follow her, but Rig put a hand on his shoulder.

"She's my woman," the mariner said simply. "We're gonna be married in a few months. I don't like the way you're always looking at her. And I'm tired of you occupying her time."

Maldred grinned. "I'd say she's her own woman. And you're not married yet." Then he pushed in front of the mariner before the astonished Rig could say anything.

The mariner stood alone on the ridge for several minutes, listening to the rain pattering against the rocks and glancing down at the village, which looked like scattered doll houses, the people and goats merely bugs meandering around in senseless patterns amid the puddles that he hoped would become a lake and swallow Knollsbank up.

❖ ❖ ❖ ❖ ❖ ❖ ❖

Little light filtered in from outside, but it was just enough for Dhamon to see this wasn't a normal cave. He stood inside the tall, narrow entrance, on an ancient mosaic floor made of variously colored stone chips. Six lofty pillars stretched from floor to ceiling, at least forty feet high. They were gigantic tree trunks, practically uniform in girth, and he wondered what engineering feat brought them up this mountain and then fitted them inside this place. They were practically white with age, and carved with the images of dwarves standing atop each others' shoulders. The one at the very top of each column wore a crown, and their upreached arms seemed to support the cavern's roof.

"By my breath!" Rikali slipped in beside him, Fetch sliding between the pair.

"A torch," Dhamon began. "I want to get a better look at this."

"Fee-ohn-a has them in her pack," Rikali said unpleasantly.

When the others finally joined them and a torch was lit, many more dwarven images were revealed. Carved into the walls of the cave, each visage was different and incredibly detailed: men, women, children, some warriors by their helmets and scarred faces, others religious folk by the symbols worn around their necks. A myriad of emotions were displayed on the faces: happiness, pride, grief, love, wonder, and more.

The floor was smooth and level. The chips of painted stone were tiled across it to form the face of a most impressive dwarf, wild hair flaring out to touch the cavern walls, the pillars practically framing an aged, wise-looking leader. The color had faded, but Dhamon surmised the braided beard was bright red at one time, and the beads woven into it were tinged with silver and gold. The wide-set eyes were sunken and black, forming braziers that might have been used in some long-ago ceremony.

"Reorx," Dhamon said, his hand drifting down to the pommel of his sword. The nape of his neck was tingling. Something didn't feel right in this place, but he couldn't identify what was wrong. He stared into the image's eyes. It was like someone was watching him, a sensation he learned to identify when he was with the Knights of Takhisis. He wanted to be back in Blöten, with his new sword and on his way. He glanced away and to the pillars. "This must be one of Reorx's temples."

"Who?" Rikali tugged on his sleeve. "Who is Re-or-ax?"

"You don't know?" This from Fetch.

The half-elf shook her head.

"A god," Dhamon said softly. "A dwarf I once knew, Jasper, told me a lot about him. Jasper considered himself a priest of Reorx. Even after the gods left."

"And this Jasper, did he ever meet Re-or-ax?"

Dhamon shook his head.

Rikali made a tsking sound and whispered it was foolish to revere someone you'd never met. She raised her voice. "Well, did this Re-or-ax accomplish much when he was around? Other than to have temples built to him high in some stupid mountain?"

"According to dwarven tales, Riki, the High God

was disturbed at the jumbled chaos all around him.
He whittled twenty-one sticks, the stoutest of which
became the god Reorx." Dhamon pointed at the
image on the floor. "Reorx said he would make a
world, round and sturdy, in his own likeness. He was
called the Forger, and by striking his hammer at the
jumbled chaos, the sparks became stars. The last
blow birthed Krynn. I'd say that's accomplishing
quite a bit."

"So the tales say," the half-elf laughed. "You don't
believe all that nonsense, do you? Not that it matters
none, what with all the gods being gone anyway."

Dhamon shrugged. "When the gods were here,
the dwarves considered Reorx the greatest of all the
powers. Humans saw him merely as Kiri-Jolith's
helper. But the dwarves. . . ." His voice drifted off
and again he found himself staring at the pits that
made up the image's eyes. "It is said that Reorx's
next-greatest creation was the Greystone of Gargath,
which led to the creation of dwarves, gnomes, and
kender."

"So the tales say," Fetch added.

"Greystone. So he made a rock. And did you ever
worship this Re-or-ax, lover? You seem to know a lot
about him."

"The only vanished god I ever revered was Takhisis," Dhamon answered flatly. He recalled being
regaled with tales of the Queen of Evil Dragons from
the time he entered the Knights of Takhisis. But none
of her priests' old worship halls were as impressive
as this place. This place definitely intrigued him,
perhaps in part because he still had that tingling sensation. He decided he would look around for a few
moments, then head back down the mountain,
demanding Donnag relinquish the blade.

"And why are you so terribly certain this place

was a temple to Re-or-ax? Not just a palace belonging to some old rich dwarf?"

Dhamon brushed by the half-elf and glanced toward the far end of the chamber, where there was an altar carved to look like a forge with an anvil atop it. Two shadowy alcoves extended behind it. "Aye, this was a temple to Reorx the Forge. Wonder that the Knollsbank folk didn't mention this, especially the mountain dwarves."

Maldred was at the entrance, examining the stone. "Probably didn't know it was here. The rocks are sharp, Dhamon, not worn like they are everywhere else on the mountain and around the other cave openings. I'd say one of the tremors opened this place up, and not very long ago." His fingers fluttered over the edges, drawing back as he cut himself. He licked the blood away and joined Dhamon. "I would guess this hasn't been open more than a month. Feel how dry it is inside here? Despite the rain?"

"It *smells* old," the half-elf said, wrinkling her nose. "Smells like a musty cellar in someone's house." She stood in front of one of the pillars, fingers tracing the features of a face at eye-level. "Said I had my fill of dwarves, I did," she mused aloud. "But I might make me an exception. Might be something valuable here in this temple to Re-or-ax." She pointed to the image of a dwarven priest a dozen feet above the floor. The figure had chips of onyx set for eyes.

"We shouldn't try to take anything." Fiona was looking at another pillar, this one filled with the broad faces of female warriors. "To defile a temple is wrong. Sacrilege, no matter your faith."

The half-elf cackled and adopted an exaggerated hurt look. "I have no faith. The gods are gone, *Lady*

Knight. So this is a temple to nothin'. Absolutely *nothin'.* Pigs! I can take whatever I please. I won't be defiling anyone or anythin'. And there ain't no gods around to come and damn me for it."

Fetch had begun climbing a pillar, using the ears as handholds and the mouths for his toes.

Maldred glanced up at the kobold and shook his head. "Come on down, Ilbreth," he said sternly.

The kobold's head spun in surprise at Maldred using his real name—which he did only when he was very mad or earnestly wanted to get the creature's attention—and the kobold nearly lost his grip.

"Dwarven gods are of no concern to us. We've got giants to find, my little friend, and then . . ."

Fetch was holding onto an ear with one hand and gesturing wildly with the other. His mouth was open, as if to speak, but his surprise kept the words from coming out.

Dhamon spun instinctively, retrieving his bow in the same motion. He pulled an arrow from the quiver, fitted it, and aimed—at what?

"Thought I saw the cave move," the kobold finally managed to gasp. "I really thought I . . . there! A giant!"

Something was watching us! Dhamon released his arrow at a huge creature that suddenly came shambling out of the wall. But it wasn't a true giant. It was only a little larger than an ogre, with overlong arms and clawed hands. It looked like it was made of stone.

The creature reached out, batted Dhamon's arrow away before it could find its mark, and snarled ferociously. The creature had the face of an old man, wrinkles looking like cracks in stone, cheekbones exaggeratedly angular, nose long and curved down like a beak. Its eyes were pupiless and dark gray, and its teeth were jagged and shot through with black lines, making them look like shards of granite.

Dhamon immediately set another arrow and fired, this missing the creature by several inches. His hand moved lightning fast as he fitted a third and aimed more carefully this time. The creature's eyes locked onto his, just as Dhamon pulled the bowstring back and released it.

"Damn," he swore, as he watched the arrow glance off the thing's bony-looking shoulder. He dropped the bow and shrugged out of the quiver. "Wasted my coins on this in Blöten. Should stick with what I know." He drew his sword and advanced.

The others were doing the same, drawing weapons and moving in cautiously, studying the creature—the likes of which none of them had seen. They formed a semicircle about it, the creature keeping its back to the wall and eyeing all of them.

"Wh-wh-what is it?" Fetch squeaked from his perch on the pillar.

"Pigs if I know!" Rikali spat. "It's ugly, whatever it is. Probably the giant that's been eatin' all the goats."

"I don't know what it is, but it ain't a giant. Giants look a lot more human than that," Rig mused. "Yah! Over here!" His shout drew the thing's attention. The creature took a step toward the mariner and opened its maw, snarling now like a maddened beast. "I'll gut you like a—"

"Wait, Rig!" Fiona cut in. "We're the intruders here. We shouldn't just attack the beast. We don't know what it is. And we don't know if it truly means any harm."

"You're right," Maldred told her. "I revere life and. . . ."

"Oh, it means us harm all right," Rig shot back. "Just look at it."

The creature stood still for several moments, its head moved jerkily, taking in Rig, Fiona, Maldred, Dhamon, and Rikali. A thick, black tongue wagged out to wet its bottom lip, then it snarled again, and with a speed that seemed peculiar for its malshaped body, it rushed toward Maldred.

Dhamon moved in that instant, too. He was quicker than the stony creature, darting in between it and Maldred. "I could use the exercise. I'll take him!" he hollered, as he drew a deep breath, pulled back, and swung. He braced himself, expecting to be jarred for striking the creature's stony chest. But the creature's flesh was soft like a man's, yielding when the blade connected, and the bones beneath crunching from the violent impact.

Both it and Dhamon were surprised. The creature glanced down at the line of dark green blood forming across its middle. It rubbed a hand against the wound and brought its claws up to its eyes, as if to study its own blood. It howled then, long and angrily, and it slashed at Dhamon.

Dhamon barely managed to drop beneath the swipe of its needlelike claws. Then he swung again, connecting with the creature's distended abdomen this time. The creature cried in pain, the sound echoing hauntingly off the cavern walls and bringing a squeal from Fetch.

Out of the corner of his eye, Dhamon saw Rig and Maldred edge closer. "I said he's mine!" Dhamon called to the mariner. It wasn't that he didn't mind help defeating the creature, he just had no desire to fight side-by-side with Rig again. "Back off!"

"It's your neck," Rig said as he retreated.

Dhamon slid to the side so he would be between the mariner and the creature. It howled once more, remaining fixated on Dhamon, who noticed that the wounds on its chest and stomach had stopped bleeding.

"So you heal quickly," he commented. "I can fix that."

Dhamon feinted to his right, the creature following him with both arms stretching out as far as it could reach. Then he spun to his left, crouched beneath the beast's claws, and drove his blade up, running the creature through. Blood spilled out, releasing with it the overpowering smell of decaying leaves. Dhamon gagged and stepped back, tugging the sword free and expecting to watch the creature fall.

Instead, it screamed maddeningly and clutched at the wound, eyes darting from the blood that flowed over its claws to Dhamon.

"Pigs, lover!" Rikali shouted. "Just kill the beastie and be done with it!"

"Tough to kill," Dhamon grumbled as he made a move to step forward again.

"My turn!" Maldred cut in. The big man darted up, his great two-handed sword held above his shoulder. "Stay low!" he called to Dhamon as he swept the blade in a high, wide arc. The metal shimmered as it connected with the beast's flesh, then it continued on, passing through the neck. The head plopped to the floor, the creature's body falling a heartbeat later.

"Impressive," Dhamon stated.

"Guess the two of you didn't need any help," Fiona said. She brought the torch nearer so she could get a better look at the creature. She glance at Maldred, then at Dhamon. "But I still think you were a bit hasty. It might not have been hostile. Dhamon attacked it first. Provoked it with the arrows. Not everything that looks different from us is an enemy."

The half-elf sheathed her knife. "It was mean, all

right. And ugly. What were you gonna do, Fee-oh-na? Talk it to death? Or maybe invite it to join the Solamnic Knights?"

The mariner padded up to Fiona's side, glaive grasped tightly in his hands. He stared at Maldred's sword, the dark green blood on it. He watched the big man pull a cloth from his pocket and wipe the blood off, pausing to sniff the cloth before tucking it into his belt.

"Smells very strongly of copper," he commented to the mariner.

"Blood is blood, doesn't matter what it smells like, or what color it is. At least the thing's dead." After a moment's pause, Rig nodded to the two-handed sword. "Nice blade."

"It was a gift from Donnag. To replace a weapon I lost many days ago."

The mariner prized weapons. The glaive he carried was magicked, able to pass through armor as if it were parchment. And he had a penchant for collecting weapons, especially coveting enchanted ones. He glanced at Maldred's blade again, wondering if there might be some magic about it because it so easily cut through the creature. Shrugging, he quickly decided he didn't care; if it was a gift from *Lord* Donnag, it wasn't anything he was interested in. Then Rig knelt by the slain creature and examined its feet. "Had to have been one of those giants they were talking about. It would make big enough tracks for a common man to *think* it a giant."

"Probably," Dhamon said, padding closer. "But we might as well make sure. We can check down those alcoves, see if we can find any goat carcasses and. . . ." The tingling sensation was back for just an instant. Was something else watching him? He turned and glanced at Rikali.

The half-elf was against the cavern wall, studying some of the carved images of dwarven children, tracing something with her fingers and making faces. For an instant it looked like one of the carved heads was making a face back. Dhamon blinked and looked closer.

"Riki!" He warned.

Too late! A second beast separated from the wall and grabbed for the half-elf, one claw completely circling her slender waist and raising her above the floor. As Dhamon dashed forward, the creature drew the other claw to her throat and growled loudly.

Dhamon skidded to a stop, the others behind him. Rikali struggled frantically, but couldn't break the thing's grip. It was larger than the first, though not quite as tall. It had a wide chest and a big pot belly. Its legs were thick like tree trunks, and its feet were long and ended in claws that curled in on themselves. It met Dhamon's gaze, and as he inched forward it squeezed Rikali tighter. She screamed.

"Stop!" Maldred called to Dhamon. "It's threatening us."

"Aye," Dhamon returned. "That's clear enough. We come any closer and it kills her, it seems." Behind him, he heard a soft "shushing" sound, recognizing it as Rig tugging daggers free.

"It probably wants us to leave," Maldred continued. "Doesn't want to end up dead like its friend. Fiona's right. We're the intruders. But if we leave . . ."

"It'll probably still kill Riki," Dhamon finished. With that, he sprang toward the creature, pulling his sword over his shoulder and swinging hard, biting deep into the beast's side. He jumped back quickly. The creature howled in surprise and savagely flung the half-elf to the ground, stepping on her as it advanced on Dhamon.

Fiona dropped the torch and rushed forward, and found herself being flung toward one of the pillars by yet another creature. This third beast had also emerged from the walls, shrugging off its camouflage and soundly striking the Solamnic Knight again, sending her weapon and the torch flying. The torch sputtered at the entrance, making it more difficult to see the two creatures.

Stunned, Fiona made it to her knees and shook her head to clear her senses.

"By all the vanished gods, what are these things?" Rig cried in disbelief as he peered into the shadows and pivoted to face the creature that was pressing its attack on Fiona. The mariner swept the glaive out, completely slicing through an arm and lodging the crescent blade in the thing's ribcage. "They certainly aren't true giants."

Unlike its dead brother, this creature didn't cry in pain. It only glanced at the stump where its arm had been, at the blood spurting from it, and at the glaive lodged deep in its flesh. It snarled once at the mariner and tugged the weapon free with its remaining hand, tossing it far across the cavern where the weapon was lost in the darkness. Then the beast returned its attention to Fiona, who was just now struggling to her feet.

"What are these things?" the mariner repeated as he drew a long sword and a dagger and advanced again. Fiona stepped back to give Rig fighting room, as she scanned the floor for her sword.

Despite its grievous wounds, still the creature fought fiercely, reaching out with its remaining arm toward the mariner. Rig's sword was held high above his head, and was coming down like an executioner's axe. With all of his strength behind it, the blade cleaved the creature's other arm. Without pause, the mariner moved in closer and repeatedly drove a dagger into its stomach, groaning when green blood erupted to splatter him. It fell to its knees, but refused to die.

Meanwhile, Maldred was concentrating on the other creature, drawing it away from Rikali and giving Dhamon a chance to slip around behind it.

Dhamon scooped up one of Rikali's daggers and leapt in, intending to stab the beast in the back. The creature sensed him, swiping with one claw at Maldred, then whirling and clawing at Dhamon.

Dhamon ducked beneath the beast's arms and jabbed upward into its rib cage with the dagger, while in the same motion he swung the sword into the thing's thigh. Dark green blood spattered down at him, blinding him. But he thrust and swung again and again, even as Maldred came at it from the other side.

Out of the corner of its eye, the beast spotted Rikali, who was grumbling and sluggishly picking herself up. Ignoring Dhamon and Maldred, the creature moved the fight toward her, viciously kicking out with a leg and raking its curled nails across her leg. She gasped and fell back.

"Pigs! Can't the two of you kill that beastie!"

"Trying," Dhamon replied, as he drove the dagger so deep into its stomach it was lodged there.

At the same time, Maldred swung down hard, slicing through the creature's leg and crippling it. As the beast fell and twitched on the floor, the big man continued to slash at it. Dhamon crouched over it and plunged his sword into where he guessed its heart would be, slamming his eyes shut as more blood spurted on him.

Behind them, the mariner continued to struggle with his creature.

"Tough to kill!" Rig shouted. Though the beast had no arms, it still lunged toward him, crawling on its knees and snapping. It managed to stand, and as Rig stepped back to ready another swing, it kicked out with a clawed foot.

Fiona recovered her blade and joined him.

"No harmful intent, huh?" he mused to her as, exhausted, he shoved the long sword through its stomach. The creature sagged forward onto Rig, toppling him and burying him beneath its heavy body. Fiona rolled the thing off him, and the mariner got to his feet, stabbing it one more time to make sure it was dead.

"What a mess," the mariner observed, plucking at his blood-soaked shirt. Then he headed toward where the creature had thrown his glaive. "Ah, here it is."

Meanwhile, Rikali was holding her throat and coughing violently. "Pigs!" she spat. "I thought that horrible beast was going to kill me!" She shook out her arms and legs and stumbled toward Dhamon. "But you saved me, lover." She kissed him loudly on his cheek, then bent over the creature, with some effort tugging the dagger free. "This is mine!" she said, waving the dagger at the body.

Dhamon sheathed his sword and studied the wall the creatures had been hiding against. There were no hidden niches he could find. Their coloration seemed to be all the camouflage they needed.

Rig was poking at the wall with the butt-end of the glaive, making sure there were no further surprises. Fiona had rescued the torch and held it high behind him.

"Three of them," Rig said, after he'd checked all of the walls. "Just like Kulp's folks said they'd spotted tracks for. Guess that means you can come down

now, Fetch." He looked up at the kobold, still clinging to the pillar. But the kobold shook his head, gesturing wildly. "We got them all. You're safe."

Fetch shook his head even more exaggeratedly,
almost comically.

"He's right," Rikali said, her face paler than
normal. "We didn't get them." The half-elf pointed to
the first one that had been slain, the decapitated one.

The head and body had somehow moved toward
each other, and the companions stared as the two
pieces began to reattach themselves. The rocky-hued
flesh flowed like water from the stump that had been
its neck, capturing the base of the head and adjusting
it until it fit properly. At the same time, the wounds
on the rest of its body were closing. The chest began
to rise and fall regularly, and the eyelids fluttered
open. A moment later it was climbing to its feet,
snarling.

Maldred rushed forward, tugging his sword free
and swinging.

"This one, too!" Dhamon pointed. Then he turned
and joined Maldred to fight the creature who had
raised itself from the dead.

The armless body of the creature Rig had slain
was twitching, the wounds on its chest and stomach
sealing as they watched. Its face was drawn together
in concentration. A barely discernible "skritching"
sound came from nearby.

"In the name of Vinus Solamnus," Fiona hushed.
"Look at this."

The noise was made by claws moving across the
tiled floor. The arms the mariner had cut off the
downed creature were crawling back toward the body.
They moved purposefully, arranging themselves
against the shoulders, the skin flowing to reattach
them.

"Awh. . . ." Rig grumbled. "They're definitely not giants. They're damnable trolls." He stomped forward, pinning one of the wriggling arms beneath his boot, and picking up the other and yanking it away from the shoulder before it could completely reattach. He heaved it out of the cave. Then he drew his sword and struck the torso again and again, sending a shower of blood spraying in the cave. "Keep hitting them," he explained between swings, "or they'll come back to life."

"I thought trolls were supposed to be green," Fiona said as she moved to the third creature, which Maldred had sliced the leg off of. The leg was rolling toward the body, and she thrust the flame at it and watched the skin bubble and pop.

"Well, most are," Dhamon said, as he and Maldred simultaneously skewered their foe. "Good idea, what you're doing, Fiona. You can burn trolls. They can't come back to life if they're cinders. Bring your torch over here when you're done."

"I thought these stinking things were only found in swamps and forests," she continued. Her free hand drew her sword and she hacked at her target, which was futilely attempting to hobble away. She heard movement behind her and whirled, thinking it another troll coming up behind her. It was the half-elf, edging closer for a better look.

But the moment's distraction served to the troll's advantage. It reached a hand out and swiped at Fiona's face, the claws digging into her cheek and causing her to cry out. She spun back instinctively, swinging hard and slicing through the creature's arm at its elbow. The claws remained attached to her face, as if the limb had a life of its own.

"That's disgusting," the half-elf spat, as she tugged the arm free, taking some of Fiona's flesh with it. Then she dropped the limb to the cavern floor and snatched the torch from the Solamnic, thrusting the flame to the arm and gagging at the smell of the burning troll flesh.

"Damnable beast!" Fiona cursed. Her free hand held over her injured cheek, she swung at the creature more fiercely, severing its other arm. It howled angrily at her and tried to roll away, but she pressed her attack, repeatedly hacking at it until it was still. Then she threw the dismembered pieces away from the torso and glanced about for her torch.

The half-elf had carried it to Dhamon, who was burning the troll he and Maldred had slain for the second time. The Solamnic reached for her backpack, retrieved a second torch, and quickly lit it and went to work.

Behind her, Rig was calling for some fire.

"Yuck." This came from the half-elf, who had picked up a troll foot, the toes of which were jerking. She tossed it Fiona's way, and busied herself by retrieving the other pieces the Solamnic had scattered, and complaining each time she found something that wriggled.

"Here!" Fetch hollered. "Look over here!" He was gesturing toward the base of the pillar he clung to. A head had rolled there, and was continuing to roll toward the entrance as if it were attempting to make an escape.

"I'll get it," Rig returned. He tromped over to the pillar and hauled back on his leg, intending to kick the head out of the cave.

"Stop!" Dhamon brought his torch over and applied it to the head, grimacing when it opened its mouth and screeched. "There are tales that amputated troll limbs can regrow entire bodies."

"Since when did you believe everything you

heard?" The mariner brushed by him and checked on Fiona.

It took the better part of an hour to cut up the trolls and burn them in a large bonfire, which made the cavern reek of charred flesh.

"I'm not certain we got all the pieces," Dhamon said as they stood at the cavern entrance, where everyone had retreated for clean air. He kept his eyes trained on the blaze, occasionally glancing to the walls and the pillars, where the carved dwarven images were more illuminated now.

Then, while Maldred and Rig took turns watching the fire as it dwindled, using their swords to push back fingers and feet that tried to crawl away, Dhamon tended to Fiona.

"It might scar," Dhamon told her as he cleansed her torn cheek with a little of his alcohol. "But the healer in Blöten, Grim Kedar, is amazing. He might be able to help you."

"I will be fine."

"You're cut to the bone. I'd like him to look at you. No telling if you might get some infection or disease. You shouldn't take any chances with something like this. Those creatures' claws were filthy."

"I'm surprised you care."

"I don't," he said flatly. "But it's pretty clear that Maldred does."

"Fine. All right then. I'll see this Grim Kedar fellow when we return to Blöten."

Rikali glided up to the pair. "Oh, I don't know, lover, I think a scar would give the Lady Knight a bit more character." Then the half-elf glided away, before Fiona could think to reply. Dhamon stifled a chuckle.

"Couldn't you have done that outside?" Fetch asked the companions, finally climbing down from the pillar and holding his nose. He pointed to the pile of smoldering ashes. He had refused to budge until he was positive the trolls would not be coming back to life. The kobold waved his hand in front of his face. "It stinks worse'n me."

"That's debatable," said the mariner. "Anyway, it's still raining, so we couldn't've burned them outside." He sharply added, "And thanks for all your help with this." He gestured at the smoldering remains.

"Any time." The kobold wandered away, inspecting the altar Rikali was sitting on, ogling his reflected face in its smooth surface for a few minutes before getting bored with that activity and disappearing to explore one of the alcoves.

"Most certainly these were the 'giants' the villagers were being pestered by," Rig said after several minutes of silence. "Don't have any souvenirs from them to show Donnag as proof we fixed the Knollsbank problem, though." He glanced at Maldred. "Will the ogre take our word?"

"A better question," interjected Fiona, "is will he keep his?"

"He will." Maldred was looking out at the dark gray sky. There was no hint of light, telling him the sun had set more than an hour ago. "Either the trolls were trapped in here and got out when this fissure opened, or they've been in the mountains a while and started after the goats when whatever it was they were eating ran out—or was washed away by all this rain."

"Does it matter?" Rikali asked. "The beasties're dead. And we call this job done, pry the gems out of the pillars, and get out of here. Besides, we're—"

"They were the giants for certain!" Fetch was dragging the carcass of a kid into the chamber. "All sorts of bones back there. An' some stairs. But I wasn't going down them alone." He paused and dropped the bones. "Just in case there're more of them trolls."

Maldred motioned for Fiona, plucked another torch from her backpack. "We ought to make sure there aren't three more." Softer, for her ears alone, he added, "You are indeed an impressive warrior, Lady Knight. I watched you wield your blade. A match for any man I know. Probably any two."

"It shouldn't matter if there are more." Dhamon snatched up the torch they'd used to light the troll bonfire. "But to make you happy, Mal, I'll take the right passage."

"And I will take the left, my friend."

"Whoa!" Rig tromped past them, then whirled, hands held up to block them. "I agree with the half-elf. We met Donnag's conditions. We killed the 'wolves'—giants—whatever you want to call them. Now let's go back to Blöten and see if *Lord Donnag* keeps his end of the bargain. He promised Fiona a chest full of treasure and men to guard it on the way to Takar. Let's not take any more chances."

Rikali clung to Dhamon's arm. "Let's go explorin', lover. I'll come along—for just a little while. Might find all manner of pretty little baubles for my pretty little neck." She snaked out a hand and touched Rig's shoulder. "We can go back to stinky old Blöten in a bit. After we take a quick look downstairs. Then I want to come pluck me those onyx eyes," she gestured at the pillar, "before we return to Donnag. Stay up here if you're 'fraid." Then she tugged Dhamon toward the alcove, and a moment later they'd disappeared inside.

Rig growled. "I don't trust either of them."

"Then go with them," Maldred answered. "I'll stay here with Fiona."

The mariner drew his lips into a thin line and met Fiona's gaze. His eyes told her he didn't trust Maldred either.

"I'll be all right," she said. "It's a good idea to keep an eye on Dhamon."

The mariner turned to follow Dhamon, though his thoughts were on Maldred and Fiona.

"Three hours at most!" Maldred called after Rig. "Try to judge your time and meet back here in three hours! Your torch won't last much longer than that." Softer, he added to Fiona, "to the left, then, my love." He carried the torch and led her into the darkness. "Fetch," he added, "stay right here and wait for us."

The kobold scowled. He knew that tone. He sat down, staring at the embers glowing amid the pile of ashes.

CHAPTER TEN
LOST FACES

Fetch poked the end of his hoopak into the troll ashes and grumbled. "Fetch, do this for me. Fetch, do that for me. Fetch, carry this. Fetch, stay here. Fetch—you stink when you get wet. Fetch, quit playing with the fire. Fetch. Fetch. Fetch." He stomped his foot against the tiled floor. "My name is Ilbreth."

His red eyes glowed like hot coals in the ever-darkening cave, fixing on the closest pillar, which bore the image of priests and religious warriors. "And since no one's watching Ilbreth, he might as well help himself." He strolled boldly over to the pillar, eyes darting to the alcoves to make sure Maldred and Dhamon weren't coming back right away, then he started to climb. When he was even with the first priest's visage, he dug his sharp claws into the eye sockets and pulled out the chunks of onyx. He examined them, smiling when he saw how smooth and large they were. A little higher and he found pearls serving as the pupils to another eerie face, these also a good size. Skittering around, he retrieved several polished balls of gold and brass on the back side. They felt comfortably heavy in his hand.

Only two of the pillars had such treasures, and these were the closest to the altar. Fetch guessed that in ages past other visitors helped themselves, then either were forced to leave before gobbling up the rest of the treasures or . . . well, he couldn't think of another reason why they wouldn't have taken everything. Only four pairs of eyes had been gemstones, the rest precious metals he suspected the dwarves had forged, perhaps from ore taken from this very mountain. The polished balls clinked together pleasingly in his pocket, and he made a game of thrusting his fingers into the pocket, naming the metals—gold, silver, or bronze—and seeing if he pulled out a ball that matched. But the game did not last long, and he quickly tired of it.

After about an hour had passed, the cave grew darker still, and the rain that pattered against the rocks outside began to sound threatening. Fetch felt like a nervous rabbit in a deep, dark hole and imagined the raindrops were footsteps of trolls and goatherders and gem-craving dwarves from the far valley of crystal come to rob him of his precious metal eyeballs.

"Don't like this dark," he muttered to himself. Though the kobold had unique vision that allowed him to see through the blackness, he detested the night. All manner of horrible things came out when the sun went down.

"A fire," he decided. "I'll start a fire and stay nice and cozy warm and it'll lighten up this cave for me." He rubbed his shoulders. Indeed, he thought, even though it was the heart of a very hot summer, it was getting a little chilly this high up. "Nice and warm and so I can see."

He padded around the cave looking for something to burn. Nothing much was left of the trolls. The altar was made of some rich, black stone that felt smooth to the touch and had no hope of catching fire. Neither did it register any heat, and that unnerved the kobold. He considered it unnatural. His hoopak was made of wood, but he had no intention of sacrificing it. The weapon was acquired from a kender who had befriended him years past and who Ilbreth turned on and killed during negotiations over a certain dubiously acquired treasure. So finally the kobold settled on one of the middle pillars to set on fire, the one with the carvings of female dwarven warriors. He didn't think it quite as artistic as the others, it had not yielded any metal eyeballs, and it looked like it would burn real good.

Sitting down in front of the pillar, he traced the outline of an ugly harridan who must have had more muscles than brains to be able to carry all the others on top of her shoulders. He took one more glance down the alcoves, then started humming, a magical tune Maldred had taught him—the first spell Maldred had ever taught him, in fact. And it was his favorite. He searched for the spark within him, that essence of magic Maldred said he sensed when he met the kobold in the wilderness. Feeling it, his tune increased and was cut through with a gargling noise that wasn't part of the enchantment but which the kobold added for effect. He felt the energy flow from his chest into his arms, into his fingers, and into the face of the carved dwarven woman.

"Make us a little light," he told the carving. Then a heartbeat later the carved figure started to burn. It was slow at first, the flames difficult to catch on because the wood was so dense, old, and dry. But Fetch was persistent. He puffed on the flames—he was extremely accomplished at setting fires. Then he sat back, satisfied, as the pillar became engulfed with flames.

It's just one pillar, he thought, although it was burning fast and merrily. There were still five left to pay homage to the departed dwarven god. What was the name Dhamon said? Rocks? No. Rork? The kobold paced around the pillar, warming his hands and tipping his face to catch the welcome heat. His gaze roamed to the far wall, where the light was catching the other faces carved in stone. The dancing flames made it look as if the faces were laughing. Fetch joined in their revelry, cackling and snorting and dancing and pretending to pray to Rork, god of the carved dwarves. The kobold liked to dance— though not when Maldred was around. Dancing was frivolous, and the kobold did his best to present a serious and studious image to his master and mentor. But Maldred wasn't here, so he danced faster and wilder until his chest burned from the exertion and the altitude.

Panting, he approached the laughing stone faces, his shadow darkening some and turning them sad. Running his fingers around their features he created another game to occupy himself. He began naming each face he touched. "Laughing Lars, Laughing Dretch, Laughing Riki, Crying Mo"—this for one who seemed to be looking directly at him, sorrowfully.

Then he skated over to the black altar. He worked at his other magic, the spell that allowed him to take on the form of various creatures. Within the span of several minutes, he looked like Laughing Lars, though he gave his face the healthy ruddy red color he imagined the dwarf would have if he were alive. For more fun, he took on Laughing Dretch's image and left his skin stony gray. But Fetch quickly tired of this game, too, and returned to the burning pillar. The flames had reached the topmost carved dwarf and was burning very quickly.

He thought the scent almost pleasant—much better, at least, than the troll flesh and the perfume Rikali had drenched herself with. He sniffed and tried to imagine what a young wild pig would taste like roasted on the pillar fire. Not quite able to decide, he gave up and returned to simply staring at the fire, mesmerized by it.

"Maldred says I play with you too much," he told the flames. "But I don't think so. I really like fire."

A moment later he was standing inches from another pillar, then sitting in front of the face of an old male dwarf, who had deeply carved wrinkles and squinting eyes—another that hadn't yielded any valuable gems. "Don't look at me like that," Fetch said. "Oh, won't listen to me, huh? Well, I'll just have to burn you, too."

He started humming, searching for the spark, and grinning wide when the old carving caught fire.

❖ ❖ ❖ ❖ ❖ ❖ ❖

Maldred and Fiona carefully picked their way down a staircase that was at times winding and circular, then sharply angled and steep. It seemed to stretch downward into the darkness forever. The steps were smooth with age, and they were shiny from the numerous feet that must have traipsed over them. For more than an hour they'd been heading down, pausing at alcoves where wood and stone statues of Reorx were nestled. Beneath the statues were ceramic bowls with offerings so ancient and brittle that they were unidentifiable. As they continued on, they tried to gauge just how far beneath the great chamber they were.

"I wonder how old this is?" Fiona mused. She was running her fingers along the wall, where she'd found more carvings of dwarven faces. Many of the mouths were "O" shaped, and she took the torch from Maldred and inserted it into one of the mouths, which was obviously meant to serve as a sconce.

Then she tugged the last torch free from her satchel and lit it. "I'll carry it for a while," she said to Maldred. "But we can't be gone much longer or we'll have to find our way back up in the dark. So . . . how old do you think?"

"Hundreds and hundreds of years, maybe. Perhaps a thousand," he said finally, stopping also to examine a face similar to one he'd spotted on a pillar above. "Donnag and his people have claimed this land for a very long time. He is keenly aware of what comprises his holdings, like a greedy dragon who can account for every coin in his horde, but I'm certain he does not know about this. Else I would have heard of it, too. We will make him aware when we return, perhaps taking one of the smaller wooden statues of the god for proof, and he will be most happy with the knowledge. And you're right. We should think about returning to Fetch. It'll take us a while to make the climb back."

"A thousand years," she repeated. "The gods were very active then."

"Krynn is better off without them." Maldred looked down. They should head back. They had been gone more than an hour. Maybe two. And it would take them longer to climb up than it had to go down. But it seemed like the steps didn't go much farther. "Maybe just a little more." Then he laughed. "Wonder if this'll take us to the foot of the mountains—or beneath them. I wouldn't be surprised." He gestured for her to follow him. "Maybe we'll emerge near Blöten! I'll take you straight to Grim's and he'll mend your face in . . ."

"What about Rig? And Fetch is above. . . ."

He touched her chin. "They're grown-ups. They'll be all right, and if need be they can find their own way back. Besides, Dhamon and Rig are together. And I know for certain that Dhamon will be returning to Donnag's."

Then he headed down the steps.

She followed, one hand holding the torch, the other feeling along the wall and touching the images carved there. A disturbing question tugged at her mind, and she finally voiced it. "How can you say that Krynn is better without her gods? The gods gave us so much. And Vinus Solamnus who founded my order . . ."

"The gods never did anything for me," Maldred said evenly. "In truth, I'm glad they're gone." He stopped when a shrill noise echoed up from below, and he drew his hand back over his shoulder, gripping the pommel of his sword. He relaxed when a large bat flew by. "Though I suppose the gods kept the dragons in check."

There was a sharp intake of breath behind him, and he turned. Fiona, two steps above, was eye to eye with him.

"I don't like the way you talk, Maldred. The gods are important to Krynn, and I believe they will come back," she said, thrusting her chin forward. "Maybe they won't return in my lifetime. But it will happen. And dwarves will use this temple again. I would certainly like to think so, anyway. I can imagine their deep voices echoing in prayers to Reorx." Suddenly she blinked and shook her head. "Where's Rig, anyway?"

He brushed the tip of her nose with his fingers, locked his eyes onto hers. "Rig is of no concern, and you should abandon all thoughts of marrying him," Maldred said, his voice sonorous and melodic, enchantingly pleasant. "Lady Knight, you need be concerned only with me, and with seeing what's at the bottom of these never-ending steps."

She found herself enjoying his words again, as she had the first night she met him at the campfire. His eyes sparkled then, and now—the light from the torch was hitting them just right. "Concerned only with you," she repeated. Then she was again following him down the worn stone steps.

❖ ❖ ❖ ❖ ❖ ❖ ❖

"Pigs, but these go on forever, lover," Rikali complained as she stopped to rub the backs of her legs. "Bad enough all that climbing up the mountain. And you'd think these wouldn't be so steep, being built by dwarves and all with short, stubby legs. Bet these lead straight to the Abyss! My fine house ain't going to have such steep steps! Ain't going to have any steps at all."

"A while ago you thought exploring was a fine idea," Dhamon told her. "In fact, I think it was your idea."

"A woman can change her mind, lover."

Dhamon continued down the steps, glancing at the wall where he noted carvings of dwarves that were every bit as elaborate as the ones in the large chamber above. They weren't just faces this time, though, as they were at the very top of the steps. They were full figures, presented sideways, as if they were moving down the steps with him. He spotted one with a short beard, and it made him think of

Jasper. "I wish Jasper could be here to see this," he mused. He noted the writing above the figures, and made out some of the words, his eyes narrowing with realization.

"Well, from what you told me of him, he probably wouldn't've liked these steep steps either."

Jasper never complained so much, Dhamon thought.

"I don't recall Jasper ever complaining about such things," Rig said aloud.

That brought a rare, big smile to Dhamon's lips. "I can't imagine the steps going on much farther, Riki. In fact. . . ."

He paused and took a closer look at the nearest carvings, as he had at the very top of the stairs. More writing. He brought the torch closer so he could see the words better, and he traced the faintest ones, fragments of sentences, with his fingertips.

Amid the words he continued to read as he traveled down a few more steps were carvings of dwarves digging in the earth, followed by dwarves making homes underground and becoming miners.

"It reads like a diary," Dhamon explained. "In fact, I'm pretty sure that's what it is. 'Kal-thax we leave behind this day. Calnar thane to the Kalkhist Mountains to delve a new home. New Hope it will be called. Thorin.' " He took in a deep breath. "If I remember what Jasper told me of his race's history, that would make this about 2800 precataclysm." He whistled softly. "This place is indeed very old."

"Well, how do you know it wasn't done more recently, and they were just reminiscin' about the old days? Who'd keep some stony diary anyway? Too much work if you ask me." Despite her words, Rikali tried to feign interest in the carvings, thinking that might please Dhamon.

"Because I can see the bottom of these steps. And because the carvings at the top are even fainter than these, older, and they talked about the Graystone being forged and Kal-Thax built. So this is more recent and written as if it is happening now, not written like history. All of it is written that way."

"Wait, lover." Rikali placed both hands against the wall. "Feels cooler here."

Rig snorted. "We're deeper underground. Been walking for better'n an hour. Maybe two." He was thinking about Fiona, suspecting she was in the cavern above impatiently waiting for them. He didn't like her being alone with Maldred. Rig told himself not to be jealous, that Fiona truly loved him, that they would be married one day soon and would be far away from these thieves. Still, he couldn't keep his suspicions entirely at bay. And he couldn't help wishing he'd gone with Fiona rather than with Dhamon and that gabby Rikali.

The half-elf shook her head and darted up a dozen steps to press her hands against the wall. Then she came back down. "It's cooler here, I tell you."

Dhamon felt about, finding moisture in one spot. "There's an underground stream behind this wall," he said. "Maybe it opens up below and we can take a bath. Get all this troll blood off."

"Oh, I like that idea, lover."

Dhamon moved down slowly now, ignoring the half-elf's request to hurry so they could clean the dirt off themselves and find the valuables that must surely be somewhere in this place. And he pushed aside Rig's complaint that this was all very interesting but wasn't getting them back to Blöten any faster and that they would be late rejoining Fiona in the chamber so very high above.

"Here," Dhamon pointed. "This is the last of the

carvings, and they're etched deeper, not as old, definitely. Carved about eight hundred years later than the last ones I showed you—if I understand the history." There were images of dwarves and a forge, a replica of a great hammer. "The Hammer of Reorx," Dhamon whispered. "That's the forging of it, about two thousand years before the cataclysm. The Time of Light, I think it was called. The hammer shown here was used a thousand years after its forging to make Huma's dragonlance."

Rig was honestly interested now, as weapons of any kind were a passion of the mariner's. "It was later called the Hammer of Kharas, right? After a hero of the Dwarfgate War."

"How can you two talk so much about dwarves? I've had my fill of them."

"Maybe it was forged somewhere down here," Rig said. There was a tinge of excitement to his voice.

"I just want to find me some pretty baubles, something valuable, and have me a nice bath."

"Riki, this entire mountain is valuable."

"But I can't fit it in my pocket now, can I lover? I can't hang it around my neck."

Dhamon let out a deep breath. "To the dwarves, this would be priceless. To historians, too."

"To Palin," Rig added.

"Thought you wanted to get back to Blöten." The half-elf harumphed. "I know I certainly do. I'm tired of . . . Wait." Rikali put a hand on Dhamon's shoulder. "I smell somethin'. Thought I smelled somethin' before, smells stronger now." She turned and glanced up the steps, the top of which she hadn't been able to see a few minutes ago. But now the stairs were faintly visible to her oh-so-keen eyesight because of a soft light streaming down from high above. "I think I smell fire!"

"Fire?" Rig said, turning and squinting to see whatever it was she was looking at. He saw only darkness in the distance. "The trolls were done burning before we started down."

Dhamon sniffed the air. "I think she's right."

"But what could be burnin'?" the half-elf asked. Then her eyes grew wide. "Fetch!" she cried. She started up the steps, then stopped as the cavern rocked with a tremor. This time the quake wasn't coming from below, as all the others had. This one originated from above.

◇ ◇ ◇ ◇ ◇ ◇ ◇

Fetch wasn't certain how he'd done it—managing to set all six pillars on fire. They were too far apart for the blaze to have spread on its own accord, so he must have done something to help.

He scratched his head. He remembered setting two or three on fire, maybe it was four, picking out the heads on the bottom to roast. But certainly not all of the pillars. Or had he? Perhaps he'd simply lost track of the time. Maybe he'd merely gotten so caught up with the new dance he'd created—his flame dance he'd dubbed it—that he'd just let everything else slip his mind.

Not that it mattered. The fires would burn themselves out eventually, or maybe the wind would pick up and blow some rain inside and the water would put the fires out. It definitely was raining harder, he could hear the rain clearly, and the wind was blowing.

The fires would burn out—and in the process everyone would be done a great favor. Why, if there were gems or gold hidden inside those carved columns, he'd surely find them when he sifted through the ashes. Maldred would be exceedingly pleased.

"No, he won't," the kobold muttered to himself. "He'll tell me to stop playing with fire spells." He sat and watched the flaming pillars, trying hard to be ashamed of the whole incident, though actually he was awed by the great blaze he had birthed.

All around him the dwarven faces laughed, the shadows and the light playing across their grotesque features. The kobold mused to himself that Maldred would have to admit he'd breathed life into the carvings.

He glanced up and saw the flames dance along the very roof of the cavern, where the tops of the pillars rested, their crowned dwarven kings nothing more than kindling now. It was incredibly beautiful. The red and orange, the white and yellow.

Such intense color and all of it was his doing. Fetch grinned, then frowned, remembering he was trying to scold himself for his bad behavior.

Then his mouth dropped open as the first pillar collapsed, sending embers everywhere and sending him scurrying behind the forge-altar for cover. With a "whoosh" and a "pop" the second came down, the fallen chunks burning on the floor. Fetch poked his head above the altar and his eyes grew wide. It looked as if the god-image on the floor was lit up with smiles, pleased with Fetch's fiery magic.

For a brief moment the kobold thought all the pillars would collapse and burn out before Maldred returned, then he could sweep the ashes out of the cave entrance and no one would be the wiser. But Maldred might notice the wooden columns were gone. And he might smell the scent of charred wood.

"Maldred'll be mad," the kobold muttered to himself. "Really mad. Maybe I can convince him it was an accident." Then he ducked as the third pillar burned itself out, and the fourth also collapsed with a loud "whoosh!" He poked his head up again and breathed a sigh of relief. It would be some time before the last two pillars went. He must have set them afire several minutes after the others.

Then the kobold looked up at the ceiling, where the fire illuminated great cracks that had formed, and more carved dwarves he hadn't noticed before. "Didn't really think the pillars were holding the roof up," he admitted. "Figured they were just for decoration."

The cracks widened as Fetch watched. Then the kobold stood up and backed away, eyes darting between the two shadowy alcoves and the cave entrance.

"This is not a good place to be," Fetch warned himself, as he heard the stone groan and crack. "Not a good place at all. I gotta get out of here." The only question remaining in his childlike mind was which direction.

A glance at the entrance. It was the safest bet, but also the wettest. A glance at the alcove Maldred and Fiona had disappeared into. Maldred should be warned, he was the kobold's master and mentor, after all. But Maldred would be mad and would scold Fetch and perhaps punish him.

A glance at the alcove where Dhamon went. It was closer, by a couple of feet. Well, maybe not that much closer, but Dhamon wasn't likely to yell at him.

When the cracks widened and the rocks groaned louder, and when stone dust started falling every bit as hard as the rain outside, the kobold whirled, his small feet racing over the tile as fast as his heart was hammering in his chest. The first significant chunk of ceiling hit when he still had several yards to go.

It thundered against the floor, sending shards

flying through the air. Fetch lost his balance and pitched forward, arms and legs flailing for any purchase. Then another chunk fell and the entire cavern started to shake, the walls wobbling and the carved dwarven faces dissolving. Laughing Lars and Laughing Dretch turned to stone dust.

He forced himself to his knees and into a crawl, moving as quickly as possible, wincing when the first fist-sized rocks struck him as more of the ceiling fell. He made it to the alcove just as the world seemed to explode. Without a second thought, Fetch hurled himself down the steep stairs, apologizing profusely to the carved dwarves he passed and focusing on a faint light far below, which he hoped was the torch Dhamon had been carrying.

The steps were terribly steep, but fear spurred the diminutive kobold on, as the mountain continued to rumble, and rocks and stone dust belched down the stairway after him. He felt like he'd been running for an eternity when he tripped on a crumbling step and tumbled head first for several dozen feet before he was able to right himself, his body a mass of aches and pain. Nonetheless, he got up and hurried on, the mountain still rumbling.

The air was so very close in the stairway, musty smelling, tinged with the scent of rocks. And an odd taste. Enough stone dust had found its way into his mouth. He didn't care for the taste. The light below was bobbing, coming up to meet him. He slowed his course and almost stopped, he was so tired. He let out a sigh of relief when the human came into view.

"Dhamon Grimwulf," Fetch huffed. "Am I so happy to find you."

Rikali was hissing at him and brushed by Dhamon, caught the kobold's throat in her hands and shook him.

Fetch sputtered, arms flailing about, lungs crying for air.

"Put him down, Riki."

"Dhamon, the little rat did somethin' and you well know it." She shook Fetch again and then dropped him on the step. The kobold gasped, more for effect than out of any real pain. He tried to get Dhamon's attention, but now the human was racing past him, feet pounding up the steps, taking the light with him, finally stopping. Several moments later, Dhamon returned with a grim expression.

"There was a cave-in," he reported. "And I think it's impossible that one little kobold could have caused it."

Rikali still glared.

Fetch coughed and pretended he was hurt, that it was difficult for him to breathe. "Was what I was trying to tell you," the kobold began. "Those trolls. You thought you'd burned them. I thought you'd burned them. They was nothin' but ashes. But that arm you threw out of the cave mouth." Fetch gestured to Rig, "It crawled back up into the cave, was growing a whole 'nother big-as-you-please troll on the end of it. I tried to beat it with my hoopak, but it was too much for me. Then it started rummaging around in the ashes, caught fire, and I thought it would destroy itself." He paused, gulping in air, still feigning injury.

"Go on," Rig said.

The kobold could tell from Rig's expression that the mariner had bought the story. Let him think it's all his fault for throwing the arm away. Indeed, Fetch considered, it might have happened that way. The arm probably would have come back if the cavern hadn't collapsed first, and it could have happened just as he was explaining. "Well, the troll arm brushed against one of them pillars and it caught on fire. Soon they were all burning. I couldn't put them out, and I ran down here to get you—and just in time, too, I might add. The pillars must have collapsed and took the cave down with 'em."

Dhamon looked skeptical, but said nothing. Rikali was still hissing, trundling up a few steps, peering ahead, then running back down.

"So what do we do?" the half-elf asked nervously.

"We got to go down," Rig said, signaling for the torch. Dhamon gave it to him.

"Down? Pigs, you can't be serious!"

"Too much rock up there," Dhamon said as he fell in step behind Rig. "We have to hope that we'll find a way out down below."

"And if we can't, lover?"

Dhamon didn't answer that question.

"And what about Maldred?" Rikali mused, as she slowly followed the procession.

Maldred'll be mad, Fetch thought. If he's still alive.

◇ ◇ ◇ ◇ ◇ ◇ ◇

As Maldred felt the mountain shake, he looked up. The walls were cracking, the faces carved in them twisting into weird shapes that no longer looked dwarven. Many feet above, the torch Fiona had lodged in a sconce popped free and disappeared, its light going out.

He grabbed Fiona's hand and raced down the remainder of the steps, wincing as rocks crashed down from the ceiling and struck him.

"Are you all right?" he called to her, not slowing his pace and tugging her to get her to move faster.

"Yes!" She was having a difficult time keeping up with him.

The mountain continued to shake, spitting rocks at them and showering them with dust that filled the air and made them cough.

"Hurry!" Maldred urged. Then suddenly his feet flew out from under him as a step crumbled beneath him. He released her hand, but too late, she was falling down with him. Tumbling down the last fifty feet of stairway, their bodies pummeling each other, the torch flying from Fiona's hand, singeing her tunic and the flesh beneath, then going out amid a shower of stone and dust and plunging them into absolute darkness.

She heard the cry of bats, panicked, perhaps hundreds of them. Then that sound faded and she heard Maldred's breathing. She reached forward with her fingers, exploring, finding rocks, the edge of the stairs, feeling his chest, incredibly broad and muscular but rising and falling quickly. He moved away from her, his feet fumbling and pushing rocks away, then standing and finding a wall to lean against.

"Fiona?" he gasped.

"Here," she answered. She moved some rocks aside that had landed on her, felt her legs to make sure they weren't broken. Then she stood and groped about, connecting her fingers to his. He didn't move away this time. "Are you hurt, Maldred?"

He shook his head, then instantly realized she couldn't see him. "Sore," he answered. "That's all."

"So dark," she said as she groped behind him and felt the wall, searched with her foot and found the bottommost step. "We've got to get out of here somehow."

"Not by climbing up." He pulled her close and felt the gash on her cheek from the troll. It was bleeding again. "That way was sealed with the cave-in."

"Can you see?"

"I can sense it."

"How?"

"I just can, that's all," he said, with a slight edge to his voice.

"Rig and Dhamon!"

Maldred closed his eyes and hummed, shut out her questions and felt the wall behind him, fingers from one hand splayed over it, fingers from the other wrapping around hers to hold her in place. He was performing an enchantment, a simple one as far as he was concerned, but one of great importance to both of them. Within the span of a few heartbeats, he'd sent his senses into the stone, his mind flowing through the rock, up the rubble-strewn steps, through a thick wall of collapsed rock, and into the chamber that wasn't a chamber any longer. It was as if the top of the mountain had broken off and poured down on what was left of Reorx's temple. "No Fetch," he whispered. Then his mind was searching through the rocks, expecting to find the crushed body of the kobold. "Not here. Not here. Not dead."

Fiona was listening to his voice, realizing he had cast some spell, and surprised at his ability to do so. She had thought him merely a brigand. But she wasn't offended by this secret he'd kept, rather she was pleased—as it meant he might find a way out. She wanted to ask him about Rig and Dhamon, but waited, fearing if she interrupted him she could ruin the magic.

"Down this way," he was whispering to himself, his voice almost melodic. His mind flowed through what was left of the other archway, slipped around boulders, caressed the shattered images that had been so painstakingly carved so many centuries ago into walls now forever ruined. "Not as blocked. Light at the bottom." He focused on the torchlight as his senses moved down the passage, noting it was even deeper than the one he and Fiona had taken. There were side passages that had been concealed by the faces and figures on the wall, which were revealed by all the ruptures.

Maldred's mind flowed through a crevice and caught a glimpse of a room beyond. There was a feast hall with a great stone table and stone benches, all carved out of the very mountain and all now unreachable—a great prize destroyed before Donnag could claim it. There was another room, featureless, which he surmised had served as a barracks, with rotted planks of wood and sheets lying about. A third room contained a smaller altar, a miniature replica of the destroyed chamber above, though it lacked the same array of ornate pillars.

Maldred focused again on the light.

"Dhamon," he said finally, sighing. A measure of relief Fiona could not see crept across his face. "He lives. Rikali. Fetch." He paused, his senses trained on the kobold, on his explanation of the troll catching the pillars on fire. And he let out a clipped laugh. "Only Rig truly believes the little liar."

"Rig is alive?"

• Maldred's senses travelled farther, past them and down the last of the steps, to an ironbound door partially blocked by rubble. "They're near a door. Some digging and they can reach it," he continued to himself. He wanted to talk to Dhamon to tell him to pass through that door, there was certainly another way out somewhere behind it. The dwarves who carved this place would not have allowed themselves to be trapped with only one entrance and exit. But his magic couldn't let him break inside Dhamon's thoughts—at least not without actually being face-to-face with him.

So then he pulled his mind back away, leaving Dhamon and Rikali and flowing back through the rock toward himself and Fiona, discovering other hidden chambers as he went, nearly all destroyed. He was bolstered by the fact that his good friend was brave and resourceful. "Dhamon will find a way out," he whispered.

Then he sagged against the wall, let out a deep breath, smiled broadly, and released Fiona's hand. "Dhamon, Rikali, Fetch. They are all right. Rig, too. A little beaten down by the rocks, but their passageway did not suffer so much damage as ours."

"Your magic," Fiona began, her tone indicating she was impressed as well as surprised. "I didn't know that you're a sorcerer, that you could—"

"I am far from a sorcerer, Lady Knight," he said with a chuckle. "I am a thief. Who occasionally dabbles in magic. And I just happened to know a simple enchantment that lets me peer through rock. I've found us a way out. It'll take us a while, but the way looks clear."

Fiona wished she could see him, see anything but this blackness. "How can we get to them?"

She was reaching out with her hands again, and he took both and pulled her face close to his. Despite the rain and the stone dust, the faint trace of sweat, she had a fragrance about her. He inhaled deeply. Then, bending, his lips brushed hers.

"Lady Knight, we can't get to them."

CHAPTER ELEVEN
REFLECTIONS OF TRUTHS

Pigs, but I'm not gonna die here! I won't have it!" Rikali ground her teeth together and squeezed by Dhamon and Rig, nearly stepping on Fetch in the process. "I'm gonna have me a grand house on an island. Far away from here, and no cave-in is gonna stop me." She felt her way down the staircase, careful not to trip over chunks of rocks and collapsed steps. "Wonderful idea this was, lover, comin' down here lookin' at all of the carved dwarves. I've had my fill of dwarves, I have! All I was lookin' for was a few baubles. Haven't gotten much that sparkles lately. Damn little—everythin' considered—from riskin' my pretty little neck in that valley of crystal gettin' gems so you can buy some old sword from Donnag."

Dhamon shot her a withering look. The mariner's eyes narrowed and he studied Dhamon, his expression souring.

"Well, you ain't got nothin' now, lover. Donnag's got all of the gems and that sword too. Donnag's the better thief, I'd say. This is all truly wonderful. Shoulda stayed upstairs and picked the eyes outta those wooden dwarves. Desecrating a temple to a dead god. Pigs to it all! Never thought much of the gods, anyway."

Fetch started to say something, but the half-elf cut him off with snarl. He shrugged his small shoulders and decided keeping quiet was wiser.

"There's a door down here!" Rikali yelled. "But the damn thing's rusted shut."

Dhamon brought the torch down to her, Rig and Fetch following. There wasn't much left of the torch, a half an hour of firelight at best.

"It better lead outta here," Rikali continued to grumble, giving the door a good kick. "Better be a back door at the bottom of this mountain. Huh?" She put her ear to the door and listened, furrowing her brow in concentration. "I hear somethin'. Maybe the wind whistlin' through some trees. By my breath, that's a good sign." Then she was fumbling in her belt, pulling small metal picks from behind her jeweled buckle. "Prefer to use my fingers," she said more to herself than to Dhamon. "But my nails haven't grown back yet. Pigs on my luck. That light, put it down closer. Hey, not so close it burns me!"

Dhamon crouched next to her and watched in fascination as she moved the picks in and out of the rusted lock with a skill he wasn't close to mastering, turning them first one way and then the other, putting her ear to the lock, making clicking sounds with her tongue against her teeth as she finally left two picks in and retrieved a third.

"It's an old lock," she said to explain why it took so long. "Things are rusted inside. Don't want to move."

"Could just break it down," Rig suggested, his eyes on the waning torch.

"Barbarian," Rikali whispered. "No genius to kickin'. No skill and thinkin'." Louder, she said. "I'll have it in a minute, just hold on and . . . there!" With a self-satisfied nod of her head, she pulled the picks out and replaced them in her buckle and wriggled the latch, grinning triumphantly when she heard a soft clacking. She tugged on the door. "Pigs! Probably swelled too much for the frame with all the moisture down here," she decided, as she wrapped both hands around the latch, braced her feet, and pulled again. Dhamon tried to help, but she shouldered him away roughly. "I unlocked it, I'm gonna open it. Be the first one to see inside. You just step back and watch me."

Dhamon did just that, listening to Rig grumble that he could have had it open with a single kick and that she had better hurry because there wasn't much left of the torch. Fetch suggested they pull some of the wood planks out of the door, and he'd be happy to make another torch from them, but everyone ignored him.

"I know I can get it!" she hissed between her teeth. "Just a little more. See, it's comin'. Just a—"

It came open with a roar as water rushed into the stairwell, sweeping Rikali behind the door and pinning her against the wall. Dhamon turned and scrambled up the steps, holding the torch high and staying just beyond the water's reach. Fetch was dumbstruck, barely able to scream, "I can't swim," before the water surged over his head. Only the mariner managed to stay anchored. He braced himself and spread his arms across the stairwell, hands firmly against each wall and slamming his eyes shut. When the wave hit him, he kept from being swept up in it, and when the surge stopped, the water settled down around his thighs and he opened his eyes.

Rikali was sputtering and splashing, jammed between the door and the wall. Rig sloshed down the steps and threw his weight against the door, budging it just enough for the half-elf to slip out. She struggled against him for a moment, then relaxed and gulped in some air. The water came up to her shoulders.

"Suppose I should thank you," she managed.

The mariner felt claws against his back, and he instinctively thrust his hand to his waist for a dagger, stopping just as his fingers closed on the pommel and he realized the source. The kobold had climbed up and wrapped his scaly arms around Rig's neck, coughing up water and cursing in a language the mariner couldn't understand.

"Dhamon!" Rig called.

The faint light from above became brighter—but only a little—as Dhamon climbed down the stairs and joined them, holding high what was left of the torch. His face was impassive, as if their predicament didn't in the least bit concern him. His eyes hinted at other thoughts working furiously and they were fixed on the way ahead. A minute later he was past them, sloshing through the doorway and into the chamber beyond.

"What do you think you're doing?" Fetch hollered at him. "Where're you going?"

"Hey, you stinking kobold!" the mariner cut in. "If you're going to hitch a ride, don't scream in my ear. I'll drown you like a rat so fast you're—"

"Dhamon!" Rikali hissed.

"The way we came down is blocked," Dhamon called back. The light was getting softer as he continued to move away from them. "So forward is our only option."

"Well, I don't like our option," Rikali moaned as she followed him, walking on her tiptoes and letting her arms float out to her sides. "I'm too young to drown, Dhamon Grimwulf!"

Rig swiftly followed, trying to shut out their words and concentrate on the water. His element, whether fresh or salt, he felt it flow about him, pleasantly cool despite the summer, as it was part of an underground stream shielded from the heat by the tons of rock that cocooned it. He concentrated on the flow, determined to discover how the water entered the chamber.

"No other way out," the mariner growled after a few minutes. Softer, he said, "Always figured I'd die by drowning. Just didn't want to die with Dhamon."

Dhamon's torchlight danced spookily against the water's surface and the elaborately carved rock walls. The light touched softly on hundreds of images of dwarves. The dwarves were forging weapons, cooking, mining; a fat couple was dancing around the image of an anvil; a child was stacking rocks. On the ceiling was a tiled image of Reorx, almost identical to the one they'd seen on the floor above. There was a great gash in one of the walls, and Rig gestured to it.

"That has to be where the stream broke through. But it's more like a river now because of all the rain," he said, quickly moving toward it. He bumped into something and pitched forward into the water. He came up sputtering, the kobold on his back complaining shrilly. He felt about beneath the water—a stone bench, a stone table, a few other objects he couldn't readily identify. He forced himself to move slowly, bumping into more things hidden beneath the inky surface, and he sent a shower of water Rikali's way to get her attention. "Over here! And be careful."

For once he cursed all the weapons he'd loaded

himself down with. He'd be swimming with ease now, and not slowly navigating around, if he didn't have the glaive on his back. But he wouldn't allow himself to drop it. "All this damn rain," he said to himself when he finally reached the gash in the wall. "It must have swollen the stream so much that it broke through a thin section of wall. Yep, it's thin here." He broke off a piece of rock.

The half-elf was treading water at his side, for the water had risen and she could only touch bottom with her toes. "Well, that's good to know," she huffed, "we're all gonna drown 'cause of all the rain."

Dhamon had sloshed up behind her. He looked nonplused, his face ever stoic, eyes flitting to his left and right. His breathing was regular, and he moved deliberately, as if he knew where he was going, and was not in the least bit worried about what lay ahead.

The mariner shook his head at Dhamon's apparent lack of concern, took a deep breath and entered the gash, holding onto the rock wall so he wouldn't be swept away. Fetch coughed and tightened his grip on the mariner's neck. The torchlight showed Rig's fingers inching higher on the wall.

"What's he doing, lover?" Rikali had her hand on Dhamon's shoulder. He was helping her to stay above water.

Dhamon didn't answer as she continued to fret and shower him with useless questions. He was watching the mariner's fingers, becoming harder to make out as the torchlight faded. There was a final sputtering, then the flame went out, smothering them in a thick and absolute darkness. Rikali moaned and dug her fingers into his shoulder.

"Lover? I can't see anythin'."

A sloshing and a string of high-pitched curses from Fetch signaled the mariner's return.

"Dhamon?"

"We're here, Rig. What did you find?"

"There's about a foot of air between the stream and the rocks—for the moment anyway. And the water's moving pretty fast. I think it's our best bet. Follow it and pray it spills us out somewhere."

"I don't pray," Rikali whispered.

"You're insane!" Fetch spat at the mariner. "Go in there?"

"And you've a better idea?" Dhamon asked as he dropped the useless torch and felt about with his hands, finding Rig and then the gash in the wall. Rikali continued to hold onto Dhamon, her breath coming in ragged gasps as she worked to keep her chin above the water, all the while muttering about the dark and drowning.

"Yes, I've a better idea!" the kobold squawked. "I can see! A little. Maybe if we stay here, really search this room, we can . . ." The rest of his words were drowned out as the mariner followed Dhamon and Rikali through the gash and into a corridor the stream had cut ages past.

In the darkness, they moved through the water, sometimes swimming awkwardly, Rig struggling the most with the glaive and the kobold on his back. Their heads bumped against outcroppings in the ceiling, bringing curses, and the stream pushed them against jagged spikes protruding from the walls. Dhamon felt something slick brush against his leg, a fish or a snake—he hoped it was nothing worse as he continued feeling his way.

For a few hours they followed the stream as it twisted and turned through the mountain, sometimes cutting back so that they thought they were close to where they started. Eventually its course straightened, and they could hear the water sloshing loudly against the stone, and from time to time they discerned the screech of bats coming from somewhere ahead. Rikali announced that was a good sign, as it meant there was still air in front of them.

"Wrong, Riki," Fetch countered, as he continued to hold firmly to the mariner's neck, his cloak swirling about his legs, which were floating behind him. "It's a very bad sign. It means the bats are trapped. An' so are we."

The half-elf dug her fingers tighter into Dhamon's shoulder as he increased his pace. She felt the warmth of blood around her fingertips. Dhamon didn't complain.

A heartbeat later Dhamon lost his footing as the bottom of the tunnel sloped away and the water deepened. He and the half-elf bumped into Rig.

"What?" the mariner asked.

"The current feels different here," Dhamon said. "Not the depth. Something I can't quite—"

"Yeah," Rig interrupted. "I can feel it, too. The current's splitting. The stronger goes straight ahead, but there's a branch heading to the left, and the water there feels warmer, maybe heated from something farther underground."

"And. . . ." the half-elf cut in. "This means what?"

"We could separate," Dhamon suggested. "Rikali and I will take the left and Fetch and—"

"Bad idea," Rig argued. "We're all tired. It has to be well past midnight by now. Nobody splits up. Follow me." The mariner moved past them, pausing only to peel the kobold off his back and pass him to Dhamon. "Your turn." Then he was awkwardly swimming ahead, shifting the glaive to his hand, and nearly losing it. He shut out the complaints of Fetch and Rikali.

"Wish Fiona was here," Rig whispered as he continued to struggle along. "Hope she's all right." He told himself she was fine, that she and Maldred hadn't dawdled so long, that they hadn't journeyed so deep into the mountain, and that they'd managed to get outside before the cave-in. "She's all right," he reassured himself, adding that he would make sure when he got out of here that Maldred didn't get any cozier with the Solamnic. And he would do his best to help her gain the ransom for her brother. "She has to be all right. I think I'd die without her."

Then a dark thought crossed his mind. Perhaps Maldred had caused the cave-in, and the kobold had lied to cover up his master's deed. The burning troll arm causing the fire above did sound a little farfetched. Eliminating Rig would make it easier for Maldred to win Fiona. His heart beat wildly with that possibility.

The current was moving faster now, the corridor widening. The speed made it easier for the mariner to maneuver with his glaive. Rig guessed they'd covered several miles already when the sound of the rushing water became even louder, the channel narrowed, and the pounding drowned out the chattering of Rikali and the sloshing noise of Dhamon swimming to catch up.

There was only a few inches of air, and the mariner found himself clinging to the ceiling, taking a few deep gulps, and then submerging to swim some more. He hoped Dhamon and the half-elf were close behind and that they hadn't given up and tried to backtrack. Still, he told himself, he wasn't going to lose a precious minute worrying about his companions. Time to put his own skin first and to let the stinking thieves save themselves. Concentrate on getting back to Fiona.

"Awww. . . ." he breathed, as he held on to an out-cropping and let his arm drift out in a sweeping pattern, his nose pressed against the ceiling. His fingers brushed against cloth. "Who am I trying to fool? Dhamon? You all right? Dhamon!"

There was a muffled reply, and they were off again, another hour passing, the mariner guessed, as they followed the stream in the pitch darkness, gulping in air when a pocket presented itself. The water was warming, evidence of something underground, perhaps volcanic heat.

Dhamon was thinking of the dragons: the green who slew his men in the Qualinesti Forest; Skie, who could have killed him and Rig and everyone else at the Window to the Stars; the Black he'd encountered in the swamp and who would have slain him save for the scale on his leg—which at the time had branded him as a servant of the red overlord.

Death didn't frighten him anymore. Everyone died. It was just a matter of when. Drowning would not be so painful. Then his jaw tightened and he scolded himself. Dying would be the easy way out. And there was the sword to consider—he had no desire to let the ogre chieftain keep the sword *and* the gemstones. His musing was interrupted by needlelike claws against his neck—Fetch. The kobold was stretching for air. Rikali's fingers brushed his shoulder, Rig's hand reached out again to make sure they were all nearby.

Then a hint of green intruded.

The kobold started clawing Dhamon's back, jabbering frenziedly and pointing.

"I see it!" Dhamon spat, as he took in a deep breath against the ceiling, dove under, and swam toward the light. Rikali moved past him, feet kicking furiously, knocking Dhamon and almost dislodging the kobold from his back as she went. He saw her outline as they neared the green glow, then he saw her rise. Dhamon kicked faster.

Rikali's hands struck stone. Frightened she'd hit a dead end, she panicked and gulped, drawing water into her lungs. Her hands flailed about, feeling angular stone. Stairs! She pulled herself out of the water, climbing on the steps, gasping, and instantly rolling onto her back to stare up incredulously at a smooth oval rock that formed most of the ceiling of the otherwise rough-hewn chamber. The rock was reflecting the mysterious green light. The underground river continued to rush by her, and she turned to watch it.

"Dhamon. Come on, lover," she breathed. "Come . . . oh!"

Dhamon's head appeared above the surface, in the narrow space between the water and the rocky overhang. Fetch's craggy face craned around Dhamon's neck. The kobold was coughing and spitting as Dhamon gulped in air and hauled himself out. A moment later, the mariner materialized and followed them.

Rikali was yawning. "We could sleep here. I'm so very tired. Just an hour or so, all right, lover?"

"No time for sleep," Dhamon said. But his yawn and his drawn expression hinted at how terribly tired he was, too.

Fetch dropped off Dhamon's back and started wringing out his robe. "Good thing that we found this place, huh? Breathe in that stuffy air! Damn. My hoopak. Lost it in the water." He turned to glare at the river, most of which was obscured by the rocky overhang. "Now how am I gonna get me another one? Sure ain't gonna find a kender in Blöten. Maybe Donnag's got one in his—"

"You might not have to worry about it, Fetch," Dhamon suggested. "If we can't find a way out of here, you won't need a weapon."

While the kobold continued to bemoan his misfortune, loudly mulling the possibility of dying at his spry age, and while Rig speculated that they might want only to take a quick breather here and then continue to follow the river, Dhamon joined Rikali in taking a good look around the chamber. They searched along the closest wall, hoping to find a staircase leading up, or a natural chimney they might climb. They'd heard bats a while ago—but there wasn't a trace of them here, not even guano on the floor.

There were no carvings on the walls, nor on the collapsed columns that at one time likely reached to the glowing rock high above. Dhamon had expected to see more images of dwarves, but everything appeared untouched, except for the pillars, which had been ground smooth. There were no symbols to Reorx. The remains of stone and wooden benches littered the floor, the rotting wood adding to the fusty smell. The only area intact consisted of a raised dais at the back of the chamber, and three black half-moon steps leading up to it. On either side of the steps were black pedestals, atop which perched perfectly round black stones, polished to a mirror finish and eerily reflecting the green light.

Oddly, Dhamon thought, the pedestals and globes looked to be devoid of the stone dust that covered everything else.

The mariner whistled softly. "Now I wonder what all this is about." Forgetting the river and their dire situation for a moment, he padded to the center of the chamber. He stopped halfway, bent, and studied something on the floor. "I bet this isn't part of that dwarven ruins," he mused, his hand stretching out and closing around an object. He brushed the stone dust off, coughed to get Dhamon's attention, and held it up for him to see. It was a skull, human or elven, and a thickly rusted knife with a carved bone handle protruded from the top of it.

"Several more if you want your own souvenir," Rig said. "They all look pretty much like this. Lovely place beneath the mountain." Then he replaced the skull and yawned. "I think we better get out of here."

Rikali slid up to Dhamon and took his hand, interlocking her fingers with his. "I don't see a way out along these walls, and I don't like this place, lover. Shivers dancin' on my back. I want out of here. Place makes me feel . . . creepy. I want to see the sky. And I so very badly want to sleep. Maybe we better go swimmin' again. Follow the river." Much softer, she added, "Please, just get me outta here."

Dhamon tried to extricate his hand, but she only held it tighter. He returned a gentle squeeze, and listened to the kobold persist in his high-pitched frettings about his hoopak and imminent demise. Then he tugged the half-elf forward, not sure why he felt impelled to investigate this place further rather than returning to the river and leaving. But there was a prickly feeling at the back of his neck, an unnerving sensation that might cause other men to flee, but that only made Dhamon determined to discover what was causing it.

A scrabbling sound over the rocks indicated Fetch had finally decided to accompany them. "Still have my old man in my pouch," the kobold announced. "The tobacco's worthless, though." He picked it out and tossed it to the floor, adding to the debris.

"You're worthless," Rikali hissed at the kobold. She shuddered when she glanced down at a dozen skulls, all with protruding daggers. A few were small, kender, or perhaps human children. She hoped not children. Although she didn't care for dwarves, she was certain they wouldn't have done this. Not to children. But who would have been capable? "By my breath, that one had to have been a tiny baby." She paused to stare at a particularly tiny skull. "Who could've done such a thing, and why? Who . . ." She stopped herself. No use asking Dhamon, she decided, he didn't seem in the least bit interested.

Dhamon had stepped away from her, finally extricating his hand, and was climbing the narrow black steps. He glanced only perfunctorily at the pedestals. Standing at the edge of the dais, the green light haloed about him, casting a sickly hue across his skin and making his wet hair look like strands of seaweed. He moved near the center of the dais and stared at the floor. "Odd."

"What is it?" Rikali asked. She edged ahead of Rig, who was also moving toward the dais. "What? Is it valuable?"

Dhamon knelt and stretched out with his hand. Rikali scampered up the steps, settling herself next to Dhamon. Fetch was curious, too. The kobold, still wringing out his robe, arrived close on her heels.

"All right, what is it?" Rig found himself asking. "I don't suppose you've found a way out."

"No," Dhamon replied, pushing himself to his feet. He was still looking down at the dais, the prickly sensation persisting on the back of his neck. "And that's what we need to be looking for, not staring at this all day."

"It's beautiful," Rikali said. "I want to touch it, and. . . ."

"Well, don't touch it," Dhamon sternly reproved her. "We don't know what it is or what it does, if anything. And we don't need to know. You want to live to see the morning? Then we need to get out of here. And I shouldn't've let myself get distracted."

"Beautiful," she repeated, reaching out.

"Don't touch it!" This from the kobold, who was pulling the half-elf's arm back. "Riki, stay away from it."

Rikali started to argue, but there was something about the kobold's uncharacteristically serious expression that checked her. *What is it?* she asked him with a cock of her head.

"It's magic," he answered. "And not necessarily the good kind." The kobold looked over his shoulder at Dhamon, then glanced down at Rig, who was standing at the bottom of the steps. "Supposed to be looked at, not touched. Not ever touched."

Dhamon and the kobold stood staring at it, Rikali stayed on her knees. The only sound in the chamber now was the rushing of the underground river.

"Fine," Dhamon said. "Let's leave it be and move on."

Rig shook his head, running his fingers through his hair. "Aww, I guess I should take a look, first." He moved up the steps and slid between Dhamon and Rikali, extending a hand to help the half-elf up. "I'll be careful. Hmmmm. Interesting."

At the center of the dais was a pool, almost oval in shape. But light, not water, swirled inside it. One moment it was a dark green color to accompany the glow from the ceiling, then it turned sapphire blue, the colors undulating as if they were alive and warring. Sparkling motes of a bright yellow-white appeared, looking like stars captured deep in the pool struggling to breathe. They were all but overwhelmed by the aggressive colors.

"So what is it?" Rikali's curiosity had gotten the

better of her. "I mean, it certainly looks like magic. You got a clue, Fetch? Or are you just tryin' to scare me? Bad magic, hah. You wouldn't know magic, good or bad, if it climbed out of a lamp and—"

"Hush!" The kobold paced around the edge of the pool, until he was standing opposite her. He was watching the yellow lights as they flashed and flickered with a pattern he seemed to comprehend. "This is old," he said in a voice tinged with awe.

"Pigs, I could have told you that, you worthless little rat."

He scratched at a wart on his diminutive palm, narrowing his eyes in concentration. "Not so old as the dwarven stuff, though, I don't think. Or maybe it just wasn't built as well. This here's the only thing left standing."

Rikali sighed. "Think anythin's at the bottom of the pool?" She was stretching out a finger, just to feel its wetness.

"I said, don't touch it! Don't think it would be a good idea. Just listen to me for once. All right?" The kobold edged away from the pool and retreated down the steps, studied the pedestals and murmured to himself in his native tongue. "With knowledge comes death," he whispered in the common tongue. Then he was off babbling in kobold again.

"I hate it when he does that," Rikali told Dhamon. "Wish you'd make him stop that gibberish. Although I can't tell if he's cursing you or reciting some kobold recipe for lizard steaks. It's like trying to listen in on—"

"There's some writing on the pillars," Dhamon interrupted. He'd silently left the dais while she was talking and had moved to stand behind the kobold. "I can't make it out. Didn't see it at first." He leaned over Fetch to get a closer look.

"I can't read," she whispered.

"Well, I can read it," the kobold interjected. "Some of it, anyway. It's magical symbols, mostly."

"And . . ." Rikali waited. "If it's nothin' much interestin' I'm all for headin' into the river again and tryin' to find a way out before it rises and there ain't any air pockets left. Ain't anythin' valuable here that I can see. Shoulda plucked them onyx eyes out of them wooden dwarves when I had the chance. Ain't never going to get them now."

"We need to leave," Dhamon said. He was a few feet away, no longer haloed by the green light. His skin had dried, his hair and clothes were starting to dry, too. His black locks curled gently around the base of his neck. "We've wasted too much time."

The kobold ignored him and climbed the steps again, circled the pool, sat opposite Rig and Rikali and started more of his magical humming. He paused and looked up at them. "I don't have to hum, you know," he informed them. "Just makes the magic easier fer me. I can concentrate better."

"Magic?" Rig let a breath out between his teeth. "The kobold *really* knows magic? He's a sorcerer? A kobold sorcerer? I thought him lighting that pipe was just a trick."

Fetch made a great show of pushing back the sleeves of his robe and twisting the gold ring in his nose. "I'm not familiar with the kind of magic the people who built this placed used," he said officiously. "See those globes? They represent Nuitari, one of the moons of magic that used to be in the night sky. 'Course that was quite a while before I was born, back when magic was something most anybody could pick up—before you had to have some special spark inside of you. Wizards of the Black Robes and such, I think they called 'em. Raistlin. He was one of 'em."

"Ray-za-lin." Rikali echoed. "Never heard of no Ray-za-lin." She was looking back and forth between the kobold and what she could see of the river. Had it risen a little in the past few minutes?

Fetch shook his head sadly. "Don't have a whisper of Raistlin's mastery. Never will. But even though that kind of magic isn't around anymore, I figure I can do this. Or at least try. Be a shame not to try."

"We need to leave." This came firmly from Dhamon. "I intend to get out of here. With the three of you, or alone," he added. "I'm not waiting much longer." Softer, "I can't afford to."

But they weren't listening to him, as Fetch's humming and the mysterious pool continued to hold their attention.

"It represents an eye," the kobold stopped to explain. "Even shaped like one. See? Works like one, too, in principle. At least if I understand what I deciphered on that . . . that . . ."

"Pedestal," Rig supplied.

"Yeah, the pedestal over there. You look through the eye and see things. Whatever it is you want to see. Now be quiet, the both of you, an' let me do some scrying." Then he was off humming again, a fast, off-key melody intercut with bits of gargling. His fingers were waggling in the air, for effect, not out of necessity, but he wanted to put on a good show for Rig and Rikali. He cursed himself for revealing that he didn't need to hum. *Have to remember not to talk about the machinations of spells*, he scolded himself. Then he placed his hands just above the water, fingers splayed, thumbs touching.

He felt the energy in the pool, the swirls of green sending faint waves of heat against his palms, almost relaxing him, making him warm and comfortable and making it difficult for him to keep his eyes open.

The blue swirls made his skin itch, though not as bad as the itch of the callus on his palm, and he concentrated on the latter to keep himself alert.

Concentrating harder than he ever had before, trying to awe his small audience and master what he had decided was a buried treasure of Raistlin and the Black Robes, he focused on the motes of yellow light. Feeling them with his mind, he coaxed them to the surface, as the pedestal had instructed. The kobold wished he would have taken the time to translate both pedestals, but his fear of being trapped here if the river rose unexpectedly demanded haste. Besides, he knew Dhamon didn't have the patience for his magic. When he thought he saw one flash of light rising, he closed his eyes and pictured all of the yellow-white flashes, imagined them all surging above the dark colors and performing their twinkling magic just for him.

Then the sensations against his palms faded to nothing, and the warmth that was threatening to lull him to sleep disappeared, making him feel oddly chilled. And just as he was about to give up on all of this and sink into disappointment, he heard Rikali gasp, and he opened his eyes. The surface of the pool had turned bright yellow, like the sun on a cloudless day. In the very center of it, however, was a conspicuous black spot—the size of one of the globes on the pedestals. He blinked, but the spot didn't change shape or size or go away.

"That's it?" the half-elf finally said. "That's all it does? I thought we were gonna see somethin' excitin'. Like maybe a way out of here. You said we'd see somethin'. Worthless, Fetch."

The kobold grinned, showing his yellowed teeth, and he made a motion with his hands, as though he were stirring the pool, careful not to actually touch it, however. "Well, if that's what you want to see," he tittered. "A way out for you. Indeed, you shall have it, Riki dear."

The black spot in the center started to grow and widen, until it took up most of the surface area. Then it seemed to blink, as if it were a pupil in the middle of an eye that had just closed and opened again. It blinked once more, and an unmistakable image appeared in the center of it, hazy at first, but swiftly taking focus as they watched. It looked like a portrait of the foothills, and rising above those foothills a section of the Kalkhist Mountains. Pouring from the top was a waterfall, one that from the position of the sun and the topmost visible peak looked to be just south of Blöten. The water plunged into a basin in a niche in the hills that in turn fed a river leading into the Black's swamp. The tops of homes could be seen, evidence that a village had been flooded. The sky above was dark gray, and rain continued to fall steadily.

"So you've made a pretty picture, Fetch. Interesting. Hardly what I was hopin' for, though. What's that got to do with gettin' out of here? And what's . . ."

She hushed as a new sound filled the chamber. Water, not the underground river rushing by, but the pounding of the falls—an almost deafening sound. There was a fresh scent with it—air and grass and the hint of flowers.

The eye blinked and the image focused again on the base of the falls.

"There's a cave behind it, the falls," Rikali added, now impressed. "And water's coming out of the cave, too." She looked closer and spotted wood and debris floating in the basin. The remains of another flooded village perhaps.

"Is it this river?" Rig risked a question, gesturing

behind him. "Is that what it's showing? Is this where our river comes out?"

Fetch shrugged. "I asked it for the way out."

"Well, ask it if that's our river," Rig insisted.

The kobold stirred the air with his fingers, concentrated harder, and felt suddenly fatigued, as if the pool was absorbing his energy. But the eye finally blinked and the scene shifted again.

"That's us!" Rikali exclaimed. They looked at a mirror image of the half-elf and the kobold peering into the pool, the river rushing by behind them. Another blink and flowing water filled the orb. Now they could see the underground river, which was lit green by the magic of the chamber. There was a fork, a branch of the river veering crookedly, and an equally wide one that went straight ahead. The magical eye swept along the wide, straight path, then angled down a narrow cutoff. The image blinked, and again the scene with the cave and the waterfall appeared.

"That must be the way out! Fetch, you're wonderful!" She stood and whirled toward Dhamon, pointing at the river. "We take that river until we find a narrow branch to the west. And that will get us out of here."

The mariner kept looking at the pool. "Ask it something else."

The kobold cocked his head. "What?"

"Ask it about Fiona. See if she's all right."

Fetch scowled, but was quick to oblige when the mariner shouted, "Just do it!"

The eye blinked and Fiona came into focus. She was standing on a rocky slope, face tilted up and catching the rain. It was pouring all around her, the sky a dark gray. At her side was Maldred, and Rig growled deep in his throat as he saw this. The big

man was extending his hand to the Solamnic, helping her climb up the side of a mountain, was brushing her injured cheek with his free hand. She didn't
recoil from Maldred's touch. Indeed, she moved
toward him as he lowered his face to hers.

The eye blinked and was black again.

"Well, enough of that," Fetch said awkwardly.
"Mal and the Knight made it out all right. They're
somewhere at the base of the Kalkhists, probably
headed back to Blöten. And it looks like it's headed
toward morning outside. No wonder I'm so tired. I
could sleep for a year."

Dhamon padded slowly toward the river.

"Another question," the mariner's tone was vehe-
ment and demanding.

"What?" the kobold seemed exasperated. "We
know the way out, just gotta feel for it in the dark, so
let's go . . . unless you want to ask if there's some
great treasure nearby." This idea instantly appealed
to Fetch, and he started stirring the image, a big smile
stretched across his face. "Something magical, maybe
a few enchanted trinkets, coins and gems and . . ."

"Treasure," Rikali whispered.

"No," Rig barked. "Shrentak. Ask it about
Shrentak. The Solamnic Knights who are being held
there. Probably in the dungeons, if it has such a
place. It must have such a place. Do it, you little rat!
Ask it about Fiona's brother."

"Aw. . . ." Fetch wriggled his nose in disgust.

"His name's Aven."

Fetch shook his head. But once again he twirled
his fingers. "Maybe there's treasure in Shrentak," he
whispered. His lungs ached a little, as if he'd just
raced a great distance. Indeed, he was tired from the
ordeal of the fire and running down the steps, all
the hours without sleep, plunging into the river and

swimming and finally arriving here. His joints ached terribly, come to think of it, his hips especially, and now his fingers. But, there was this great magical artifact at his command. . . .

"Aha!" The mariner clapped his hands. The image inside the eye displayed a dark interior, catacombs filled with mud and muck and cramped cells. A thick gray-green ooze dripped from the walls and along the ceiling, and lizards scurried down the hallway. The image shifted to a corridor lined with . . .

"Cells!" the mariner practically shouted. "I want to see *inside* the cells!"

Fetch concentrated again—harder. He dipped his index finger below the surface for the briefest of moments, then tugged it back and twirled the air again.

"Amazin'," Rikali gasped. "Fetch, I had no idea you could—"

"There, that's it!" the mariner cried, cutting off the rest of the half-elf's words. One instant he was gazing into the pool, and the next, the image of the dank corridor sprang up around them, transparent and ghostlike. But at the same time it was frighteningly real. It was as though they had been transported into the middle of the rough-hewn hallway, which stretched in both directions as far as they could see. Cell doors lined the hall, doors made of thick, rotting wood laced with heavy rusting bars. They clearly heard slime dripping from the ceiling, saw the ethereal green globs drop to the floor and vanish. There was a stench of urine, so strong it made their eyes water, and the worse smell of death.

Rig took a tentative step forward, then another until he found himself at the entrance of a cell. He peered through the bars, found his face passed right through, a sensation similar to walking through a cobweb. Beyond were a dozen men, all human and so emaciated they looked like skeletons with skin hanging on them. They breathed shallowly, huddled together and squatting in their own waste. Their sunken eyes took him in emotionlessly. One struggled to reach out a hand. Rig fought the bile rising in his throat, then he forced himself to leave and look at the next cell.

Rikali had silently padded up behind him. "Solamnics!" she gasped. Their plate mail was gone, but a few had tabards identifying themselves as members of the Order of the Rose. There was no trace of Knightly pride in their suffering frames, and no hint of defiance on their gaunt faces. They were thoroughly broken. Some had no eyes, just vacant scarred sockets, a few were missing limbs. Nearly all of them were terribly maimed, testaments to burns and torture.

The mariner's body shook with pity and revulsion, and his fists clenched in anger. "Horrible," Rikali whispered. Then she edged away from Rig and closed her eyes.

Rig continued to scan the faces, swallowing hard when he thought he recognized one. "Aven," he stated. Scraps of what was once a Solamnic tabard clung to the man's scrawny frame. His skin was as gray as the stone walls and was laced with boils and thick recent scars. The red hair was long and matted and dotted with the husks of insects, and his heart-shaped face, once full and flawless, was gaunt with hunger. He could have passed for Fiona's twin at one time. Now he was barely identifiable. "Aven," Rig stated louder.

With considerable effort, the man lifted his head and appeared to meet Rig's stare. There was a flicker of recognition in the sad eyes. "Fiona's brother,

Aven," the mariner told Rikali. "Fiona and me, we set our wedding on her birthday so Aven would be there. He was supposed to have leave from the Order then."

The Knight looked like a corpse and moved sluggishly. He stared at them, but even that simple act seemed to take all of his strength and cause unbearable pain.

"Aven, he can see me somehow. Aven. . . ."

All of a sudden, the Solamnic tried to rise, pushing against the floor with his skeletal arms while his feet slipped on the slime-covered stones. Finally, he stood, swaying on scabrous feet and shuffling toward Rig. His mouth opened, as if he wanted to say something, but only a rasping wheeze came out.

The mariner took a step forward. "No!" he shouted as the Solamnic fell to his knees, eyes still fixed on Rig. "Aven, we'll get you out of there," Rig said. He tried to reach for the man, but his hand passed through the apparition. "Hold on and—"

Aven coughed dryly and clutched his chest. He seemed to watch Rig for a moment more, then he fell back and crumpled to the floor. A sigh escaped his lips, and then he stopped breathing.

"By all the vanished gods," Rig said in a hushed voice. He stared at the body for a few minutes. "Aven's dead." Then he pulled back from the door to look at the half-elf. She was peering into another cell, whispering about humans, elves, and kender. Something about a smattering of dwarves.

"I think there's a gnome in there, too," she said to herself. "A little man with a really big nose." Then she stepped back and glanced at Rig and then down the hall, which was an illusion but more than an illusion. Her eyes asked if they should continue their exploration.

Curiosity had gotten the better of Dhamon, and he had entered the corridor, too. He was at the far end, peering into a cell and then moving on, rounding a corner. He was impressed by the magic, able to smell the foulness of this place rather than the mustiness of the cavern he knew he was inside. But everything here seemed so disturbingly . . . palpable.

There was a door, narrower than the others, with a tiny window in the center of it. Dhamon crouched and looked through the opening, coughing because of the strong smell. He didn't notice the man inside, not immediately. There was a jumble of other things competing for Dhamon's attention—wooden bins and chipped crockery stacked high on shelves, alongside metal and bone implements, the use of which he cared not to contemplate. It was obvious this place was used for storage. There were chains hanging on the far wall. Most of them were rusted because of age and all the moisture, but a few were newly forged. From the ceiling more chains hung, along with ropes and barbed whips.

It was when he craned his neck, and discovered his face could pass through the wood, that he saw the man. The man was naked, back to Dhamon, skin covered with massive sores and tangled hair fanned out around his shoulders like a lion's mane. He was sitting upright, almost proudly so, and his bones stood out in appalling clearness, reminding Dhamon of the cadavers the priests in the Knights of Takhisis demonstrated battlefield surgery techniques on. There was a copper bowl filled with scummy water sitting next to him, and a few moldy crusts of bread near it.

Dhamon wondered why the man hadn't used some of the implements in this room to escape. There were certainly sharp enough objects on the shelves to

worry at the wood of the door. But when the man
turned, Dhamon had his answer.

There was an iron collar about his neck, and it was
fastened with a short length of chain to the wall, so
short as not to permit the man to stand. He could not
reach any of the objects that might help to gain him
his freedom. The man was young, Dhamon could tell
from the smoothness of his gaunt face and the dark
blue of his eyes. And he was important.

There was a tattoo on his arm just below his
shoulder, artfully rendered and colorful, depicting
the claw of a blue dragon holding a red banner.
Dhamon wasn't about to go close enough to read the
writing on the banner. He didn't need to; he'd seen
he symbol before. It belonged to a particular Taman
Busuk wealthy military family that had allied themselves with the Dark Knights. So the prisoner was
from money and was from Neraka, was likely connected to the Dark Knights there, if not one of the
Order. Perhaps Sable was ransoming him, and perhaps there was some merit to Fiona's belief that the
dragon would take treasure in exchange for her prisoners—some of them, anyway.

The man's eyes widened and he opened his
mouth, as if he wanted to speak to his visitor.
Dhamon pulled back from the cell and continued on,
not wanting to hear what the apparition had to say.
This vision alone was disturbing enough, no need to
add to the gloom with words.

He rounded another corner, still more cells. How
many people did the dragon keep locked up in her
dungeons? From his quick glances he could tell most
were human, and by their conditions it looked like
they'd been here anywhere from a few hours to several months.

Dhamon had been in dungeons before, when the

Knights of Takhisis kept prisoners for political reasons. He'd ushered his share of prisoners into cells. But never had he been in a prison so deplorable as this vision indicated. The suffering was even almost too much for Dhamon to bear.

"Enough of this," Dhamon said finally, when he spotted a cell where no living prisoners remained. Corpses had been stacked like cord wood along one wall. "It's past time to leave this hellish place." He shook his head, as if to clear it, then strode away from the image and toward the river, which he was certain had risen further.

"No," Rig objected. The mariner had been following Dhamon, staying a few yards back and watching his reaction to the scene. "I want to see more," Rig continued. "Fetch, show me all of Shrentak. I want to know how to get into that damnable dungeon!"

The kobold sighed, his shoulders drooping. He looked to Rikali for support. But for once, she said nothing. She was glancing down the ghostly corridor and toward the river, where Dhamon was standing.

"More, Fetch! Show us a way in!"

"No!" Dhamon spun, returning from the river's edge. He walked back through the prison corridors, which were growing more transparent, striding resolutely up the dais's steps. His face retained its stoic mask, but his eyes had lost their hardness, and his lips twitched. He'd caught a glimpse inside several more cells along the way, and the sight bothered him. However, he wouldn't admit that, even to himself. "The river's rising," he said evenly.

At that warning, the half-elf sprang away from the magical pool and hurried down the steps, brushing by Dhamon. "I don't want to drown," she softly wailed. "I want me a fine house."

The mariner let out a deep breath and swept his

hand to the side. "If this vision is to be believed, and I think it is, Fiona's brother is dead. I have to tell her. If, or when, I see her again."

The kobold started to rise.

"Wait, Fetch!" Dhamon said, an idea forming. He saw Rig's eyes narrow. "One more question."

"I thought you decided we were done with the magic pool," the mariner muttered.

The kobold's shoulders sagged. *I'm tired*, he mouthed. Indeed, he looked spent, and the green light that haloed him made him look shriveled. "I can't," Fetch said in a strained voice. "I just can't."

"Ask it about the rain," Dhamon persisted. "Where is all of this coming from?"

"The sky. The clouds," Rig said. "That's where the rain is coming from. I really don't know you anymore, Dhamon Grimwulf. You're a selfish churl. Look at him. He's exhausted. I pushed him too hard as it was."

"What is causing it to rain?" Dhamon's words were clipped.

The mariner moved to leave, but something stopped him. The Shrentak vision had melted and again the pool showed a black spot on its surface, as Fetch resumed stirring the magic at Dhamon's demand. "The swamp. So what?" Rig grumbled. "The rain's somehow coming from the swamp. But it ain't even raining there, according to that image. So . . ."

"This rain isn't natural, Rig. Can't be. It's rained more in Khur in the past few days than probably the past couple of years. Simply out of morbid curiosity, I want to know what's responsible. The information could be valuable. And this . . ." He waved his hand at the pool. "This apparently is one sure way to find out."

The image focused more sharply on a marshy

glade ringed by a tangle of ancient cypress trees with roots that sank deep into the muck. Lianas flowed from the branches, forming a flowery curtain. Colorful parrots were thick in the trees, and a dawning sun managed to peek through a break in the closest canopy.

"There, ask it about that." Dhamon was pointing at a shimmering, yet shadowy image behind a veil of purple flowers. "There's something hiding there. Ask it if that thing's responsible for the rain. Can't hardly make it out. Might be part of a dragon."

"Dhamon, I can't. So-o-o tired."

"Hurry, Fetch," Dhamon ordered. "I want an answer."

The kobold sighed and summoned just enough energy to stir the air above the pool again, fought to catch his breath and felt his heart flutter in his chest. The shadowy image came into better focus. "A dragon. Hah! Isn't big enough to be a dragon. Why . . . it's a little girl," the kobold said.

The flowers parted, showing a thin waif of five or six with long coppery hair and blue eyes. She was delicate, and dressed in a filmy garment that looked to be made of pale purple and yellow flower petals. There was a slight smile on her unblemished, cherubic face, but it was a sly smile, not a pleasant one. She raised her hands—they were misted in silver-gray—and she made a beckoning motion, as if she had somehow spotted Dhamon and Rig and Fetch in this cave beneath the mountain and was motioning them closer. The scent of flowers became intense, almost suffocating. Then suddenly the image was gone, the black spot was shrinking, swallowed by the bright yellow. A heartbeat later the yellow was fading, becoming sparkling motes forced to the bottom by the oppressive blue and green swirls. The sickening fragrance was gone, too, replaced by the musty smell of the cave.

"Wait, I've another question!" Dhamon practically shouted.

Fetch sagged onto his back. The kobold was shaking, staring at his hands. "I've been robbed," he said in disbelief. "I'm older. That foul device stole years from me! Dhamon!"

The kobold's voice was different, softer, and the words were less distinct. The kobold was different, too. The scraggly hair that clung to his bottom jaw turned white as the companions watched. Then it began fluttering to the floor, like dry pine needles falling from a dead tree.

He opened his mouth, as if to say something again. His eyes were wide with fright and disbelief, and his fingers, which were feeling frantically about his face, were trembling. Fetch's scaly skin was flaking and losing its color, becoming as gray as the stone on which he sat. His eyes had lost their glossiness, the red fading to a dark pink. The kobold gasped, a rattling wheeze escaping his lips, and he glanced between Dhamon and Rig as his chest heaved.

The mariner stared slack-jawed. "Dhamon. . . ."

"I see him, Rig."

"Magic. The little guy mentioned something about the magic exacting a price."

Rikali sucked in her breath. The half-elf had been watching the river, and only now truly noticed that the kobold had changed. "Pigs, what happened to you, Fetch?"

The kobold didn't reply, though he gestured feebly to the pool.

"Well, make it change you back," the half-elf stated. "Wiggle your fingers and make it fix you."

Rig shook his head. "I don't think that's possible."

"Well, maybe it'll wear off."

"I feel . . . " Fetch began in his soft voice. "Cold."

"Dhamon, what are we gonna do about him? Can Grim. . . ." Rikali's words trailed off as she glanced again at the river. "Dhamon, the river really is risin'! We have to hurry. Please, lover! Let's just grab Fetch and get out of here. We'll take him to Grim Kedar's. That old ogre'll fix him up, just like he did you and Mal."

Dhamon glanced at Fetch, his face an unreadable mask, then he turned and hurried toward the water. He tugged his boots free and tucked their tops under his belt in the back. The half-elf followed him, asking what they should do about Fetch and would Dhamon carry him. He didn't answer her, simply grasped Rikali's hand and eased into the water, taking several deep breaths. Rikali clung to the edge for a moment, looking at the dais.

Rig padded closer to the kobold until he was towering over Fetch.

"Shouldn't we wait for them, lover?" she asked.

Dhamon took several more deep breaths and shook his head. "No, the river's rising too fast." His tone was emotionless. "I'm not waiting around for them. It might have been a mistake to wait this long." He dropped below the surface, beginning to swim with the current. Rikali took a last look at Rig and Fetch, then followed after Dhamon, the green light fading as they swam from the chamber and were swallowed by the absolute blackness.

✧ ✧ ✧ ✧ ✧ ✧ ✧

Rig stared at the kobold. Was the green light playing tricks? Simply making the kobold look . . . older? An illusion. Perhaps it was something from the pool, maybe it took the kobold's energy. And, perhaps when the kobold rested he would revert to his more youthful appearance. The mariner wished Palin Majere was here. The sorcerer would know what to do. Though he wondered whether Palin would have toyed with the pool to begin with.

"We have to leave," he said finally, scowling when the creature twitched and wheezed. "You all right? Fetch?"

The kobold shivered and wrapped his arms around his chest. His eyes had faded further. "No, I'm not all right," he hissed. "Damn Black Robe magic. Said there was a price. I paid it all right. A big one."

The mariner seemed genuinely concerned for the creature and took a closer look at him. The usual mix of scales and skin beneath the robe, though the color had changed, still had the stench. But when the kobold looked up to meet his stare, the mariner noticed something else different. It was an illusion or a trick of the green light.

There were wrinkles about his eyes, like an aging human would exhibit, and the hairs that grew in scattered clumps along the sides of his head were a smattering of red and gray, and there weren't as many of them. Rig extended a hand, and the kobold took it, grimacing a little when he got up.

"Ache a lot," Fetch said. His shoulders shook as he turned from the mariner, stuffing his fist in his mouth to choke back a sob. "Stolen," the kobold repeated. "Years."

"What's a few years? Besides, whatever happened, it'll probably just wear off. Just like Dhamon suggested. And there is that pasty-faced ogre in Blöten." Rig adopted a light tone, hoping to get the creature moving. "Grim, right? We'll go see Grim."

He looked at the river. *If I had any sense,* he thought to himself, *I'd leave this little thing right here and swim for it.*

The kobold had squared his diminutive shoulders. "It stole more than just a few years. My arms and legs feel stiff. Hurts to move 'em. Don't see quite so well. Everything's a little fuzzy."

By the blessed memory of Habbakuk, I'm feeling sorry for the little rat, Rig cursed himself. *I'm the one who demanded a couple of questions, so I'm partly to blame. Still, the creature's a thief,* he continued. *A thief and probably a murderer who doesn't deserve any sympathy.*

"We have to go, Fetch," he repeated. The sound of the river seemed louder, and he glanced at it again. It had started to spill out onto the floor of the chamber. There wouldn't be much of an air pocket now.

"Ilbreth," the kobold answered after a moment. His voice was soft and raspy. "My name's Ilbreth. And you're not so bad. For a human."

It's Fiona, the mariner thought. *She's rubbed off on me and made me soft.* Aloud, he said, "C'mon, Ilbreth." He turned and left the dais, kicking at a few rocks and skulls. "I ain't waiting any longer on you," Rig added unnecessarily. But he did wait, and when the kobold didn't join him, he turned and glanced back.

Fetch was lying on the ground, not moving.

CHAPTER TWELVE
RETURN TO BLÖTEN

Dhamon stopped swimming shortly after he
turned to follow the narrow branch-off, which
he'd nearly missed; there was no reason to
put in the effort. The current was so strong he was
like some bit of flotsam being propelled along. He
concentrated on keeping his legs straight and his
arms tucked in close, hoped he didn't brush up
against any sharp rock walls. His head pounded and
his lungs cried out for air, but there was none to be
had—not a single air pocket since he'd gulped his last
breath in the green-lit chamber. There was only this
total darkness and a sound constant and deafening.

He felt himself growing lightheaded, found himself thinking of Feril and the dragons and of the night
at the Window to the Stars. His leg was tingling, had
been since they'd started exploring the old chamber
of the Black Robe sorcerers. It began to radiate its
waves of intense heat and bone-numbing cold just as
he'd asked Fetch to discover the source of rain. And
it became worse just before he left the chamber—

which was the real reason he left Rig and Fetch behind. When the pain took hold of him, he could think of nothing else.

The corridor angled sharply and threw him against a jagged rock. For a brief moment, he thought that drowning here might be a blessing—no more pain. Someone would find a corpse with a souvenir from a dragon overlord affixed to its rotting leg. Then he felt a surge, felt rocks brush his stomach, felt himself sinking, being propelled through a curtain of pummeling water that drove the last of the air from his lungs and pushed him under. His eyes were still open, but all he could see was dark, murky gray. Then the water turned paler, the color of dense fog, and he was borne down deeper. He made out shapes. Odd—a stone home? A covered well? A wagon? All underwater.

Dhamon was forced all the way to the bottom by the powerful water of the falls. He felt his feet touch something solid, and he was able to push himself up, and then he thrashed when he broke the surface. It was all he could do to tread water, the pain was so intense from the scale, threatening to overwhelm him and send him under again. The violent tremors started in his muscles, and he mindlessly drove himself toward the shore, concentrating on a patch of muddy ground, gulping in air, and trying to blot out the possibility of death. He managed to reach the bank and pull himself halfway out of the water when he finally surrendered to exhaustion and the icy-hot pain, and slipped into merciful unconsciousness.

Rikali's head broke the surface just behind him. She greedily swallowed the fresh air. "Pigs, but I thought we were gonna die, lover! Never thought I'd be so grateful to see all of this rain. It's beautiful!" She tread water and breathed deeply, listened to the roaring of the falls behind her and the near-silent patter of the rain. "Dhamon? Where are you, Dhamon?"

Panic gripped her heart when he didn't answer. She furtively glanced about, spotting him on the bank, half in the water. Then she hurriedly swam toward him, pulled herself out, and turned Dhamon over onto his back. She let out a deep breath when she saw his chest rising and falling, and then she busied herself with cleaning the mud off his face. His limbs were quivering.

"It's that damnable scale," she hissed. "Together we'll find a cure for it, lover. Should've asked that pool, made Fetch wiggle his tiny fingers and ask about healing you. About how it could be done. Finding you help is more important than Shrentak and this rain. Why hadn't I thought of that? Am I so selfish I didn't think of that?" Then she was smoothing his hair away from his face, which was tight with pain. She tugged him out of the water, glancing up at the falls and idly wondering about the kobold. "He's worthless, Fetch is. If he had been thinkin', he would've asked the pool about your scale. It's his fault, it is. Not mine. All his fault. He thinks he's so smart. Well, he isn't smart at all. Worthless. But don't you worry, lover. After it stops rainin' and all of this water dries up, we'll go back there to that cave and have another look at the pool. We'll find a cure for that scale. I promise."

She did her best to cradle Dhamon, rocking him and brushing the mud from his tunic. "And when you're all healed we'll find a spot for our grand house. We'll have a dinin' room bigger than the one in Donnag's palace and rooms for little ones that'll grow up handsome and look just like you. And we'll have a garden that goes on forever filled with strawberries and raspberries, and I'll plant grapes, too.

Maybe we'll learn how to make wine. The sweet kind. You'll see, lover, it'll be . . ."

Just then Rig's head broke the surface, the mariner sputtering and gasping, his glaive held firmly in his hand. He took a deep breath, then dove again, surprising Rikali and bringing her to her feet.

"What're you doin'?" The half-elf glanced at Dhamon to make sure he was still breathing, and then padded to the edge of the basin. She stared through the mist and saw the mariner surface again, the kobold cradled against his chest. She waved to get the mariner's attention, then returned to Dhamon. His eyes fluttered open, and she grinned.

"Feelin' all right?" she asked.

Dhamon nodded as he struggled to his feet. He was still sore, but focused on the mariner and the kobold. Rig's face was cut in several places, likely from colliding with sharp rocks underwater, and the kobold's cloak was in tatters. The mariner wiped at the blood as he dragged himself out of the basin, dropped the glaive onto the shore, and gently laid Fetch's body down.

"What's wrong with Fetch?" Rikali took a tentative step toward them.

Rig plopped down next to the kobold's body and stared at the falls.

"Fetch?" she repeated hesitantly, then adopted a scolding tone. "I was wonderin' if you two were gonna make it. All of that playin' with the magical pool. You might have hurried up a little. . . ."

"Ilbreth's dead," Rig said simply.

The half-elf sucked in a breath and stumbled toward the bank, dropping to her knees and gently shaking the kobold's body. "Die on me?" She glanced at Rig, looking for an explanation. "Fetch wouldn't die on me. He just wouldn't."

He continued to watch the falls.

"Poor Fetch," she cooed. She fussed over the body, fighting back tears, then her thin fingers searched, tugging free the gold nose ring she coveted and thrusting it in her pocket. She found a few pearls and an uncut amethyst in a small pouch, the latter no doubt a souvenir from the valley of crystal. These, too, she claimed. Then she jerked free the pouch containing the old man pipe. Rig's hand shot out, surprising her, and his fingers closed around the pouch. The mariner took it from her and solemnly placed the pouch on the kobold's chest.

Dhamon moved to a section of bank several yards away. He waded into the water and began washing the rest of the mud from his clothes and hair, keeping his back to the dead kobold and keeping his shoulders square. His head was thrown back as he looked up into the mountains, the tops of which were obscured by the clouds. He rubbed his arms, trying to work some of the soreness out of them, and turned his neck this way and that.

"Gonna save these pretty baubles to remember poor Fetch by," Rikali said as she joined him and began washing the mud from her clothes and hair. "We'll keep them in the library on a shelf where all of our company can see them when they come to visit."

"You can't read," he said tersely. "What would you possibly want with a library?" He cupped his hand over his eyes to help keep the rain out as he continued to study the nearest cliff face.

"I'm very smart, Dhamon Grimwulf. I could learn to read," she said, tucking the amethyst and pearls into a pouch at her waist, retrieving the nose ring and pushing it on her little finger. She thrust her chin out defiantly. "You could teach me to read."

Dhamon pointed to a narrow trail. Water was running down the trail, and at first he mistook it for a stream. But there was a signpost next to it, and he decided that marked it as a road. "We can follow that back to Blöten. Rig?"

Rig was hunched over beneath a tree, using the blade of his glaive to scoop at the mud and dig a grave for the kobold.

"Now ain't that touchin'?" Rikali noted, glancing at the kobold's body, then at the mariner. "Thought they couldn't stand each other."

Dhamon was studying the trail. "Probably the shortest route, but it doesn't look like the easiest. We could take the long way around, but Maldred's probably well ahead of us, and I want to get back to Donnag's as quickly as possible."

"But Dhamon, I'm so tired," Rikali pleaded. "We been walkin' and swimmin' the whole night. It's so early in the mornin', probably not much past dawn. Can't we sleep for just an hour or two? Ain't slept in more than a day. And find us somethin' to eat. Please. I'm so hungry."

He paused for a moment, considering the idea. Then he shook his head and started off. The half-elf glanced over her shoulder. Rig was still working on the grave. Without a second thought, she hurried to catch up to Dhamon.

Dhamon and Rikali had difficulty climbing the slippery trail. They held onto the signpost and rocks to help them keep their footing. It was slow going, and occasionally the half-elf peered down at Rig, who was still busy.

"First I want to have a little chat with Donnag about this fool's errand he sent us on. Then I want to tell him about the little girl in the vision, the one that perhaps is causing all of this rain. He might know what it's about," Dhamon explained to the half-elf. "Of course, that information is going to cost him."

"Cost him a lot," Rikali said.

"I think it's raining 'cause his last patrol killed some of the Black's spawn. A lot of them, according to that tale he told us at dinner. The rain is some kind of retaliation. I just don't know what precisely the little girl has to do with it."

"Lover, you can't be serious. It was a vision, a magical dream Fetch called up out of that pool. You don't even know if it's real."

"Real? The first vision showed us the way out, didn't it? I'd say that makes it real. Shrentak seemed real enough."

"A girl making it rain? Hah! I bet Fetch was asking it a different question, nothing about rain. That's what brought up the girl. I bet he was thinking about some place nice and warm and dry where he could find some sweet company and . . ."

Dhamon vehemently shook his head. "No. *The girl is the cause*. She's drowned out villages, one at the base of these falls. Knollsbank could well wash away, too. This rain is far from natural."

Rikali cocked her head and furrowed her brows. "Why'd anybody want to make it rain that much? Why'd anyone want to flood out villages of goatherders and farmers? Doesn't make sense."

"It does if you're a black dragon wanting to make your swamp bigger and seeking revenge."

They continued to pick their way up the trail, which in fact had become a widening stream now. They had to periodically grab onto rocks to keep their feet from slipping out from underneath them. Rikali glanced over her shoulder again. Rig was nowhere in sight.

"Besides, it was a little girl, not a black dragon," Rikali continued.

"Dragons are powerful, Riki. The dragon could take the form of a girl, or the girl could be the agent of a dragon."

"A little dragon girl? How do you know so much about dragons, lover? Must come from all that readin' you can do. You should teach me readin'. I thought you were through with dragons, anyway."

Dhamon let out a curt laugh. "I am through with them, Riki dear."

The half-elf beamed and worked to keep up with Dhamon.

"I don't want to have anything more to do with them. But the information about the girl is valuable. I suspect the ogre will pay me a good bit of coin for it—in addition to the sword I want."

Rikali tittered and reached out to grab Dhamon's elbow. But her hands went flying as she stepped on a moss-slick rock and her feet shot out from under her. She landed with a smack in the center of the stream, sending water showering around her. Dhamon whirled to reach for her, but too late. She started to slide with the stream down the mountainside.

Rig had finally finished his task and was coming up from the base of the trail. He rushed and made a grab for Rikali, but only managed to tear her sleeve as she passed by pell-mell. Rig dropped his glaive and dove in after her. A moment later he surfaced and waved to Dhamon.

"Dhamon, you better get down here!" He was wiping blood away from a gash on her cheek. "She's hurt." There was blood on her forehead, too, and running from her nose. She moaned softly, her fingers and lips twitching. The mariner gently opened her lips to look inside her mouth. Two teeth were broken, the remnants of one buried inside her cheek. He tugged it out.

Rig gingerly prodded her ribs. "Nothing broken here. Dhamon!"

Dhamon hadn't moved. He stood a few dozen feet away, up on the mountain, watching them.

Rig continued to shout. "Heard you say something once about treating Knights on a battlefield! How about a little help? She's your girlfriend, after all."

"She only thinks she is," Dhamon said so softly Rig couldn't hear. He waited a moment before sliding down the trail to join Rig. "We don't have time for this . . . delay," he said, his voice heavy with irritation. He knelt over the half-elf and smoothed the hair away from her face. He thought she looked pretty, with her expression serene and her face devoid of the usual heavy makeup. He felt around her neck, turned her head this way and that, his ministrations as gentle as possible.

"She's okay," he told Rig. "Her head hit a rock, see?" He tilted her head slightly, showing the blood that stood out amidst her silver-white locks. "Nothing too serious. She's breathing regularly." He felt around the head wound. "She'll have a good-sized bump when she comes to." Then Dhamon stood up and held his hands to the rain, letting it wash away the blood. "And she will come 'round soon enough. This rain will help." He turned and started back up the mountainside.

"Wait a minute." The words flew angrily from the mariner's mouth. "She's *your* woman. *You're not going to leave her here.*"

"Riki'd understand," Dhamon replied. "I've got to pick up an important package from Chieftain Donnag and sell some valuable news to him. The sooner he learns about the rain, the more it'll be worth. And I've got to find Maldred. He'll want to know about the rain, too. Riki'll catch up with us. She's more resourceful than you think."

Rig stared incredulously. "First Fetch, now Riki. . . ."

Dhamon's face was impassive. His hands hung loosely at his sides, his lips were a thin line. And his eyes were cold.

That image of Dhamon would remain etched in the mariner's mind for the rest of his days, showing him how callous a person was capable of being. Might as well be stone beads—they held no hint of compassion. There was only calculating purpose. Rig saw that. Dhamon's eyes showed cunning and selfishness. There was no trace of the man he'd known in the past, they were not the eyes of the former Dark Knight who'd answered Goldmoon's cry for a champion and who'd intrepidly led them to the Window to the Stars; no shadow of the hero who dared to stand up to the dragon overlords and who, though not gaining Rig's friendship, had most certainly gained his respect.

"Get used to it Rig," said Dhamon, reading his thoughts. "I'm not the man you knew."

Had Dhamon just said those words? the mariner wondered, or was he remembering what Dhamon had said one night in the Kalkhist Mountains? It didn't matter. They were true. Rig was staring at a stranger. The mariner had known thieves in his younger days, and had proudly kept company with pirates—whom he considered a few notches above common thieves. None of them had been like this Dhamon, a Dhamon he really didn't know.

"You're not human," Rig said softly.

Dhamon laughed. Then, without a further word or a gesture, he turned and started climbing the trail again, going a little slower and holding onto rocks so he wouldn't take a spill like the half-elf.

The mariner reached up to his shoulder with one

hand and yanked until one of his sleeves came loose. He wrapped it around the half-elf's head, trying to stop the bleeding. The mariner gazed up at the watery trail, then at the half-elf, scooped his arms under her knees and shoulders and picked her up. "Awww . . . by the blessed memory of Habbakuk!" He saw her left arm hung crookedly, and there was an ugly knob where a bone was trying to break through her skin. "It's broken, I'd guess." He laid her back down, started looking around. "I'll need some wood," he said to himself. "Never set any broken bones before, and I'm not going to start now. Might cause more harm than good. But at least I can keep it from flopping around."

He sloshed over to the partially submerged remains of what appeared to be a house and pulled a board free. "Yeah, something like this will do." Then he took off his shirt and started ripping it into strips to fashion a crude splint. "Damn Dhamon Grimwulf to the bottom layer of the Abyss," he growled.

Rikali moaned softly. Her face contorted in obvious discomfort as she fought her way back to consciousness. The fingers of her good hand fluttered down to touch her stomach. "The babe," she whispered. "Please let my baby be all right."

Rig stared in shock. "You're with child? Does Dhamon know?"

She shook her head. "And you won't tell him." Then she drifted away into unconsciousness again.

The mariner worked to juggle all of his possessions. All his daggers were strapped across his chest, the long sword dangled at his side, the glaive he strapped to his back again. He had to move things around a bit to get comfortable. It was difficult for him to carry everything, and the half-elf too, but somehow he would manage.

Rikali groaned as he shifted her weight in his arms. Rig looked up the mountain. "Guess we'll have to try this trail," he decided. "But we'll take it slow."

◇ ◇ ◇ ◇ ◇ ◇ ◇

Fiona stood rigidly in her Solamnic plate, which she had polished to a mirror finish upon her return from the dwarven catacombs. The job had given her something to do while she waited for Rig and Dhamon, and while Maldred was secreted away in his meeting with Chieftain Donnag.

Her hair was tied uncharacteristically in twin tight braids at the back of her neck. The gash on her cheek had been healed by the ogre shaman—at Maldred's insistence and expense. Her limbs still ached a little from the arduous adventure up the mountain and into the dwarven ruins and then back to Blöten. But her appearance didn't give any hint of her real fatigue.

She squared her corners as she paced in the mud in front of the men Donnag had provided as escort for her ransom. It was just as he'd promised. They were hardy ogres, forty of them, the shortest towering above her at nine feet. All wore bits of armor, mostly boiled leather plates with metal studs scattered in random patterns. Perhaps the designs signified something in the ogre language. A few had chain shirts and leather greaves, and some of the armor pieces looked almost new. Nearly all wore some kind of helmet, and a few sported long cloaks of a thin, dark fabric—made darker by the continuing rain. They stood at attention, shoulders straight and with an impressive posture unlike the stooped appearance exhibited by most of Blöten's residents.

Though she suspected they resented her because she was a human—a female—and above all a Solamnic Knight—she was certain she had their loyalty, as Chieftain Donnag had instructed them to follow her every order unto death if need be. She also suspected they were being paid handsomely, though she did not know if Donnag or Maldred had handled the costs, and she did not care to know.

Only a few of them could speak her tongue, and those who spoke it haltingly also mispronounced half the words. Maldred said all of the men were well-trained fighters who had skirmished with the dwarves of Thoradin, hobgoblins and goblins of Neraka, and the spawn and abominations that encroached into Donnag's foothills from the swamp. Their muscular appearance and thick scars hinted at numerous previous battles.

They were certainly a homely bunch. Most had warts and boils dotting their exposed skin, the rain plastering their scraggly hair to the sides of their heads. Others had teeth protruding upward or downward from their lips. A few were missing pieces of ears. One had an almost cadaverous nose. Their skin ranged from a light tan, the color of sand, to a dark brown, the shade of a walnut tree's bark. There was one trio of brothers, who had skin that was tinged green, which Fiona thought made them look perpetually ill. And there was one whose skin was nearly as white as parchment. Maldred had explained this individual was a burgeoning shaman, schooled a little in the healing arts, and that his presence might be a boon—depending on what swamp denizens crossed their path.

Some of the ogres carried only one weapon, this being a large curved sword that she'd learned was forged here in Blöten and given to those who'd found favor with Donnag. Others were practically as weighted down as Rig—axes strapped to their backs, crossbows meant for human hands hanging from their belts, long knives in sheaths strapped to their legs, spiked clubs clutched in their fists. They'd need all these weapons and more, Fiona thought. They'd need luck and the blessing of the absent gods.

And what did she need? Fiona mused. A good dose of common sense? What was she doing here? Committing one impropriety after another, she admonished herself. Consorting with thieves, who were also likely considered murderers, making a deal with a despicable ogre chieftain, commanding a squad of ogres. She was certain the Solamnic Knighthood wouldn't approve. Deep down, she didn't either. Perhaps they would release her from the Knighthood if they discovered all that she'd done. And her brother? What would Aven think of the lengths she pushed herself to in her effort to ransom him?

"Aven," she whispered. It will be all right, all of this, she told herself, if she could gain his freedom. Time enough to atone for her deeds after her brother was at her side.

Still . . . second thoughts were nagging at her sensibilities. Perhaps she should give up on all of this now.

"Fiona!" Maldred called to her. He was emerging from Donnag's palace and jogging toward her, a smile spread wide across his face. "Dhamon is all right, and is on his way here."

She pushed her concerns to the back of her mind and waited for him. He rested a hand on her shoulder.

"That is good news," she returned, looking up into his clean-shaven face. "I am glad no misfortune befell him in the cave-in." Despite her words, Fiona seemed unruffled by the news. She was making it a point to appear stoic and detached in front of her ogre troops. "And you know this about Dhamon because . . ."

"Remember? I am a thief who dabbles in magic." Maldred's eyes locked onto hers. "Dhamon found a way out of the mountain many miles away from where we came out. He will be at least another day or two in arriving here."

"And Rig?"

Maldred's lips tugged downward. "The mariner is trailing behind him. He is all right, too. Do not concern yourself with him."

"I will not concern myself with him," she echoed softly.

◇ ◇ ◇ ◇ ◇ ◇ ◇

In fact, it was two mornings later, the rain slowing to nearly a drizzle, when Maldred came out of Donnag's palace and approached Fiona in the ogre chieftain's garden. There were no flowers, just a myriad of weeds nurtured by the rains. Most were thorny, with twisting gray-green vines that tried to claw their way up the few statues scattered about or that sent runners across the cobblestone paths. The garden filled a circular courtyard off Donnag's grand dining room, and it scented the air with a mix of pleasant and pungent fragrances.

She had been summoned to meet Maldred here, and he softly touched her cheek to get her attention. "Dhamon was spotted entering the south gate a few hours ago. He is meeting with Chieftain Donnag as we speak."

She stood straight, her eyes wide. "And Rig? Is he with Dhamon?"

Maldred shook his head. "It seems Rikali is injured. The sentry reports that Rig arrived later and took her to Grim Kedar's."

The Solamnic looked a little puzzled that they would not all be together. She pursed her lips, thinking for a moment. "What about the kobold?"

"Dead," said Maldred, rubbing his chin ruefully.

"I must go to Grim Kedar's, then," she said finally. "If Rig is there, I certainly should . . ."

Maldred's eyes flashed. "Why? They will find their way here soon enough."

She cocked her head. "I suppose they will. But I should go to Rig."

"Why?" Maldred moved closer and took her hands. He gazed into her eyes. "Do you love him so terribly much, Lady Knight?"

She returned his look. Fiona knew she could so easily lose herself in Maldred's enigmatic eyes. "I don't know. Months ago I was certain I did. I had no doubts. But now . . . I don't know."

"He doesn't deserve you," Maldred said. "He does not appreciate you, so few of his words are filled with compliments." His sonorous voice had turned melodic. "He is so unlike you."

"Unlike me," she repeated softly, still staring into his eyes, wanting him to talk some more just so she could listen to his mesmerizing voice. Rig used to talk to her at length, when he was first trying to impress and woo her.

"You must not marry him," the big man said. "Your heart belongs to me."

"I will not marry him," she repeated. "My heart belongs to you."

Maldred smiled. Had Fiona not questioned her own feelings toward the mariner, the enchantment would be so much more difficult. But her doubt gave him room to manipulate his magic. He bent close to her, brushed her lips with his.

She stepped into his embrace, tracing his jaw with her fingertips, easing away from him finally, almost reluctantly. He extended his arm and nodded to a canopied wooden bench. They walked there together, slowly.

"I will check on Dhamon. Wait for me here, Lady Knight."

"Of course I will wait for you."

Chapter Thirteen
Donnag's Promise

Dhamon stood at the base of the stairs, looking out on what served, decades past, as the manse's dungeon. He wondered where the current dungeon in Blöten was—where the ogre chieftain locked away those who crossed him or who fell out of his favor. Or perhaps he simply killed all the scoundrels and saved the paltry expense of housing, feeding, and guarding them.

Dhamon was certainly dressed for a dungeon—his clothes filthy and torn from his arduous trek, his hair dirty and matted, the stubble on his face thick and uneven. He stank of sweat, so strongly that he even offended himself, and his boots were thickly caked with muck.

Iron manacles dangled rusted shut from the tall ceiling and dripped with moisture. In a near corner sat a weathered wooden rack, discolored with what Dhamon was sure was blood, and behind a veil of cobwebs was suspended a cage filled with pieces of a human skeleton.

Just beyond the torture implements were massive chests filled to bursting with steel pieces, elegant golden statues, high vases, and coffers spilling strings of pearls into puddles caused by rainwater seepage. The great chamber was illuminated with expensive crystal oil lamps that glimmered between once-exquisite tapestries that had been irreparably damaged by mold.

Weapons hung on one wall, their blades catching the light. Another wall displayed shelves of baubles and trinkets—carved animals with wings and horns and jeweled eyes, precious shell arrangements crafted by Dimernesti artisans, and vials of exotic perfumes, that—though stoppered—still sweetly scented the air.

And there was more. He padded toward the center of the great room.

Inside the former cells, the doors of which had long ago been removed, more wealth could be observed—coins and carved ivory tusks, ornate chests as valuable as whatever was locked up inside them; gem-encrusted busts of minotaurs and other creatures.

"This is our main treasure room, Dhamon Grimwulf," the chieftain said proudly. He stepped out from an alcove, taking Dhamon by surprise. The chieftain had not used the same staircase as Dhamon, suggesting the existence of secret passages. "The rough gemstones you gifted to us are being cut as we speak. Then they will be given a good home here among our rare and esteemed collection, some set into fine pieces of platinum and gold that will adorn our fingers. We so like gems. It gives us much pleasure to look at them. Others will be stored away so we can admire them later—when we tire of what we normally wear."

Dhamon looked away from Donnag to study an

urn that appeared to be made of solid gold.

"And we can never have too much wealth, can we?" This was not truly a question. Donnag came farther into the room, drawing his cloak up around him before stepping over one of the puddles. He strode toward a platinum-edged throne and eased himself down, sighing and yawning and steepling his big, fleshy fingers. From this position, he could better keep an eye on Dhamon and the array of treasure. "Wealth makes rulers more respected, we think. But it makes us more envied."

Dhamon padded toward a case filled with necklaces and rings. He leaned against it nonchalantly. Out of the corner of his eye, he spotted Maldred entering the room. The big man must have used the same hidden staircase as Donnag.

"Take as much as you desire—within reason—for you and your half-elf harlot," the ogre chieftain continued. "We do not mind. Indeed, we wish to be generous to you, who have aided Knollsbank. We so love our milk and goat meat."

Dhamon nodded a greeting to Maldred and selected two gold chains, thick and dotted with emeralds and sapphires. He added a pearl and ruby ring, suitably flamboyant for Rikali's tastes, and a thin jade bracelet that was elegant and cool to his touch, something he would prefer she wear. There was a jade egg, the size of his thumb, sitting on a small wooden base. The egg had a colorful green and orange bird painted on it, with dabs of white to simulate clouds. She might like this, too. He tucked them all in a pocket and made a mental note to ask Maldred just how familiar he was with Donnag and the manse—and how friendly.

"You have an eye for what has value, Dhamon Grimwulf," Donnag observed.

Dhamon was picking through a coffer filled with jewels now, selecting a few and holding each up to the nearest lamp. One ruby that caught his eye was the centerpiece of a hammered gold brooch. After a moment's consideration, he claimed this prize, too.

"There will be more. Much more," Donnag said, "after you return from the swamp. Another small errand for us."

Dhamon laughed long and hard, not stopping even when Donnag's eyes narrowed to slits. "You think I'm going on another *errand* for you, your lordship? You claimed wolves were slaughtering the goats in the mountain villages. And yet, the villagers had informed you about what they believed was the real threat. I don't think I trust you. Your errands are far too deadly."

"We have been very busy," Donnag quickly replied. "And sometimes in our crowded schedule we do not listen closely to messengers from villages. We apologize if we did not communicate the true threat that menaced the village of Knollsbank."

Dhamon selected a dark sapphire cloak clasp, intending to keep this one for himself. "Nor will I join the ogres you're sending with the Solamnic to the ruins of Takar. Believe me, her brother's dead. Rig saw it in a vision inside the mountain. Her trip is a fool's errand."

Donnag's lips formed an exaggerated scowl, looking almost comical with his dangling gold hoops. Then he, too, laughed, the sound echoing oddly off the mounds of riches. "And you think we are sending our men into the swamp at the behest of a woman? To Takar? For her brother, whom we've never met? For a woman? A *human* woman? Pfah! You are most amusing, Dhamon Grimwulf. We should have you in our lofty presence more often.

We have not laughed so hard in a very long time. We like you."

Dhamon pocketed a few small gems, flawless specimens, he believed, and likely more lucrative than all the baubles he'd already claimed. "Then why send the men? And why bother with the Solamnic's ransom?"

Maldred moved closer, his boots crunching softly over scattered coins. Dhamon was preoccupied with inspecting the treasure and did not see the big man and Donnag exchange meaningful glances.

"Why would you—ruler of all of Blöde—stoop to help a Solamnic Knight? Or why pretend to?"

Donnag's gaze left Maldred. He grinned. "Why, Dhamon Grimwulf, the Solamnic Knight is helping us, rather than we helping her. We have been told she is exceptionally able in a fight—as good as any two of my best warriors! And therefore she might prove unwittingly useful to us in the swamp. Besides, we so love the thought of a Solamnic Knight at our beck and call. The treasure we gave her to lure her along is insignificant as far as we are concerned. And it will be returned to us anyway. As for the forty men, they are to help us strike at the Black again. You see, we have a plan . . ."

" . . . which on second thought really doesn't interest me," Dhamon shot back. "Sorry I asked about it." He stood, smoothing his hands on his leggings and glancing around to see what other items might appeal to him. "However, what does interest me is my sword. I'd like it now."

"I'm interested in your plan, Lord Donnag." This from Maldred.

Donnag nodded to the big man, who had moved to stand between two marble sculptures of dancing faeries, his elbow resting on the head of one. "Ogres used to supervise the humans and dwarves at the

Trueheart Mines. Ogres, that at one time, were loyal to us."

Maldred cocked his head.

"The Trueheart Mines. In the swamp. Ogres who have switched their loyalty to the Black are in charge there. Perhaps they crack the whips."

"And what do you intend to do with these traitorous ogres?" Maldred seemed genuinely curious.

"Nothing. We are interested in the ogres' workers. Ogres of our kin have been captured, as we explained before, in vile retaliation for the slaying of many spawn. They are being slaved to death there, and we will not permit that!"

"So you want those ogres freed," Dhamon observed. "That seems like a reasonable goal." Much softer, he said, "That ought to make the rain continue for at least another month or so." From several feet away, he was eyeing the wall of weapons now. "But Fiona thinks your men are going to Takar," Dhamon added.

Donnag didn't reply. His attention was directed to a silver buckler, in which his toothy visage was clearly reflected.

"Ah, Takar and the mines are in the same general direction," Maldred observed. He was idly rubbing his chin. "Lady Knight has never been to either place, and she won't discover the ruse until it's too late. And then she will be forced to help anyway, as she abhors slavery. Yes, I like this plan. I think I will go on this errand for you, Donnag."

"Maldred, Fiona will believe you are helping her," Dhamon said, his voice cautious. "You told her . . . "

". . . that I am a thief," Maldred finished. "It is her fault if she does not understand that I am also a liar. At least she will have an escort into the swamp, and she has gained what she sought—a ransom for her brother—though it will do her no good, and eventually it will be returned to Lord Donnag. And I will have gained what I prefer, a bit more of her charming company. She is truly easy on my eyes."

"So you want to steal her away from Rig," Dhamon whispered. "Like you stole the merchant's wife. And many others. Always the thief, my large friend. I wonder if you'll keep her any longer than you did the others?"

Maldred smiled warmly and gave a shrug of his big shoulders. He paced down a row of chests. "I saw her fight those trolls. A great swordswoman! Indeed, she must have been truly formidable to have helped you at the Window to the Stars. A swordswoman with a fierce heart and fire in her blood! Ah, I do fancy her, Dhamon. Perhaps I will keep her around for a little while."

"And if she shirks off that spell you have cast to win her favor. . . ."

"Then what have I lost? Love is fleeting, after all. Eventually I will let her go anyway, unharmed, in honor of your friendship with her. To you, Dhamon Grimwulf, I have always kept my word. "

"I don't care what you do with her," Dhamon said. "I just want my sword, as promised."

Maldred's face took on a strange expression. "Doesn't it at all bother you, Dhamon, that your Solamnic friend is being so deceived?"

"Former friend." Dhamon edged his way closer to the weapons. "And, no, it doesn't bother me. In fact, I find the whole business amusing." He paused at a coffer brimming with jewels and drew a handful of necklaces from it. He carefully reached behind him and placed them in his satchel, fastened it, and decided he was finished with petty baubles. "The sword, Donnag?"

The ogre chieftain frowned, his attention finally drawn away from his own reflection. "Maldred is going into the swamp at my request. He says you are his friend and partner. We think you should join him. Fight for me, Dhamon Grimwulf, and we will reward you beyond your dreams."

"No thanks. The trolls provided enough exercise. I'm not going along to the mines, or to anywhere else in Sable's domain for that matter." He cast a quick glance at the alcove from which Donnag and Maldred had entered the room. There was no indication of anyone else back there. The three of them were alone.

Donnag raised his hand to object. "But you are a warrior and. . . ."

"The sword. Our deal. Remember? I'm not going to ask again." Dhamon pointed to the wall. "You have the gemstones from the valley. Knollsbank and the other villages are safe from the 'wolves.' Now I want what's mine. My weapon of choice."

"Very well, Dhamon Grimwulf." Donnag gripped the arms of his throne and pushed himself to his feet. "You shall have our very special sword. As promised." The ogre chieftain walked slowly toward the wall of weapons. His face was somber, his eyes fixed ruefully on the weapons, as if he was loath to give away even one and diminish his fine collection.

They were arranged from left to right, shortest blades to longest. The former included daggers, some of which were no longer than a few inches. The latter would have been impossible for Dhamon to use because of their size, though some of the largest and strongest ogres in Blöten might have managed them. More than a hundred daggers and swords in all, and all valuable either because of the workmanship, materials, or because they were richly enchanted from a time when magic was plentiful in the world. There were a few axes in the mix, also ornate, twin glaives, and a dozen dwarven throwing hammers.

Donnag sighed and reached up and carefully took down one long sword just above his head. He pivoted slowly, as if to let the blade dance in the light of the torches, and held it out. "The sword of Tanis Half-Elven."

Dhamon stepped forward and took the blade, his fingers reverently clutching a pommel that was striped with silver, bronze, and blackened steel. The crosspiece was platinum, formed in the shape of muscular arms that ended in talons grasping bright green emeralds. He passed it back and forth between his hands, feeling its perfect balance and noting the exquisite blade etched with dozens of images— wolves running, eagles in flight, great cats crouching, snakes entwining boars, horses rearing.

"A magnificent weapon," Dhamon said appreciatively. He pivoted, moving the blade with him, as if he were fighting an unseen foe. "A work of art."

"It suits you," Donnag said. "A famous sword for a famous swordsman—for Dhamon Grimwulf, who dared to make a stand against the dragon overlords."

Dhamon continued to work with the sword, then relaxed for a brief moment, holding the long sword parallel to his leg. He tightened his grip on the pommel, and then suddenly leapt forward, clearing in a heartbeat the space between himself and the ogre chieftain, and slamming his elbow into the ogre's massive chest.

Surprised and sputtering, Donnag stumbled, his shoulder striking a coffer and tipping it, sending coins and gems clattering across the floor. Dhamon kicked out as hard as he could at Donnag's unarmored stomach. The blow was enough to completely unbalance the ogre, and he fell heavily to his back, knocking over several small sculptures and shattering crystal vases.

Without pause, Dhamon shot forward again, grinding his boot heel into Donnag's stomach and sweeping the blade down to menace the ogre's throat. "Don't move," he hissed, "Or Blöde'll be looking for a new leader." He cast a quick glance to the alcove—no ogres stepped out. "A leader who brings guards into his treasure room."

"What in the layers of the Abyss are you doing?" Maldred shouted. He made a move to approach, but Dhamon warned him back by pressing the tip of the sword in Donnag's throat until it drew a drop of blood.

"Keep back!" Dhamon returned. "This is between Donnag and me."

Even as Dhamon glanced at Maldred to make sure the big thief was staying put, Donnag acted. Using his great size to his advantage, he rolled to the side, dislodging Dhamon. At the same time, his massive hand caught Dhamon's ankle and he pulled, yanking him back into a marble pedestal and momentarily stunning him.

Maldred leapt over a small chest and tried to insert himself between Donnag and Dhamon. "Stop this!" Maldred hollered.

The ogre chieftain brushed by the big man, reached down and grabbed Dhamon's ankle again, hoisting him until he was suspended upside down, his dangling fingers brushing the stone floor.

"We shall kill him for this atrocity! We give him Tanis Half-Elven's sword and he tries to slay us with it! Unbelievable, this is! We shall kill him slowly and painfully!"

Maldred was at his shoulder. "There must be a reason, a fit of madness. He is my friend and . . . "

" . . . he has signed his death warrant!" Donnag ranted. "We shall skin him and leave his flesh for the carrion to feast on. We shall. . . . argh!" The ogre doubled over and dropped Dhamon, who had regained his senses and managed to stab the ogre's calf with the pin of his sapphire cloak clasp.

Dhamon rolled away from the cursing ogre, fumbled about on the floor for the ornate long sword and crouched, ready to meet Donnag's charge. When it didn't come, Dhamon stood up and slowly advanced.

"How dare you, insolent human!" Donnag yelled. His ruddy face was reddened further by anger. "We shall . . . "

" . . . die if you don't give me the real sword of Tanis Half-Elven," Dhamon finished. He darted in and swept the sword at the ogre's legs, slicing through his expensive trousers and drawing blood.

The chieftain howled and retreated. At the same time Maldred rushed in, planting himself firmly in Dhamon's path.

"Get out of my way, Maldred," Dhamon spat each word with emphasis. His eyes were dark, his pupils invisible, his lips were curled in a feral snarl. "I've been deceived for the last time by this pompous, bloated creature!"

Maldred stood pat, ready to intercept his friend. "He leads all of Blöde, my friend. He's powerful. He commands an army, here and scattered in the mountains." The words rushed from the big man's lips. "You can't fight him, Dhamon! Take the sword and run! Flee the city and I'll find you later."

"I'm not running anywhere." With that, Dhamon lunged to his right and Maldred stepped to meet him. Too late, the big man realized Dhamon's move was a feint. Instead, Dhamon spun to his left, feet churning over stone and coins, leg muscles bunching and pushing off.

Dhamon vaulted a long iron box and bowled into Donnag, knocking him back again. The ogre fell heavily to the floor, and lay awkwardly across a mound of steel pieces. Dhamon drove the pommel of the sword against the ogre's face, satisfied when he heard the bones crunch. Donnag moaned as Dhamon continued the onslaught, hammering the pommel down repeatedly and breaking several teeth. Again Dhamon pressed the blade to the ogre's throat, glancing over his shoulder at Maldred.

"Back off, Mal!" Dhamon hissed. Maldred was quick to comply. "I'll separate Donnag's head from his ugly royal shoulders without a second thought." Dhamon's chest was heaving from the exertion, his body slick with sweat. The pommel felt slippery in his grasp, and he pressed the blade down a bit more.

Maldred looked uncertain, glancing between his friend and Donnag. "Dhamon, leave him be. Let's get out of here. He's truly good for Blöde. Kill him and you'll throw this country into one petty war after another. You've got the sword, plenty of gems. I know a hidden way out of the city and—"

"You don't understand, Maldred, I don't have the sword." Dhamon had moved his free hand to Donnag's throat, pressing on his windpipe. The ogre gasped and flailed about with his massive arms. Maldred crept close and looked down over Dhamon's shoulder into the chieftain's rheumy blue eyes.

"Is that true?" the big man asked.

Donnag didn't answer, couldn't as nearly all his air supply had been cut off. But the expression in his eyes served, and Maldred nudged Dhamon. "Get off him." Maldred's words were cold but commanding, and after a moment's pause, Dhamon relented. Still, he kept the long sword aimed at Donnag's thick neck.

The ogre chieftain rubbed his throat and glared at Dhamon, swallowed hard, and then made a move to get up. This time it was Maldred who kept him in place, setting his foot squarely on the chieftain's chest. He spoke to Dhamon. "How do you know that's not Tanis's sword?"

"I know." Dhamon studied the ogre's ugly face. "I know because I know Donnag. He deceived us about Knollsbank's woes, he intends to deceive Fiona. The truth and he are strangers, Maldred. Why would he give me the real sword when he can deceive me with a pretty piece like this?" Dhamon spat at the ogre and tossed the sword away. He drew the broadsword he still carried, the one stolen from the hospital, and waved it in front of Donnag's eyes.

"We have guards," Donnag managed.

"Not down here," Dhamon cut in. "I noticed that you left them all upstairs. Don't trust them down here, do you? Afraid they'll take a bit of your horde? Your fear has made you vulnerable. Your treasure is your weakness, your lordship. Well, you won't have to worry about your precious collection any longer. Dead men can't spend steel. And since you haven't got any heirs, Maldred and I might as well help ourselves to whatever we can carry. Then we will let the guards down here for their turn. Rig and Fiona can take whatever they want, too. And your whole country be damned."

"Wait!" For the first time there was real terror in Donnag's eyes. All of his haughty indignation vanished. His lower lip slightly trembled. "We will give you the real sword. We swear! Let us up, Maldred."

"No." Dhamon waved the blade closer. "Where is it?"

"In . . . it's in that steel box." Donnag's chest heaved in relief as Dhamon backed away, toward the box he had leapt over to reach the ogre.

"Watch him!" Dhamon said to Maldred. Then he was kneeling in front of the box, ramming the tip of the broadsword into the lock—snapping the sword and breaking the lock. Sweaty hands threw back the lid, which clanged loudly against the stone floor.

The sword that lay inside was not held in velvet or resting in a sheath, as befitting a weapon of its status and history. Rather, it was at the bottom of the box, amid silver pieces, leather thongs from which dangled rough gems, small pouches, and other knick-knacks.

Dhamon carefully moved the coins aside and lifted the blade, an eager gleam in his eyes. It was a long sword, the edge etched in an elvish script he couldn't read. Its crosspiece bore the likeness of a falcon's beak. It was not nearly as ornate as any of the other weapons hanging on the dungeon wall, and its workmanship was not as fine as the sword the ogre had tried to pass off to Dhamon. Still, there was something remarkable about it. He held his breath as he stood and slowly swung the weapon in front of him.

"Wyrmsbane," he whispered. Dhamon raised the blade parallel to his face, his dark eyes reflected in the polished steel. Was it his imagination, or did the metal give off a faint light of its own? Perhaps it was the elvish script, a written spell that caused the soft glow.

"Dhamon?" Maldred was at his shoulder.

Dhamon's attention snapped back to Donnag,

who was standing against a pillar, the great leader of Blöde nervously watching them. "I asked you to watch him."

"It's all right," Maldred said. "He'll do nothing against us now." As an afterthought, and much softer, he said, "And I am watching him . . . very closely." The big man nodded to the sword. "Wyrmsbane, you said?"

"One of the names the sword was given."

"And you're sure this is the fabled weapon?" Maldred's eyes darted to the wall of swords, then back to Donnag, who hadn't moved an inch.

Dhamon nodded. "It fits the description the sage gave me."

"The sword of Tanis Half-Elven."

"It's had many owners through the decades. Many names. Most know it as Wyrmsbane, sister sword to Wyrmslayer."

"Wyrmslayer? The blade the elven hero Kith-Kanan wielded in the second Dragon War?"

Another nod. "Wyrmsbane was said to be not as powerful, though it was forged by the same Silvanesti weaponsmiths during that Dragon War. Legend says this blade was given to the kingdom of Thorbardin. And from there it went to Ergoth, where it fell into Tanis Half-Elven's hands. It was said to be buried with him."

"The thief claimed to have robbed Tanis's grave," Donnag croaked.

Dhamon glanced into the steel box and idly wondered if some of the other trinkets also once belonged to the famed hero of Krynn's past. "Redeemer, it was also called," he continued. "What Tanis called it, I believe. Because it was forged to redeem the world from the clutches of dragonkind."

Donnag cleared his throat. "You have what you

want. Now leave, the both of you." There was no power behind the words. It was as if the chieftain was pleading with Dhamon rather than ordering him.

"A test first," Dhamon told Maldred. "Just to be absolutely certain. And just make sure, Maldred, you keep your eyes on Donnag." He went over to what he believed was the very center of the old dungeon and slowly turned to take it all in, though in truth that was impossible, as he could not see into the reaches of all the cells that extended from the chamber. Then he gripped the pommel with both hands and closed his eyes. The other two watched him intently.

❖ ❖ ❖ ❖ ❖ ❖ ❖

" 'Tis a very old blade, this one ye be askin' me about." This from a slight man so bent with age he looked like a crab folded in a shell. Wispy hair, like a spiderweb, clung to the sides of his head, and a thin beard extended from the tip of his chin down to the folds of a drab weather-worn robe. He was hunkered over a table in a dingy tavern in the rough section of Kortal, a town east of the northern Kalkhist Mountains in the territory of the red dragon overlord.

"I'm interested in old weapons, Caladar," Dhamon said as he reached and grabbed the old man's tankard, brought it toward him, and from a jug he'd purchased—the second of the night—refilled it. The old man's hands closed greedily around the tankard and he drank deep, his eyes bobbing shut in pleasure.

"I've not tasted anything quite so sweet in quite a few years," Caladar mused. He carefully set the tankard on the table, his fingers feeling clumsily thick after imbibing so much alcohol. "I haven't been able to afford it."

Dhamon reached beneath the table and glanced around the room. It was very late, and only a few other tables had patrons, who were engrossed in their own drinks and tales. He tugged free a brown leather bag and pushed this across the table toward the old man.

Caladar's right hand shot forward. The speed of his acquisitive gesture surprised Dhamon. "Ye think that by plyin' me with drink and coin I'll tell ye more?"

Dhamon didn't answer. His dark eyes locked onto the old man's pale gray ones.

"Ye'd be right." The sack disappeared in the folds of the robe. "Ye wouldn't've been a decade ago, when I had me more money and more respect, and I had some righteousness about me, too, and a good dose of morals. But I figure now I haven't got me that many more years left, and so I could use the means to enjoy them." He raised the tankard to Dhamon in a toast.

"The sword . . . " Dhamon prompted.

"It be called Redeemer. Be ye lookin' for it 'cause ye need to be redeemed?"

Dhamon shook his head, his eyes never leaving the old man's face.

"It was laid to rest with Tanis Half-Elven—after he was brutally slain. Skewered in the back, according to the story I heard, an ignoble way for a noble man to die. Buried with him, hands placed around the pommel. The story says." Caladar shuddered. "If the gods hadn't abandoned Krynn they would've watched over Tanis's body, wouldn't've let some common thief . . ."

"Shhhh!" Dhamon drew a finger over his lips, as the old man's voice had been rising.

Caladar wrapped both hands around the tankard and shakily raised it to his thin lips. He took several big gulps, then carefully set it back on the table and wiped his lips on his shoulder.

"Old man. . . ."

"Caladar," he corrected. "Caladar, Sage of Kortal."

"Aye, Caladar. This sword . . . "

"Ye should have known me in my younger days. Hah! Even as recent as a decade ago, I was truly a great sage. A wise man people came to see for miles and miles around, askin' advice, hearin' the old tales, learnin' of Krynn's ancient secrets. My mind was so keen that . . ." His words trailed off to note Dhamon's fingers drumming on the pitted tabletop.

Caladar edged the tankard toward the center of the table, and Dhamon refilled it, scowling slightly to note that this second jug was now empty. He motioned for a serving girl and plunked two steel pieces in her palm. *Another,* he motioned. *How could that old man drink so much and still stay alert?* Dhamon himself had finished only two tankards of his own, and felt a little sluggish because of it.

"Redeemer," Caladar stated, eyes smiling as he watched the young woman return with another jug.

"Aye, Redeemer."

"Also called Wyrmsbane." Caladar took another pull from the tankard, and his words faltered. "Elven made and elven enchanted. Elven script along the blade. The significance of that? That'd be your guess?" He shrugged. "Crosspiece in the form of a bird. Odd, considerin' it was supposedly forged to fight dragons and their kin. Ye would think it would have the likeness of a dragon on it. Maybe its maker just favored fowl." He paused and chuckled, leaned back in the chair and scowled when Dhamon glared at him impatiently. "Against scaly folk it is a shockin' thing to behold, Redeemer—or so the tales say. Tanis supposedly slew many draconians with it, the blade inflictin' grievous wounds quickly and with frightenin' accuracy. Scaly folk cannot harm the blade, or so . . ."

" . . . the tales say," Dhamon finished.

The old man nodded. "Not that they couldn't harm the sword's wielder." He giggled, a thin cackling laugh that raised the hackles on Dhamon's neck.

"There's more . . ." Dhamon pressed. He reached for the man's tankard again, but Caladar waved off a refill.

"I intend to take that jug home with me," he stated. "And if I drink me another drop now, I won't be finishin' my tale or findin' me way to bed."

Dhamon softly drummed on the table top and again fixed his eyes on the old man's.

"Yes, there is more. Or so the tales say. Redeemer, though not as strongly enchanted as its sister sword, was magicked with the ability to find things." The thin cackle again. "Perhaps Tanis was a might forgetful and needed the sword to tell him where he put his boots when he took them off at night. But I think not."

Dhamon drummed a little louder.

"Redeemer *can* find things, somehow. Was said to find as many things in a day as there were moons in the sky—which was three when the blade was forged by the Silvanesti. But mind ye it was also said not to function all of the time. Perhaps only when it wanted to. Perhaps it could only find things nearby, within the distance of the magic. Or perhaps it would only work for certain individuals. A legendary sword such as that must surely have some rules of its own. Or maybe it has a will of its own."

Dhamon glanced at the entrance as a few patrons

left, slamming the tavern door shut. The barkeep was cleaning up, getting ready to close. "These things you speak of? Material goods?"

"Wealth?"

Dhamon nodded.

"Probably."

"Intangibles?"

"Like the perfect woman? Like happiness? Hah! I doubt anyone can find happiness with all of these dragons in control. And as for a perfect woman—there is no such thing—human, elven, or any other race for that matter. A *good woman*—now that is another matter. But you look for her with your heart, young man, not some legendary elf-forged artifact." He hunkered even closer to the table, his voice dropping as he rested his chin on the lip of his tankard. "I truly doubt Tanis Half-Elven used the sword to find him riches—or anything else for that matter. Only a thief or a desperate man would so use a fine blade in such a way."

Dhamon eased himself several inches back from the table. "And it's here in town, you say? This Redeemer? What does this grave robber want for it?"

"More than the likes of ye could afford."

"Maybe," Dhamon returned. "But I intend to bargain sharply for it. Where is it? Who is this thief and where can I find him?"

The old man let out a clipped laugh. "And now ye come to the heart of just why I let ye ply me with drink and steel. The sword *was* here. And the thief *was* here. Last week or the week before. The days blur for me, ye know. Me friend Ralf got a look at it, and said it was a beauty—said it was the real thing. No question."

"I don't understand. . . ."

"Word on the street and among the guild was that

the grave robber indeed intended to sell it—and some other trinkets he came by which he stole them from dead folks. But Kortal was only a stopover for him, a place to spend the night and buy some supplies. He wasn't expectin' to sell the sword here in Kortal. Town's too poor. He was headed to Khuri-Khan, a larger city with larger coffers and where the men and the creatures who roam the streets would have a keen desire for such an artifact, and the steel to pay for it. The thief would have gained a likely fortune for it there."

"Would have?"

Caladar yawned and eased himself away from the table. Standing, he held onto the back of his chair for a few moments to steady himself. Then he reached for the jug. "Would have indeed. But ogres are thick in the Kalkhists, and Kortal sits at the edge of the mountains. Ogres found out about the thief and sought him out. And Ralf told me they took him to Blöde—where some high-and-mighty lord was gonna give the little grave robber just the fortune he was lookin' for."

❖ ❖ ❖ ❖ ❖ ❖ ❖

Dhamon focused on the sword, running his fingers over the crosspiece and tracing the bird's head and beak. He expected it to tingle, the pommel or the blade, if it was so richly enchanted as legends claimed. But it felt no different than other swords he had wielded. Metal against his skin. Though he admitted to himself again that it was very keenly balanced.

Perhaps if he could read the elven script. Perhaps Maldred could read it. His big friend always seemed to amaze him. Or maybe . . ."

"Wyrmsbane," he pronounced. "Redeemer."

It wasn't a tingling. He'd held other enchanted weapons that seemed to vibrate slightly in his grip. But there was . . . something. A presence almost, a sense that the sword was aware of him. He concentrated intensely and closed his eyes, shut out Donnag's labored breathing. Dhamon was aware only of the sword now, the metal pommel in his grip, initially cool to the touch, then warming a little.

"Wyrmsbane," he repeated softly.

What do you seek?

His eyes flew open and stared at the blade. Did he hear the words, or were they just in his head? He glanced at Maldred. His friend was keeping an eye on Donnag, occasionally looking Dhamon's way. His face would have registered something if he would have heard the blade speak.

What do you seek?

Dhamon swallowed hard and thought quickly. How to test the sword of Tanis Half-Elven? "Wyrmsbane, what is the most valuable bit of jewelry in this room?" There were certainly plenty to pick from. Maybe that crown in the case, Dhamon mused. "What is most valuable?"

The sword did nothing, communicated no message and formed no picture in his head. Perhaps he'd only imagined it speaking to him. What do you seek? Hah! He was so tired, after all. It was nothing more than a waking dream. He saw Maldred watching him, Donnag, too. There was a look of trepidation on the latter's face—perhaps because he feared Dhamon would get angry if the sword didn't perform some magical trick. If so, Dhamon might slay him in retaliation.

Donnag saw Dhamon studying him, and the chieftain quickly looked away. So that's it, Dhamon thought. This sword isn't the right one either. Sure, it matched the description the old man in Kortal gave him, but it wasn't especially exquisite—like the other enchanted swords he'd seen had been. A copy? That certainly wasn't beyond the ogre. Deceiving others came so easily to Donnag.

I just might slay him, Dhamon thought. Maybe with this forgery. He sighed and took a step forward, still pondering whether to leave the chieftain alive. He intended to keep the sword anyway, if only because it was so well balanced. He needed to search about for a suitable scabbard to fit it. Likely Donnag had plenty of them around here, too, studded with jewels.

He turned toward the wall of weapons, then abruptly stopped moving when his palm grew cool, as if he'd thrust his sword hand in a mountain stream. Then his hand began to move, though not of his own volition. The sword he still grasped was moving it, turning Dhamon toward the far reaches of the treasure room where the light was dim. It began to tug him there—gently. He could have easily resisted, dismissed the sensation as part of him being so tired.

What you seek.

Did he just hear those words? Did Donnag and Maldred, too? Had he imagined them again? A trick of his hunger and fatigue? No matter, he took a step in that direction and then another, the sword leading him as if it was a divining rod.

"Dhamon? What are you doing?" Maldred's voice dripped with curiosity.

"Watch him," Dhamon answered.

The big man pivoted so he could keep an eye on Donnag and Dhamon, though he realized the ogre chieftain didn't really need watching—not at the moment, anyway. He was riveted to the spot watching Dhamon handle the sword.

Dhamon stopped amidst shadows thick and ominous. He stood in an alcove brimming with gilded vases as tall as a man and thin pedestals displaying dainty figurines of elves and sprites. He imagined they would be breathtaking, if there was enough light to make out their features. His hand grew cold and dry, as if the pommel he gripped was ice. It was an odd sensation, as the rest of his body was hot from the oppressive heat of the summer, and he was sweating. The sword seemed to be trying to draw him farther into the small room, and after a few deep breaths, he obliged. He realized the place wasn't an alcove after all, but another cell. His eyes picked through the darkness and spied manacles on the wall, high up and too large to be used on a human, perhaps even too large for an ogre. Had there not been so many valuable trinkets sprinkled here and there, and had there been a proper light source, he might have investigated further out of curiosity.

But the sword was pulling him over to a corner, to a pedestal and a water-damaged black wooden box that rested atop it. Dhamon opened it, running his fingers over the small object inside.

"Beautiful," he said, imagining what it must look like.

"No!" Donnag moaned.

Maldred swung on the ogre chieftain and with a pointed finger kept him from budging. "Dhamon? What is it?"

Dhamon held the sword with one hand as he reached out with the other to grab a gem about the size of a large lemon. The chill dissipated from his hand, and the gentle urging of Wyrmsbane stopped.

He retreated from the alcove and stepped beneath a lantern.

The gem, dangling from a long platinum chain that sparkled like stars, fairly glowed. It was a pale rose in hue, and it was shaped like a teardrop. The light sparkled over its facets.

Donnag made a sound, like a choked sob.

"It's a diamond, isn't it?" Dhamon asked. He headed toward Maldred and Donnag.

The ogre chieftain nodded, a great sadness in his eyes. "The Sorrow of Lahue, it's called. Named for the Woods of Lahue in Lorrinar where it was found. No one knows where it was mined. I came by it—"

"I don't care how you acquired it," Dhamon interrupted.

"Don't take it. Please. Anything else. Whatever you can carry."

"Flawless," Dhamon observed.

"Priceless," Donnag added.

"And now it's mine."

The ogre made another move to object, but a glance from Maldred stopped him.

"Consider it my payment for this information," Dhamon began. "The rain that assaults your kingdom, and all of the Kalkhists, is not natural. It was called down by a being in Sable's swamp—one who wears the guise of a child. I suspect it is all in retaliation for your forces slaying so many spawn. Or maybe it's just the dragon's attempt to enlarge her swamp. The rain has flooded many villages in the foothills. Perhaps it will ultimately wash away Knollsbank."

Donnag paled, the gem forgotten for the moment. "How do you know this?"

"A vision. From deep inside your mountain."

"Then the rain, the child, must be stopped. But how?"

Dhamon shrugged. "I've no clue. And it doesn't concern me. I've no intention of staying in these mountains, so the rain won't be bothering me for much longer anyway. Certainly you have sages under your royal thumb who can provide you with more information. Maybe they can tell you how to preserve your kingdom." He turned to Maldred, tossing him the Sorrow of Lahue.

The big man was quick to catch the impressive gem and thrust it into a pocket.

"Your share in all of this," Dhamon told him. He hefted the long sword. "I have what I was looking for, and I've some shiny knickknacks to amuse Riki. We will meet up again, my good friend. Perhaps in a few months. After you've run Donnag's errand to the mines. And after you've finished playing with the Solamnic."

Maldred nodded. "I'll stay here a bit longer—with Donnag."

Dhamon smiled knowingly. "Thank you, Mal." Then he was taking the rusted stairs two at a time, wanting to quickly put some distance between himself and a very angry Donnag.

The chieftain's ogre guards, who seemed to be aware of much that transpired in town, revealed that Rikali was at Grim Kedar's. He stopped by there briefly and discovered she was sleeping.

Dhamon told Grim not to wake the half-elf, and left a leather pouch for her. It was filled with small baubles from Donnag's treasure room—something shiny to help speed her recovery and to ease any ire she might have because he left her wounded in Rig's company. Of course, he also tossed a valuable trinket Grim's way to pay for Rikali's care. Then Dhamon was moving again.

He found a dead-end alley far from the manse,

dark because of the dense clouds that filled the sky and because of the closeness of the decaying walls that rose on three sides. He stripped and let the pouring rain wash him, cleansing the stink from his skin while at the same time invigorating him. For the better part of an hour he relished the sensation, unseen by the few ogres who shuffled past on the far end of the street. Then he scrubbed his clothes against a wall, beating out the blood and dirt and sweat that had clung to them.

When he was finished, he dressed and stood still for quite some time, concentrating on the rain, breathing deep of the air that smelled much sweeter than the musty atmosphere of Donnag's treasure chamber. Next he tended to his hair, cutting the matted ends with Wyrmsbane. He used a dagger to shave, careful not to cut himself and wanting, for some reason, to look more presentable than he had in some time.

"A scabbard," he remembered, as he peered out of the alley. "Should've looked around at Donnag's, was going to. But I wanted to get out of there too badly." Still, he suspected he could get a scabbard from the weaponsmith he had visited here before his Knollsbank trek. He'd trade his broadsword for it. "And something else suitable to wear." He considered returning to the ogre seamstress, where he had earlier acquired his trousers and boots. Perhaps she had something else that would fit him. But he would wait until the sun was starting to set and he couldn't be so easily spotted. Donnag might seek a little revenge for Dhamon's stunt in the treasure room. Certainly the ruler had eyes and ears throughout the city, and Dhamon intended to be very careful until he could slip out under cover of darkness.

Come to think of it, there was another matter to

address—the one that had brought him to Blöten in pursuit of this very sword. He'd been putting it off, dallying in the rain, fearing the consequences.

Dhamon padded to the back of the alley, finding a crate to sit upon. Gripping the pommel of Wyrmsbane with both hands, and extending the sword forward until its tip rested in a puddle, he closed his eyes and considered how to phrase this unusual request.

"A cure," he stated simply after several minutes had passed. "A solution. An end." Not to the rain, which was still drumming down steadily. "Redeemer, where is the cure for this damnable scale?"

He waited several minutes more, listening to the incessant patter of the rain, feeling the water pelt him, neither pleasant nor unpleasant, simply constant—as if it had been raining forever.

"Nothing." He sighed and swirled the tip of the sword in the puddle, watching as the blade cut through his dark reflection. "What did I expect anyway? The perfect woman. Happiness. Intangibles. A way to escape this hellish curse." He chuckled softly and closed his eyes. "No escape."

What you seek.

Dhamon's eyes flew open and the pommel grew chill in his hands. There, in the puddle, was an image, clouded and indistinct because of the shadows and the overcast sky. He leaned closer, seeing a little clearer. Leaves, tightly packed, the green color intense and so dark it looked almost black.

There was no physical tugging, as there'd been in Donnag's treasure room when he sought out the most valuable trinket. Just leaves and branches, and a colorful parrot nearly hidden by a clump of vines. There was a lizard, too, but it skittered out of his mind's eye, and also insects, as thick as the clouds overhead. He thought he glimpsed a shadow among the leaves, the size and shape of it impossible to discern. Perhaps merely the breeze rustling a limb. The shadow passed by again.

"The swamp. Something in the swamp."

The pommel tingled slightly, perhaps telling him yes, perhaps arguing with him. He wondered briefly if he was hallucinating, so desperately did he want to be free of the scale's pain. But the pommel grew colder still, and the vision persisted for several moments longer.

Afterward, Dhamon sat still, listening to the rain and feeling his heart pound inside his chest. It was beating excitedly, his breath coming raggedly. *A cure*, he told himself. One exists. The sword said so, said there was a way to get rid of this damnable scale or to make it stop hurting.

He laid Wyrmsbane across his legs and bent over it, smoothing the water away from the blade and keeping more from falling on the elvish script. He traced the foreign words with a fingertip, and for a moment he wished Feril was with him—she would be able to read this. But Feril was far away and Rikali couldn't read either the elf or common language. The half-elf wouldn't even recognize her written name.

One more look at the blade, and then he sat straight, back set firmly against the wall. He decided to wait here until the sky darkened to announce sunset. "Then a scabbard and clothes," he repeated to himself. "After that, I'll see if Riki is awake."

And then, he thought, he'd do something about investigating the cure.

A smile tugged at the corner of his mouth. But it quickly vanished and his fingers twitched about the sword as the scale on his leg started to throb again. Gently at first, so gently he tried to deny the sensation.

Then within the passing of a few heartbeats, the pain grew intense and his body feverish. Dhamon's hand hurt terribly, and he realized that he had unintentionally squeezed the blade of his sword and sliced through his skin.

He pulled his left hand back and stared at the cut flesh, blood pouring out over his palm and pantsleg. He cupped the hand to his stomach and rocked back and forth, as the scale began to send waves of agony through his body. His right hand still gripped the pommel, refusing to release the legendary sword, and his mind focused on the weapon in an effort to lessen the pain.

He gulped in the damp air as the tremors started, then he pitched forward into the puddle, his legs jerking and kicking, his head turning this way and that. Water filled his nose and mouth; he was face-first in the puddle now, gagging.

"I'll not die here!" he managed to gasp. Through a curtain of pain, he summoned all of his strength and rolled onto his back, coughing up the rainwater, still clutching Wyrmsbane. Then the shadows of the alley seemed to reach out and engulf him.

Dhamon awoke hours later, lying on his back nearly submerged in the puddle, which had grown bigger because of the persistent storm. It was dark, well past sunset. He forced himself to his feet—awkwardly, then stumbled to a wall and leaned against it. His head was pounding, perhaps the aftermath of the episode, certainly in part because he was so hungry. His stomach growled.

He would eat after he saw to a scabbard, he told himself. And clothes. He would eat his fill, and then he would visit Grim Kedar's again—to tend to his swollen, wounded hand and to see Riki. He would have to be exceedingly careful at the healer's, as

Grim would have been summoned to the manse to mend Donnag's broken cheek and jaw. He would have to trust Grim.

"A scabbard," he repeated, noting that the pommel tingled pleasantly in his uninjured palm, as if agreeing that was a good idea. He had more than enough wealth in his pockets to coax the ogre proprietors into opening their doors to him this late in the evening. "The finest scabbard available."

CHAPTER FOURTEEN
ENTANGLEMENTS

At dawn the ogre mercenaries gathered outside Donnag's palace, standing at attention in the drizzle. The chieftain was with them and impressing upon them their mission, which was to follow the Solamnic Knight to the ruins of Takar. There she would deliver the ransom, and there they were to help her regain her brother or her brother's body, if it came to that.

"Guard her and the baubles as if you were guarding us," Donnag intoned.

Passersby gawked at the assemblage, some murmuring how unusual it was to see Blöten's ruler out at this early hour, others wondering why the ogre force was gathered and why a Solamnic Knight was walking around so freely and why she seemed to claim the chieftain's favor.

Donnag was regally dressed. A long, dark red cloak trimmed with gems and gold brocade dragged in the mud behind him. His posture was stiff and imperious, his stride purposeful. He'd spent the past two days inside his bed chambers, recovering from the injuries Dhamon had inflicted upon him, and he felt *good*. Grim's magic was strong, making him as healthy as he was prior to the incident, perhaps even healthier. But the old healer's magic was not good enough to regrow the few teeth he'd lost in the brawl or to soothe his ire over being bested by a human.

"I'm surprised Donnag lived up to his word, Fiona," the mariner whispered. He nodded toward a wooden chest filled with gems and coins. Donnag had paused in front of the chest. He was eyeing its contents and dropping a few more bits of jewelry inside. The ogre chieftain motioned for the lid to be closed. Two thick leather straps were wrapped around it, and it was fastened to the back of the largest ogre.

"The world gives us surprises," she answered the mariner.

"Maybe. But, you still can't be serious about this." Rig raised his voice slightly, after Donnag was pacing again and was now a good distance away. "I told you I watched your brother die. One week ago to this day. Inside that . . . that . . . mountain. Fetch used this eye-shaped pool left behind by the Black Robes, and he conjured up an image of Shrentak's dungeons." The mariner had spent most of the evening telling the Solamnic about their trip to the ruins and along the underground river, and about the visions Fetch had called forth. "I watched Aven die, Fiona." *And then I watched Fetch die too,* the mariner added silently to himself.

She met his gaze, her eyes bright with determination, though rimmed with the tears she fought to keep in check. "Rig, you don't know that for certain," she said stubbornly, repeating the words she told him last night. "It was a vision. You weren't actually there in Shrentak. He might still be alive."

The mariner shut his eyes and took a deep breath, opened them and noticed that her lip trembled almost imperceptibly. "It was real enough, Fiona. How many times do I have to describe it?"

"And even if it was real," she said, "I want his body back. If he is dead, he deserves a proper Solamnic burial. I'll not have him rotting in the Black's lair. I'll use the ransom to rescue his body."

She drew her shoulders back, thrust out her chin, and forced her tears back. "A very proper burial." She made a move to walk away from Rig. But his hand reached out and gently closed around her arm, and he gently turned her to face him.

"Fiona. . . ." he began.

"You're not going to change my mind." As an afterthought, she added softly, "I'll understand if you don't want to come along."

"Oh, I'm coming with you, all right. I'm not going to leave you and . . ."

She tugged on his shirt, interrupting him, turning her face to the ogres and pointing to one in the center of the front line. "That man has been to the ruins of Takar before. He'll guide us."

He was a barrel-chested ogre in boiled leather. His skin was dark brown and wart-riddled, and his eyes were as gray as the rain clouds overhead.

"His name is Mulok, and he's old, I'm told, for an ogre. He was at the ruins when the Black was just settling down in her swamp."

Rig rolled his head to work a kink out of his neck. He released her arm and lowered his voice. "I could lead us to Takar. Alone. You and I and that chest of gems."

"Neither you nor I have been there, we've directions only. It is fortunate one of Donnag's men has actually been to the ruins."

"But we have reliable directions."

"Having Mulok with us is better, I think." She took a step back. "Maldred has confidence in him. Besides, you 'steer by the stars,' and we haven't seen anything but clouds for quite some time."

"I don't know about this." Rig thrust his thumbs behind his belt, his fingers drumming against the leather. "I don't like it, Fiona. I don't like this plan."

She let out a long breath and steepled her fingers, let the silence settle around them. He was used to the gesture, which she subconsciously practiced when she was upset. After a few moments, she continued, "Rig, the plan is simple, and we've been over it before. The bozak, the old draconian who approached the Solamnic Council, is stationed in Takar. I'll recognize him. The gold collar studded with gems, the scars on his chest. When I saw him . . . well, he was so distinctive that I'll have no trouble picking him out. We find him. We give him the gems. And he releases my brother—or my brother's body. There's enough gems and coins that we should be able to ransom other prisoners as well. The plan will work. It has to."

Rig frowned. "I don't believe you can trust Sable's minion—this old draconian. He might not be waiting for you at Takar. He might have given up waiting. Or he might have been lying to you and the council all along, which is what I suspect. I don't trust or like his *Lordship* Donnag. I certainly don't like Maldred—he admitted to being a thief. And I don't like Dhamon. Not anymore."

"Did you ever?" Her voice had an edge to it. She opened her mouth to say something else, but Maldred's approach drew her attention.

He was dressed in black leather armor, and a dark green cloak hung from his massive shoulders. A two-handed sword stuck out behind his neck. His hair was cropped close to his head, making his face seem even more angular and striking.

Dhamon was at his side, wearing a green leather vest, dark and embellished with an intricate leaf pattern. It was laced across the front, but was open enough to reveal the muscles of his chest. His trousers were short, ending at mid-thigh and made of a tightly woven canvas dyed black. Dhamon was making no attempt to hide the scale on his leg. His cloak was made of an olive-hued reptile hide, thin and supple. His hair had been trimmed a little shorter, just below his jawline, and his face was clean-shaven. A long sword hung from a tooled black leather scabbard, and Dhamon kept one hand on the pommel as he walked. The other hand had a bandage wrapped around it.

"I am glad you changed your mind," Maldred said to Dhamon.

"I haven't . . . exactly." Dhamon had explained to Maldred a few minutes ago about his question to the sword and the vision it gave him of the swamp.

"Nevertheless, I'm glad you're coming with us—even though it was Wyrmsbane that apparently convinced you."

Dhamon shrugged. "I'll come with you for a time."

Maldred glanced at the sword. "Until it gives you more information?"

Dhamon nodded. "The sword hints that I need to journey into the swamp. And I'd rather do that with company. Aye, at least for a time. So I'm swallowing my words. I'll help you with the mines first. And then we'll part company, and I'll pursue my own quest."

Maldred lowered his voice when he caught Rig watching them. "We'll not be parting company, my friend. I am with you to the end. We will find a remedy for that scale that vexes you. So after the mines, with or without the fair Solamnic at my side, I'll follow wherever that sword might lead you."

Dhamon caught the mariner's stare, then pivoted so he faced away from Rig. "We'll discuss this sword and where it might lead later . . . "

"When we're far from Donnag," Maldred finished.

"Aye, I fear he will seek retaliation."

"His lordship will do nothing at all to you," Maldred said. "He'll not raise a hand against you. But he'll likely never make another deal with you."

"That is a certainty on my part."

"In any event, Donnag and I had several long talks over the past two days—while Grim Kedar was summoned on and off to tend to him. About how you had the sword you wanted, and he had his life. About keeping one's word, and the price for deceiving others."

Dhamon raised an eyebrow.

"He deceived me too, my friend. Wolves. Hah!" Maldred grinned slyly. "And if he wants to keep our friendship, leaving you alone is the price."

"He is full of lies." Dhamon's voice was flat. He was watching Donnag out of the corner of his eye. The ogre chieftain was parading in front of his mercenaries again.

Maldred softly chuckled. "Well, here's one lie you'll find amusing. He told Grim he tumbled down the stairs in his manse and broke his jaw. And Donnag told his guards the same tale." Maldred reached up and fingered a platinum chain that hung about his neck and extended under his leather tunic. There was a bulge on his chest, where the Sorrow of Lahue was nested. "It wouldn't do for the ruler of all of Blöde to admit to being tromped by a lowly human."

"Still," Dhamon began, "I'll feel better away from here."

Maldred slapped his friend on the back. "And what of Rikali?"

"She's still mending at Grim's. The injuries she suffered from the fall were evidently worse than I thought. She'll be there another few days."

"And does she know you're not waiting, that you're leaving with us?"

Dhamon nodded. "Aye. And she's not too happy about it."

Maldred's expression clouded. "Does she know you're not coming back?"

Dhamon knew from a brief conversation with Rig that the half-elf had drifted in and out of consciousness on her return trip to Blöten and wasn't aware Dhamon had left her behind. Rig hadn't told her, apparently considering the whole matter none of his business. Dhamon visited with her late last night at the ogre healer's, and told her he would see her when they returned to Blöten from their trip into the swamp.

"No," he answered. "She doesn't know. And at least I don't have to worry about her following us. She hates the notion of slogging through a swamp."

"To the bottom layer of the Abyss with you, Dhamon Grimwulf," Rig whispered. The mariner had crept close enough to hear the last bit of their conversation.

◇ ◇ ◇ ◇ ◇ ◇ ◇

The swamp closed about them. It was muggy, hot, and stifling, and though what little they could see of the sky was notably overcast, it was devoid of the rain that was continuing to batter the mountains. Fiona struggled to stay in step with the ogres. Her Solamnic armor made her miserable. Still, she refused to remove it. Not even Maldred could convince her.

Their lungs felt saturated with the heady fragrance of lianas mingled with the fetid odor of stagnant pools. Hundreds of eyes watched them—snakes that dripped like vines from cypress branches, bright red and yellow parrots that flitted down from high above to pass just above their heads before disappearing again in the foliage.

Green became their world—vines, leaves, moss, ferns, even the green scum resting on the pools of water. The huge trees formed a vast canopy, and on the rare days when the sun poked through the clouds in the afternoon, only diffuse rays made their way down to the boggy forest floor. Sometimes the ogre mercenaries resorted to torches, as the swamp was so close and dark it seemed perpetually night. Dhamon wondered how anything managed to grow here. Dragon magic, he decided.

Lizards darted out from under their feet. Something in the brush moved to the side of the ogre column, unseen but obviously paralleling their course. A great black cat lounged on a low-hanging branch, yellow eyes trained on them, giving a yawn. There were noises that hinted at other watchers. The chitter of monkeys, the snarl and snap of an alligator, the mournful cry of an unfamiliar creature that sounded uncomfortably close. There were a few tracks of massive creatures with webbed feet. The ogres talked about hunting giant crocodiles come evening, wanting to supplement the rations Donnag had provided with fresh meat.

A mist hung above the ground everywhere. This,

too, was green and was birthed by the summer's heat
evaporating some of the swamp's moisture. It put
Dhamon on his guard, as he suspected it could hide
all manner of things. The swamp took on an almost
haunted appearance, the mist a chorus of pale green
ghosts they had to walk through.

Dhamon spent the first few days trailing behind
the ogres, who were forging their path through the
foliage. He queried the sword each day, asking it
again about a cure. Sometimes he received nothing.
And sometimes he gained more visions of the
swamp, mirror images of what he first pictured in
that Blöten alley.

Fiona was at the head of the column. She was
paying far more attention to Maldred than to Rig,
who sometimes drifted back to walk with Dhamon,
though they did not speak. Often Rig stayed toward
the center of the column, where he could keep an eye
on the Solamnic Knight, and take occasional glances
over his shoulder to watch Dhamon.

Dhamon mused that the mariner had become
practically invisible—or forgotten, as no one paid
him any heed. Dhamon was pleased Rig was leaving
him alone. He preferred to keep to himself, talking
only when Fiona or Maldred wandered back to check
on him, or when one of the ogres tried to engage him
in a game of chance.

The morning of the fifth day brought them to a
river. The insects were thick around the water, which
at its deepest point was up to Dhamon's armpits. But
the insects didn't seem to bother the ogres—or the
alligators and crocodiles that lounged in profusion
along the banks. Dhamon suspected it was only the
number in their entourage, and the size of the ogres,
that kept the swamp denizens from making a meal of
them.

Later that morning, Rig drifted back to walk with Dhamon again. The two men didn't acknowledge each other, though they slogged over the marshy ground practically shoulder to shoulder. When the shadows became so thick they knew the sun had set, the column slowed, and the ogres began to set up their camp. Rig moved forward to find Fiona. The Solamnic Knight was deep in conversation with Maldred, so the mariner drifted away, becoming invisible again.

Dhamon distanced himself from the camp, careful to keep it in sight, however. Stabbing the end of his torch into the ground, he crouched in front of a stagnant pool, drew Wyrmsbane, and stirred the water with the sword's tip. "A cure," he whispered. "A remedy for this scale."

He was concentrating fiercely, hunkered in front of the pool until his leg muscles stung from being forced into this position for so long. There was no tingling from the sword, no image, no chilling pommel. Nothing. "A cure," he repeated.

Dhamon recalled that the old Sage of Kortal said the sword did not function all the time, that it had a will of its own. And indeed it hadn't responded to him every day. So Dhamon refused to give up hope of finding what he wanted. He held his position a few minutes longer and focused all of his thoughts on the sword and the scale on his thigh. "A cure."

Nothing.

He let out a deep breath, the air whistling out softly between clenched teeth. He would try again in the morning, before they were on the move again. He would return to Maldred and . . . the pommel grew cool in his hands. It was a welcome sensation, cutting the heat of the swamp and causing his heart to leap. He stirred the water and again focused all of his thoughts on the scale on his leg and on finding relief from it. A moment later he saw an image in the pool.

It was a green vision again, thick leaves and vines, lizards and birds moving in and out of view, swamp flowers and massive ferns. Again, there was no tugging to tell him which direction to proceed, and no sun or moon visible in the pool to help point the way. But this time there was more. Through a slight gap in the leaves, Dhamon made out stone—bricks or a statue, he couldn't tell. But it was something made by man, smooth and worked. When he concentrated on that, the pommel tingled.

He mentally begged it to show him more, but the vision dissolved. He rested back on his haunches and sheathed the sword. Maybe he would wait to try again when they reached the mines. Perhaps it would give him more distinct images if he gave the magic a rest.

Dhamon returned to camp, settling himself several yards away from the mariner—on the only solid patch of ground that hadn't been staked out by the ogres. He saw Rig watching him. The mariner had rested his glaive against the trunk of a massive shaggybark. Dhamon mused that Rig seemed to collect the weapons he discarded. The mariner wouldn't be getting this sword, as Dhamon knew he wouldn't be discarding Wyrmsbane while he lived.

Then Dhamon leaned his back against the tree, a gnarled root prodding discomfitingly into his leg, and he closed his eyes and futilely attempted to sleep. The sounds bothered him too much, festering in his mind. The cries of hidden birds and great cats, the movement of leaves in the lowermost canopy. More than that—the conversations of the ogres bothered him. He wished he could understand them better and could pick out more than a few words here and there.

He couldn't bring himself to trust them, as they were mercenaries of Donnag. He wanted to know exactly what they were talking about, and he wanted Maldred to share his concern about their loyalty.

He heard the squishing of footfalls and opened his eyes. The ogre called Mulok was approaching. Dhamon considered waving him away, preferring to be alone. But the big ogre carried a large skin of spirits with him, and so Dhamon gestured Mulok closer.

Dhamon noted that Rig was still watching him. Fiona was several yards away. She was softly illuminated in the light of a tall torch stuck into the ground. She gave Dhamon an occasional glance, but most of her attention was conferred on Maldred. She was standing close to the big man, and his hand had enfolded hers.

Mulok took a long pull from the skin and passed it to Dhamon. The ogre knew a smattering of the common tongue, and tried to engage Dhamon in a conversation about a large boar he had spied earlier in the day and tried unsuccessfully to catch. Dhamon listened politely and took several long swallows of the alcohol. It was slightly bitter, but not at all unpleasant. He found it heady, and after one more swallow passed it back and nodded his thanks.

Mulok dug in his pocket for painted stones, elements of a simple game the ogres enjoyed. Dhamon reluctantly agreed to play, and was fishing about in his pocket for a few copper coins when the howl of an ogre cut across the camp. Dhamon jumped to his feet and drew his sword. Mulok dropped the stones and reached for his club.

With only two tall torches burning, there was little light—just enough to make the clearing the ogres had made by tromping around seem truly spooky. The ogres had been milling around, flattening the last of the saw grass, their dark shapes difficult to discern because of the tall, thick foliage that ringed the clearing. Dhamon moved toward the nearest torch—to where he'd last spotted Fiona. Mulok was tromping behind him.

But before he took more than a dozen steps, Dhamon felt himself being lifted, snakes dropping from the canopy and wrapping around his arms and chest and hoisting him skyward. The air was filled with the hissing of hundreds of snakes.

Within the passing of a heartbeat, Dhamon's left arm was pinned. But his sword arm remained free. With it he slashed out at more snakes dropping down on him and seeking to entwine him further. His frenzied swings managed to stop any more from slithering closer, at least for the moment. Keeping his eye on other snakes he saw massing above, he wielded Wyrmsbane against the serpents that already had a firm hold on him, swiftly cutting himself free and dropping in a crouch to the soft ground below.

Dhamon suspected only a few minutes had passed. And in that time several of the ogres in the company were being hauled, struggling and cursing, into the lower canopy. Maldred was among them. The big man's arms were lashed to his sides, and one snake was wrapped around his legs, holding his limbs tightly. Maldred was trying with all his considerable strength to extend his arms and break his bonds. But the snakes were resilient, defying his attempts and twisting ever tighter. They cut into the exposed flesh on his arms and drew blood.

On the ground, Dhamon was barely managing to elude more of the dropping snakes. He crouched as one tried to whip about his chest. He swung Wyrmsbane at a thick constrictor that was dropping toward him, striking it, but only managing to bat it away. Veins knotting like cords in his arms and neck, he swung a second time, slicing through the constrictor and releasing a spray of gray-green blood.

In a matter of moments, he had cleaved several snakes in two and was standing on a severed section that continued to writhe. In the scant light of the torch he could see the mouth that snapped open to reveal rows of needle-fine barbs. Odd. He looked closer. Not teeth, exactly. There was something else unusual about the dead and dying snakes that lay around him.

They looked more like vines, like the lianas that hung everywhere in the swamp. He dropped beneath a hissing serpent, and his hand shot out to feel one of the dead snakes. They felt like vines, too, devoid of scales. "What are these beasts?" he said to himself. Then he was shaking off his curiosity, rising and slashing at another approaching serpent.

"Dhamon!" Maldred called from above. He was hidden in the lower canopy, but Dhamon could hear him thrashing. "Some help here!"

More ogres were caught and disappeared aloft. Others were swinging swords and clubs at snakes that continued to drop from the canopy and lash about for more victims. The snakes made a hissing that grew in intensity, the sound virtually blotting out the shouts of the ogres.

Fiona sliced through an especially thick snake twisting toward Dhamon. He saw her and nodded, then dropped to his stomach when he felt the brush of a serpent against his back. He rolled and slashed upward, cutting off the head of another one. With his free hand, he reached up and grabbed another snake that had dropped to entwine him. Holding his magical blade between his teeth, he climbed up this last snake as if it were a contorting rope.

"Dhamon!" Fiona called to him. "I can't see Maldred!" She had cleaved through at least a dozen of the creatures and parts of them were wriggling and snapping on the ground. The torchlight revealed that her silver mail was spattered with dark green slime. Her face grim and eyes wide. "He must be above with the others. Dhamon!"

Dhamon couldn't reply, the blade in his mouth as he continued to climb. He stopped about twenty feet above the ground. Hanging on tight with one hand, his feet clamped about the constrictor to keep it from jostling him too much, he swung out with his sword wildly, cutting through a black snake hurtling toward him. He sliced through it easily, slamming his eyes shut as the blood sprayed him. Acidic, it burned his skin, and he almost fell off in surprise. He could see a few other black snakes among the green majority. They were wrapped around ogres, biting at their faces and hands. After a few moments of struggling, the ogres hung limply in their coils. Dhamon called a warning to the ogres fighting on the ground to beware the dark snakes. But the hissing of all the snakes had grown so unbearably loud that the ogres weren't able to hear him.

He climbed higher still, marveling at the length of these snakes. He was more than fifty feet off the ground, and the snakes were longer yet—Dhamon couldn't see the end of the one he was climbing.

"Maldred!" Dhamon screamed his friend's name. "Maldred!"

He tried to blot out the hissing as the snakes continued to lower themselves through the canopy to the ground. He thought he heard his friend's familiar deep voice coming from somewhere above him. He climbed higher, then paused again, when the snake he was clinging to began to thrash wildly, threatening to dislodge him. He stretched across to à thick branch, releasing the snake he'd been climbing, then with a quick motion he sliced through the snake. The thing fell to the ground, and he swung about and continued up the tree, disappearing amid the broad leaves of the lowermost canopy.

Far below, the cagey ogre named Mulok had put his back to a cypress tree and was swinging an axe in front of him like a scythe. With his other hand he was jabbing his sword above his head, keeping additional snakes from dropping on him.

Fiona darted about, continuing to wreak havoc among the creatures. Only one had managed to wrap around her, but she killed it before it could lift her. Her Solamnic plate was helpful—the only good thing about wearing it into this swamp. The snakes found it difficult to get a hold on the metal. They slid off and became easy marks for her swordsmanship.

The ogres quickly noticed her success, watching her as they battled their own snakes. They instantly developed a respect for this human woman whom they previously only tolerated.

Suddenly there was a crashing overhead, twigs snapping. The body of one of the green-skinned ogres dropped like a boulder, the impact spraying marshy water around on the ground. The nearest ogres howled in anger. Their fellow was clearly dead, his mottled skin a mass of bites and wounds.

Another fell, and Fiona shouted orders to the dazed ogres, hoping some could understand her. One did, the white-skinned shaman Maldred introduced her to. She couldn't recall his name, but she waved to him. He interrupted a spell he was in the midst of casting, and shouted in the ogre tongue in an effort to translate her words for his fellows. A moment later the ogres had regrouped alongside the Solamnic Knight in the center of the clearing, backs together and blades flashing in the meager torch-light. The ground was covered with the severed pieces of snakes, still writhing and snapping, some finding boots to bite, others being crushed beneath heels.

"Maldred!" Dhamon continued to howl from high above. He had managed to climb out on a sturdy branch between canopies, which were draped with snakes. As he made his way toward the trunk, he sliced through a number of them. Other snakes hung from higher branches, and he side-stepped these and occasionally hurled one down as he went. "Maldred!"

"Here! I'm up here, Dhamon!" The deep voice was muffled, but clear enough.

"Keep talking so I can find you!"

Another voice intruded, which Dhamon recog-nized—Rig's. The mariner also had been captured and carried aloft by the serpents. He seemed to be close by. The moonlight that filtered down through the higher canopies showed the dark-skinned man trussed up against the trunk of an adjacent tree. Four thick snakes had wrapped around him, while a fifth was snapping at his face. Dhamon sliced through another snake as he started toward the mariner, then decided against it and turned instead toward the sound of Maldred's voice. Like a skilled tightrope walker, Dhamon balanced on another branch, leapt to one extending from a massive elm, and edged along, grabbing at the snakes that hung down and using them to help keep his footing. He paused twice to pluck the sword from his mouth and slay a pair of offending black snakes, grimacing when the acidic blood stung his skin.

Maldred was nearly twenty feet above him, tied with snakes to a thick branch. All around him the foliage of the cypress moved, alive with the creatures that were as long as a hundred feet. Dhamon climbed hand over hand up a thin, ropelike snake, slaying it when he'd reached the next branch. Then he sidled in toward the trunk, dodging another pair of black vipers. He used the sword to help him climb, the blade sinking into the wood as he made his way up to Maldred. The snakes were thicker here, sheathing the big man. Dhamon fought his way through a curtain of thin green snakes, then nearly toppled from his lofty perch when he felt one slip down the back of his vest. His free hand groped for the offending snake while the creature bit at his flesh. Finally feeling the snake with his fingers, he tugged the creature out of his vest, flinging it away. He cut through a few more serpents before he reached Maldred. The big man's face was dotted with bite marks, his cheeks badly swollen.

Dhamon started hacking through the snakes as if he were sawing through rope. Green and black blood sprayed him, and he stopped only to bat away a thin one that dropped down and tried to wrap itself around his neck.

"Nearly there," he told Maldred. A large green snake dropped down and clamped its teeth into his exposed thigh. Dhamon jammed the pommel of the sword down hard on the creature's head, stunning it. "Just a few more and I'll have your arms free."

"And that will be a third time you've saved my life, my friend," the big thief managed to gasp. "I'll owe you. . . ."

"Nothing," Dhamon finished. "You helped me gain Wyrmsbane. There. Almost through just a little . . ." Dhamon stiffened. He felt something tightening painfully around his waist. "A little more," he gasped, as he bent to finish the task.

He hadn't quite cut all the way through the snakes that imprisoned his friend when Maldred finished the job by flexing his muscles and tearing the last one from his body. Gasping, the big man's hand shot forward, fingers closing on the constrictor wrapped around Dhamon's waist and squeezing hard. He crushed the creature, ooze seeping out to stain his massive hand.

"It has no bones," Maldred said, as he brushed the dead creatures away and shakily balanced on the branch. "Sorcery was at work, my friend, and I would love to study this if the circumstances were different. Someone of considerable power has animated the vines."

"Aye," Dhamon agreed, motioning toward other branches where ogres were held. "And that someone is making a mess of Donnag's army."

They hurriedly made their way from branch to branch. Staying together, they kept the snakes off each other while liberating the remaining ogres. Those freed in turn worked to release their brethren, the ogres having a much harder time of maneuvering their large bodies on the branches.

Far below, Fiona continued to command the ogres to shift their circle, never staying in the same spot for more than a few moments. No more had been grabbed since she had maneuvered them into a circle formation. The white-skinned ogre stood in the center, weaving his hands in the air. The air shimmered around his fingertips. Then the shimmering spread outward to resemble a cloud of fireflies. The lights danced yellow and pale orange and swarmed around the snakes that continued to drop from the canopy. As the lights grew brighter, the snakes stopped writhing. After several moments, they hung, unmoving, appearing to be nothing more than flower-covered vines amid dissipating lights.

The Solamnic Knight directed the ogres to shift the circle again to accommodate the magical reach of the shaman. Soon they were beneath another myriad of writhing snakes, and again the ogre's fingers began to flutter.

High above, Rig peered through the shadows and watched Dhamon free Maldred and then several ogres. The mariner continued to struggle against the tightening serpents that had pinned him to the shaggy-bark trunk. His cheeks stung, and he felt the blood running down his face. "Stinking snakes," he spat, as one darted in to snap at his nose. "To the Abyss with Dhamon Grimwulf and all these snakes." He realized Dhamon wouldn't be helping him soon, if ever, and that if he didn't do something quickly to free himself, he'd die. It was getting very difficult to breathe. He nearly managed to escape twice, but each time more snakes came to take the place of those he had cast off.

It seemed hopeless, but Rig concentrated—not on his own situation but instead on the romance budding between Fiona and Maldred. "Won't let him have her," he managed to gasp, as another serpent dropped down threateningly. Opening his mouth wide, his teeth clamped down on the black snake, and he bit hard until it stopped moving. Rig gagged when the acidic gore filled his mouth. He spat it out and continued struggling. "Won't leave her alone with him and Dhamon Grimwulf. Won't, can't. . . . Finally!" he cried, as he slipped a hand free. His fingers immediately fumbled about his waist, closing on one of his numerous dagger pommels, and tugging the blade out. "You're carrion now, you slimy serpents," he hissed, as he viciously slashed through one snake and then another, and then two or three more, heaving the ropelike bodies away as far as he could.

After several minutes, he cut off the last one and sagged against the trunk to catch his breath. He spat repeatedly, trying to get the taste of blood out of his mouth. Then he fumbled at his waist for a waterskin and poured its entire contents down his throat. That seemed to help a little, but his tongue still burned. His dark eyes scanned the leaves above, alert for more snakes.

Spotting three descending on him, he leapt to another branch. The starlight spilled down here, from a gap in the uppermost canopy right above him. Rig glanced up, grateful for even a glimpse of the sky. It had been quite some time since he'd seen the stars. Fiona was right, he used them to "steer by," always had—steering each ship he was on to some new port of call. The mariner contended that he could never get lost, not so long as there were stars to guide him. He felt better, seeing them, felt like he was in the company of old friends—ones who wouldn't change and become thieves and who wouldn't stare wide-eyed at men named Maldred.

"Waitaminute," he hushed. The mariner actually *looked* at the stars now, not just admired them. Rig climbed a little higher, oblivious to the sounds of battle below. He could see more of the sky from his improved vantage-point, studied a few of the constellations. They were different before the Chaos War—he'd seen plenty of star charts from the time when three moons hung in the sky to know that. And he was acquainted with a grizzled old caravel captain who sailed under those constellations.

But these were the ones he grew up with and had come to consider his friends. He raised a hand, tracing the outline of a dragon's wing. He wanted to study the sky a bit longer, but a loud hiss sent him scampering to the branch below. It was like climbing around the rigging of a ship, not especially difficult to him, though he'd been away from the sea for several months. Too many, he thought.

Below the mariner, Dhamon was cutting his way through a veil of descending serpents and making his way to a low branch. Dhamon leapt to the ground, the marsh absorbing his weight and sending a shower of malodorous water spraying in all directions.

Dhamon heard the hissing again, louder echoing off the thick trees, heard Fiona snapping orders, heard an ogre growl a series of garbled words in response, heard Maldred jump to the ground.

Fiona was nearby, and Dhamon and Maldred made their way toward her voice, lashing out at serpent-vines as they went. It seemed like forever before they were back in the clearing the ogres had made. Maldred was quick to join the circle of ogres the Solamnic was expertly directing. Dhamon stayed back, eyes darting about for more snakes, slashing at the ones descending on him.

Dhamon wrinkled his nose, deciding that the blood smelled worse than the healing balm they'd put on him in the hospital in Ironspike. He wouldn't have minded the rain now, to wash some of the odor away. So many serpent-vines had been slain that he was practically tripping on them, and the stench was growing. He gagged as he concentrated on sweeping Wyrmsbane at the serpent-vines that continued to drop, though in decreasing numbers now. There were fewer snakes here simply because he and the ogres had already hacked through most of the vines that had been ensorcelled.

He ignored Maldred's plea for him to join the circle. He certainly didn't want to fight shoulder-to-shoulder with ogres that were swinging so wildly with their weapons that they were liable to hit him in the process. Besides, here, away from the throng of ogres, he could concentrate on keeping himself safe, not having to worry about protecting anyone around him.

There was a thick curtain of snakes at the edge of the camp, where none of the ogres had been fighting, and Dhamon made his way toward it, slicing through a few black serpent-vines as he went. He was careful as he approached, their hissing drowning out the sounds of the ogres in the circle, which was well behind him now.

"What magic birthed you?" he muttered, as he came at the curtain from one end, slicing through several serpents with one swing. "What could have possibly caused all of you to . . . argh!" A serpent-vine had dropped behind him, needle teeth sinking into his shoulder. The snake started wrapping its body around Dhamon's neck, forcing him to drop Wyrmsbane. His hands shot up to his throat, tugging at the coils. Then suddenly the snake went limp, and he could easily unwrap it.

"Don't bother to thank me." It was the mariner. Rig had made it down from the canopy and slew the snake.

Dhamon quickly retrieved Wyrmsbane, and without a word he went back-to-back with the mariner as they worked their way along the curtain of serpents, eventually slaying all of them.

More than an hour after the assault began, the last vine was dispatched, and Rig gulped down the contents of another waterskin, still trying to get the taste of the blood out of his mouth. He retrieved the long sword he'd dropped, while Dhamon kicked small piles of serpent-vines, making sure they were all dead.

Nine ogres had died, either to venomous bites or falls from the canopy. A tenth remained missing. Fiona considered the fellow lost and decided no one should climb into the canopy to look for him. Then there might be two men missing.

"Our numbers have been cut by a fourth," Maldred announced.

"By someone who doesn't want us here," Dhamon added.

"Obviously," Rig muttered.

Murmurs of "Sable" rippled through the pack of remaining ogres, that one word distinguishable in their otherwise guttural language.

Dhamon turned to Mulok and spat out a series of simple words in ogrish, pointing at the corpses. Then he regarded Maldred. "Maybe the Black, like some of the ogres say, but I don't think so. More likely one of her minions. If it had been Sable, we'd all be dead." *And if it had been her or another dragon*, Dhamon thought to himself, *I would have sensed it. The scale would have told me.* Like it did when the dragon flew over the Vale of Chaos, and like it warned him of the big green in the Qualinesti Forest. "I would have known," he said aloud.

Rig was rubbing the blood off his cheeks, gently pressing at the bite wounds and tugging free his last waterskin, upending it over his face and knowing he could refill it in a nearby stream. The wounds stung, and several felt swollen and tender. Maldred seemed to have fared just as badly, but was doing nothing to tend to his injuries. The ogres were taking good care of themselves, using their water, some spreading the sap from roots they were digging up. Rig considered trying that, too, then decided better of it. Perhaps such ministrations were why they were covered with boils and warts and overall looked as ugly as they did. Dhamon seemed to have suffered only a few bites, and he blotted at these with a scrap of cloth soaked in alcohol.

Satisfied there was nothing else he could do for his wounds, the mariner began searching around the base of the shaggybark where he'd propped the glaive. He was certain he had found the right tree, as he recognized knobby roots that looked like giant spider legs. Yes, this was the right tree.

"Where?" he whispered. "Where is my weapon?" He knelt and felt the ground, found the impression the haft of the glaive had made. It was too dark to see any details, the tree was so far from the torches. "We'll see," he said, rising and striding toward Fiona. He stopped a few yards short of her, tugging a torch free and carrying it back to the shaggybark, unaware that she was following him and that Dhamon and Maldred were watching. The mariner stuck the torch in a solid patch of ground and knelt again.

"What are you looking for?" she asked him.

"My glaive. Sat it here when I tried to sleep. Before the snakes came. This is the right tree. It was right here. See?" He stabbed his finger at the impression. "Then the snakes came and. . . ."

"Maldred says they were enchanted. Not really snakes at all. Simply vines brought to life through a spell. He knows because he dabbles in magic."

"Well, he's just full of surprises, ain't he?" Rig's fingers were prodding at the ground. "Anyway, it must be a powerful spell to bring all of those slimy creatures after us. Something that would've been out of Feril's realm."

"Dhamon thinks—"

"Yeah, I know, maybe a minion of the black dragon. Or Sable herself. I got ears. But I don't think so. Dragons leave bigger tracks. And besides, I don't care what Dhamon thinks."

"He didn't say a dragon, he said a—"

Rig dismissed her words with a beckoning wave of his hand. He found a footprint, a small one, no longer than his open hand. Then another and another, narrow and childlike. He pointed to them. They led off into a bog.

She crept closer and examined them herself. "Maybe an elf," she said. "Maldred!"

Rig scowled when he heard the big thief sloshing over. Maldred knelt next to Rig, and Dhamon padded a few feet away, examining more of the small footprints.

"Fiona is right," Maldred said. "It could be an elf. There used to be plenty of elves in these woods before the Black moved in and turned everything into a swamp."

Rig moved away from Maldred and Fiona, edged closer to the bog, which spread to the west as far as he could see in the torchlight. "Damn. Took my glaive, some faerie or little elf, maybe whatever made it rain snakes. Maybe it rained snakes so the little demon could make off with my weapon. My very magical weapon. Better have your ogre friends look around the camp and see if anything else is missing. See if they can spot my glaive."

He tested the ground at the edge of the bog, his boot sinking deep.

"You're not going after the weapon," Fiona stated. "It's too dangerous."

It might not be too dangerous if you came with me, he mused. He almost said it aloud, but he didn't need to. She must have picked up on what he was thinking.

"If the circumstances were different," she began, "if we weren't going to Takar to ransom my brother, we'd all go with you and help you find the glaive. But a weapon isn't worth . . ."

A wave of his hand dismissed the rest of her words. A frown was etched deep in the mariner's face. He treasured weapons, had ever since he was a youth and stole aboard a ship to escape an unfortunate home life. The glaive he'd been toting around was remarkably enchanted, and he prized it above all the others he had strapped to him. An artifact, Palin Majere had called it, from a very long ago time. It had been given to Dhamon Grimwulf by a bronze dragon, discarded after Dhamon had nearly killed his friends with it—including the mariner. Rig was quick to snatch it up. It parted metal like it was parchment.

"Took my glaive," he repeated. "Now how am I gonna get it back?"

Dhamon persisted in examining the footprints as he listened to the mariner continue to grumble. For a brief moment he considered asking Wyrmsbane where the glaive was. But he quickly discarded the notion, not wanting to do any favors for the mariner. He would save the magic of Tanis's sword for his own questions, which might, tomorrow morning, involve these small footprints that troubled him.

"Too dark," Dhamon said, finally giving up on the footprints. He rejoined the ogres, seeking out Mulok and sharing some more of the bitter drink, then he began examining the ogre corpses.

Fiona backed away from the shaggybark and Rig, and instructed her charges, via Maldred, to search through the dead ogres' belongings. "Just in case other things are missing," she said. "Make sure they gather any rations they find."

Mulok and the other ogres busied themselves stacking their dead comrades around the base of a cypress tree. It wasn't practical to bury them here, or to burn them. Maldred said they'd be left for carrion—after they were first stripped of any weapons and armor that could be used.

Rig noticed Dhamon pluck a large silver ring off the hand of one corpse and stuff it in his pocket. He watched him take a silver bracer off the arm of another and slip it in his pouch, then move on, pretending to be interested in the lianas. The mariner was disgusted, shaking his head and wishing ardently that he'd never crossed paths with Dhamon Grimwulf, and that the Solamnic Knights had agreed to this ransom. They could've done it for Fiona, who had dedicated her life to the Order. It would have saved Fiona and him time—weeks. They wouldn't have had to struggle across the length of the Kalkhists following Dhamon and Maldred, and they wouldn't have gone to the village of goatherders on an errand for the arrogant ogre chieftain.

And they might have gotten to the old bozak draconian in Takar in time. Fiona's brother might have lived.

"If the dragon was to be trusted about accepting a ransom," Rig grumbled. "If the draconian was in Takar. If. If. If." He growled from deep in his throat. He wanted desperately to go after his glaive. But if the person—or creature—who took it was responsible for all the snakes, he suspected he'd be throwing his life away. And he wanted to go to Shrentak, a notion he'd allowed himself to become obsessed with, and rescue all the people held there. "Shrentak," he hissed.

The mariner spotted Dhamon and Maldred conferring by one of the torches. Clenching and unclenching his fists, he made his way toward them. Fiona was nearby. Good, he thought, she'd get an earful of what he had to say.

"The chest." Fiona was pacing in a tight circle as she talked. Her hands were shaking, her shoulders uncharacteristically rounded. "Something took the chest. With the gems and coins. The ransom for my brother!"

"For your brother's body," Rig corrected her.

Her eyes were fire when she stopped inches from the mariner. Her lips were moving wordlessly. The mariner knew what she was thinking. If they hadn't wasted time trying to collect a ransom with Dhamon and his overlarge friend—if the Solamnic Council had simply given her the coins she needed—her brother might still be alive. Maybe.

"It wouldn't have mattered," the mariner told her, though he didn't completely believe that. "Ransom or no, that dragon wasn't going to let him or any of those other Knights free. It was probably all a sick game. So we're walking through this damned swamp for nothing. This whole expedition is pointless, Fiona. How many times do I have to tell you that I saw your brother die?"

She started to say something, but he cut her off.

"So you want his body for a proper burial. That's admirable. But so far this has cost the lives of ten ogres. And my glaive. And now the chest with all the loot is gone, too. No ransom. No body. We're not where we're supposed to be. Let's just go home. We can honor your brother by—"

"You can't say that," Fiona countered desperately.

"You can't say this is all pointless. Maldred had sent scouts ahead—before the snakes came. They'll find the ruins of Takar and . . ."

Dhamon nodded. He had silently padded up on the two, listening intently to their conversation. "Maldred sent two good scouts." He gestured to the south. "They should be back soon, if we're as close to the place as Mal thinks."

"I think we're practically right on top of it." This from Maldred, who was still looking about to make sure no more snakes were descending.

"On top of what?" Rig boomed. "Certainly not Takar. We're too far south from the ruins of Takar. So where'n the layers of the Abyss are you taking us, Maldred?"

The big man offered Rig a look of puzzlement.

"You heard me. Where're you and this Mulok fellow leading us?"

"To Takar, as we agreed."

"Like hell." The mariner took a few steps back, so he could regard Dhamon, Maldred, and Fiona. He set his clenched hands against his waist, shoulders defiantly thrown back, lip curled up in a sneer. "We're nowhere near Takar. Not at all where we're supposed to be. And you know it, Dhamon."

"Rig?" Fiona moved closer, though she positioned herself so she was between Maldred and Dhamon.

Three against one, the mariner thought. "I got a good look at the stars when I was snake bait. I can read the stars, you know, steer by them. I used to make a living by them. We're south and east of Blöten. And, yes, the ruins are in that direction. But we're too far to the south, and we're not east enough."

"Is that true?" A look of suspicion crossed the Solamnic's face. She glanced up at Maldred.

"Impressive," the big man stated. He thoughtfully rubbed his chin and met the mariner's glare.

"So tell me, Maldred, Dhamon," Rig persisted, "just where are we going, and why?"

Chapter Fifteen
Trueheart and
Battered Spirits

A noise in the brush caused Maldred to jerk away, his hands reaching for the pommel of the sword strapped to his back, stopping when he recognized the two ogre scouts he'd sent out a while back. The creatures looked shocked by the aftermath of the battle, and Maldred gave them a curtailed version of the events.

The scouts reported quickly, Maldred and Dhamon listening attentively, while Fiona gave Rig an inquisitive look.

"Are you certain we're not near Takar?" she asked.

Rig nodded. "But I don't know where we are."

"I do. We're less than a mile from the Trueheart Mines," Dhamon said, squarely facing the mariner, his eyes dancing in the torchlight. "If you want to rescue somebody, there are plenty of prisoners there in need of it."

Fiona looked incredulously between Dhamon and Rig, then let out a deep breath from between her teeth and angrily took a step toward Maldred. Dhamon's hand slammed against her breastplate, stopping her. Maldred was talking to the scouts in the ogre tongue, gesturing at the force of the mercenaries, and then to the south.

"He's getting them ready," Dhamon explained. "Issuing a few orders. You know how that is, Fiona. Soldiers need instructions before a fight."

Rig batted Dhamon's arm down. "You and Maldred lied to her. You promised her a small army of mercenaries."

"I didn't promise her anything."

"Maldred, Donnag. . . ."

"Well, Rig, there're thirty mercenaries left—after the snakes."

"For Takar," Rig stated flatly. "They were to be for Takar."

"We didn't *want* to go to Takar," Dhamon returned. "I certainly had no intentions of going there—or anywhere else in this blessed swamp, for that matter. You should have realized that days ago, Rig." His voice was icy, his stare hard and unwavering. "Maldred had his own agenda, and he thought he could use your sword arms. You're good in a fight, the both of you. And he seems quite fond of Fiona."

"Fiona," Rig stated softly. "This is all about her. Maldred is more than fond of her. He lied to her just to keep her around."

Dhamon didn't reply to that. "I suspect you two would've gone along with us from the beginning if you weren't so bent on going to Takar to ransom a Solamnic Knight. Sorry, a Knight's body. Maldred's plan is equally as noble as yours. Just not quite as dangerous—or futile."

"We're not going any farther." Fiona stepped

back, wrapping her fingers around the pommel of her sword. "With any of you." Her tone was as venomous as Dhamon's, her posture rigid. "Rig was right all along, and I was a fool not to listen to him. What was I thinking? Are my senses so muddled that. . . ."

Rig took her arm and pulled her a few feet away from Dhamon. "We can't afford too much of a confrontation here," he whispered, his eyes darting back and forth between Dhamon and Maldred, who was still occupied with issuing orders. Several ogres had joined the big man.

"Wish I could understand them," he grumbled. "Can't trust them. Don't know what they're saying." His expression softened when he looked at her heart-shaped face. "Listen, there're way too many of them, and I know for certain now that there's not a single one of them that can be believed."

"I agree. Can we find the way to Takar alone? If my brother is truly dead . . ." She let that thought trail off, inhaled deep and adopted her military posture again. "It is my fault for not finding another avenue to raise the coins and gems. And now the ransom I had managed to extract from Chieftain Donnag is gone." She eased her fingers away from the pommel of her sword and steepled them in her nervous gesture.

"Fiona. . . ."

"Oh, Rig. Maybe I don't need the coins. If we go to Takar I can find that old draconian. I'd recognize him in a heartbeat. Perhaps I can persuade him to tell me for certain if my brother is truly dead. I must have something more than your vision. Maybe, just maybe, the black dragon might release him. . . ." She paused. "My sword has value, my armor. Perhaps everything isn't lost."

Rig placed his hands on her shoulders. "Fiona, please. Let's stop this. Forget Takar. If you want to honor your brother, forget his plight. Forget all of this. Let's go to Shrentak instead, try to rescue the prisoners there who are still alive. Maybe where a garrison of Knights failed, two people could succeed. Unnoticed. Slipping in and out. That would be an *honorable* thing to do."

Her face softened for a moment, her eyes watering, her posture relaxing. It looked as if she might agree with him, but then Maldred strolled over, reached out and thumped her shoulder, drawing her attention. Fiona's eyes met his and instantly brightened.

"Fiona," Maldred began. He was holding a torch, which sharply revealed the planes of his face and the injuries he had suffered, his wide, dark eyes that held hers despite her fury. "We mean to free the ogres that the Black works as slaves in the Trueheart Mines. They're Donnag's people, good men all of them, and the dragon's killing them with the work. Dhamon and I want your help."

"We don't intend to help!" Rig said, glaring venomously at Dhamon and Maldred. "We don't intend to go another step with the likes of you!"

"We had our own agenda," Maldred admitted. "It just happened to be convenient that you wanted to travel through the Black's swamp. We thought we could use your fighting skills along the way. You're good in a brawl, the both of you. We certainly would have lost more ogres to the snakes if you'd not been with us."

Maldred made a gesture with his hand and turned. Fiona followed him. Rig watched dumbstruck as the two of them walked toward the assembled ogres. Maldred addressed them now.

"Fiona? What are you doing?"

She kept pace with Maldred and did not acknowledge the mariner.

"Wish I could understand you, Fiona," Rig grumbled. "Can't. Can't trust them either. Can't understand anything of what they're saying." His expression softened a little when he looked at Fiona. Her face was calm, which troubled him.

"Lady Knight," Maldred began. He talked softly, so Rig would not hear. "Dearest Fiona, it is true that we have our own agenda, one I was obviously wrong to keep from you." His voice was deep and even, so pleasant to listen to, almost like a melodic chant. "But I honestly want to rescue your brother in the process. We'll free these ogres, then go directly to Takar. You have my word. You can trust me, my love."

She continued to stare into his eyes. "Rig believes my brother is dead. He said he saw a vision. . . ."

"I heard him. And Dhamon told me that as well. But you cannot trust a vision, Fiona. You cannot trust Rig. Remember, he does not deserve you. Above all, you must have hope that your brother is alive. I would very much like to meet him, you know. Continue to the mines with us and then we'll go to Takar and find this old draconian you spoke of."

"The scarred one," she said softly. "The one with the heavy gold collar."

"Yes, we'll find him. Stay with me. And we'll gain your brother's release."

"But I've got no ransom."

"We'll think of something. The mines themselves are filled with silver."

She shook her head, her red braids lashing behind her like a whip. Still, her eyes did not leave his, and her fingers remained clenched around the pommel of her sword. Fiona blinked furiously, as if trying to clear her head. For a moment she felt faint, and bent her knees to steady herself. When she regained her composure, her eyes were bright and filled with ire.

Fiona met Maldred's surprised stare. "No. I don't know what I am thinking. Talking to you. A thief. And a liar. You'll get no help from me in these mines you're going to, Maldred. This deception you've contrived, leading me away from Takar. I'm leaving your little band. I believe Rig. I believe my brother is dead. And I believe I could have prevented this tragedy if I had found another way to raise this ransom. If only I would have acted sooner."

Rig was silent, watching the two, his glance occasionally resting on Dhamon, who was only a few feet away. All around them the ogres were gathering into a column and inspecting their weapons, chattering softly in a tongue that sounded primitive and coarse. Finally, Rig crept closer to Fiona, intent on hearing the conversation between her and Maldred.

"Fair Lady Knight." Maldred's words grew softer, more musical, his expression relaxing, too. A hand hidden in the folds of his cloak began gesturing to aid in his incantation. Her anger had lessened his hold on her, and he had to correct that. "Lady Knight, from high above when I was held captive in the trees I watched you battle the snakes. You are worth any four of these men, more formidable than I originally believed. I *need* your help. Please."

Her expression calmed a little, and her fingers eased from the pommel of her sword.

Maldred's lyrical voice continued. "Dozens of ogres are being forced to work the mine. They are beaten, fed barely enough to live. It is slavery, Lady Knight, of the worst kind. And it needs to be stopped. It is a problem I had intended to rectify before you

came along. You merely make the task less onerous."
The fingers of his hidden hand fluttered even faster.
"I should have been honest with you, I realize that
now. But I feared you would not accompany us. I
promise you, Lady Knight, if you help us free the
ogres, then we will discover the truth about your
brother. If he lives, he will be freed. You have my
word. Stay with me."

"All right. I will stay with you."

"No!" Rig roared. He had inched close enough to
hear some of what the big man had said. "Fiona, you
can't trust him. Can't trust Dhamon. Can't believe
any of this." He interposed himself between the
Solamnic and Maldred. "You can't be serious."

Her expression was odd, her eyes unblinking.
"Slavery is wrong, Rig, and freeing the ogres from
the mines is just and honorable. I will help Maldred.
And then we'll all go to Takar." She turned and took
a position at the beginning of the column. Dhamon
moved to stand at her side.

Maldred appraised the mariner for a moment.
"She has fire," he said finally. "And a rare sword
arm."

"This isn't like her," Rig stated. "Agreeing to help
the likes of you. Thieves. Liars. Freeing ogres. I don't
understand it."

Maldred shrugged and headed to the front of the
column.

"Not like her," Rig repeated. "By the blessed
memory of Habbakuk, what is going on with her?
And with me?" *I should leave,* he told himself. *But I
can't leave her. Not alone with the likes of these people.
And I want my damn glaive back.*

The column was moving. Rig took a last look at
the ogre bodies encircling the massive cypress tree.
Already lizards were scampering over the corpses,

biting at the exposed flesh. A raven was perched on a
stout ogre's stomach, plucking at the skin through a
rent in the armor. Shuddering, the mariner followed
the last of the ogres, fingers still squeezing the
pommel of his sword, eyes darting all around looking for movement in the vines. For a moment he
wished more serpent-vines would appear and whisk
away Dhamon and Maldred and all the ogres. Then
it would be just he and the Solamnic Knight again.

The mercenaries were forced to make their way
single-file, the swamp so overgrown that at times
they were practically squeezing between cypress
trunks. Rig lost sight of Fiona, Maldred, and Dhamon
shortly after they'd left the clearing. He was worried
about the Solamnic, furious over the loss of his
glaive. In the back of his mind he kept visualizing the
small footprints and telling himself he should talk to
Fiona again, make her listen, cut their losses, and get
out of here. Around him all he could see were the
dark shapes of trees, barely discernible in the light of
the few torches the ogres carried.

"I'm going to die here," he thought, not meaning
to say the words out loud. "To snakes or treachery."

They hadn't traveled far, a mile or perhaps a little
more, when the night's blackness gave way to the
lights of torches and fires burning merrily ahead.
There were sounds—snaps, cries, curses, grunts. The
ogres were moving quickly now.

At the front of the column, Dhamon brushed aside
a veil of moss and caught a first look at the Trueheart
Mines. Crates of rocks filled a stretch of marshy
ground that had been cleared with axes and was now
dotted with decaying stumps. The mine itself was a
great hole in the ground, a gaping pit from which
light beamed out, and into which thick ropes tied
about a few cypress giants led. There was a smaller

maw, this set into a low hill, and light shone out of that, too.

Ogres were moving around, shadows of the creatures that followed Dhamon and Maldred. They looked emaciated, their flesh and what was left of their clothes hanging on them, their eyes vacant. Some were climbing up the ropes out of the hole, crates filled with ore strapped to their backs. It looked like it was all they could do to make it to the surface, crawling on hands and knees until their black spawn guards undid the clamps that held the crates. The crates emptied, they were again strapped to the ogres' backs, and the creatures returned to the mines.

The spawn were hideous, resembling draconians to an extent, but they were jet black like a starless sky. Their wings were short and dull compared to the scales on their torsos that gleamed wetly in the light. Their snouts were vaguely equine, covered in tiny scales, and their eyes were a drab yellow, narrowed in malevolence. They had stumpy black tails, which were constantly twitching, claws that were constantly opening and closing. A stunted spiny ridge ran from the tops of their heads to nearly the tips of their tails. Their breath escaped from them in a hiss, making the clearing sound like it was filled with snakes and instantly bringing back memories of the ensorcelled vines.

The sight of the spawn sent a shiver down Dhamon's back. They were repulsive and unnatural, and he wondered just how many of them Donnag's forces had managed to slay in the "nest" the ogre chieftain said they'd found. Dhamon knew from his association with the sorcerer Palin Majere that spawn were created by the dragon overlords. The great dragons used something of themselves and something from a true draconian, and they used human captives for the bodies. Those ingredients, coupled with a powerful spell, brought the spawn into existence, and somehow made them unswervingly loyal to the dragon who created them. They did the dragon's bidding without question, and they seemed to take delight in killing things.

Dhamon had fought their like before, namely the red spawn of Malys. His lip involuntarily curled up in a snarl at the memory mixed with the sight before him.

Several spawn had whips, and they obviously delighted in using them on the ogre slaves. Dhamon watched as an especially frail-looking slave didn't move fast enough for one of the spawn. The spawn lashed at the ogre viciously, then moved in and spat a gob of acid that sizzled on the ogre's lacerated back. The ogre didn't howl in pain, as Dhamon expected. He merely shuffled back to the ropes and returned to the hole in the ground for another load.

From the smaller hole set against the hill, humans and dwarves brought out more crates of ore, followed by two additional ogre slaves who were so hunched over it looked as though they were crawling on the ground.

Fiona shuddered. "You could have told me the truth of this place and I would've come," she said to Dhamon. "For this reason alone."

"I didn't know," he replied.

"Maldred did."

Then my friend Maldred would not have needed to use his ensorcellment on you, Dhamon thought, recalling how righteous the Solamnic Knight was when she accompanied him to the Window to the Stars. She was saying something else, talking softly again, this time to Maldred. Dhamon wasn't listening. He watched the spawn whip the miners, spit at the ones who moved too slowly, claw at the sturdiest of the lot to keep them in line. He was counting the spawn, searching for other guards and taskmasters and wondering if he should have left all of this business to Maldred and his Solamnic puppet and struck out deeper into the swamp on his own, in search of his cure. Dhamon's right hand drifted to his sword. It tingled slightly, and this puzzled him.

There were a dozen spawn on the grounds, nothing else that he could see in the foliage along the perimeter. But there were more in the mine, he was certain of it. And he needed to know just how many more.

He motioned to Maldred, making a few gestures with his fingers—the silent language of thieves Rikali had taught him. For an instant he wondered how the half-elf was doing. Angry that she'd been left behind, for certain. Still, she was safer this way, Dhamon told himself. And he was better off without a relationship. Still, he found himself missing her.

The big man nodded and gestured back to Dhamon, his fingers fluttering. Then he began whispering orders to the ogres.

Dhamon raised his arm, the blade of Tanis Half-Elven flashing in the light. Then, dropped it down as a signal and he raced forward, the ogres and Maldred charging behind him. Fiona joined the charge, heading toward an impressively large spawn that was lashing a recalcitrant dwarf. She nearly slipped, as the ground was marshy despite the absence of rain. The pounding of their footsteps was like muted thunder, and water and mud sprayed in their wake.

The spawn were startled, but were astonishingly quick to react. A few grabbed slaves and used them as shields. Others inhaled sharply, then puffed out gouts of acid to coat the charging ogres. Donnag's men cried out in surprise and pain, but didn't retreat.

"Spread out!" Maldred barked in the common tongue, repeating it in ogrish.

The words haunted Dhamon. It was what Gauderic had called to the mercenaries in the Qualinesti Forest when they faced the green dragon. For a moment, Dhamon saw the forest again, the elves and humans racing along the river and toward the green dragon—racing because he countermanded Gauderic's order that they flee. "Spread out!" he heard Gauderic cry inside his head. But that forest was a very long way from here, the men who fought the dragon all dead. And Gauderic, Dhamon's friend and second-in-command, was dead too, by Dhamon's hand. Dead and buried.

"Spread out!" Maldred hollered again.

Swallowing hard, Dhamon raced toward the closest spawn, crouching beneath a cloud of acid spittle and leaping forward, ramming his shoulder into the creature's stomach. His arms pumped. Tanis's blade stabbed into the beast's chest again and again as the pommel tingled merrily.

The creature lay struggling, and Dhamon thrust the blade in one more time, noting that the elvish script along the blade glowed faintly blue. Then he pushed himself off the beast, just as it dissolved in a shower of acid, which miraculously did not settle on him. He heard the sound of whips cracking and the thud of weapons striking spawn flesh all around him. Without pause, he pressed his attack on another spawn, darting around a pair of gaunt ogre slaves who stood staring in disbelief at what was transpiring. He vaulted over a crate of ore and slammed his foot into the chest of another spawn, knocking the beast off balance and sending the whip flying from its clawed fingers. But its wings beat furiously to keep itself upright, and it inhaled sharply and spit furiously at Dhamon, the acid breath striking him in the chest and its claws tearing through what was left of his leather vest. The acid didn't affect Dhamon, though it fell around him, and he realized it was the sword's magic keeping him safe. The tingling persisted.

"It signals the presence of dragonkind," he speculated of the tingling sensation. And the spawn were certainly birthed by dragon magic. Then Dhamon concentrated solely on the battle. He slammed his teeth together and drew his blade back and swung it with all his strength at the creature. He struck it in the side of its head, easily cleaving through the bone and through the beast's brain. Then he pulled his sword free and sprinted away, as the spawn melted into a cloud of acid that rained down on the ground.

He headed toward the smaller mine, where a mal-shaped spawn was emerging.

"An abomination," Dhamon whispered.

As grotesque as the spawn were, this creature was far worse. Its head sat on a thick neck on which rope-like veins stood out. Its wings were stunted, one being scalloped like a bat, the other rounded and a little longer. The beast had three arms, the third growing out of its right side, several inches below the more normal-looking arm. And the hand that extended from the third limb looked small and smooth, the size of a kender's or a gnome's. The abomination's eyes were overlarge and bugged away from its head, perched on either side of a wide, pug nose. It had a tail, longer than the spawns', and at the end of it was the snapping maw of a snake.

"Monster," Dhamon spat. Abominations were created through the same process as spawn, he had learned. But rather than humans, the dragon substituted elves, kender, dwarves, and gnomes. No two abominations looked the same, and the other dragon overlords were not known to purposefully create them. Save the Black. The corrupt overlord of the swamp favored her corrupted "children."

"You're next," Dhamon said to it.

But Fiona was nearby and beat him to the creature. Her sword arced above her head and cut through its third arm. It clawed furiously at her with its two remaining limbs, the nails raking uselessly against her plate.

As Dhamon looked about for another target, he saw her raise the sword high and bring it down on the beast's collarbone. There was a sickening crunch, then she turned away as the thing burst into a stinging cloud of acid. Their eyes met for a moment, hers filled with a mix of anger and eagerness for the fight, Dhamon's with an equal and fierce determination.

Without a word Dhamon raced toward Maldred. While the ogre mercenaries were dealing with the remaining spawn, the big man was questioning one of the slaves.

"How many in the mines?" The words were in the ogre tongue, but they were simple, and Dhamon knew enough of them to understand. "Spawn. The black creatures. How many?" The slave didn't answer. "The masters," Maldred tried. "Your masters. And tell me about the mines below."

A response came, but the ogre slave's voice was indistinct, and Dhamon wasn't close enough yet to hear the words.

"Ten spawn." Maldred called to Dhamon, pointing to the smaller mine and using the common speech. "Another dozen in the larger one. A few draconians." He nodded toward the gaping maw in the ground. "Fiona and I will take the large mine."

Dhamon scowled. His sword made him the better man to deal with the spawn and draconians, and any abominations that might be around. And for an instant he considered arguing that point. But the smaller mine presented the lesser threat. "All right," he answered. "Then Rig and I will take the other mine."

Maldred nodded. The mariner was already in the clearing, threading his way through the ogre mercenaries and weaving around dumbstruck slaves and crates of ore. He had a long sword in one hand, three daggers clasped in the other. He was heading toward Fiona, who'd just dispatched another abomination.

"Lady Knight!" Maldred boomed across the clearing. "I need your help!"

She glanced up and saw Maldred, hurried in his direction, either not seeing Rig or ignoring him. The mariner stared as she rushed by. He intended to follow, but saw two dark shapes emerging from the smaller mine. A spawn and an abomination. He shook his head and ran toward them, feet churning up the marshy loam. Drawing back, he hurled his daggers, all three landing in the chest of the abomination and turning it into a cloud of acidic vapor. The spawn advanced to meet him.

The Solamnic could barely hear Maldred above the sounds of battle and the cries of the ogre mercenaries. He was gesturing, eyes locked onto hers. "Lady Knight. You and I will venture into the main mine." Even as he was explaining his plan, a spawn emerged from the gaping hole. Dhamon charged it, bringing his sword down on its spiky crown and cleaving its head in two before it could clear the entrance.

"There are many ogres toiling below. And some

humans." This last Maldred told Fiona as almost an afterthought. "We must kill the spawn and free the miners. Dhamon and Rig will deal with the other mine while the mercenaries stand watch up here and handle any spawn we might chase out."

She nodded, her eyes fixed on his. "As you desire," she said.

"This is so unlike you, your spirit dampened. You give in to me far too easily," he said, perhaps regretting the spell he had cast over the Solamnic. He took her by the arm and led her to the main shaft. Soon they were lowering themselves down the ropes.

Dhamon was running toward the smaller mine. He waved his sword to get Rig's attention. The mariner had just vanquished a spawn, his skin was a mass of boils from the acid, his shirt shredded from the creature's claws. Coupled with the snake bites on his face and hands, he looked like he shouldn't be standing. But his shoulders were square, his eyes clear, and he was watching Fiona and Maldred climb down the ropes. "Fiona!" he called. "Don't go with him!"

Dhamon shook his head and pointed to the smaller mine entrance behind Rig. "There are ten spawn inside there. Maybe more," he told him as he entered the shaft. "We've got to take them before we can get the rest of the slaves out."

Rig stood indecisively for a moment, then, shaking his head, he followed Dhamon, thrusting his aches and pains to the back of his mind and telling himself when they were done here, he and Fiona would be on their way and all of this would be a bad memory. They would never have to look at Dhamon Grimwulf again.

The smaller mine had narrow tunnels that were barely six feet tall. It was being worked by human and dwarf slaves, diligently mining the thick veins of silver. Rig and Dhamon found their way through the winding shafts, guided by guttering torchlight and the sound of whips and snarls.

They came upon two spawn who were unaware of what was transpiring above. The sounds of picks against the rock was loud enough to drown out the battle overhead. Dhamon killed one before it could react, slamming his eyes shut when the cloud of acid came. Then he bowled into the second, ramming the sword into its chest. It clawed him deeply as it went down, then melted into acid and a stringent cloud.

"So the spawns' dragon-acid cannot harm me," Dhamon muttered. "Thanks entirely to you." He glanced at Wyrmsbane. "But the creatures' claws are another matter." He wiped at a line of blood running from a slice across his chest.

Rig didn't pause to see how Dhamon was faring. "I don't want to be here," he hissed, admitting to himself, however, that freeing these people was far from a bad idea. He bolted down the tunnel, shouting to the humans and dwarves to drop their picks. Then he was pulling on their chains, which were weak and rusting from the moisture of the Black's swamp. His muscles bunched, and he tugged free link after link, shutting out the grateful voices. "If I had my glaive, I'd be cutting through this metal like it was parchment."

Hands touched him in thanks. "Shrentak," he mumbled as he picked up other chains and tugged them apart and told those freed to head for the surface. "I should be doing this in Shrentak."

After they freed more than a dozen slaves, Dhamon and Rig worked their way down another corridor, crouching and readying their weapons when they spotted the dull yellow gleam of spawn eyes.

❖ ❖ ❖ ❖ ❖ ❖ ❖

In the main tunnel, Maldred and Fiona were busy freeing ogres. They'd found one too weak to move, starving and beaten. Maldred killed him quickly, speaking softly in the ogre tongue and closing the dead slave's eyes. "A righteous enough cause for you, Lady Knight? Even though these are ogres?" he asked. He frowned when he saw Fiona's blank expression. Had he spent too much effort on his last charming spell, and was she too far under his influence? "Have I put out all of your fire, Lady Knight?" he asked. "I must see later about giving at least some of it back."

She didn't seem to hear him. Instead, she headed toward a hissing sound coming from a shadowed alcove. A draconian stepped into the torchlight, and from a few yards away it cautiously regarded her.

The creature was a bozak, birthed from a corrupted bronze dragon egg a long time ago when Takhisis walked the face of Krynn and she used these creatures as commanders during the War of the Lance. His bronze-hued scales glimmered in the light of the torch, making him appear almost regal. The scales were the size of coins across most of his frame, smaller along his face and hands where they were flat and smooth like the scales of a fish. His wings were short, too stunted to allow him to fly. But were he not in such tight confines, he could use them to glide short distances.

The bozak was not much taller than Fiona, and was not as muscular as Maldred. But he *looked* powerful. Battle-tested and old. He wore a gold collar about his neck. It was studded with bronze spikes, and at irregular intervals chunks of onyx, sapphires, and garnets were scattered. It was a singular piece of jewelry, and some part of Fiona's mind recognized it.

Recognized that and the deep criss-crossing scars across its chest.

It was the draconian who had appeared before Fiona and the Solamnic Council, the one that was supposed to be in Takar, and the one that had information about her brother. But only a small part of Fiona's mind registered this ironic fact.

The creature opened his mouth as if to speak, but Fiona cut it off.

"Foul beast!" she hollered as she raised her sword high above her head.

Momentarily puzzled, the bozak took a step back and began gesturing with his hands, instantly forming a shimmering gray web in the corridor to keep her and Maldred away from it.

"Foolsss," it spat. "Ssshining Knight, you'll not take thessse minesss. The missstressss holdsss them. As she holds others, and you might. . . ."

Fiona stabbed her sword into the web and fought her way through the sticky mass. Then she pressed her attack, even while it was in the midst of another spell. She sliced into the creature's belly, not letting it finish its vile speech. Deep under Maldred's enchantment, she was oblivious that this was the creature she had planned to meet at the ruins of Takar, the creature she had raised the ransom for. The creature that was her hope of regaining her brother. Only a small part of her mind noted that the Black's minion was instead at the Trueheart Mines, where she was tricked into going.

She drew her sword back again and struck out at its neck. The head lopped forward as the thing dissolved into bones, leaving the gold collar behind. Maldred tugged her back just in time—for the bones burst apart, sending deadly shards through the air while bouncing off her armor.

Then she and Maldred were rushing down the tunnel.

It took nearly two hours for both silver mines to be cleansed of spawn and abominations, and of two enormous constrictor snakes that had been used to keep the slaves in line. Maldred and Fiona searched niches and cutbacks, she calling out in the common tongue and he in ogrish to find more slaves. The mines were immense, and it could have taken more than a day to fully explore them. Maldred wasn't willing to devote that much time, as he wanted to get the freed ogres back to Blöten before any more spawn or other swamp denizens came by. He told Fiona that perhaps Donnag would send more men back here later—if those ogres who were freed provided information that necessitated a return trip.

"After you, Lady Knight." Maldred bowed and extended a hand, and Fiona grabbed the rope and pulled herself up.

He followed. "She has served her purpose," he mused aloud. "A most fine sword arm."

Dhamon and Rig were already in the clearing above, marshaling the freed slaves into some semblance of order and placing those who could barely walk under the care of the ogre mercenaries. Three mercenaries had died to the spawn and abominations, including the white-skinned shaman.

The mariner had a new concern. He didn't want to return to Blöten, and he didn't want the freed humans and dwarves going there either. He knew how badly nonogres had it in that city. His stomach knotted. Taking them farther away would mean that much more time lost from his plan of slipping into the Black's lair and freeing whoever was still alive in her dungeons. "Shrentak," he said. The word sounded like a curse.

"Shrentak? And what would you want with that most wondrous and hallowed place?" The voice was lilting and silenced the murmurs of the freed slaves and mercenaries.

Rig cocked his head and looked around for the speaker. All he could see were the wart-riddled bodies of the mercenaries and the beaten and frail forms of those they'd rescued. Fiona was just emerging from the larger mine. It wasn't her voice. Maldred crawled out behind her.

"Lose your tongue, o' man the color of night?" the voice persisted.

Dhamon was looking for the speaker, too, the hairs standing up on the back of his neck. He clutched his sword and motioned for Donnag's men to circle the freed slaves and protect them. Then he took a step toward a line of cypresses. He thought he saw something dart behind a trunk. He squinted and took another step.

"Dhamon!" Maldred shouted. The big thief was gesturing at the canopy.

Dhamon glanced up, and his eyes widened in surprise. The leaves of the cypresses were falling, as if the tree were dying in a moment's time. But the leaves didn't flutter to the ground, they began hovering. A heartbeat later they were rising and swooping—heading straight toward Dhamon and Rig.

"What in the blessed memory of Habbakuk . . ." Rig began. He drew his sword to meet this new threat, which Dhamon was already attempting to engage.

The leaves shimmered in the torchlight, the green melting from them to be replaced by grays and blacks and browns, many of which were difficult to discern against the shadows of the swamp. The leaves continued to transform, growing wings and tails.

"What are they?" Rig hollered.

Dhamon shrugged and readied to meet this new mysterious threat.

There were hundreds of the things—roughly the size of blackbirds, though they were not birds. They had batlike wings that were more membranous than leathery. Their heads resembled that of mosquitos—complete with needlelike noses that dripped something viscous.

Dhamon reached up to knock one away, discovering that their bodies were segmented and hard like the shell of a beetle. He swung at another, slicing it in two and releasing a foul red gore.

"Stirges!" Fiona hollered.

"What?" This from Dhamon.

"Stirges. They're . . . they're insects. They'll drain your blood!"

Dhamon was quick to react, for the creatures were already swarming him. Though he swung his sword high above his head, cleaving some in two, several dove at his chest, their needlelike stingers stabbing into his flesh. He hollered, in surprise and pain, as they began feasting on his blood.

He heard Fiona behind him, sword whistling as she cut through the foul creatures. The Solamnic was protected by her plate mail, the stirges flying at her and stunning themselves by colliding with the metal. She was careful to cover her face with one arm. And she continued to strike at one after another as she made her way toward Rig.

The clearing was filled with growls from the ogres, who had never encountered such malevolent insects and who were plucking them off their bodies and squishing them in their bare hands; screams from the freed slaves; the soft thud of the dead stirges hitting the ground; smacking sounds from the creatures gorging themselves.

Bare-chested, Dhamon was an easy mark for the little beasts. A dozen were latched onto his chest and his back. He scraped some off his legs, stomping on them before they could take to the air again.

"They're not that difficult to kill!" Maldred was shouting.

"No," Dhamon muttered, as he jabbed at the stirges who flew in to take their dead brethren's place. "There's just so many of them! Too many!" He felt weak, and realized it was because so much of his blood had been drained. "They could destroy us," he shouted to his friend.

"I'm not going to die here, Dhamon Grimwulf!" Maldred returned. "I promised to help you with that scale, remember?"

I won't have to worry about the scale, Dhamon thought. If we can't get rid of these deadly pests, soon the scale will be the smallest of my concerns. He hefted Wyrmsbane with one hand, using it to fend off the creatures diving on him. With his other hand he began plucking at the insects, squeezing them in his hand until the chitinous shell broke, then hurling them on the ground and stomping on them for good measure. His hand was slick with his own blood that they'd drained, and he whirled about to see that the ogres' hands were bloody as well. They'd all abandoned their weapons, using their hands to squeeze the life from the stirges. Dhamon considered doing that as well, but he was loath to drop the long sword, and wasn't about to leave himself too open by taking a moment to sheathe it.

There was a snarl behind him—Mulok. The big ogre was plucking the stirges off Dhamon's back. Dhamon felt blood spatter him with each creature the ogre squeezed. Then he felt the ogre's back against his, slick with blood. Others were copying

Mulok, standing back to back; those who didn't were falling.

"No! Mugwort!" Maldred cried to the largest ogre, the one who toted Fiona's chest of gems through the swamp. The great ogre dropped beneath a cloud of black, winged bodies. He flailed about on the marshy ground for a moment, then lay still. More of the creatures descended on his body, their smacking noises hideous.

"Enough of this!" Maldred was battling several of the creatures. He tugged a few free and then began gesturing. An instant later, Mugwort's body—and all the stirges blanketing it—were engulfed in a crackling ball of flame.

The ogres nearby began plucking the stirges off themselves and throwing them on the bonfire, the insects shrieking and popping and releasing a nauseating stench. There was another burst of flame, and then another, as Maldred ignited the corpses of other fallen ogres and slaves.

Finally he tended to himself, tearing one bloated insect after another from his arms and legs, backing toward a pair of Donnag's ogres and shouting for them to pull the last ones off his back.

Rig and Fiona were standing back to back, a ring of dead stirges at their feet. The Solamnic battled the insects without a word, one hand clenched tightly on her sword, the other reaching up to grab stirges from the air and crush them. Rig was vocal, cursing the swamp and the insects, Maldred, Dhamon, the chieftain Donnag, all the lost gods. The faster the words flew from his lips, the faster his hands moved; he had abandoned the sword, dropping it at his feet in favor of grabbing and squishing the creatures.

"Stirges, huh?" Rig said. "Damn big mosquitos, if you ask me. Fought them before?"

"Hu-uh." Fiona, too, was busy.

"This many of them?"

A shake of her head.

"Where?"

"Once. When I was visiting the isle of Cristyne. But there were only a small number of them. We'd disturbed a nest. We got out of there fast."

"We're winning!" Maldred shouted from across the clearing.

Only a few dozen of the stirges remained, and soon they were dead, too. The ground was covered with black bodies, an insect carpet that crunched as the ogres and slaves trod across it to see if any of their fallen comrades survived.

Rig kicked through the mound in front of him, finding his sword and quickly retrieving it. He shook his head. It was covered with blood—his and the stirges. He scowled as Dhamon approached him, Maldred behind him.

The fires were burning out all around the clearing, but Dhamon was peering into the dense cypresses that surrounded them. "I was certain I heard a voice. . . ."

Maldred nodded.

"I heard it right before these creatures came."

"Yeah," Rig said. "Soft and pretty—these . . . stirges . . . were anything but. Bet she brought the snakes, too, our mysterious lady. Doesn't want us in the swamp. Or maybe she just doesn't want us near Shrentak. The stirges came right after I mentioned that place."

Dhamon's eyes narrowed. He thought he spied something with a metallic gleam moving between the fern leaves.

"Shrentak. . . ." The voice was feminine and breathy, the same one they'd heard before the insect onslaught. "Shrentak would welcome you, o' man the color of night," the voice continued. "There are always a few empty cells." A veil of lianas parted and the figure of a young girl glided into the clearing, her coppery hair disturbed by continuous motion. She appeared no more than five or six, yet she spoke like a much older woman, with a seductress's voice. And in her small hand she clasped Rig's glaive, a weapon she shouldn't have been able to lift. The blade glimmered in the light.

"The girl . . ." the mariner began.

"From Fetch's vision," Dhamon stated.

Their eyes grew wider as a silvery-gray mist formed and encircled her free hand. Dhamon darted forward, able to take only a few steps before he found himself rooted to the spot, the stirge-covered ground shimmering around his boots and holding him fast like a vise. The silvery mist poured from her hand now, blanketing the ground like a low-hanging fog and swirling around everyone's legs.

Twisting around, Dhamon saw that Rig and Fiona were likewise held. But Maldred was free, the mist somehow was unable to hold him. Now the big man was charging toward the child, bringing his two-handed sword from his back as he moved.

"Fool," she said simply, gesturing again. "My mistress Sable, who waits in Shrentak, will be angry with you. She'll order more than my little rain and earthquakes to gnaw at your kingdom."

A streak of silver shot out like a lightning bolt from her tiny hand, grew to a diaphanous, sparkling cloud, and then draped Maldred like a net. In its misty light, the big man's form shuddered and expanded, his ruddy skin rippling with even more muscles, and its rich color fading until it became practically white. Then it changed hue again, becoming a pale blue dotted here and there with warts and boils. His short ginger hair grew and thickened, turning stark white and flowing over his shoulders like a lion's mane.

"What is she doing to him?" Fiona cried.

"*Revealing* him," the waif replied evenly. "Chasing away his spell that paints a beautiful human form over his ugly ogre body. Revealing the son of Blöde's Donnag—my mistress's enemy!"

When the transformation was complete, Maldred stood more than nine feet tall, an ogre more awesome and imposing, physically, than any of those who accompanied them to the mines. His clothes were now in tatters, barely covering his massive body.

Dhamon stared dumbstruck at the creature he had considered his closest friend. There was no trace of the Maldred he knew, not even the eyes were recognizable.

Fiona and Rig were likewise astonished. The Solamnic felt faint at the sight, the shock of which was enough to drive off at least some of the magic Maldred had cast upon her. She shook her head, trying to chase away . . . something, she couldn't tell what. Fiona's memory seemed hazy. Still, a dozen thoughts rushed at her: the deceptions played upon her and Rig, the trip through the dwarven ruins, the fight in the mines. An image flashed in the back of her mind, of a bozak draconian. One with a gold collar. Had she slain him?

Dhamon shook his head in disbelief, as if the vision of the blue-skinned ogre might disappear and Maldred return in its place. He twisted his head about to face the girl again.

"You're not revealing anything!" Dhamon spat. "You're making us believe our friend is a creature! Just like you created the stirges and the snakes!"

"Your friend is an ogre mage," the girl continued. "Soon to be a dead one. I will relish giving this news to my mistress personally. Sable will reward me well." She threw back her head and laughed, a cackling sound so incongruous to her small form. Miniature silver lightning bolts arced from her fingers and danced toward Maldred, who was still held by the shimmering mist. "Very well, indeed!"

"No!" Dhamon screamed. He tugged free of his boots, which were held by the child's magic, and raced toward the girl, drawing Wyrmsbane as he went.

The child was faster. Lightning bolts struck the ogre in the chest, skin sizzling and popping and burning. Maldred twitched, but didn't cry out. Rather, he fought against the cloudlike spell that held him in place, gesturing and humming loudly with his own incantation.

Dhamon was nearly upon the child figure when more bolts flew, again aimed at the huge ogre. They struck their mark once more—but a heartbeat after Maldred had retaliated with his own magic.

His spell complete, a burst of flame erupted from the ogre mage's flailing hands. It was a riot of color, green and blue, crackling wildly and shooting forward like a gout of dragon's breath. It grew and changed color, becoming a great fiery red-orange ball that, with a near-deafening "whoosh," engulfed the child and several of the trees around her. Despite the wetness of the swamp, the trees burned, becoming cinders in an instant.

Dhamon skidded to a stop and stared at the smoldering trunks. The girl had been vaporized and was gone. Or was she?

He turned to Maldred, face filled with anger and a dozen questions.

The ogre mage sagged to the marshy floor, hands pressed against his blue chest as if that might lessen the pain. Dhamon rushed to his side and ripped strips from what was left of his own cloak, pressing them against the wounds.

"I am what I appear, my friend," Maldred stated, his pained voice difficult to hear.

"It seems you are an expert at deceptions," Dhamon replied. "You are every bit as accomplished a liar as your father." He kept his words low, not wanting the others to hear. "I thought you were . . . are . . . a man, like me."

Maldred gasped, fighting for breath. "Sometimes deceptions help to build friendships," he answered. "But other than the form I wore, I have never lied to you, Dhamon Grimwulf. I think you know that."

"You just never bothered with the complete truth." Dhamon continued to blot at the wounds, relying on the skills he learned on numerous battlefields. "Does Rikali know?"

Maldred shook his head. "Fetch did. One of the few secrets he managed to keep." The ogre's eyes searched Dhamon's face. "I'm sorry you had to learn this way. I . . ."

"Doesn't matter, I guess," Dhamon said. "A body's a shell, after all. Just let me know if you've got any more interesting secrets. I hate surprises."

Rig and Fiona moved toward them, for they too were released from the girl's magic. The ogres and freed slaves had gathered in a circle around them, a few of the scouts cautious to keep a lookout toward the mines and the ring of cypresses.

"Donnag's whelp," the mariner said bitterly. "No wonder you fit in so well in Blöten." He shook his head, then edged by a group of ogre mercenaries and slipped to where the child had been standing. "Told you he couldn't be trusted."

Fiona said nothing, her chest was so tight she

couldn't have talked if she'd wanted to. The Solamnic tried to picture the face of the human Maldred, the one with the mesmerizing eyes. There was only this blue-skinned ogre, which made her shiver in anger and disgust. Her hands trembled, the palms clammy. She tried to grip the pommel of her sword, but her fingers fumbled over it.

The image of a bronze draconian slipped into her mind again. She saw a golden collar fall to the floor of the mines. Had she dreamed that? Seeing the creature she was supposed to meet in Takar? Watching him die? Did she kill him? Indeed, how much of what she'd been through was real?

Suddenly Maldred's eyes caught hers, holding them like he had done when he looked human. With a gesture and a concentrated thought, he released her completely from the enchantment, and she blinked furiously, shaking her head to clear it.

Dhamon helped the ogre mage to his feet, astounded by just how large and heavy he really was.

"We will take these people back to Blöten," Maldred said. His voice was deeper and louder now. "Grim Kedar will see that they are healed, at my father's expense. The humans and dwarves will be given a place to stay."

"And then. . . ?" Dhamon asked. He intended to press deeper into the swamp, and though his friend was a blue-skinned ogre, he would still prefer to have Maldred at his side. Wyrmsbane had given him visions of the swamp when he asked it for a cure to the scale on his leg. He had no intentions of leaving this place until he was free of the scale and the pain.

"I don't know about the likes of you, but I'm going after the girl," Rig said. "She's got my glaive. And I intend to get it back."

"She's not dead?" Dhamon seemed surprised,

was certain he had seen her burned to ashes like the trolls.

Rig shook his head. "Hardly. I see her footprints leading away. And since she's still got my glaive, I'm going to follow them. She's heading west. We're going in the same direction. Toward Shrentak."

Dhamon left Maldred and stepped toward the mariner, who was intently studying the tracks. Wyrmsbane was still in his hand. He felt the pommel tingle, then grow cold.

What you seek.

BETRAYAL

The Dhamon Saga · Volume Two

Jean Rabe

CHAPTER ONE
NURA'S CHOICE

Inside the cave the darkness was an impenetrable blanket that cloaked the creature sleeping within. Only its breath gave it away—this raspy and uneven, echoing hauntingly against the stone walls and escaping as a breeze to tease the coppery curls of the child who stood just beyond the entrance.

She was no more than five or six, cherubic and clothed in a diaphanous dress that at first glance appeared to be fashioned of pale flower petals, but on closer inspection seemed instead to shimmer like it was made of magic. The fingers of her left hand were clenched about the haft of a glaive, an axe-bladed pole-arm more than twice her height and looking far too unwieldy for her to manage. The fingers of her right hand fluttered playfully across the giant fern leaves that helped to conceal the cave mouth. The green of the ferns was intense, struck by a fiery late afternoon sun and made slick with humidity, droplets of water beading up and gleaming like diamonds.

"Mumummmm-ummm," she sang when she spotted a furry caterpillar, striped orange and golden-brown and standing out starkly against a diamond-dotted frond. She stared at it for several long moments, then gently plucked it up and held it before her wide, blue eyes. "Soft," she pronounced. "Very pretty." The thing slowly wriggled, and in response she laughed in a voice that was not at all childlike. Then she popped the caterpillar into her mouth and swallowed it, just as the darkness of the cave swallowed her as she stepped inside.

"Master?" she whispered, as she instinctively padded forward, her bare feet slapping against the stone. It was an enormous cave, one which she couldn't have seen the far reaches of even if a dozen torches were merrily burning. And it was one of several the creature had in this part of Ansalon, all connected through underground tunnels that the child was occasionally permitted to wander–this particular cave was the most familiar to her. Though well shielded from the sun, the interior was nonetheless stifling, the air feeling damp and close and filled with the strong, sweet-sour stench of decay. The child inhaled deeply, holding and relishing the scent, then almost reluctantly releasing it. "Master?"

A pause, then again she repeated the word, no longer a question now, and she effortlessly tossed the glaive to the floor, its blade clanging against the stone. In response, twin globes of dull yellow appeared in the middle of the blackness. They were eyes, larger around than wagon wheels and cut through by murky catlike slits. Though there was a thick film on them, they gave off a faint light, eerie and just enough to illuminate the creature's massive snout and the child who was dwarfed in front of it. The girl stood on her toes and almost reverently stretched a hand up to graze the edge of the creature's jaw.

"You summoned me, O Very Old One?" Her voice was husky now and had an edge to it, a sultry's woman's voice.

The creature's raspy breath was broken by a rumbling– words so sonorous and loud they chased a tremor through the ground. "Nura-Bint-Drax," it said, each syllable excruciatingly drawn out and allowed to return as an echo. "Nura. My very young servant."

"Your chosen one." The child smiled and shifted back and forth on the balls of her feet, spread her arms wide, and turned her head this way and that so the hot breeze of the creature's fetid breath could better wash over her. "Your very loyal servant."

There were no more words for a time, the creature silently regarding the child and the child basking in the creature's presence. But then the great eyes blinked and the child haltingly stepped back, thin arms falling to her sides, shoulders squaring, unblemished face fixed forward like a soldier at attention.

Then the rumbling started again–ponderously slow words that the child had to concentrate on to understand.

"Yes, Master. I have made a selection, a most suitable one. You shall be quite pleased."

She felt the reply as much as heard it, the tremor racing through the stone floor and against the bottoms of her feet.

"His name is Dhamon Grimwulf, Master. A human."

There was another silence, this one seemingly interminable, as Nura's legs and arms tingled from remaining straight and motionless for so long. She breathed shallowly and somehow managed not to blink. Finally the creature's breath quickened and it raised its head, tucking its jaw into its neck and tilting it so as to look farther down upon the child, eyes narrowing disapprovingly.

"A human," the creature stated, the two words uttered with such contempt and strength that when the ground shook Nura had to struggle to keep her balance.

The child bravely thrust out her chin. "Yes, Master. Dhamon is a human. But he is the one."

The creature growled, and bits of rock and dust fell from overhead like rain. "You are certain, Nura-Bint-Drax? You have no doubts?"

"He is the one." She tipped her head and a corner of her mouth turned slightly upward. "I have been testing him, O' Very Old One."

The ground vibrated softly this time, as if the creature was purring. It opened its eyes wide again, giving faint light to the cave interior. "Tell me of this . . . ."

"Dhamon Grimwulf." Nura's head went back as far as she could manage, her wide child eyes meeting the creature's immense and steady gaze. "He was a Knight of Takhisis, Master, a commander of men who once rode a great blue dragon into battle. But he turned from the Dark Knights, touched by the powerful goodness of an aging Solamnic, further touched by Goldmoon, who made him her champion. Proof he can be swayed."

Nura paused, picking through the complex rumbling that followed. "Yes, Master. Dhamon Grimwulf was the man who led a band of mortals to the Window to the Stars to confront the five dragon Overlords. He was victorious that day, though not a single dragon died, victorious because he took a stand and lived. Pity he did not recognize what he achieved."

The rumbling intensified, and Nura put all her effort into staying on her feet and deciphering the words. When the ground quieted, the child waved her hands in front of her face and shook her head. "No, O' Very Old One, he is Goldmoon's champion no longer. And he no longer struggles against the Overlords. Now he has no cares beyond his own pleasure. And there are very few who call him friend."

"A fallen hero," the creature stated.

"Yes, Master."

"A common thief."

There was a near-painful skritching sound, of something sharp being scraped across the stone, and then a throaty growl that encouraged her to continue.

"Master, I believe Dhamon Grimwulf's spirit died

when he decided the dragon Overlords were unstoppable. His beliefs in a better world, and in himself being a catalyst to achieve that, are deeply buried. Hope is a thing that does not exist for him."

The creature canted its head and gave a nod.

"Dhamon has been battered by life . . . or rather by death that seems to pursue him and instead claims the lives of close friends and charges. To be close to Dhamon Grimwulf is to risk death, it seems."

She moved closer to the creature, and it lowered its great head so she could tease the barbels that hung from its chin. "A young green dragon slew his men in the Qualinesti Forest," Nura added. "Then he killed his own second-in-command in the throes of drunken self-defense. Though there were many things that went wrong in his life, I think that act was the final blow that turned him completely inward. He has lost confidence in himself and in Krynn. Yes, he is a fallen hero, Master. *But he is the one.*"

The cave was plunged into darkness then, the creature having closed its eyes. A series of vibrations danced through the stone, the sensation intense and the noise echoing and forcing the child to throw her hands over her ears and step away. The creature rested its head on the floor, and eventually the vibrations slowed, then ceased, to be replaced by the raspy uneven breath of its slumber.

When it awoke several hours later, the child was still there, patiently sitting a few yards away. The eerie light of the creature's eyes showed Nura's own eyes sparkling with anticipation.

"More," the creature stated.

"Regarding Dhamon Grimwulf?"

"Yes. More. You must do more so that I can be certain, too."

Nura digested the words and put a meaning to them. "You wish me to test him further, Master?"

There was a harsh grating sound that the child understood as a yes. "Then indeed I shall test him some more," Nura said, the excitement thick in her voice. "I shall test him to the very limits of his existence. And if he dies, I shall have been proved wrong and I shall search for another. But if he does not die, and if he can be thoroughly broken, swayed to our side, made useful . . . ." She let the words hang in the foul air. "If this Dhamon Grimwulf can survive . . ."

". . . *then indeed he is the one,*" the creature finished. It turned its head, eyes looking past Nura and through the small gaps in the fern leaves beyond the cave entrance. The child wheeled to see what the creature had spotted. It was night outside, but there was the faintest hint of a flickering—a torch passing by.

Nura's keen eyes recognized the torch-bearer, and she softly laughed. "That human," she whispered, "and the one following . . . they are of no consequence."

The creature snarled almost imperceptibly.

"As you wish, O Very Old One. I live to serve you."

The War of Souls
THE NEW EPIC SAGA FROM
MARGARET WEIS & TRACY HICKMAN

**The New York Times bestseller
—now available in paperback!**

Dragons of a Fallen Sun
The War of Souls • Volume I

Out of the tumult of a destructive
magical storm appears a mysterious
young woman, proclaiming the
coming of the One True God.
Her words and deeds erupt into
a war that will transform
the fate of Krynn.

Dragons of a Lost Star
THE WAR OF SOULS • VOLUME II

The war rages on . . .
A triumphant army of evil Knights
sweeps across Krynn and marches
against Silvanesti. Against the dark
tide stands a strange group of heroes:
a tortured Knight, an agonized mage,
an aging woman, and a small,
lighthearted kender in whose hands
rests the fate of all the world.

April 2001

STORIES FROM
THE CHANGING FACE OF KRYNN

Bertrem's Guide to the Age of Mortals:
Everyday Life in Krynn of the Fifth Age

NANCY VARIAN BERBERICK,
STAN BROWN,
AND PAUL B. THOMPSON

Countless legends, histories, and sagas have told of the great heroes and villains of Krynn. Now, delve into the life of Ansalon in the Fifth Age as seen through the eyes of the common people, through articles on everything from arms and armor to festivals and clothing!

TALES FROM
THE WAR OF SOULS
Don't miss this new collection of short stories detailing the era of the War of Souls, newest chapter in the continuing saga of Krynn. Contains stories from Richard A. Knaak, Paul Thompson & Tonya Carter Cook, Jeff Crook and other popular Dragonlance authors.

October 2001

BERTREM'S GUIDE:
A WAR OF SOULS JOURNAL
The War of Souls has begun, and Ansalon will never be the same again. See how these world-changing events affect the lives of the everyday people of Krynn. Includes articles from Nancy Varian Berberick, Mary H. Herbert, John Grubber, and Jeff Crook.

September 2001

The tales that started it all...

New editions from **DRAGONLANCE** creators
Margaret Weis & Tracy Hickman

The great modern fantasy epic – now available in paperback!

THE ANNOTATED CHRONICLES

Margaret Weis & Tracy Hickman return to the Chronicles, adding notes and commentary in this annotated edition of the three books that began the epic saga.

SEPTEMBER 2001

THE LEGENDS TRILOGY

Now with stunning cover art by award-winning fantasy artist Matt Stawicki, these new versions of the beloved trilogy will be treasured for years to come.

Time of the Twins • War of the Twins • Test of the Twins

FEBRUARY 2001

New characters,
strange magic,
wondrous creatures.

ADVENTURE THROUGH THE HISTORY OF KRYNN
WITH THESE THREE NEW SERIES!

THE BARBARIANS
PAUL THOMPSON & TONYA CARTER COOK
Follow a divided brother and sister as they lead rival tribes of
plainsmen amidst the wonders and dangers of ancient Krynn.

Volume One: *Children of the Plains*
Volume Two: *Brother of the Dragon*
August 2001

THE ICEWALL TRILOGY
DOUGLAS NILES
Journey with an exiled elf to the harsh, legendary land known as Icereach,
where human tribes battle for life and ogres search to reclaim lost glories.

Volume One: *The Messenger*
February 2001

THE KINGPRIEST TRILOGY
CHRIS PIERSON
Discover for the first time the dynastic history of the Kingpriest
and how his religious-political rule of Istar influenced the world
of DRAGONLANCE for generations to come.

Volume One: *Chosen of the Gods*
November 2001

CLASSICS SERIES

THE INHERITANCE
Nancy Varian Berberick

The companions of Tanis Half-Elven knew of their friend's tragic heritage—how
his mother was ravaged by a human bandit and died from grief.
But there was more to the story than anyone knew.

Here at last is the story of the half-elf's heritage: the tale of a captive elven princess,
a merciless human outlaw, a proud elven prince, the power of love, and how
tragedy can change a life forever.
May 2000

THE CITADEL
Richard A. Knaak

Against a darkened cloud it comes, soaring over the ravaged land: the flying citadel,
mightiest power in the arsenal of the dragon highlords. An evil wizard has
discovered a secret that may bring all of Ansalon under his control, and it's up
to a red-robed mage, a driven cleric, a kender, and a grizzled war veteran to
stop him before it's too late.

DALAMAR THE DARK
Nancy Varian Berberick

Magic runs like fire through the blood of Dalamar Argent, yet his heritage denies
him its use. But as war threatens his beloved Silvanesti, Dalamar will seize the
forbidden power and begin a quest that will lead him to a dark and uncertain future.

MURDER IN TARSIS
John Maddox Roberts

Who killed Ambassador Bloodarrow? In a city where everyone is a suspect, time
is running out for an unlikely trio of detectives. If they fail to solve the mystery,
their reward will be death.